# GLOBAL CONSPIRACY

## DAVID SHOMRON

# GLOBAL CONSPIRACY

## A Thriller

## DAVID SHOMRON

SAMUEL WACHTMAN'S SONS    DEKEL PUBLISHING HOUSE

# GLOBAL CONSPIRACY

DAVID SHOMRON

Copyright © 2016

**Dekel Publishing House**
www.dekelpublishing.com

North American rights by
**Samuel Wachtman's Sons, Inc.**
ISBN 978-1-941905-06-7


**English translation:**   Alex Eshed
**Language editing:**   R. Reinprecht
**Proof reading:**   Eilath Giladi, Pnina Ophir


*Cover images*
*Racing boat © Pixabay / Dreamstime.com*


*Design and typesetting by*

**For information contact:**

**Dekel Publishing House**          **Samuel Wachtman's Sons, Inc.**
P.O. Box 45094, Tel Aviv          2460 Garden Road, Suite C
6145002, ISRAEL          Monterey, CA 93940, U.S.A.
Tel: +972 3506-3235          Tel: 831 649-0669
Fax: +972 3506-7332          Fax: 831 649-8007
Email: info@dekelpublishing.com   Email: samuelwachtman@gmail.com

# PROLOGUE

## *Pyongyang, two hours before Revolution Day ceremonies.*

The President of North Korea, called the Great Leader by the people, paced up and down his office, mentally going over his annual message to the people. Everything had to be in place, nothing left to chance. He had to be especially rousing and exciting in order to counterbalance his earlier statement of withdrawing his country's plans for nuclear development. The pressures from the United Nations Security Council—including sanctions—were just too great. But his own people, not to mention the rest of the world, saw this as back-pedaling, caving in, bowing to external influences. His prestige was seriously damaged, and the morale of his supporters was losing ground.

He had, therefore, decided to make this occasion more spectacular than anything seen before. The speech would stir the faintest heart, the military parade would be on an unprecedented scale. Millions would throng to the central square and overflow into the adjoining streets and alleys. They would hear the Great Leader's fiery oration and witness the might of the marching military forces, the armored vehicles thundering past them and the fighter jets screaming overhead.

The Great Leader called his Chief of Ceremonies, General Pak, into his office.

"I want to hear the latest rundown on the preparations for the speech and the parade," he announced. "Everything should be in place by now." The tone was calm, but General Pak knew the power the leader could wield with a single word.

"Most certainly. With your permission, I'll mention only the highlights. First, we have Your Excellency's speech from the grandstand, which will be broadcast over all the radio and television channels, including satellite transmission. Huge monitors have been erected at almost every intersection to allow the public to view Your Excellency during your speech and the following parade. The infantry will march past the grandstand in blocks of 400 soldiers each, preceded by the military band. The armored vehicles will roll past, and they will be followed by the trucks towing the missiles. The parade will wind up with dancers who will also throw flowers into the crowd."

The general glanced at his clipboard.

"At the same time," he continued, "twenty-five formations of fighter jets will fly overhead streaming the colors of the flag behind them. Right now, patriotic music is being pumped out of over a thousand loudspeakers installed within an area of three kilometers radius from the grandstand."

The Great Leader smiled softly and turned to the huge window overlooking the central square. He crossed his hands behind his back and, without turning, inquired:

"What about security?"

"Six thousand combat soldiers, hundreds of plain clothes Secret Service agents and nearly half the police force will be spread along the routes. Another eight hundred will mingle amongst the crowds and maintain order. All are equipped with the latest communications devices. Snipers are positioned on every rooftop in the vicinity, and the emergency operations room has been on red alert for the past three hours. I can assure you, Great Leader, that there will be no disturbance of the peace." The general was beginning to perspire heavily despite the air-conditioned environment.

"I distinctly requested you to prepare something extraordinary for this occasion. So far, all you have told me relates to size and quantity." The Great Leader turned from the window and fixed a steely gaze into the general's eyes. "That, from my point of view, is insufficient."

General Pak made a supreme effort to keep his voice and breathing normal.

"Indeed you did, Great Leader." He turned a few pages on his clipboard. "There are some items never seen before in any of our parades—in fact, to the best of my knowledge, in *any* parade worldwide."

The Great Leader continued to stare, but a ghost of a smile appeared on his face, and his nod was almost imperceptible.

"The first block of soldiers will perform extremely intricate exercises involving juggling and interchanging of their weapons. The flag bearers will form outlines of scenes and texts glorifying our nation and its leadership. The jet fighters will perform aerobatics involving thirty-six planes weaving in and out of each other's courses at almost touching distance. The training for all these maneuvers has taken up over four hundred man-years."

There was a moment of silence. General Pak was sure that his heartbeat was audible. If the Great Leader was not satisfied....

A wave of the hand, and the general was dismissed.

The Great Leader strode into his dressing room. His butler and his barber were ready. He donned the snow-white tunic, buttoned up to the neck, without a single ribbon, medal, or sash. His custom-made shoes had extra thick soles and heels. He ordered the barber to give him a particular hairdo to lengthen his face, thereby giving the impression of additional height. All his life he had suffered the indignities of a small stature, and his only consolation was that a surprising percent of the world's most prominent people were of less than average height. When he left the dressing room he felt fit and ready.

A short knock at the office door preceded General Pak's entrance.

"It is time, Your Excellency."

Together they left the building and were driven in the limousine to the grandstand on the other side of the square. The military march music blared through the loudspeakers. The huge piazza was packed with myriads of citizens, all cheering wildly while being held in line by uniformed soldiers. At the appearance of the Great Leader, the cheering rose to a frenzy, flags were waved wildly, and several people were in danger of being trampled by others craving to get a glimpse of their leader.

The Great Leader exited the limousine and walked past the guard of honor, waving and nodding to the dignitaries lining his path to the podium—the highest point on the grandstand. When he finally appeared there, now visible to everyone, a roar erupted from the crowd, threatening to drown out the raucous loudspeakers. The roar was gradually transformed into an ear-splitting chant—a continuous repetition of the Great Leader's name.

The Great Leader smiled at the throng for a few seconds, nodding once to the left and to the right. He then extended his hand, and an immediate hush fell on the square. The world awaited the words of North Korea's Great Leader.

CRORO

Eight hours earlier, approximately thirty kilometers west of North Korea in the Yellow Sea, a yacht flying a Panamanian flag sailed on a southbound course. Five of its crew were ex-soldiers of Her Majesty's Special Forces—more commonly known as "commandos." They had all fought in Iraq in 1991, in what was known as the "First Gulf War." Great Britain had joined the coalition armies to defeat Saddam Hussein, the Iraqi dictator, who had invaded and annexed Kuwait several weeks earlier.

The five had all been part of the "Desert Scorpion" unit. Captain Martin Cooper had led seven daring and highly motivated fighters in special missions behind enemy lines. They were either parachuted or used stealth to infiltrate the Iraqi forces, where they sabotaged, kidnapped, and photographed in accordance with the orders they received. They never questioned these orders—total obedience was the key to their success. Even when their most carefully planned raids met with a hitch, they always found their way out, either by brute force—of which they had no lack—or, more usually, by their wits and the uncanny guidance of their captain. They had adopted the musketeers slogan of "one for all and all for one," and their mutual loyalty was absolute. Two Scorpions had not survived the war. The remaining six had been duly decorated for their bravery and accomplishments.

The crew's current mission had gone off flawlessly so far. The "main event" was yet ahead of them, the next morning, and following that: sail south, avoid being intercepted, and get out of these waters as soon as possible.

One of the ex-Scorpions was now at the helm of the yacht. He checked the course once again. So far so good—thank God for computers. His instructions were to keep an eye on the monitor: true, if the line turned red, the siren would go off automatically, but it was his job to alert the admiral immediately just the same.

*Well, that was easy enough*, he thought. *I wouldn't know the first thing about running a boat, anyway. Give me solid ground any time. That's where the real action is. Nothing much since that last mission in Iraq—now that was action!* He grinned at the memory. *That would have been—well, years ago....*

*We are surrounding the house where the Iraqi officers are sleeping. Well, they were supposed to be, but they surprise us and open fire. Captain Cooper orders us to storm the place, so we do. As I aim the bazooka at the doorway, I notice the flashes of automatic fire from a window to its left and see Roger and Edwin fall. Damn. So I turn my weapon to that window and score a bull's eye.*

The firing stops. I drop the bazooka and we all charge in with our pistols ready. Nine Iraqi officers are splattered all over the place. The other Scorpions spread out in the *remains of the house to make sure we haven't missed anyone. I remain by the shattered door with one eye on the mutilated officers and one eye searching outside in case reinforcements arrive.*

*I see one of the Iraqis slowly reaching for his holster and I shoot him in the head. He lies still. There is a gold pendant around his neck in the shape of a hand and I yank it off and put it in my pocket. I look around for anything else to salvage as a memento. There is an open shoulder bag on the floor and it is full of Iraqi money. I grab a handful of notes and hear Coop yell 'Drop it! Put that back! I'll have you court-martialed!' I curse and drop the cash. I'm pretty sure he hasn't seen me take the 'hamsa' pendant off the corpse. We make our way out of the house. An Iraqi hiding outside the door jumps Coop with a dagger. I shoot the Arab without thinking, and he drops like a sack of potatoes. Coop says 'Thanks, mate. Forget the court martial.' I grunt something and pick up my bazooka. We collect poor Roger and Edwin and hoof it back to base.*

*And a good thing, too, forgetting the court martial. If I were tried, they'd find out all the other stuff I have in my collection of wartime mementos—my gallery, I like to call it. Rings, weapons,*

*coins, wallets, necklaces, bracelets, watches—quite a collection—*
*all gone by now, of course.*

*Sure I work for Coop today, too, but our relationship is just this*
*side of cordial. I'll do everything he asks, of course, I owe him that*
*much, but I sure would like to quit and go it on my own. And you*
*can bet I will.*

He grinned again. Another look at the monitor. All was as it
should be. Yes, this would definitely be his last mission.

# EIGHTEEN MONTHS EARLIER

# ONE

Sir Cedric Norton, English aristocrat and the very model of the perfect gentleman, eagerly anticipated his rendezvous with Anne. It was his habit to visit Paris from time to time and meet with Anne, whom he considered to be his protégée, now that Raoul had died. As usual, he was dressed in the height of fashion, his almost bald head carefully groomed and his Clark Gable mustache trimmed to perfection. He preferred the staid life of an active scientist, owner and director of Norlaser, one of the most advanced research institutes in the UK, specializing in laser technology. Today, approaching seventy, he could enjoy his successes and his well-established reputation throughout the scientific world.

He had met Colonel Raoul Dupré, a military attaché at the French Embassy in London, several years ago at one of those cocktail events he so thoroughly disliked. The young French officer had hit it off with him right away, displaying a remarkable familiarity with some of the more intricate aspects of lasers and their implementation. And when he introduced his wife, Anne, the old knight was entranced. Not only was she beautiful and vibrant, she was as British as he was.

Sir Cedric sat impatiently in their usual restaurant awaiting her arrival. His aperitif remained untouched on the tablecloth, and his eyes never left the doorway. He had taken a very special interest in Anne. She was an exciting person, though at times somewhat contradictory. On one hand she possessed a calm outward aura that made everyone in her presence feel comfortable. On the other, she could occasionally resort to alarmingly independent action if she suspected an injustice had been committed. She had told him of at least two "little incidents," as she called them, one in which she had rescued a student from a rather repugnant altercation with the law, deriving from a jealous roommate, and the other where she had interceded for another student who got mixed up with a drug dealer—and both could have turned out rather nastily for her. And yet he considered her as having sound judgment and, more often than not, as making very accurate decisions.

Sir Cedric was still musing when Anne finally walked into the restaurant, hardly two minutes late. His face broke into a radiant smile as he rose to greet her.

"My dear Anne," he murmured as their cheeks met. "How wonderful to see you again. You look positively ravishing, I do declare."

"Thank you kindly, Sir Cedric, m'lord." She gave a mock curtsey, gave him a mischievous grin, and they both sat down. "How are things back at the shire?"

He gave her a paternal smile. At forty-two, Anne still looked stunning. She could easily have passed for thirty though she made no effort to do so. True, following Raoul's death she was a wreck, but an iron-strong will and a ferocious dedication to live life to the utmost brought her back to the world of the living. Indeed, Sir Cedric was of the opinion that his companionship and guidance were more beneficial to her than her own parent's comforting.

"Absolutely boring, thank goodness," he replied without missing a beat. "I had one three-hour board meeting during the past fortnight and that was quite enough. I really can't be expected to be at their beck and call every other month, now, can I? I won't have time for my research or my chess matches with the admiral. And that would never do, would it?"

"You poor thing," commiserated Anne. "The pressure you must be under. I imagine you had to fight your way through layers of snoring peers at the club in order to get out in time to meet me here."

"Ah, you mock me, cruel lass. But it is my sworn duty to put my welfare well below the interests of those who need me. Never let it be said that my elevated position hath turned me into a despot, treading the masses under my heel as I reap the ill-gotten ..."

"Funny you should bring it up," interrupted Anne. "I had quite an interesting dialogue on despots and tyrants with one of my students just an hour ago. Interested?"

"To be sure, to be sure," boomed the old gentleman. "But first, let's order our meal, shall we?"

The waiter came and left. Sir Cedric leaned back in his chair and folded his hands on his slightly protruding abdomen. Anne pictured him removing an imaginary monocle from his right eye, which, of course, would never have occurred to him to wear.

"Well, now," he commenced, "despots and other dastardly bad guys. What have you to say in their defense?"

Anne laughed. Every now and then she wished she could spend more and more time with this kind old man. He gave her that sense of true comfort, that warm feeling of "I'm home with daddy." After losing Raoul, he was a true godsend. Without him, she would have probably sunk into deep depression.

"Not much, I'm afraid," she retorted. "As a matter of fact I didn't voice an opinion at all. It wasn't the topic we were discussing. A student actually challenged me as to why we need to learn history, claiming that all that study did not teach us how to get rid of those 'bad guys.' He said, and I think I'm quoting verbatim: 'Barbara Tuchman's March of Folly pales in comparison to the utter stupidity, the total denseness, of the leaders of what we jokingly call the 'free' world.'"

"Well, my dear, those are two separate issues altogether, aren't they? History, as I understand it, is an academic pursuit. It has nothing to do with the behavior of power-mad lunatics."

"I believe I made that point very clear at the lecture, Ced," Anne said. She was the only person who called him that. *I can't address you as Sir Cedric every time we talk—that's ridiculous!* she had explained. *And frankly, I never liked the name Cedric. It'll have to be Ced or 'hey, you!' Take your pick.* And he had, and liked it, too. Though he would *never* have tolerated anyone else to even dare breathe that name within hearing distance, and he even made Anne promise never to call him Ced in public. "I was actually mulling over the points brought up regarding the dictators. And I found myself quite disturbed by them."

"Indeed, my dear? And why, pray, is that? I believe we all hold people like Hitler and his ilk in total abhorrence. There'll always be an Attila or a Stalin somewhere, won't there? And some people pay a heavy price to be under their influence. It's regrettable, I admit, but not really alarming. I really don't see why that disturbs you, as you put it."

Sir Cedric wondered if the rather fierce arguments he had had with Raoul would surface again now.

"Obviously you haven't chewed a bit on the dilemma as I have, Ced. Your tyrants of yesterday are quite different from the despots of today. Today they wield power that endangers democracies all over the planet."

"Come, come, my dear." Sir Cedric leaned forward, deliberately taking the opposing argument. "Aren't you carrying this a tad too far? Today's democracies can squash any loud-mouthed towel-head that dares put his words into action. Witness what happened to Saddam Hussein. They know better than to—"

"No, Ced, that's not the point at all!" Anne was quite flushed. "It's not those bastards that concern me, though they're bad enough. It's how the world *reacts* to them that really worries me."

The soup arrived and Sir Cedric took advantage of the pause it provided to assess the conversation so far. This was not the

Anne he knew—not the playful, giggling, carefree woman he had resurrected from the darkest hours of despair. This was a serious Anne he was less familiar with, an Anne about to make a statement regarding world affairs that, in the past, had been Raoul's forte, not hers. And he *had* discussed this very topic with Raoul on several occasions—sometimes almost violently.

"And what, exactly," he prodded, "is wrong with the world's reaction?"

He could see she was choosing her words carefully as she delicately sipped the consommé.

"It's the system, I'm afraid," Anne said quietly. "They say there's no better government than democracy. But that holds true only when democracies relate to each other. When a 'wolf' appears in their midst, the democracies become 'sheep.'"

*There we go,* thought Sir Cedric, but he remained diplomatically silent.

"Democratic leaders are elected by large populations whose main concern is in bettering their lives. A very legitimate endeavor. But politicians, relying almost solely on public opinion polls, use this as leverage in their own propaganda. And that's what current politics looks like today—the main concern of those elected leaders is to be re-elected again and again! Their decisions in office seldom have any bearing on the needs and concerns of their nation. Instead, they cater to the sway of public opinion, which usually has very little knowledge of foreign policy or national security, but a lot to say about their own comfort."

There was a prolonged pause. Sir Cedric watched Anne as she collected her thoughts. These were pretty strong words coming from her. Raoul couldn't have put it better, though his approach to this issue was in stark contrast to Anne's. *It's time to put the cards on the table.*

"I think I know what you're getting at, Anne," he said, finally. "And I think you have made a good point. Modern history shows that the price for getting rid of dictators and tyrants is rising all the time. Let's see if you, as a historian, can clear up a couple of questions that have been nagging me for quite some time now." Anne was staring at him now, her hand holding the soupspoon halted in mid-air on its way down to the bowl.

"Let's take World War I to begin with," he continued. "Victory was achieved only at the intervention of the United States. How long did it take them to make that move, Anne?"

"Not really my specialty, Ced," Anne replied, "but let's see now. I make it about two and a half years. The war began in 1914 and the US entered it in 1917...."

"Why, Anne? Why so late? Because of public opinion, that's why. You just said so yourself. President Wilson could not intervene without the support of his people, could he? And they opposed the move for two and a half years! In that time a lot of people were killed in Europe. Do you happen to know the approximate number, Anne?"

"Eight million. I see where you're heading, Ced." Anne's voice was excited. "As I recall, in World War II the figures were even worse. It took President Roosevelt about as long to make sure the nation would support US intervention. *And* he needed German and Japanese provocation as well before doing anything. This time fifty-two million lives were lost! It's appalling!"

"You're the historian, Anne." Sir Cedric took hold of Anne's hand and spoke very quietly. "Now tell me in simple terms—where does this lead us?"

Anne grew pale.

"I ... I never thought about it that way. Obviously the enemies of democracy today hold threats far beyond what Germany and Japan could come up with then. Today, in a world armed with

intercontinental ballistic missiles carrying nuclear warheads …"
Sir Cedric noticed her voice was rising. "… flying crisscross over
the globe…. If and when things erupt— My God, Ced!" Her eyes
opened wide.

"Total devastation," she whispered, staring into space. "Hundreds of millions dead."

Her head snapped toward him.

"You knew!" she accused him. "You knew this all along, and
you led me right into it." Her gaze softened and she smiled at him.
"I can't get mad at you, Ced, even if you did manipulate me there.
Actually, I'm relieved that we share our opinions on this. Of all the
people in the world, you'd be the last one I'd want as opposition
on this topic."

"Thank you, my dear." Sir Cedric felt himself relax. "I really
didn't want to get you upset. Let's finish our meal with nicer things
on our minds, shall we?" He beckoned to the waiter for the main
course. "And by the way, I believe I shall bring this matter up with
the admiral."

C3�

By nature Anne Dupré was a calm and neat individual. She was
born Anne Cooper in England in 1966. Her parents—her father
was an English Literature lecturer at the University of London—
had sent her to the best schools in Reading. She had studied
history at Cambridge and earned her Master's degree in History,
Literature and Culture in the Middle Ages. Then she had gone off
to Paris and got her PhD in Ancient and Medieval Worlds.

During her studies she had met a young French officer,
Raoul Dupré, fell in love, got married and had two children. He,
meanwhile, progressed along his military career, rising to the

rank of colonel. She was offered a position as history lecturer at the Sorbonne, but, as fate would have it, Raoul was posted to the French Embassy in London.

They all moved to London, and Anne—with her father's assistance and connections—began teaching at the University of London. The children now studied in schools in their native tongue, which they had spoken at home even while in France. Here, Raoul and Sir Cedric had the good fortune to meet and develop a deep friendship.

Three years later disaster struck. Raoul contracted cancer of the liver and died a few months after being diagnosed. During her mourning period, Anne received an offer from the Sorbonne in Paris for a full professorship in the History Department. She couldn't turn down this opportunity. But to take the children with her would be a second major upheaval in their lifestyle and educational program. So she reluctantly left them in the care of her parents in Reading, and moved back to Paris alone. She was quite well off, having not only a decent salary from her employers but also a pension from the French government as the widow of a French officer.

Raoul's parents lived in Montpellier near the Mediterranean Sea. When Raoul was still alive he, Anne and their children would visit them twice a year. Since Anne was widowed she and her children only visited during the summer vacation, so that the youngsters could meet with their grandparents. The Duprés and Anne would call each other every two or three weeks and exchange information on the children and their health. The old couple was very proud that their daughter-in-law was a university professor, and their only regret was that the children went to school in England instead of in France.

Anne had a large number of friends and acquaintances—French academicians, naturally, were her closest environment.

But the British academic world was also no stranger to her, due to her father's connections. And, of course, the diplomatic world in France and in England alike, because of her late husband's occupation.

Anne today was a relatively young, attractive widow who drew men's attention wherever she went. She knew that, but taking advantage of that fact was the furthest thing from her mind. Her lifestyle was modest, even somewhat old fashioned—she did not drive a car, wear fancy clothes, use a cellphone or attend glamorous events. She expected that one day she'd meet someone to take Raoul's place, but she wasn't anticipating it anytime soon. Or even later, for that matter.

## *TWO*

Trim and Fit Ltd. had started out as a tiny workout gym in Earlsfield, not far from the Southern bend of the Thames. Over the years it had developed into a profitable enterprise. Clientele was increasing almost weekly as its reputation spread throughout the city. The manager and owner, Martin Cooper, ex-Special Forces major, had done well with his staff of five. They were fully employed the year round and none could complain of lack of income.

Martin assembled the boys for their weekly briefing.

"Lads, as you all know we've been doing pretty well for the past couple of years. Don't you think it's time for a big break? Well, that's what it seems like right now. We may be getting into an easy expansion deal abroad."

The five staff members exchanged questioning glances.

"Do you remember the Frenchman we showed around about two months ago? Leblanc? Well, it seems he was more than just impressed. He wants to open a gym just like ours near Paris. He even wants it to carry our name on it, as if it were our Paris branch."

As the news sank in, there came a round of hand-clapping and table-pounding. Questions flew around, and Martin raised his hands for silence.

"We wouldn't have to do much. Of course, I'll need to visit there quite frequently to begin with—Leblanc will need me on hand at the founding and running in stages—but later on it'll be only once every few months to see that our standards are met. That's all. Leblanc will supply all the rest. Staff, fixtures, accessories—the works. And we'll collect fifteen percent of all their earnings. In a couple of years, I believe we'll be able to afford to expand here, too."

When the cheering had died down Martin added: "I'm flying to Paris soon to finalize with Leblanc. I don't know how you can keep up the good work without me, but I'll give it a try." He winked at the burst of laughter from the men. He was frequently absent for several days leaving George in charge, and business was no worse for that.

The rest of the meeting related to current issues.

## THREE

The neat apartment on rue Gay Lussac didn't need any preparation for guests. Anne always kept it tidy. Besides the hallway and the living room, there were three bedrooms, one for herself and one for each of her children. When they visited her, she wanted them to have their privacy, if they so wished. The living room also served as her study, and right by the window was a medium-sized desk on which her files and work papers were neatly stacked next to her computer. A cabinet for serving drinks stood by the opposite wall.

Anne also took meticulous care of her looks. She knew she was attractive, yet—and perhaps because of it—she regularly visited her cosmetician and her hairdresser. She had a floor-to-ceiling mirror installed in her bathroom, and she never left her flat before she had taken a full two-minute check-up on her appearance. Face and figure combined to a very appealing picture. Add to that a dash of poise and dignity, chestnut hair, and you have a typical blue-eyed "looker" to some, a comely figure of a woman to others. None who saw her could remain indifferent. And if you knew her better, you would also discover her love for the arts—she would attend concerts, ballet, exhibitions, jam sessions and the like whenever her schedule allowed it.

Sir Cedric said he would be bringing his admiral friend along. She had never met the admiral in person, though she had heard a lot about him from dear old Ced. Besides being an excellent chess adversary, it seems the admiral was also a keen conversationalist and a staunch "defender of the oppressed" in his political views.

The two elderly gentlemen were very punctual. Sir Cedric beamed, shared a short embrace with Anne and introduced the admiral. Anne half expected Admiral Patrick Stone to be tall and in a white naval uniform, covered with medals, epaulets, and gold buttons. Instead, she saw a short, balding man with large horn-rimmed glasses, dressed in casual street wear.

"It is a pleasure to make your acquaintance, Mrs. Dupré," said the admiral, giving a stiff bow. Anne wondered if he was going to kiss her hand. "I have heard quite a lot about you from Sir Cedric here."

"Oh, I do hope we can dispense with the formalities, please," Anne said hastily, rather put off by his somewhat pompous greeting. "I'm Anne, and he's Ced … ric, and you're whatever you like to be called. Will 'Admiral' do?"

It was as if Admiral Stone had been practicing a role for the theater. His transformation from snooty officer to friendly guest was almost instantaneous. He gave an apologetic grin.

"Nasty habit I have there," he admitted. "Introductions always raise the image of being presented to the Queen, know what I mean? Yes, almost everyone calls me Admiral or Patrick. Your choice. Am I forgiven?"

Anne gave him a warm smile, indicated the chairs around the small table she had prepared and offered drinks. After the regular chitchat that usually starts off such get-togethers, the admiral finally straightened up in his chair and said:

"I have ideas of my own on the topic you and Cedric discussed. I am very concerned about the inadequacies of the democracies of the world. Iran is developing nuclear weapons and long-range missiles, and their president is openly and arrogantly threatening everyone opposing him. North Korea is conducting underground tests with atomic bombs and has already sent missiles towards Japan. And the best thing the democracies of the world can do is to complain to the United Nations."

"True, true," muttered Sir Cedric.

"Here's what we can expect," continued the admiral. "The Security Council will propose sanctions. Vetoes will fly in from all over, so the Security Council waters down the sanctions proposal until it is totally ineffective. Is it any wonder that nobody takes them seriously?"

"Not to mention that these people in the UN are all earning a decent salary for warming their seats," Anne chipped in.

"Then there's this deputy to al-Baghdadi who keeps popping up every now and then. At least he doesn't mince words. He very clearly states that his aim is to destroy the civilized world and instate Islam rule in its stead. And in South America," the admiral noticed he was getting agitated and took a sip of his whisky, "we have another clown who graduated from the same academy attended by Idi Amin and Kaddafi. But this South American dictator in Venezuela is extremely dangerous, not only to his own people—these despots always are—but to the world."

"You're not painting a very rosy picture, Admiral," Anne said. "All those you've pointed out are not only very influential today, but are gaining power every week."

"Just how long do you think this can go on?" Sir Cedric had remained serene throughout the admiral's speech. "I mean, until it all blows up on our faces? A year? Two?"

There was a short silence. Anne looked from one man to the other.

"Gentlemen," she said softly. "You did not come here all the way from London just to air your views. Not only did you know beforehand that I sympathize with these opinions, you have also entertained ideas of what can be done. So let's put our cards on the table, shall we?"

"Just what do you mean, Anne?" Sir Cedric asked.

"All right—here's my opening gambit." Anne took a deep breath. "I say something has to be done about the situation. Emphasize the word done! Talking is fine, in fact necessary, but nothing will happen unless action is taken."

"You realize, of course," Sir Cedric said carefully, "that we are too old and not that internationally influential to cause superpowers to alter their behavior. But do go on, Anne."

"These tyrants must be stopped. I don't know how, of course, but I can assure you that I oppose the use of force. Violence is a decision that is up to those who can wield that kind of power, and we all know that far too many lives will be lost before and after it is deployed. So I'm trying to think along unconventional lines."

"I'm afraid you'll need to clarify yourself a bit more, my dear." The admiral set down his empty glass. "When we mention 'unconventional means' we are actually speaking of nuclear, chemical and biological weapons. Surely you were not referring to them."

"No, of course not!" Anne felt a bit miffed. "I have already stated that I abhor violence of any kind. No—I was thinking about quite a different approach. But first, please let me ask you both a preliminary question. And I apologize in advance if it seems too ridiculous to you."

The two men looked at her expectantly.

"You both claim to be too old to do anything. I think this is because for you 'doing' means either fighting or diplomacy. I would like to try and offer something else. So my question is—if you could do something towards this cause without leading an army or winning an election, would you commit yourselves? I know I would."

Sir Cedric and the admiral exchanged glances.

"Cedric was right," the admiral said. "And you came to the correct conclusion as well. Cedric and I had discussed what could be done and gave up after a while. Then he suggested we pay you a visit and review the situation. Because we do feel that if we could do something, we would. Cedric thinks you may come up with an idea we hadn't thought of. And now I think so too. Please continue."

Anne looked into both their faces. She was convinced they were both sincere. Let's give them a bit of drama, she thought.

"Hitler's pants," she said.

"What was that?" "I beg your pardon!" "Excuse me!" "Could you repeat that?" The men exploded with comments. Anne smiled and let the consternation die down.

"I apologize for jumping to conclusions," said the admiral with an embarrassed smile. "I thought you just said 'Hitler's pants.'"

"I did," Anne said quietly.

Silence…. Then Anne went on.

"Imagine Adolf Hitler, leader of Nazi Germany, standing on a terrace of one of those gigantic squares with millions of devout followers watching every move he makes, listening to every syllable he utters, the newsreel cameras grinding away. Imagine him raising a fist in the air to emphasize a point. Imagine his pants dropping at that moment."

Sir Cedric chuckled. "I say, that's quite a bizarre scene."

"Even more so if his underwear was pink and flowery," guffawed the admiral.

"Or if he didn't have any on at all!" The two men laughed long and loud. Anne frowned, but she couldn't hide the smile on her lips. She waited until their merriment subsided.

"Now imagine you were one of those millions in the crowd watching him. Or a German in some other city hearing about the incident by word of mouth or by reading it in the paper. Or even a non-German but a sympathizer of the Nazi regime. What would you think?"

"That he'd made an utter ass of himself!" the admiral said.

"Far more than his maniacal ranting and gesturing!" Sir Cedric added. "I think I'm beginning to see where this is going, Anne."

"I hope so," Anne said. "Don't you think his prestige would have been severely damaged? Wouldn't his influence on the masses be markedly diminished? Isn't it just remotely possible that the course of history would have been altered?"

"Very likely," Sir Cedric said. "Quite dramatically, too, in hindsight."

The admiral shook his head.

"This is all well and good from an academic point of view, Anne," he said. "But you've described an illogical incident—or accident—that only has entertainment value. Therein lies the humor. Somewhere deep inside all of us is that feeling of relief that something comical happened to someone else and not to us.

And many accidents, sometimes even deliberately designed as pranks, cause laughter in the viewer at the expense of the victim. But no one could have engineered Hitler's pants to fall or Stalin's moustache to catch fire. That's patently impossible."

"I think you used the right word, Admiral," Anne said. "*Prank*. No, I'm not thinking of that kind of practical joke, but I lack a better word for what I'm about to describe. Listen, gentlemen, the pants and the moustache cannot be engineered because we cannot turn back the clock. But I think that with the appropriate planning certain things definitely can be engineered. I don't know how— you gentlemen are far more experienced than I am in solving these kinds of problems. I only know—in fact I'm certain—that these insane leaders can be made to lose face in the most embarrassing of circumstances, thereby losing their credibility and their leadership."

"Are you saying that we—" Sir Cedric began.

"I don't know if it's 'we' or someone else," Anne blurted out. "Not by terror or propaganda, not by force, and not by sanctions or by diplomacy. I'm looking at the end result. The tyrant is so publicly shamed that his leadership is compromised, perhaps even toppled. He will become an outcast, perhaps even have to face an uprising against him."

"How?" Both men asked the question together, and smiled guiltily at each other.

"Well, thanks for not torching the issue right away, gentlemen." Anne sounded pleased. "I don't know how. It's still a jumble of ideas. Perhaps interfering in an important 'speech to the nation.' Or messing up their computers. I wouldn't have the faintest idea of how to even begin such an operation. Over to you two now...."

The three of them sat in silence for several minutes. Anne got up quietly, turned on the electric kettle and returned to her seat.

Sir Cedric got out a small notebook and was making a few marks in it with a pencil. The admiral gazed at the ceiling as if planning a second Sistine Chapel. He suddenly stood up, cleared his throat and glanced at Sir Cedric, who gave a small nod.

"Anne, my dear, not only are we not 'torching' your concept—I, for one, endorse it. Your earlier question of commitment to the cause was very appropriate. I find myself agreeing with the fact that something can be done—at least, brainstorming for applicable ideas seems to be the next step to take. Creative thinking, you know…."

Sir Cedric was grinning from ear to ear as he, too, stood up.

"If I know you, Patrick, you're already scheming jamming traffic, energy disruption, disabling weaponry and so forth. And by subterfuge, sir—no violence involved. We need to work out these ideas—and I have a feeling it won't be easy at all."

"Yes, yes, of course," muttered the admiral, his thoughts obviously elsewhere.

A piercing whistle came from the kettle.

"How about a nice cup of tea?" asked Anne, getting up as well. "I can't believe I just said that—I sounded like a matron in a British sitcom."

They all laughed, and Anne served tea and chocolate cookies. Between mouthfuls she said:

"I see that we all need more time to think about this. Why don't we meet again in a few days' time? We could meet in London sometime next week, and I'll combine it with a visit to my children and parents in Reading. Okay with you both?"

CHAPTER THREE

## *Excerpt from article in Governments Today, by Reginald Koffey*

... Tyranny has to do with the internal affairs of a nation: it has to do with how a leader and a people interact. Lately, however, it has to do with its foreign policy as well.

There is a long list of tyrannies on our planet: we can begin with Ahmadinejad's Iran, Castro's Cuba and Kim Jong-il's North Korea and easily continue with unsavory candidates such as the military dictatorship in Pakistan, Azerbaijan, Uzbekistan, Kuwait, or Oman. Maybe Myanmar, Morocco, or Colombia, too.

There is an anti-tyranny crusade led by the USA. It would seem, however, that this crusade suffices in waving banners and rattling sabers instead of actually mounting their steeds and going into battle....

## *FOUR*

This was the first time Anne had visited Sir Cedric's flat in Knightsbridge. It wasn't huge but it also wasn't tiny. A confirmed bachelor, Sir Cedric had a comfortable living room and bedroom, but he also dedicated two additional rooms to his den, where he kept all his paperwork and computers, and his laboratory. It was a diminutive laboratory, naturally, but Sir Cedric could test out some of his laser designs before taking them to the fully equipped laboratory in Kensington. He often referred to it as his "pet lab," deliberately teasing his dog-loving friends.

The flat was spotless, of course. Sir Cedric had a lady housekeeper who came in every day to do everything another man might expect a wife to do—mainly pick up after him. That and clean up, cook meals, make the bed, and keep the larder and bar well stocked. Sir Cedric readily confessed that he was the world's most untidy person when it came to anything beyond his personal appearance. In self-grooming he had no peer. He used the most expensive soaps and lotions, visited his barber every week, and possessed a wardrobe of immaculate sets of business suits and shoes. Of course, it was the maid's job to see that all these were in order before they were needed, and Matilda did a pretty decent job of it, according to her employer.

When Anne arrived, both men were waiting for her with drinks in their hands. After the welcoming embraces and niceties, they sat down and looked expectantly at Anne.

"What?" she asked, somewhat flustered.

"We're waiting for new ideas from you," said Sir Cedric. "Patrick here and I have had our heads together for hours on end since last we met at your place. And here's what we came up with: nothing!"

"Well, let's phrase that a bit more accurately, Cedric, shall we?" the admiral said and turned to Anne. "To all intents and purposes he's right—nothing. But that's because we've dismissed several options and ideas as impractical."

"Like what?" Anne asked.

"Well, it would be very nice to stop a military parade in its tracks, wouldn't it? That would suit our purpose just fine. So how do we do it? We thought of digging trenches, of sabotaging the lead vehicle, of painting the tanks pink and even stupider variations. Sorry, Anne—there's no way it can be done."

"Or," Sir Cedric interjected, "jamming communication lines. This would only work if we could somehow tap into them and have Mr. Dictator say ridiculous stuff when the multitudes—and the press, of course—are listening. And, also, keep the 'competition' from repairing any damage we inflict in time to save their lord and master. To rephrase Patrick's words—can't be done."

"Isn't that just like the male chauvinists you are." Anne smiled to show she was not admonishing them. "Because *you* can't think of a solution you assume it cannot be done. When *I* had a problem I couldn't solve, I looked for other people to assist me in the solution. In fact, I recall turning to two very specific gentlemen for advice on how to continue. In fact, they are right here. Come on, my dear fellows, isn't there anyone you could ask 'how do I stop a parade in its tracks'? Well, maybe not, but you could ask leading questions. As long as you know *who* to ask!"

Sir Cedric faced the admiral with a very sad face. "Patrick, I'm afraid we have just been scolded. We have shirked our duty and taken the defeatist attitude. We should be tried by a jury of our peers and found guilty of negligence and sloth. As penance we should serve…."

"I think I understand your drift, old boy." The admiral's eyes were sparkling. "You're quite right, Anne. I suppose we didn't go into further inquiries because we would seem a bit odd, if not downright ridiculous. After all, this is not our usual line of occupation or even interest."

"It is now," Anne said. "Why don't we all prepare a list of candidates for discovering information that would help us? I'm already considering approaching—"

"Hold on just a minute, Anne, please." The admiral raised a hand. "There's a point I'd like to make and a proposal to follow it. It just dawned on me, with your help, Anne, that our attitude was all wrong. I mentioned the fact that we'd look ridiculous. Cedric even went through a mock condemnation of our shortcomings … these all point to the fact that we're not taking ourselves seriously enough. No wonder we were reluctant to open ourselves to outsiders. So here's what I propose: here and now the three of us establish an alliance, some kind of partnership or association, with the purpose of finding and developing ways and means for limiting the power of dictators without resorting to violence or politics. We could thus, I hope, make a mockery of them and cause them to lose their following. The result being, we all hope and pray, the thwarting of any dastardly plans these bastards had up their sleeves."

"Now isn't that something!" breathed Sir Cedric. "An association, my word! Like some kind of triumvirate or conspiracy thing. Patrick, you're right—this *will* make us take things seriously. I'm all for it. And I'd like to nominate Professor Anne Dupré to head this newly created order."

"Hear, hear," smiled Admiral Stone. "I solemnly promise to undertake any task she presents me."

"Hey, gentlemen," Anne protested. "Why me? I'm no activist. And I have no managing experience."

"Because, dear Anne," Sir Cedric said, "you're one hell of a smart lady and we know you to have been one for quite some time now. Furthermore, *you're* the one who emphatically stated that something needed to be *done*! And in addition, you've come up with ideas and directions that none of us 'activists' had ever thought of. And, I believe, they are all feasible given adequate preparation."

"I really don't know. I'm a history professor, for God's sake ..."

Admiral Stone added: "I imagine that in the future we'll need an experienced leader to direct operations and stuff. But you'll be our chairperson, our policy maker, and what you say goes. As to the association that has no name yet—we'll need to decide exactly how we operate. We all realize we'll need more people involved, but none of them would know the whole picture behind this involvement. Well, perhaps some of them, at a later stage."

"Who, for instance?" Anne asked.

Sir Cedric responded: "Offhand I wouldn't name names without due consideration. But in general I would say we would need to consider scientists, politicians and financiers. Patrick?"

"Makes sense to me," the admiral said. "We'd possibly need a professional work crew at some time in the future. What about staff to run the management chores? I mean taking minutes of meetings, establishing a computer database, setting project timetables, charting plans against results, you know—regular office stuff."

Anne stood up. "I don't think keeping records is a good idea. At least not now. It's just the three of us and things could evaporate tomorrow as easily as they came into being today. Let's keep it this way until necessity forces us to change our views."

"Point taken," the admiral said. "No office. Anything else?"

"Actually, yes," Anne said. "I really don't like the idea of involving politicians. I have no proof, but my gut feeling is that there isn't a single one of them who would put our cause before their own self-promotion. So I move to drop politicians from our agenda. Agreed?"

"Personally," Sir Cedric said, "I'd drop politicians from a flying airplane, let alone our agenda. I think we can do without them for now, at least until we think of a really desperate reason to involve them."

Anne had never felt anything like this before. Certainly, it was very flattering to be praised by these two eminent gentlemen, but the responsibility they expected of her was a substantial burden to shoulder. This was no job for a teacher who loved her profession and dedicated most of her time to it.

"About this chairperson thing ..." she began but her voice shook. She stopped, pulled herself together, and began again.

"Look, fellows, this is a very heavy responsibility you've hoisted on me. If I reject your nomination I would be denying everything that I believe in on tyranny. On the other hand ... oh, hell. Yes, I accept, and thank you both very much."

There were calls of "good girl" and "we're counting on you" from the two men. Anne calmed them down.

"But before we make our plans for what steps to take next, there is something important that I would like to make very plain.

"This association must be kept a total secret. Not a soul outside ourselves is to know what we're up to. If we do not disband right now, then it is understood that no individual among us may back out in the future. We might decide, the three of us unanimously, that we're closing up shop—but until such time we're all dedicated to each other implicitly. I sincerely believe that if the authorities ever got wind of what we're doing they'd put an end to it immediately. Not only would we probably find ourselves in a legal predicament, but it is also my belief that no one else will be there to pick up where we quit, leaving the world to continue its march toward disaster.

"We're all going to assemble a list of contacts to approach. We'll convene again and discuss the merits of each candidate. If he or she seems eligible he—oh, hang this gender thing—will need to be recruited. Each one of them should be aware only of the immediate involvement in their own expertise and nothing beyond. I'm afraid that recruiting is going to be an extremely delicate matter. If our candidate does not respond to our approach he may tell others, and that would jeopardize our entire project. I have nothing to suggest along these lines, and I hope you'll come up with something."

"Now let's put our intended targets up against the wall, as it were." Anne smiled. "I nominate the Al Qaeda leaders, and the Iranian president—in fact, they may even be in cahoots. Anyone else?"

The admiral was smiling in admiration. "Well said, Anne! Right. I was thinking of the North Korean president, the Cuban president, the Venezuelan president, and their like."

"That'll do," said Anne. "Now we need ideas for methods of operation. It's a blank slate now, but that's where our contacts might—what am I saying, *will*—provide us with the solutions. I personally hope we can tackle North Korea and Iran first—they seem to me to be the most dangerous. So let's set out our homework for next time: besides providing a list of potential contacts, please think about methods of humiliating the targeted tyrants."

"Most assuredly, Anne," Sir Cedric said.

"Oh, and I think that henceforth we need to have an innocent excuse for our meetings. Wherever we meet we must always be prepared for an unexpected interruption or visitor, and it must seem like a normal social get-together. Think up something, please."

"If I may," the admiral said. "I have had some experience in clandestine activities during service in Her Majesty's forces. With your permission, Anne, at our next meeting I would like to impart to you how we should proceed in recruiting collaborators. A few rather simple rules could make all the difference between success and failure."

"Let's have our next meeting in Paris, shall we?" Sir Cedric said. "I have a scientific conference there next week, and I'm sure Patrick can think up some reason for being there."

"Works for me." The admiral addressed Anne. "Our cover story is that your friend Cedric is bringing me along to visit you at your flat. Pretty flimsy, I agree, as we've done that already, but truth, no matter how flimsy, is almost always the best cover. We'll prepare something more elaborate for future meetings. Agreed?"

Anne was beaming. "Agreed," she said.

## FIVE

Martin Cooper had a window seat on the British Airways Airbus A321 and anticipated a comfortable flight. The departure from the gym was uneventful. George Graham didn't need much updating—this wasn't the first time he'd been left in charge. Although Martin would have trusted anyone on the team to do the job perfectly, he and George seemed to be more in tune than any of the others. He had a college education and was an accomplished athlete, horse rider, and pilot—having luckily been born into a wealthy family. He seemed to know what Martin wanted even before Martin did.

The team had performed well during the First Gulf War. They had saved each other's lives at one time or another, mostly Martin's own—without them he would probably have been left for dead in the Iraqi sands on several different occasions. Naturally, this brought about a tight bond between them, individually and as a team. Besides George, there was John Carmichael, the expert machinist who could literally revive a jeep after a direct hit with a mortar shell. Philip Brown could easily have won the Olympic sharp shooting event—his uncanny knack at finding the chink in the enemy's armor had led to more than one near-instant victory. Bernard Webb had almost superhuman strength, knocking down doors and extracting vehicles from sand pits just by putting his shoulders to them. Spencer Partridge could work semi-miracles with a knife when necessary, though he much preferred whittling wooden figurines.

Martin leaned back in his seat and shut his eyes. If the deal with Leblanc worked out, he could give the lads, and himself, a rise in pay. Or he could expand the gym and hire more staff—the lot next door, though not cheap, was available.

He smiled. *What a convenient opportunity,* he told himself, *to meet Anne. She'll get the surprise of her life. True, there weren't many opportunities to meet with her in the past, and, quite frankly, there never seemed to be a need to. Even though she and I are second cousins, we went our separate ways. If I hadn't seen her name in the Times concerning an imminent student's strike in Paris, I wouldn't have remembered she existed. But now, memories are flooding back—childhood memories, to be sure, but very pleasant ones. Anne, the chubby tomboy. Anne, the quick-witted leader of the strategy games with her neighbors. Anne, whose worst embarrassment was when she had to wear braces on her teeth to correct the slight overbite she had. Would she like the perfume I bought her? Would she remember me at all? Oh, well, if she turned out to be a cold fish, nothing would be wasted—Jennifer would love to have that perfume.*

*Maybe I should finally settle down, marry Jennifer and raise a family? I'd better make up my mind soon. Jennifer is sweet and she'll do anything for me—I know that. But for some reason I don't see her as Miss Right, know what I mean?* Martin felt a bit stupid asking himself this question. *I'm thirty-nine now, but I still don't think it's that urgent.*

*Back to Anne. This should be exciting, even if it's a dismal flop. I remember mother saying something about Anne marrying a certain Dupré fellow a long time ago. The last time I saw her was some twenty-five years ago when we were both in our teens, and I think she was a couple of grades ahead of me. Theoretically she could be a grandmother today, if she and her children married quickly enough. Hah—imagine! Pigtailed Annie Cooper with a husband and children and a career in the Sorbonne—history, wasn't it?*

*No, I won't alert her of my arrival. A surprise is a surprise all the way! I'll finish whatever I've got to do with Leblanc and then— roulette time! Anne and I will either hit it off for old times' sake, or we'll bore each other to tears and remain remote strangers for the rest of our lives.*

The PA system ding-donged, and the flight attendant announced their approach to Charles De Gaulle Airport. Martin smiled again and fastened his seat belt.

CRID

The slight afternoon drizzle irritated Anne only marginally, as she stepped out of the university's massive portals and into the hubbub of rue Saint-Jacques. There was usually an hour or so of daylight this time of the year, and she loved strolling down the paths of Jardin du Luxemburg, observing the groomed flowerbeds and watching children playing. But that was the roundabout way to her small apartment in the 5th Arrondissement, and today she felt she wanted to get home early and get some work done.

She couldn't get rid of the memories of last week's meeting with Sir Cedric and Admiral Stone. Probably nothing so exciting had happened to her since she had lost Raoul. Bang—just like that, she had become a leader. As if it were the most natural thing in the world. True, as a child, and later as a teenager, she was the one who always made the decisions: which games to play, when to end them, which role each participant would play—and all the other children would accept her authority without question. So maybe she *was* a natural leader. As an adult and a teacher this quality became a valuable asset. Sir Cedric and Admiral Stone probably sensed this, and she was not a little scared that men of their caliber had called on her to take the reins. Oh, well....

Gilbert hadn't called for a few days now, and Anne wondered if his wife had found out about them. Not that it mattered much. It was pretty obvious to both of them that their relationship had no future. Strong as he had seemed to be three months ago, the fifty-six-year old Chemistry Professor seemed to wilt away at every meeting they had—she couldn't bring herself to call them dates. His conversation grew less and less interesting, and their single attempt at sex the last time they met was a dismal failure. *Well, she thought, if he calls, I'll give it just one more chance. And if he doesn't—au revoir, Gilbert, I certainly shan't call you. And I don't approve of your smoking, anyway....*

Actually, she was a bit ashamed of this "little fling," as she thought of it. She had a habit of giving nicknames to experiences she went through, and this was named "little fling" from day one. Since Raoul died she hadn't had a close relationship with a man. She didn't really feel the urge and necessity to have a man at her side, but she wondered if she was at all capable of getting one, after such a long period without "practice"—another euphemism for her love life.

She headed for her apartment in Rue Gay Lussac, not more than twenty minutes away from the university at a brisk walk. She hugged her purse across her chest and waited for a break in the traffic. A tall man stepped toward her and covered them both with his open umbrella.

"May I?" he asked in English.

Anne stopped and turned toward the stranger. Was she being picked up by a foreigner to Paris? Not that it hadn't happened before, but usually the approach was at parties or lectures and involved some small talk and finesse. And in any case none of them went anywhere, and Anne prepared to brush off this encounter as well.

"You're Anne Cooper, aren't you?" Though it was a question, it sounded more like a declaration.

"Yes?" she answered, meaning "so what" and peered up at the face smiling down at her. Through the foolish looking grin she saw a clean-shaven face with a square-cut jaw and a pair of piercing blue eyes. As he was standing pretty close, well within her "personal territory" that every teacher learns to maintain fervently, she couldn't take in anything else about him without seeming to be rude. And the man wasn't really rude to her—not yet, anyway.

"Yes?" she repeated, but her expression was taking on a look of bewilderment as a spark of recognition set her brain churning. The man just stood there grinning, waiting to be acknowledged. The penny finally dropped—Anne had a near photographic memory—and her eyes widened in astonishment.

"Martin? Cousin Martin? It *is* you, isn't it?" she gasped.

"That's at least half a dozen questions we've exchanged without a single answer," laughed Martin. "So here goes. Yes, this is me and that's you, and we're related and we know each other from way back and we haven't seen each other for a very long time. Okay now?"

Anne let out a very unladylike squeal and threw her arms around his neck standing on tiptoe to do so. Her purse whacked him on his back. He returned her embrace and then they stood apart as much as the umbrella would allow and examined each other, smiling all the time.

Anne erupted in questions. "What are you doing here? What's been happening to you? Do you have a family? How are Uncle Timothy and Aunt Francine? Where do you live ...?"

Martin held up his palm.

"Easy there, Annie. I'll answer all your questions and I have a lot of my own as well. Why don't we find somewhere a bit more comfortable to sit down and talk? That is, if you have the time ..."

Anne composed herself and made a nominal gesture at arranging a wisp of hair. She was usually not given to outbursts, and she intended to cover up her embarrassment by assuming a very casual demeanor. She hoped she hadn't shocked Martin by her exuberance.

"Sure," she said, and linked her arm into his. "There's this little bistro around the corner where I usually have my morning croissant and coffee. It may be a bit noisy at this hour, but it's actually quite cozy. Okay with you?"

"Lead on, McDuff," joked Martin. Anne winced. *Lead on* instead of *lay on*—that was pretty bad, she thought. "Whither thou goest ..." Anne sighed, thoroughly delighted.

As they walked toward Place Berthelot, Martin explained. "I didn't bump into you by accident, you know. I suppose I could have looked you up and called and set a meeting, but I thought that surprising you would be more appropriate. Otherwise I would have missed seeing your face as you recognized me—Annie, let me tell you, your jaw almost hit the pavement ..."

"Well, I hope you waited for hours in the rain before I came out. Anyway, my jaw is back in place now, and I'm utterly enthralled. You said you planned this meeting? Why?"

"My presence in Paris is related to my business—let's not bother with that aspect for now. My presence at *this* particular place in Paris is specifically to meet up with you, to see how you were doing, and remember old times."

They made their way into the tiny Bistro d'Etienne, where Anne was a regular customer. The television was set to a football match, and Martin watched for a few seconds as they made their way to a table.

"Are you a fan?" Anne asked after they were seated.

"Not really," said Martin. "Here, I hope you'll like this." He pulled the little gift-wrapped parcel from his pocket.

Anne's eyes shone. "I'm supposed to say 'you shouldn't have,' right? Or 'how sweet.' I'll be original. I'll say 'thank you.'" She took out the tiny bottle of perfume.

"It belonged to Empress Catherine of Russia, and she used it only once. On her pet ocelot. And, oh yes—it's cursed." Martin kept a straight face throughout.

"Fascinating," murmured Anne, her face just as bland as his. "All I have is an orangutan, but I suppose it'll do. And I have ways of transferring hexes from objects to people, so you just watch out."

They looked very seriously at each other, as explorers would when discovering an unknown Pharaoh. Then they simultaneously burst into laughter, drawing the glares of the other patrons of the establishment. They hastily quieted down and smiled apologetically at their neighbors.

Anne remembered Martin as the son of her father's cousin and that he was three or four years her junior. They had played together in her teens and by the time she had begun her master's thesis—*Persian Influences on The Greek Empire*—he had just finished high school, and they weren't seeing each other as much. He was always the tall, lanky, fair-haired boy, usually the center of attention of whatever was happening. Now here he was again: still taller than average, fuller in physique—in fact, quite athletic looking—same blue eyes and something new she could only call charm. There wasn't any of that when he was a youngster. But now it seemed to exude from every pore. *No! 'He OOZED charm from every pore' was the correct phrase. Damn these clichés!*

"So," he was saying. "I'll save you the embarrassment of repeating your questions. Some of them at least. I am not married—never had the time and never found Miss Right. Until about seven years ago I served in the Military and was honorably discharged with the rank of Major. Since then, a few mates of mine and myself have a gym in London where we have a large clientele and we make a decent living. My parents, your great-uncle and aunt are fine, and I see them occasionally. Have I left out anything?"

"You haven't told me where you live today. I assume it's London, where you work, and that's good enough for me. Seen any action in the Service?"

"As a matter of fact, quite a lot. My mates—yes, they're the same lads I work with today—and I were in the First Gulf War in Iraq, and we were often sent on covert missions behind enemy lines. We were all decorated a couple of times."

Anne was impressed with his modesty. Through all that outward light-heartedness there was a tough interior. You don't get to be a decorated major doing raids in Iraq by being a wimp. And yet, it was always he and his pals, never him alone. They must be quite a team.

"I'm honored to be in the presence of a hero," smiled Anne. "So—why are you in Paris?"

"If you're really interested. Stop me if I bore you, which I promise I shall try to the utmost."

Martin related the aspects of the deal with Leblanc. It was in fact a huge success, and he was carrying very good news back to his staff in London.

"So," he concluded, "it looks like I'll have a good reason to visit Paris from time to time. Now let's change the topic to something far more interesting and talk about you for a while. You still have time, I hope …"

"Well, the American Ambassador expects me to be his escort to the opera tonight, after which we're flying to Hawaii for breakfast. So, I'm very sorry, but yes—I have all evening free." This sense of mischievous freedom was so refreshing. This is how she remembered all her teenage liaisons with Martin. She had long abandoned this style of language with her current colleagues— apparently the clever ones weren't clever enough to "get it," and the less bright ones just stared at her as if she had lost her marbles. She had never won these battles of wits with Martin, but she enjoyed every moment of trying to do so.

"Send him an 'oops—sorry' note tomorrow. Or next year. But back to you …"

"Right. How old are you now?"

Martin laughed out loud again.

"I'm thirty-nine, Annie. And you must be around sixty-four or sixty-five if I'm not mis—"

"All right, all right!" Anne was giggling like a schoolgirl. "I'm forty-two, widowed, and my parents still live in Reading. I'm a History Professor here at the Sorbonne, and I live in a little apartment close by."

The crowd by the television was shushing the people around them. Apparently a news flash was due. A few seconds later the announcer informed the public that Iran was continuing to defy the International Atomic Energy Agency's demands to reveal all their nuclear programs.

"They can demand all they want," muttered Martin. "But they'll never achieve anything that way." Aloud he said, "I hope you're as hungry as I am, Annie. What would you recommend in this gourmet establishment?"

They ordered dinner and continued chatting into the night. When they parted, they exchanged addresses and phone numbers and promised each other to meet again.

## *SIX*

Sir Cedric and Admiral Stone hung up their coats, Anne served refreshments and they sat by the table. No time was wasted on getting straight to the point.

"Well, gentlemen," said Anne, "What have you come up with?"

Sir Cedric raised his arm with a finger pointing upward, as if he were a seven-year-old schoolchild. When he got the others' attention he cleared his throat and said, somewhat hesitantly:

"Anne, the last time we met you mentioned the possibility of jamming up a dictator's broadcast. I have an acquaintance in

Milan, Emilio Rosetti, who owns a plant that produces musical instruments. He manufactures electric guitars and keyboards, amplification systems, wireless transmission applications, sound effect systems, and so forth—I really don't remember the entire scope of his output. It seems he's quite well known in his professional community, and he's accredited with a number of minor electronic breakthroughs. Anyway, I was about to suggest we try to find out if he could come up with anything that could serve us. What do you think?"

The admiral nodded slowly in assent.

"Sounds like a valid option to me," he said. "However, let's not approach anyone until we have agreed on a method to do so."

"*Mais certainment*," retorted Sir Cedric with a heavy British accent. "I would never have thought otherwise."

"Anyone else you want to consider?" Anne asked.

"Yes," Sir Cedric continued. "Estelle Burne is a very close friend of mine. Almost married her once. She is a freelance business consultant, retired now, and one of the most brilliant strategists I have ever met. She has found angles and solutions where top management had thrown in the towel, as the Americans say. Moreover, she loves these kinds of challenges and would, in my humble opinion, be of great service to us."

"Sounds good," Anne said. "Yes, Admiral Stone—you have the floor."

The admiral had copied his colleague's gesture with the raised finger.

"I've been giving some thought to two worthy gentlemen I know, both scientists. One is a very talented Dutch physicist named Jef van Welde and the other is a German named Gustav Lemke, who knows a thing or two about industrial chemistry. They may not be leaders in their field, but they control large factories where

… where 'things,' whatever they turn out to be, may be relatively safely built as just another internal project."

"I think," Anne said, "we'll have to know a little more about what they do."

"Well, I can't add much about Jef except that he specialized in optics and that he's a very old friend and completely trustworthy. In the past, he had evaluated a couple of optical equipment items for me—you know, telescopes, binoculars, projectors, lenses, even radars and ultrasonic devices, I think—and we became friends. I don't know the first thing about the science behind all this—perhaps Cedric here could find a common language with him in that respect—but I do know that talking to him wouldn't be a waste of time.

"As to Lemke, I have his card right here." He took out a calling card from his wallet. "Took some hunting in my files. We met years ago at some conference or other. He was very amiable and we hit it off right away. The card says: Dr. Gustav Lemke, PhD, Generaldirektor, Lemke Schädlingsbekämpfung and the phone, fax, email and the address in Hamburg. His industry is pest control—that's the long German word there. Whenever I'm in Hamburg I call him. He's quite the connoisseur of good German food and takes me to excellent restaurants. I realize this isn't much information, much like Cedric's. But we're just beginning now, and we need to talk to these …"

"Oh, that's quite understandable, Admiral," Anne said. "At this stage we have no way of knowing where these leads will take us. Three scientists and one strategist so far aren't a bad start at all, and we need to follow up on them. I'm a bit apprehensive, though, about your German friend. Pesticides are notoriously toxic, and I've read that many people have died due to misuse. He might advocate using his knowledge to build a weapon, and we've all agreed not to support chemical warfare."

Sir Cedric came to the admiral's defense.

"As I understand it, there is no intention of killing people. I'm sure Patrick was thinking along the lines of something to make people drowsy or lethargic, am I right?" The admiral nodded. "But we'll find out from the expert himself, won't we? And if we don't like his approach we'll just scratch it."

"Very well," Anne said. "We'll go along with it and see what turns up. Now it's my turn. I realize this may be overreaching as, unlike you two, scientists are not really the people I mingle with. But my late husband, Raoul, had connections necessitated by his diplomatic calling. You may have heard of the one I'm thinking of—Alfred Boulanger, who owns and manages Satellimonde. He, or rather his company, builds commercial satellites and launches them into space. He may be worth a try. I can imagine all kinds of things that can be done from space—remote controlling of devices on land, disruptions of many kinds. Thoughts, anyone?"

"I don't think you're overreaching, Anne," said the admiral. "Never heard of the chap before, but satellites have a lot of merit—except that they are so damned expensive. We could make use of them even today if only to collect information. I favor your proposal."

Sir Cedric demurred. "I have my misgivings," he said. "These pieces of equipment are so delicate, so intricately balanced, that we could never put anything of our own on them without causing major design changes. But go ahead and try anyway, Anne."

"Good. Let's get back to business, then," Anne said. "We now have candidates we wish to explore. Let's hear from Patrick how best we should do this."

"Well, let me put it this way. When governmental authorities wish to discover and eradicate underground activity, they take into account their three main weaknesses: propaganda—without which they couldn't spread their ideology, recruitment—vital, if they wish to expand their lines, and operations—which is their *raison d'être*. Propaganda requires printing and distribution or broadcasting facilities. Recruitment requires exposure to an outsider whose response is unknown: he may refuse to cooperate and then there's the danger of him informing the authorities. And of course, during operations, there is the possibility of clashing with these authorities. The first of the aforementioned does not constitute a problem for us—we have no intention to meddle with propaganda or in justifying our actions to the public. But we will need to recruit more people and therein lies our greatest danger. So we must prepare ourselves to recruit by the safest means possible. I have given this a lot of thought and would like to propose a methodical system for this."

"You mentioned operations as the third weakness," Sir Cedric said.

"Yes, I did. But we're still a long way from that stage. Every operation will need to be meticulously planned, and each plan will have its security considerations. Now, with your kind permission, here are the 'ten commandments,' if you will, to minimize danger in recruiting:

"1. While talking with the prospective recruit, mention, as if in passing, the issue of dictators and the threat they present. Watch for the reaction.

"2. If the recruit displays awareness of the dangers, ask a theoretical question—what can be done about it?

"3. If the response is that something must be done, inquire whether he himself—or she, as the case may be—would be prepared to take part in doing something.

"4. If the response is affirmative, raise the issue of how dangerous this undertaking may be and how undercover it must remain.

"5. If this doesn't faze the potential recruit, ask him how he would react if he was offered—theoretically, of course—to take part in such activities.

"6. If he claims that he would not consider being personally involved—agree with him, and switch to another subject of conversation. Scratch this candidate!

"7. If, however, he is willing to take part, we come to the riskiest part of the recruiting process: reveal that there indeed exists an organization doing exactly what was under discussion, and that you yourself would join if you knew how to contact it. If this contact were discovered would the recruit be prepared to join as well?

"8. If he agrees, he should be cautioned that, once inducted, there would be no turning back. It takes only one person to change his mind—and the whole organization would probably collapse. Therefore, he should realize that he is committing himself for life!

"9. At this stage, if he is still undaunted, you can reveal what is expected of him: we wish to exploit his high position in his field of expertise to develop tools to assist us in our common cause.

"10. Finally, you will never say anything about anyone else in this organization. You will be the sole contact person unless decided otherwise."

After a slight pause Anne said:

"My, oh my! This is straight out of John Le Carré! Normally I would want to write down everything you said, but I guess it would be best to memorize these ten points."

"Perhaps we could write them down temporarily," Sir Cedric suggested. "After memorizing, we could destroy our notes."

"Friends, please," interjected the admiral. "I agree with Anne— no notes. But I'm afraid you haven't yet told me whether or not you accept this regimen. It sounds like you do, albeit hesitatingly and reluctantly. I need to hear from you: do these points make sense to you?"

Anne and Sir Cedric immediately agreed that they did.

"Well, then," the admiral continued, "I appeal to your common sense. We are all intelligent people and we all realize that understanding the principle is far more important than memorizing a set of rules. This is not a 'how to' cookbook or a manual on the programming of a VCR. Too much is at stake here for us to risk writing anything down that may later be discovered and used to our disadvantage. So—any questions?"

There were none.

"Right, then," Anne said. "We approach the five people we mentioned, making it look as natural as possible. We employ the admiral's 'ten commandments' and see where it gets us. Also try to think of additional prospects. Agreed?" Nods all around. "Good. Let's set our next meeting ..."

"A moment, please, Anne," Admiral Stone interrupted. "What I have to say now is extremely important to our survival.... As we've noted, the next war is going to be more terrible than anything ever experienced in human history. Hundreds of millions will die, most of them in agony. What we're doing is trying to prevent that. We all need to internalize the importance of this mission—its priority is beyond anything else we encounter. As I said earlier, all followers of our cause—and that includes us as well—now have a lifetime commitment. Again, there is no turning back! If anyone, in the course of our operations, should have a reversal of opinion or show signs of betrayal, he or she will need to be silenced." He gazed carefully at the couple opposite him. "Do you follow my meaning?"

Silence. Anne and Sir Cedric both understood too well what the admiral was implying. Execution! How true—the life of an individual could never outweigh an attempt to save hundreds of millions of lives.

Anne was impressed—this was the first major decision they had made to do something. Right now she preferred to put aside the fact that in order to accomplish this she had laid her life on the line.

"There will be expenses—lots of expenses," she said. "And we need the wherewithal to finance them. Think about that, too, please. Now off you go—I have an early lecture tomorrow morning."

## SEVEN

The admiral could be charming when he set his mind to it. Despite his seventy years, his posture was firm and erect, and the silvery sheen of his moustache and very thin hair gave him a look of distinguished respectability. You could feel his powerful aura just by looking at him. His wife was always busy with one charity or another, and his two sons lived their own lives with their families in London.

He had retired at the height of his career and turned to business. He established an investment company and ran it from an office in London, employing only one secretary. Being a shrewd businessman, he also set up a nondescript company in Vaduz, the capital of Liechtenstein, for the sole purpose of having a fallback in case the necessity arose. Weekends he spent with his wife at their home in Brighton, but most of the week he could be found in his office in London or at his small but comfortable apartment in Chelsea.

The admiral could not remember when last he was so in accord with someone he had just met. This was only their third encounter and already Anne had become a dominating personality in his life.

Not, of course, in the way women dominate men, but in the sense that he was in the presence of natural leadership. And he knew exactly what leadership meant—hadn't he himself commanded a naval fleet of thousands of sailors and officers, all relying on his judgment and authority for their very survival?

So it did not take him long to begin preparing his recruiting plans. Yesterday he had his secretary set up a meeting with Jef van Welde in Amsterdam in the morning and get tickets for a naval exhibition in Hamburg in the afternoon. Now he was striding into Jef's office with an outstretched hand and a big smile.

"My dear Jef, how good to see you again," he said as hands were shaken.

"The same here, my good friend," replied the Dutchman. "And how are you?"

Niceties were exchanged, memories shared, and the admiral steered the conversation as diplomatically as he could.

"Certainly, Jef, we both know how valuable your scientific contributions were in the war. But you know what? There's a race during peacetime, too. And all the fantastic optical equipment you produce—and, I admit, other scientific breakthroughs—could serve terrorism just as well, couldn't they?"

"Well, of course, in the wrong hands…."

"I'm sure you're doing everything you can to prevent that, Jef. But don't you think Western governments are a little slack in how they tackle the threats of the dictators in the third world?"

"Come, come, Patrick—why such a gloomy outlook?" van Welde seemed quite cheerful. "Let me assure you that you have nothing to fear and that you can sleep soundly. Nothing is going to happen. The world is sick and tired of warfare. The threats you hear tossed around are all attempts at extortion and they'll all fail."

"What makes you so sure, Jef?"

"Because we have the most powerful nations on our side. I mean the EU and the USA. We have the most formidable leaders who know what's best for all of us, and they will never allow the world to deteriorate into global war again."

The admiral was taken aback by this man's innocent view of world affairs. He wasn't a stupid person, and he wasn't the gullible type—so perhaps he was secretly practicing to be a politician! But from any perspective, it didn't look like he was suitable for recruiting. The admiral would have liked to argue these points with Jef, but decided not to push the issue—and perhaps reveal more than he intended—and changed the subject.

"So your optical devices will serve mainly for peacetime utilization," he said. "Tell me, what innovations do you have in store for us?"

Jef stood up and walked around the table. He wore a huge grin. "Come with me," he said. "You will love our new microscopes."

*One down, one to go*, thought the admiral. *Let's get this over with.*

⊂߆⊃

It was nearing teatime and Admiral Patrick Stone found a vacant table at the Hamburg Stock Exchange Cafeteria on Kleine Johannisstrasse. Earlier he had called Gustav Lemke and told him he was checking up on a Naval Engineering Exhibition to be held at the Stock Exchange and perhaps they could meet up. Lemke agreed at once but insisted they should dine together. He would pick Patrick up at the Cafeteria.

The admiral sipped his tea and lazily glanced over the brochures for the exhibition. There was a time when he would have been thrilled to attend one of these prestigious events, but now they bored him to tears and he preferred to avoid them as much as possible. But they did provide a good pretext to come to Hamburg almost any time of the year. This was one of those times.

A large, fat man with a red face barged his way toward the admiral.

"There you are!" he bellowed in surprisingly good English. "I was hoping that this time *I* would be the first to arrive. How are you, my old friend?"

"Meeting with you is the highlight of my visit," replied the admiral, getting to his feet and shaking the pudgy hand stretched out to him.

Gustav Lemke was a man who loved good beer, good food, and bad women—in that order. A brilliant and innovative chemical engineer, he had several useful industrial applications to his credit, among them the usage of magnesium in paint used for shielding and a brand new technique for combining organic waste with recycled plastics. He owned a world-renowned multi-usage chemical plant in Oststeinbek, not far from Hamburg, but he always allowed himself the time to putter around in his specially constructed private laboratory.

"But my dear friend," Lemke took the admiral by the arm, "we cannot dine here. Come, you will be my guest at a brand new restaurant, the Ritz-Imperial on Lübecker Strasse. I have been there only once, but the food is exquisite and the waitresses delightful."

The admiral thanked his host and they took a taxi to the restaurant. During the meal they talked about old times and compared the food and wine to other restaurants they had frequented. Lemke was right—the food *was* delicious, though he preferred to reserve comment on the waitresses. The admiral made a mental note to pay this establishment another visit and try out other items on the menu. He decided it was time for the recruiting pitch.

"That was a very sumptuous meal, Gustav, my friend. I hope you shall give me the satisfaction of dining with me in London in a similar fashion. Soon."

"*Ach, ja!* I am looking forward to it."

"You know, Gustav, this fabulous meal makes me feel a bit guilty. For two reasons: first, I am ruining my dashing figure and shall be leaving all my lovely ladies to you. Second, there are so many people in the world that could have made use of this one meal to survive for a week. I could never understand how certain governments allow such poverty to occur in their countries."

"Well," Lemke said, "I think it is obvious. Those governments are not concerned with their people. They are far more interested in their own power and how to maintain it. You see this phenomenon happen in almost every dictatorship."

"Academically, you are right. But poverty and power are not the only issues there. Wouldn't you say that they are also attempting to expand this power of theirs outside their countries?"

"And who is to stop them," Lemke said angrily. "The United Nations? They are all talk, talk, talk, and their 'peace-keeping forces' are a joke. The United States? The EU? NATO? Come on, Patrick! You know as well as I do that they are political cripples, no spine, no guts, no balls. They have the power but behave like impotents."

"So what do you think *can* be done against the dictators?" probed the admiral.

"Destroy them of course!" Lemke noticed he had raised his voice, so he leaned toward the admiral and tried to speak normally, but his eyes gleamed just as vehemently as before. "Send in private commandos, vigilantes, mercenaries, whatever—and rip their regimes apart!"

"But outside the Western governments do you know of any entity that can actually perform these acts?"

"Of course not," Lemke replied bitterly. "There aren't any. If only there were."

"If you found out that such an organization *does* exist, would you consider joining it? I don't mean actually marching through the forests with the commandos." Admiral Stone laughed lightly. "I mean by using your expertise and the facilities at your command. Personally, I would think—"

"Let me tell you something in the strictest of confidence, Patrick. In my private laboratory, I have already developed substances that could be very damaging to these nasty regimes. I am now at the stage where I need to find somewhere to experiment with these materials, and that isn't so easy. However, I am planning...."

"But if you *had* the opportunity and the location to test your ... experiment, supplied by some organization, would you be willing to cooperate with it?"

Inwardly the admiral was shuddering. It wasn't so long ago that German chemists had experimented and had found a very effective way to annihilate millions of people.

"Yes, of course I would. Why? You don't believe I can go through with this?"

"Never occurred to me, my friend. I know you to be a man of integrity. But please explain to me—what does this substance of yours actually do?"

Lemke edged closer to the admiral and lowered his voice to a whisper.

"It looks like fertilizer and it is used the same way. It is packaged in a sealed bag, and the moment the bag is opened it starts working. The stuff is spread over an area, and for approximately eight hours it emits a certain gas. This gas is harmless to living organisms, but it has a peculiar reaction to internal combustion engines when sucked in through the carburetor. The engines simply die. They become totally useless. Think of what can be done with this. A car, a truck, a tank, even a whole convoy could be put out of commission."

Bingo!

The admiral was dumbfounded. He had not expected this kind of luck so quickly. He imagined himself reporting to Anne, and quickly guessed her response.

"How certain are you about that 'harmless business,' Gustav?"

"The gas has no effect whatsoever on living matter, I guarantee. Only when mixed with petroleum-derived fuel fumes, and then it only neutralizes its combustibility." Lemke grinned, showing yellow-stained teeth. "*Mein Gott*, I have been breathing this stuff for two years already, and all it has done is to make me slimmer...."

The admiral made a great show of measuring the German's corpulent form with his eyes.

"You would make an ideal 'after' picture." And they both burst out laughing.

Admiral Stone ordered two schnapps. "Gustav, old chap, prepare yourself for some very interesting news."

Half an hour later the German industrialist was recruited. They arranged the methods of communication between themselves and parted with a vigorous handshake.

The admiral had no idea how Lemke's experiments could be carried out. He had never expected to actually have a workable product to deal with, and he certainly could not have foreseen *what* that product was.

But that issue could be tackled later. Right now he was deliberating between flying home to Brighton and taking the train to Paris to inform Anne.

## *EIGHT*

Anne continued to conduct a normal life. She occupied herself by preparing tomorrow's lecture, having a light meal, and watching television, mainly the news. This evening she was entertaining her friend.

Since her husband's death five years ago, she hadn't developed an intimate relationship with a man. There were many men around her, to be sure—some young, some older, intellectuals, administrators, and even tycoons she had met through Raoul's military and diplomatic careers. She socialized with a few of them but nothing more ensued. She wasn't interested in a relationship and quickly rebuffed any advances made in her direction. Gilbert was the latest of her very few attempts, and it only convinced her more than ever that solitude was best for her. She kept a proper and respectful attitude toward women. She avoided gossip and personal involvement of any kind.

Tanya Gerard was the only one close friend she had. She could discuss any topic with her and they gave and took advice from each other. She had known Tanya some time before she and Raoul were married. In fact, according to prevailing norms, the two women should have been enemies, as Tanya had been Raoul's inamorata when Anne was introduced to him.

At that time, Tanya worked on stage as an actress in the evenings, and during the daytime she studied theatrical arts—acting and stage directing—at the university. Raoul was then a young and ambitious officer who dedicated all his time to the army, trying to attend all the additional training and seminars available and volunteering for every exercise and maneuver he could find. Usually, when Raoul had a free moment, Tanya was busy, and vice versa. Such a relationship could not endure for long.

Anne, on the other hand, was a bookworm and never went anywhere. Whenever Raoul had a rare free evening, Anne was always available. Tanya saw at once that it was a lost battle where Raoul was concerned, since she wasn't prepared to give up even one minute of the time she allocated to the theatre. So, no ill feelings were nurtured toward Anne—on the contrary, they found a lot in common and became fast friends. Their friendship grew even stronger after Raoul's death.

Tanya now dedicated her life to the theatre. She flirted and had affairs with almost every man she met and never gave a thought to marriage or raising a family, even though she realized she was not getting any younger. In her opinion, the theatre and a family were two conflicting concepts. A decision had to be made, and she had chosen. Her reputation grew, and she became the darling of Paris. Fans and admirers—including many respectable members of the Parisian elite—flocked to the stage door, and sent her invitations, flowers, and presents. They all fell under her spell—authors and playwrights, of course, but also musicians, professors and wealthy industrialists. And Tanya did not hesitate to pick her lovers from among them—their marital status being of no concern to her.

Because of her bohemian lifestyle, she and Anne couldn't meet as often as they would have liked, but whenever the opportunity availed itself they would spend a few hours together chatting, or just have a café crème at a bar.

It never crossed Anne's mind to mention her new clandestine activities to her closest friend. Even if she had not been bound to the utmost secrecy, Tanya just wasn't the type with which to discuss such issues. She belonged to another world, a different species of humanity, it would seem. Although Anne did not have any boyfriends, she was keenly interested in Tanya's amorous affairs, and listened attentively to all her friend's exploits. None of them, however, stimulated her enough to change her attitude toward intimacy with a man.

They were sitting on the sofa in Anne's flat. It was one of those rare occasions when Tanya could afford the time. Coffee and cookies were on the table. Anne was always impressed by her friend's beauty, an animal magnetism enhanced by fiery-red shoulder-length hair, a tiny waist and an ample bosom that she always kept almost completely exposed. A golden hand-shaped amulet rested in that glorious cleavage, and Anne noticed it for the first time.

"Is that a good luck charm you're wearing?" asked Anne. "I've never seen it before."

"*Mais oui, ma petite*," gushed Tanya in her rich contralto. "I got this one last week from a lover. He happens to be an Englishman, a retired senior army officer, or so he says. He got it somewhere in the Middle East. It's supposed to ward off the evil eye."

"You just keep wearing it there and you'll get more eyes on you than you bargained for." Anne and Tanya laughed. "Curious design, though. A hand with two thumbs...."

"Who cares!" Tanya scoffed. "It reminds me of him. I see him now and then when he's in Paris, which isn't very often. What a man! I swear, he makes love like ... like a bear. He's so strong he sometimes makes me cry out."

"I hope he isn't too violent with you," Anne said. "Does he beat you?"

"He wouldn't dare," Tanya replied. "But he *is* brutal in a loving kind of way. And I like it a bit rough, you know that. But we never overdo it."

"Go on, Tanya! You're no midget. I'll bet you give him a bruise or two yourself."

Tanya put on her dreamy look, the one she used when she remembered a particularly wild spree with a man.

"*Ma pauvre Annie*," she murmured. "I don't think you'll ever understand. It isn't a fight. It's ... it's passion! It's satisfying yourself and satisfying your man. Even animals don't have that kind of concern for each other—they don't have sex for pleasure as we do, just the natural instinct to procreate. Oh, you're too conservative, Annie, you wouldn't understand. Raoul was too gentle with you."

Anne wasn't offended. She didn't mind being constantly reminded by Tanya what she was missing, and this wasn't the first, and probably not the last time she had referred to Raoul. She bit into a cookie.

"Now tell me about your latest play, Tanya."

Tanya's eyes sparkled.

"It's not the play. I've just been invited to direct Molière's *Le Misanthrope* at the People's Theatre in Moscow. What do you think of that?"

"Why, Tanya, that's wonderful! Didn't you always say you wanted to be recognized abroad? Here's your chance."

"I really can't go into every detail right now, Annie. I've got to be home in an hour—Lucien is expecting me and I just hate to keep him waiting. But here's the conflict I'm in, and I need your advice. On one hand this is my big opportunity, as you have said. On the other hand, Paris is my home and I wouldn't want to live anywhere else in the world—I thought I'd mention that in case they offer me to stay there." The grin again. "In Moscow I'd have perfect freedom to work as I please—that would be really fantastic. But I'd be severing all my ties here in Paris, and when I return, who knows what I'll find. And I'll be a year or more older, too, remember. Here in Paris I have the lifestyle that I cannot live without."

"You don't speak Russian, do you?"

"I do, just a little, but they promised me a translator at all times." Tanya giggled. "My grandmother—you know she was a Russian émigré—used to converse with me in Russian. So although the text in my hand will be in French, I'll understand what the actors are saying."

Anne entertained a nasty thought. She could encourage Tanya to consent to the invitation, and then she would have one less obstacle to maneuver herself around regarding her new role. That way she'd need to invent less lies. But decency overcame selfishness.

"Have another coffee, Tanya?" Tanya shook her head. "Listen, this is totally up to you—it's your life, after all. I won't try to influence you in any way. But what I can do is tell you how *I* would react. Have you ever been to Russia?"

"No."

"Neither have I. But this is a fantastic opportunity to visit a huge and fascinating country. The boost to your reputation is also a considerable factor to consider. If I had been offered to lecture for a year in Moscow I would probably be facing the same dilemma you are now. Why? It's hard to say. I also feel my heart is here, even though I'm not French-born like you. But I married a Frenchman and *that* changed my life. Now my whole world is here—my work and my best friend. So I might have rejected the lecture offer. Now you tell me, dear Tanya, would you have advised me to go?"

Tanya was staring silently at Anne. Abruptly she shook herself and said, "I think I'll have a whisky on the rocks now, Annie."

"Of course," Anne said and got up to prepare the drink.

The phone rang. Anne excused herself and answered it.

"Anne?" It was Admiral Stone, and he sounded excited. "Can you talk?"

"I have company right now," Anne replied testily.

"I understand. Just take care of what you say, okay?"

"All right."

"Could you possibly free yourself and see me? I have something very important to tell you, and it's not for the phone."

*Oh, hell!* Anne thought. *I get to see Tanya so infrequently and now I have to give that up, too.* "Well, I certainly wouldn't want to miss that opportunity," she said into the phone, glancing toward Tanya. "Where are you now?"

"Excellent, Anne, excellent. Your guest is probably getting the impression that you have to leave. I'll come to your flat in half an hour. Okay?"

"Well, that doesn't leave me much time, does it? Couldn't it wait until tomorrow?"

"Well done, Anne. Now you're giving it a sense of urgency. See you soon." The admiral hung up.

Anne finished preparing Tanya's drink. She returned to Tanya and was surprised to see her putting on her jacket. She walked up to Anne and hugged her.

"Thank you so much, Annie. I've decided—I'm not going to Russia!"

"What ... but—"

"No reconsideration," Tanya said firmly. "I have to give my answer tomorrow. Annie, you have helped me make up my mind. Now I have to go and you have a date." She gave another mischievous grin. "You're off to see someone. Good for you. And this time you *will* tell me all about him! Bien—I wouldn't want my tall, blond and awesome-looking Lucien to think I was standing him up. He's a nervous and impatient twenty-year-old student, hung like a horse, and I'll tell you all about him next time."

"You've got it all wrong, Tanya," Anne protested. "It's an old friend of Raoul's. He's between trains...."

"Knock it off, Annie, *ma chérie*—I know all of Raoul's old friends, remember?" She opened the door and winked at Anne. "Have a *fabulous* time. Ciao!"

∽∾∾

Half an hour later Admiral Stone arrived.

"I came directly from the Gare Du Nord," he said. "You won't believe the international hopping I've been through today. First Amsterdam, then Hamburg, and now Paris. I'm exhausted."

"My sympathies," Anne said, with a hint of irritation. "What did you wish to tell me that was so urgent?"

"I'm terribly sorry, Anne—I didn't mean to spoil your plans. But after you hear what I have to relate, perhaps you'll think it was worth your while. Do you think I could have a drink?" The admiral sat down heavily on the sofa.

Anne realized with a start that she had been very inhospitable.

"My goodness, Admiral, I *do* apologize. Whisky, tea, coffee?"

"Whisky will do fine, Anne, thank you." He waited for Anne to pour drinks for them both before continuing.

"I have met with the two candidate recruits I mentioned at our last meeting. We can scratch Jef van Welde, the physicist—he won't do at all. But Gustav Lemke is quite another story." He reported what happened over dinner in Hamburg.

"So you see, Anne, we have a 'product'! It's supposed to do exactly what we hoped, it's safe, and its effectiveness is until about eight hours after deployment. We are on the threshold of a breakthrough. Lemke cannot test his stuff at his plant without arousing suspicion. I told him we'd take care of that."

Anne was stunned. Such a huge step in so short time was impressive indeed.

"We're moving from wishful thinking into action," she said. "I think we'll need someone who will be capable of conducting experiments of this kind in the field, as it were."

"You mean like an Operations Executive?"

"Well, I suppose that would depend on how involved he or she would be in the actual participation in our final operations. If so, he would need to be recruited into our management board. That would make us four instead of three. How does that sound to you?"

*What an amazing woman*, thought the admiral. *She's already two steps ahead. Of course, none of us could physically conduct these experiments, no matter where they were supposed to take place.*

"You're right," he said. "We'll need to have a board meeting as soon as possible. I'm off to London now, and I'll inform Cedric as soon as I arrive—and I don't care how late it'll be."

He gulped down the rest of his whisky, waved goodbye and marched through the door.


## NINE


Alfred Boulanger was a tall, thin man in his early sixties. His closely shaved head, green eyes, and hooked nose gave him an owl-like appearance. As owner and CEO—his official French title was President Directeur Général, or PDG for short—of Satellimonde, one of the most profitable conglomerates in designing, building, and launching of commercial satellites, his appearance was always at the height of elegance and his manner full of self-confidence. He lived with his family in a château about twenty kilometers southeast of Paris, but he spent most of his time at his office in the capital.

Anne assumed he would be a visitor at the space exhibition in the Grand Palais museum. Though she had never found any interest in space and satellites, she made a point of visiting the exhibition a number of times, hoping to bump into Monsieur Boulanger. Sure enough, there he was this morning, accompanied by a very attractive young lady. When he saw Anne, his eyes lit up. He whispered something to his companion, who excused herself and went to look for the ladies' restroom. Then, beaming from ear to ear, he embraced Anne and asked her how she was.

"Oh, I don't complain," replied Anne noncommittally.

"Ah, but fate has been unkind to you. You are very brave to face the world on your own. Listen, Anne, I cannot chat with you long now—as you can see, I am not alone. But I can easily make myself available for lunch. How about one o'clock at Chez Maxim's? Mind you, I won't take no for an answer."

Anne barely restrained a gasp. It wasn't often she had an opportunity to visit this exclusive restaurant.

She knew that Boulanger had a soft spot for her. Perhaps he was even slightly in love with her. But he always treated her with the utmost respect and courtesy. Sometimes she entertained the thought that were he not married and head of a family he might have had "serious" intentions about her. As she was "on duty," so to speak, she felt it was all right to take advantage of his attraction to her and accept the lunch date.

At the allocated time, he was waiting for her in the foyer. The maître d' ushered them to a quiet table by the wall. Boulanger ordered for them both. It was a lavish and sumptuous meal, and the conversation flowed as between close friends. Anne felt a bit guilty for not being able to offer anything in return to her generous host. But she had a mission to fulfill.

Over an exotic fruit salad, she decided to broach the subject and, using her student's provocative challenge to the study of history as a pretext, she asked her host's opinion on the subject.

"I'm afraid your student was more of an attention seeker than a scholar," Boulanger replied. "I don't think it was very smart to enroll for a history course and come up with that kind of question."

"Oh, there's no doubt about that," Anne said. "But in principle, don't you think he has a point? I mean, regarding the effectiveness of democratic leadership—not the value of studying history."

"Well, I wouldn't want my views to become public knowledge, Anne. If you were a reporter I'd probably brush you off with some stale slogan about democracies being the only hope for world peace, or working together for global harmony, and so on. But as it's you I'm talking to, and I know that you will not spread the contents of our conversation around, I can tell you I do not support those hackneyed spoutings."

He raised a questioning eyebrow at Anne, who nodded vigorously.

"I won't say a word," she whispered with a finger to her smiling lips.

"The Western world today is steeped in comfort and luxury, but it has lost its capacity for survival. Or should I say the *competence* for foretelling its own demise. Oh dear, this sounds like the beginning of a lecture."

"Sounds to me like a very interesting lecture," Anne said encouragingly.

"Look around you," Boulanger continued. It seemed he was not used to airing his views when they were not in line with what he thought was expected of him. This was an opportunity to share—confidentially, of course—what he really felt. "Everyone, you and I included, are like delicate flowers in the garden of global culture. We'll wither and die if we're not nurtured in time. In my humble opinion, we are *not* preparing ourselves for this. It's quite possible that when our children reach my age, or even your age, this restaurant may no longer exist. It could become a pile of rubble or a mosque. Oh, yes, there are many respectable and reputable delegates at the United Nations, but they all represent the interests of those who sent them there, and they have neither the will nor the power to fight for the lives of their people. It is a self-destructing civilization!"

*It's amazing*, thought Anne. *So many people think the way we do, yet nobody* does *anything*. She quickly reviewed the ten recruiting commandments in her mind, and delicately applied them, one by one, to Boulanger. The result was not long in coming—Boulanger did not need much convincing.

There was a short pause as the waiter cleared the table and offered coffee. A nod from Boulanger sent him off.

"This is very serious," Boulanger asked. "I say this because the outcome, as I see it, will change the face of the world. At last someone had the guts to propose some real action. I salute you and whomever you may be associated with. Listen, Anne—I have many ideas bouncing around in my head, but I need some time to sort them out."

"Perhaps I could help," Anne suggested. "Your expertise is in the satellite business and I know next to nothing about it. As a layman I can imagine snooping—I mean seeing things others cannot see, thereby gathering information—and remote control."

"You've got the main idea, Anne. The main applications are photography and relaying broadcasts. However, there's a lot more to it. Obviously, I'll refer to all the resources I have at hand to come up with something useful to our cause. *Our* cause! See how easily I can say it—something that an hour ago I would have deemed utterly preposterous! You're doing a magnificent job, Anne, and I totally understand and respect the secrecy involved. Like I said, I need time to think this over—perhaps I can provide one or two surprises for you."

"Actually, Alfred," Anne said, remembering Sir Cedric's comments, "what do you think of the possibility of a satellite carrying a piece of equipment of *our* design?"

"That won't be easy, but it's not impossible. If you get the specs to me I could give an opinion on the feasibility of incorporating it into a satellite."

"I hate to put pressure on you," Anne said, "especially after such a dramatic turn of events. But you *do* realize, I hope, that—"

"… time is of the essence," Boulanger completed the sentence. "Yes, of course, Anne. I am fully aware of that. The sooner we can implement anything, the better. Indeed, the tiniest success will help in postponing the catastrophe, even if only marginally. And that would be an excellent start. Now let's see how we can keep the ball rolling. And get those specifications to me ASAP!"

The coffee had arrived. They agreed on how to maintain communications. Anne thanked him for the "divine" meal, and they parted with a warm and meaningful shake of hands.


# TEN

Sir Cedric had arranged a convenient business meeting in Milan, from where he called his good friend Emilio Rosetti—a typical Italian who loves pasta and beautiful women. Everybody knew that he had an *amante*, a mistress, which did nothing to mar his family life with a wife and five offspring. And everyone would testify to what a devoted husband and father he was, but when you reach a certain stage of opulence, one or more mistresses were actually expected of you. And Rosetti *had* reached that stage—and had been there for some time. He enjoyed a high international reputation, and contended very successfully with his German and Japanese competition. The label "Rosetti" on any musical instrument or sound system was enough to guarantee excellence, and that was what you got if you were looking for quality and integrity. Of course, you would pay the price accordingly. It was said that his estate, just outside Milan, was something out of a dream. Unfortunately for Sir Cedric, he had never been in Milan long enough to accept Rosetti's invitations to visit him there.

The meeting between the two was friendly and informal. Rosetti took him to a superb seafood restaurant and ordered for them both. Over a delicious lobster, Sir Cedric decided to begin applying his recruiting techniques. He did not get very far. The mere mention of democracy evoked a violent response.

"Democracy? *Porca miseria!* What a useless system. Mind you, my friend Cedric, bad as it is, it still cannot compare with Mussolini's fascism. That was the absolute bottom of the barrel, that filthy bastard. Never talk to me about tyranny or dictators— they make my blood boil! You know what I think? The Americans should long ago have bombed the shit out of the nuclear installations in Iran and in North Korea."

Sir Cedric was thoroughly enjoying this conversation. It didn't take much to rile Emilio up, and apparently he had pushed the right button. Perhaps a little more persuasion....

"Emilio, old boy. Don't get so excited. After all, you know very well that the United States can't just go and bomb anyone they don't like. Actually, anyone *you* don't like. Not very fair on the rest of the world, now, is it?"

"*I* don't like? Just myself and a few hundred million people. Including, I believe, you, *Sir* Cedric Norton! That is *exactly* what I am talking about. They cannot bomb, you cannot bomb, we cannot bomb—instead, they issue complaints to the United Nations. And the members of the Security Council—*tutti essere fottuto.* All fucked up, you know. A democratic institution that is completely impotent! Not, perhaps, out of choice, but because their individual interests cancel each other out. They'll *always* be at stalemate, they know it, yet they keep on acting out this farce! *Merda!*"

"And if you had the option, what would *you* do, Emilio?"

Sir Cedric continued navigating the conversation expertly, getting all the confirming responses he needed from Rosetti. Finally the topic of Rosetti's expertise was addressed. He had calmed down considerably. Sir Cedric mentioned the option of interfering with broadcasts.

"Listen, Cedric, my friend. This is a very admirable project you are undertaking. Personally, I do not think I would have dared to initiate such a venture. But I will help you as much as I can."

He paused to think.

"You know, Cedric, it takes great skill and very expensive equipment to produce sound systems of the highest fidelity. But you are requesting noises, cacophony, disrupting communications— and that is much easier!"

"How about interfering with a closed circuit amplification system?" Sir Cedric asked. "You know, accessing a system without tapping into its wiring physically?"

"You mean a wireless audio jammer? These techniques are quite old and easily implemented. No, my friend. I believe I know what you need, and I am thinking in terms you could not understand. You have given me a challenge, and I just *love* challenges. I will work on it and get back to you as soon as possible."

"Why, thank you, Emilio." Sir Cedric was justifiably proud of his success.

## ELEVEN

It was the weekend Anne had planned to spend with her children and parents in Reading, so she had no problem agreeing to the meeting called for today at Sir Cedric's residence.

Admiral Stone was already seated in an overstuffed armchair. Sir Cedric greeted her warmly and, after taking her coat, went into the kitchen. A minute later he wheeled in a trolley laden with canapés and a tea set, all prepared ahead of time by the ever-industrious Matilda.

Anne was itching to reveal her newest recruit, Alfred Boulanger. She would gladly have agreed to hold the meeting at any earlier date, but all three had their schedules full. She forced herself to behave with the dignity that her duty as chairperson demanded.

"We're all up-to-date about our first recruit, Gustav Lemke—thanks to Admiral Stone. I mean, the admiral," she hurriedly added when she saw the beginning of a protest from that gentleman. "Before I continue with my own report, let's hear what Cedric has to say."

"Well, my friends." Sir Cedric's voice was uncharacteristically toned down. "As you may recall, I went after two candidates. I called Estelle Burns—the strategist and my old flame—first. My call was answered by a live-in nurse. She told me that she took constant care of Estelle, who had an advanced case of Alzheimer's disease."

Sir Cedric's voice caught in his throat and he stopped.

Anne broke the silence. "Have some tea, Cedric, and tell us about the other candidate."

"You're referring to Emilio Rosetti, the music man," said Sir Cedric. "Sorry about that business with Estelle. I think we can count her out."

Sir Cedric related his conversation with Rosetti. He was very pleased with the ovation he received when he ended his narrative.

Anne, in particular, was delighted. Three hits—though the others did not know yet about her own success story—was not yet a statistical sample, but a very encouraging start just the same. It was a kind of verification that their ideology was indeed justified. Anne wondered whether an opinion survey would back up her surmise that the majority of the Western world's population would have endorsed this ideology.

"Well, gentlemen," she said. "As Al Jolson remarked after the first sound movie was released, 'you ain't heard nothin' yet!'" She told them about her meeting with Boulanger down to the tiniest details. She noticed Sir Cedric getting more and more excited.

"I think this is a fantastic opportunity," Anne ended her story. "We have three …"

Sir Cedric jumped to his feet.

"My dear friends," he expostulated. "Have you any idea what this means? Anne, you have made my dream come true! For years I have been working on my pet project—a satellite-borne laser beam projector that could be aimed and fired at will from a control station on the ground. It never got past the prototype stage because I was certain I could never get it onto a real satellite. But if it works, we'll be able to hit the targets we choose, blow up explosives, jam radars, and perhaps even disrupt the functioning of atomic reactors. Or take out the tyrant himself! I'll need a few weeks…."

"No!" Anne got to her feet and glared at Sir Cedric who, though a head taller than she, got the feeling he was looking up at her. "We must, here and now, implicitly agree that there will be no 'taking out.' Not by us, ever! We'll leave that to armies or resistance movements, or even terrorists."

"But Anne," Sir Cedric tried to rationalize, "if we shame a dictator so much—which is what we *want* to do—that his people revolt against him, I'm sure blood will be shed. People will almost certainly die, and our target would probably be among them."

"Then so be it," Anne retorted. "If his people want to finish him, let them! Our job is only to make them aware of his shortcomings, to prepare the groundwork. I insist on this! If you disagree, perhaps we should redefine who we are and where we're headed."

No one spoke for a few minutes. This was a delicate issue, and Anne had declared her position almost as an ultimatum.

Admiral Stone broke the silence.

"Allow me to put it this way, please," he said. "The aim of our association is to damage the reputations of dictators. We want to embarrass them in front of their people and make them lose their confidence resulting, we hope, in their abandoning of their megalomaniac aspirations. If our non-militant actions beget major upheavals, if the targeted tyrant is executed or takes his own life, and even if there are additional casualties, that is none of our business. In fact, we could safely say that such an outcome is predictable, and that more likely than not, something resembling what I have just described will, indeed, occur. Have I made myself clear?"

Again there was quiet. This was a moral issue every way you looked at it.

"Yes, Admiral," Anne said finally. "You have hit the nail on the head. I couldn't have described it more accurately myself."

"I recall," Sir Cedric said, "that during my university days one of my bachelor friends was asked why he hadn't married. He replied that if he got married he would probably have children. The birth process involved blood and he was opposed to bloodletting of any kind. We should remember that our association is based on the fact that democracies today are very like that bachelor. By the way," he added with a smile, "*I* have totally different reasons for remaining single. Anyway, I concur with Patrick's views. But let's not fool ourselves, Anne. No matter how we define it, there'll be blood in the end."

Anne took a deep breath and let this information sink in. She decided that she'd wait until she was alone to consider the ramifications. Now it was time to switch the subject.

"Let's have another look at Herr Lemke's fertilizer. I understand that the stuff is ready and only needs to be tested out in the open, right? He says he cannot do it, but I cannot imagine any of us actually carrying out these tests. We'll need a lorry or two and an extra vehicle to tag along. We need to find a suitable location for the test far enough from prying eyes. Then, I suppose, we'll need enough of the stuff to spread on the appropriate course and drive our lorry over it, and then examine and analyze the results—perhaps even with Lemke's help. Later we'll need to conduct similar tests with the acoustic equipment. And there'll probably be a host of other manual and logistic tasks that will arise, but that we cannot handle ourselves."

"All very true, Anne," the admiral said. "What are you getting at?"

"At some stage, and I think we're there now, we'll need to address two main issues. One—finding someone to handle our logistics and experiments. Two—finding some way to pay for all we intend to do. I believe the sums involved will be quite substantial."

"Yes, it's been worrying me, too," the admiral said. "At first I believed that we could expect each of our recruits to produce the tools we needed out of their own resources. It appears I was mistaken. Before we can begin, we'll need money—a lot of it! Besides the lorries you mentioned, Anne, I envision the rental or purchase of a small aircraft. And of course we'll need our logistics men or team—the Operations Branch, if you will. Even if they're volunteers, as we are, they'll be required to travel, buy stuff and all kinds of other things that cost money. My initial estimate is in the millions—whether pounds, euros or dollars. Where do we find that kind of money?"

Sir Cedric added: "And we'll need a place to manufacture the various fittings and other accessories that will probably be required for optimal functioning of our tools. We'll need to prepare dummy targets and test environments, packaging, techniques for concealing or camouflaging our tools so that they may be carried around or across borders. I have no doubt we'll need a well-equipped workshop and, possibly, a laboratory for all that. That, too, will cost a lot of money."

"We need to recruit a financier," muttered Anne. Out loud, she said, "Does anyone have a millionaire as a close friend? Preferably a billionaire?"

"Well, I could try approaching Neil Bennett," the admiral said hesitantly. "I once knew him, a long time ago. He must be around ninety now, and he's supposed to be worth billions. He began his way in the business world by buying up derelict pieces of military equipment left on the battlegrounds after the Second World War. He paid peanuts for them—sometimes even nothing, they were so glad to have him cart the stuff away—under the heading of scrap iron. There were others who took similar initiatives, but I don't know what became of them. Anyway, Bennett invested in oil and the like and became one of the wealthiest men on earth. If he's still alive—I haven't heard about him for years—I'll try to contact him and hope for the best."

"Good," Anne said. "However, we cannot rely on just one possible candidate. I trust you'll give this some thought and come up with a couple of filthy-rich prospects. And please, find a solution for our 'Operations Manager.'"

Actually, Anne's thoughts were already churning on the prospect of the Operations Manager. She could already imagine an Op Team able to arrive at any location, plant devices, disrupt the tyrants' intentions, and so forth. Very special qualifications were necessary. They could not be like the current board, two elderly men and a woman—they would need to belong to another breed of humanity. And what about integrity and loyalty? And they'll cost money as well—young men need to be paid.

She didn't notice the others watching her. So when the admiral suddenly cleared his throat, she started and returned to reality.

"My apologies, gentlemen," she said. "I was thinking about our operations problem. I think we'll need to pay our operatives. And that brings us back to the financing issue. Oh! ..." She let out a little gasp.

They continued to watch her silently.

"... It just occurred to me ... I mean, perhaps ... oh, hell—I just met a relative of mine. He's my second cousin, Martin Cooper. I was Anne Cooper, too, before I was married. He's a retired major who fought in Iraq in 1991 during the First Gulf War. He led a commando unit and was decorated for bravery. He runs a fitness gym here in London. His staff is made up of the soldiers who fought in his unit, and he claims they are as loyal to him today as they were then. I just remembered he commented quite accusingly about the helplessness of the United Nations during a news broadcast at our café. What do you think? Shall I try to recruit him?"

Sir Cedric raised his eyebrows.

"What do you think, Patrick?"

"Couldn't do any harm. Check him out, Anne."

## TWELVE

*Lucien must be keeping Tanya quite busy nowadays*, thought Anne. *A young man in the prime of sexuality could go on and on the entire night, every night! And Tanya, at twice his age, is probably stumbling around in a blissful daze. She's quite compulsive about sex. Could I be missing something? I doubt it....*

Tanya had not called for over a week, since her last visit. Anne thanked her lucky stars for this—she was far too busy for socializing at the moment. She tried to imagine herself in bed with a young stud whose only aim was to satisfy her carnal needs. The fantasy vanished as she told herself she *had* no carnal needs.

The top item on her non-official agenda was to sound out Martin Cooper as the association's Operations Manager. She called him from her flat in Paris.

"Annie!" Martin was genuinely pleased to hear her. "I tried to call you a couple of times. When and where can we meet again? Paris? London? Dinner?"

Anne felt a thrill rush through her. *Perhaps I should have called him earlier*, she thought.

"I'll be visiting my children and my parents in Reading over the next weekend, Martin. I see them so infrequently that I've got to dedicate all that time to them. But I could extend my visit by a day. If you're free on Monday, I'd like to accept your invitation. But let's make it lunch, shall we? I've got to be back in Paris that evening."

"Fantastic!" Martin said. "How about I drop by your parent's place a bit before noon and drive you back to London to show you around my gym? Then we'll enjoy a right royal luncheon. Okay? It'll also give me the opportunity to see your parents again after such a long period and, of course, to make the acquaintance of your children."

Anne managed to blurt out "It's a date," and slammed down the telephone before her voice gave her away. Her heart was pounding and her breath came in gasps. *Am I going mad?* she asked herself. *It's just another lunch appointment in which I'll see if he's a suitable candidate for Operations Manager. I've had countless dates with men before, so why this sudden excitement? Just because I like Martin more than the others doesn't mean I need an oxygen tank now! I'm probably still fantasizing myself in Tanya's role....*

ॐ

The weekend in Reading was as if taken from a storybook. Guy and Julie, now sixteen and fourteen respectively, pranced around her like puppies. Her parents showered attention on her and made sure she had every comfort she needed. They all went on a picnic on Sunday, and in the evenings they discussed school and played board games. When the children went to bed, she and her parents caught up with all the little details that parents always want to know. When she told them about Martin they were eager to renew their acquaintance with him.

Anne had difficulty sleeping during her last night in Reading. Her thoughts kept returning to her date with Martin the next day. She found herself impatient, like a child trying to prophesy her birthday presents. But most disturbing of all was the fact that it wasn't her recruiting mission she was thinking of.

*This is really silly. It was a spontaneous kiss on the cheek between two distant relatives meeting after a long interim. Perfectly natural. And tomorrow, when he comes here? Should we kiss again? Oh, heck, it's of no importance. Let things happen any way they will.* She turned on her side, but sleep still eluded her. That future virtual kiss continued to bother her.

CO3BO

Next morning Anne felt alive and vibrant. She had eventually fallen asleep and no dreams tormented her. She took particular care to look her best, paying special attention to her dress, her makeup, and her hair. And she knew too well that this was not for the benefit of her family, but because she was going to meet a man.

Martin arrived and parked his sports car in the driveway. When Anne saw him stride toward her, tall and handsome, she decided she'd give him a kiss—and the hell with spontaneity. She had kissed very few people since Raoul died—her parents and children, of course, and Tanya sometimes—but these didn't really count. Gilbert and the two or three other "little flings" of hers were never really meaningful—just a mechanical act that went with a futile attempt at sex. Now she felt differently. For the first time since she was widowed she *wanted* that kiss.

He walked briskly up to Anne and they shared a hug and kissed each other on the cheek. Then Martin embraced Anne's mother and shook hands warmly with her father.

"It's so good to see you both again, Professor Cooper, Mrs. Cooper," he said. "You're both looking so well. I regret that we won't be able to stay for long—Annie and I have a full agenda in London."

They discussed old times, and Martin conveyed his parents' regards and invited the Reading Coopers to visit them. Both the Cooper families really had no idea why they had drifted apart for so long—it had just happened—but they promised they would do all they could to rectify the matter. Martin assisted Anne in loading her luggage into his car, they waved goodbye and departed for the capital.

The conversation during most of the ride to London mainly concerned the family. Martin wanted to know everything about them, and how Anne had spent her weekend. Anne told him about the children's school achievements, how Guy wanted a military career, as his father had done, how he was still deliberating between joining the British or the French Army. And Julie wanted to follow in her mother's footsteps and become an expert in some academic subject. Not history, however—perhaps psychology.

Then Martin told her that after being decommissioned from the army, his five subordinates stated as one: "We'll follow you anywhere you go!"

"I felt an obligation to take care of them. I got the idea of opening a civilian shooting range—something I thought was suitable for ex-soldiers. Our customers would learn how to handle firearms and practice shooting at stationary and moving targets. We found a building that was once owned by a now-defunct company and leased it. It didn't take long to discover that the building was far too large for its purpose, and one of the lads, George, who used to work out in a gym, suggested we add workout facilities as well. We did, and we now have a thriving business."

The car turned the last corner and braked. "Here we are—'trim and fit' at your service."

As they walked in, Anne saw a few people working at bodybuilding machines, and others resting on benches near the walls. The trainers gathered round Anne and Martin, who led them into his office.

"Boys, I'd like you to meet my cousin, Professor Anne Dupré," he announced. One by one they grinned and shook Anne's hand while Martin called out their names: George Graham, Philip Brown, Spencer Partridge, Bernard Webb and John Carmichael.

The "boys" took turns—in accordance with their availability—in introducing Anne to the tricks of the trade, explaining how each device functioned and the health benefits to be achieved. Anne enjoyed trying her hand at operating some of the machines. Then she was led to the more "prestigious" part of the enterprise—the firing range. She found that things were not that simple: before arriving at the range itself she had to pass through the classrooms and practice the correct procedures. She saw how a customer would have to learn to handle his weapon, take it apart, clean and reassemble it, and then load and unload ammunition into it. As if that was not enough, he also had to practice various shooting positions—only then could he enter the firing range.

Anne was taken there and earmuffs were put on her head. A pistol was put in her hand, a target pointed out, and Anne emptied an entire magazine into it. The results were surprisingly good, much to everyone's delight, considering the fact that Anne had never before held a firearm.

Anne found Martin's lads, as she now called them, to be quite charming—both in appearance and in their manner toward her.

It was close to lunchtime, so she bid the team farewell and allowed Martin to steer her out of the gym. He drove her to a fashionable restaurant and ordered lunch for both. Anne was enjoying herself so much that she almost forgot that she was on a recruiting mission.

Delicately, as if by the way, she began probing Martin's opinions on world affairs. She knew the man facing her at the table was a hardened Special Forces major, but even so she had not expected so vehement a reaction.

"From what I see around me," he said seriously, "the world is committing suicide! I see no hope at all for its salvation. Humankind is composed of pathetic half-wits! Their leaders are cowards and idiots. They have padded themselves with these so-called 'humane' laws that tie their own hands, and they'll pretty damn soon bring about the destruction of civilization as we know it. They provide 'humanitarian' aid to the megalomaniac dictator of North Korea in order to make him stop developing nuclear weapons. Now he can feed his starving people and *still* continue with his nuclear development. And take Iran … oh, what's the use! It's hopeless."

"Those are pretty strong words, Martin," Anne said softly, glancing at him over her wine glass.

"I'm sorry, Annie." Martin composed himself. "I don't usually have these outbursts. It seems you've touched a raw nerve. I've seen dreadful things in battle, and I can easily declare that most could have been avoided by the leadership taking the proper steps long beforehand. Which they could have done, but didn't! And, I'm afraid, they won't in the future either."

"It couldn't be *that* bad, Martin." Anne appeared to try to soothe him, but she really wanted to be absolutely convinced he was the right man for the association.

He looked into her eyes and took her hands in his.

"Annie, I'm not at all sure that any of our generation will die a normal death, in our beds." He paused, then let go of her hands. "Did I shock you?"

"Not really," Anne said. "Apparently there are quite a lot of people who think the way you do." She grinned at him. "I, for one. I've often asked myself if there was any way in which these dictators could be stopped. Without, of course, shedding blood."

"Can't think of any such way. You're the historian—has anything like that ever happened?"

"Oh, definitely. Kings and emperors were often intimidated into reversing their opinions or decrees—even to abdication or suicide in the face of failure. But these were all low-scale compared to what we're up against now. I was thinking of embarrassing today's dictators—make them lose face, lose their confidence, become the laughing stock of their nation. If you were approached to help in such a cause, would you lend a hand?"

"That goes without saying. But no government would even consider going into such enormous research and expenses. And no government could *ever* keep it a secret, and without absolute secrecy this kind of venture is doomed to failure."

"Ah, yes—a very valid point, Martin. But if there were a *private* organization undertaking this 'venture,' as you call it—would you still consider joining it?"

Anne continued the conversation, adhering to the recruiting rules the admiral had lain out. It didn't take long to get Martin's commitment.

"And I am authorized," she concluded, "to offer you the role of Operations Manager. I sincerely hope you will accept."

"What operations?" he asked.

Anne summarized their current need for testing newly invented chemical substances. Later, reconnaissance of the target countries would also be called for. And who knows what more besides.

Martin gazed silently into his wine glass for a few moments.

"Are you intending to commit sabotage within those countries?"

"We're not an army," Anne replied. "Neither are we a militant underground movement. The furthest thing on our minds is to handle explosives or weaponry, or to conduct guerilla activities inside dictatorships. We don't even intend to make use of the spoken or written word—I mean, we won't be doing any propaganda. Larger and more powerful instances than ourselves have tried those methods and failed. We want to make the dictators themselves appear ridiculous, to make them a mockery, to shame them in public. We want to divest them of their proud self-image and have their own people see them in their ignominy. We strive to make them fail in their ambitious projects in ways that will leave the people doubting their military powers and their authority. And, we hope, all this will result in minimizing their belligerent activities, thereby reducing the danger to the world. They would *have* to change their foreign policies and give up their megalomaniac aspirations."

"And just how will you accomplish this?"

She smiled at him.

"You're not the only recruit, you know. We've managed to hook a couple of very clever scientists, who are developing, umm … let's call them 'tools' or 'devices' or 'technological means' by which speeches, military parades, and weaponry testing may be disrupted."

"For instance?"

"Well, let me try to give you an illustration. Imagine a despot about to address hundreds of thousands of his followers assembled in the capital's central square and along the route of a grand military parade. Imagine that suddenly the public address system emits an ear-splitting screech causing the public to cover their heads and disperse. Imagine the soldiers stumbling about as if intoxicated, and that the vehicles and tanks are suddenly non-functional and grind to a halt. Now what do you suppose will follow? Would the tyrant take his own life? And if not, after lopping off the heads of 'those responsible,' would he change course? I'm no prophet, but I think I can safely say that our embarrassed dictator will probably arrive at some far-reaching conclusions. His arrogance will be greatly compromised." Anne searched Martin's face for a reaction.

He thought for a minute.

"And your people are developing these options?"

"That's right. Some of the stuff needs testing—others are still being developed and will need handling later."

"For what you have just described—well, one man will not be enough. You'll need a team. Perhaps five or six highly qualified men."

Anne gave him the sweetest smile she could muster.

"I wonder where I could find such men …"

"I have a scheming femme fatale as a cousin!" Martin laughed. "You win! I'll talk it over with my lads. Don't worry—I won't give anything away until I get your okay. Okay?"

After lunch, Martin drove Anne to Heathrow airport. At the terminal, they parted with a hug and a cordial kiss, which seemed to have become habitual.

*All well and fine*, thought Anne to herself on the Air France flight back to Paris. *But nothing can be done unless we find the funding. The admiral's lead may not be alive or his contribution insufficient for our needs. We'll need additional financiers, just to be on the safe side. There was this American billionaire at a benefit dinner for starving African children I attended. He gave quite an impressive speech, indicating his pocket was open for worthy causes—and indeed, his donation was gratifyingly generous. Something Dodson. I still have the agenda for that dinner somewhere at home—I'll have to look him up. Then I'll see if I can find a way to contact him.*

Anne dozed for the rest of the flight and awoke when the plane landed at the Charles De Gaulle Airport. She took a taxi to her apartment. The taxi's radio blared out the announcements of the Iranian president that "no one could prevent them from developing nuclear power." For peaceful purposes, to be sure, but the international community was starkly aware of his true intentions—on numerous occasions he had not troubled himself to conceal them.

*Oh, hell! We've got to hurry. In just two or three years he'll have the bomb, and that's exactly what will bring about the global calamity we're trying to prevent. If we don't come up with something in a year or two it'll be too late, and we'll witness the worst cataclysm in history. And most likely—we won't survive it.*

In her mailbox, Anne found an invitation to an international art exhibition featuring prominent artists who would arrive from the USA and Russia. *Interesting*, she thought, and noted the date and time.

## *THIRTEEN*

Sir Cedric was perusing a routine report from one of his laboratories when the phone rang. His secretary announced that Albert Allier was on the line.

*"Mon cher ami!"* the knight bellowed into the mouthpiece in his terrible accent. "It's been a long time since you last called up an old colleague!"

"True, true," came the voice over the phone. "But, as they say, better late than never. Listen, my friend, there is something I need to discuss with you quite urgently. Are you planning a visit to Paris? Or would you rather I visit you in London, which I would gladly do?"

Professor Albert Allier was the head of the Paris University Irradiation Research and Development department. He and Sir Cedric had spent many hours together on joint projects. Sir Cedric remembered him as an unpretentious man, unassuming and retiring, who would rather bury himself in solitary work than be seen in public, even on his birthday. The shy demeanor, however, belied a brilliant scientific mind that more than once came up with practical solutions for hitherto insurmountable problems. He had a knack for finding the golden path between expensive excellence and cheap workarounds, resulting in affordable quality merchandise.

Sir Cedric clapped a silent hand to his forehead. *How could I have forgotten Allier? His expertise in radiation could be just the thing we need for the association.*

"Well, what a coincidence, Albert," he said hurriedly. "I was just about to visit Paris for a private celebration. A dear friend is getting married tomorrow for the third time, and I haven't even met the poor bride-to-be yet. I'm sure I could afford some time to visit you at the laboratory. Would tomorrow do?"

"I am overjoyed that you can make it so soon, my friend. I'm sure you will find you have not wasted your time. I shall be expecting you for lunch, then."

*"Absolument!"* Sir Cedric mangled the French word. *"Au revoir."*

CVE3D

Sir Cedric and Professor Allier sat opposite each other in one of the brasseries near Jardin du Luxemburg. The professor had insisted they postpone their academic discussion until after they had "refreshed" themselves. Now, with the pleasantries over and with a full belly, they each sipped on steaming cups of coffee.

"That was delicious, *mon ami* Albert," Sir Cedric said, covering a small belch with his napkin. "Such a tiny establishment, such a gourmet meal. Your taste, as usual, is impeccable."

"Thank you, Cedric. Now, here is what I wished to discuss with you."

The professor was a medium-sized man of fifty-nine, with a short brown beard and a nervous smile. He wore a brown overcoat and gloves, and carried an old-fashioned satchel. Sir Cedric always thought that if he would also wear spectacles he could be the twin of Émile Zola.

"Three days ago," Professor Allier continued, "we were experimenting with a variant of the latest version of my irradiation machine. It's all here in my papers. Previous tests indicated it would be ideal in the control of certain kinds of pests if radiated onto fields from a low-flying plane. So we took it up in a crop duster and activated it from about three hundred meters up over a test field. We irradiated straight down and covered an area of about six hundred meters in diameter. This was an error—we overshot the boundaries of the test field."

Sir Cedric was displaying interest, but inwardly he was getting slightly bored. He was eager to question his colleague on how he could contribute to the association's cause. He finished his own coffee in one gulp.

Professor Allier paused to take a breath.

"About fifty meters beyond the edge of the test field we noticed an explosion. At first I didn't relate our experiment with this explosion—I thought it was just a coincidence. That evening I verified that the area was an abandoned quarry and that a leftover container of explosives had probably been forgotten there. Nobody was hurt and there was no damage.

"It was then I began wondering about the connection. I hurried to my laboratory and a couple of quite simple tests indicated positively that *this* particular type of irradiation would cause dynamite to detonate. Of course, the parameters like angle of incidence, power magnitude, duration of irradiation, distance of the target, and many more, all have to be taken into account, but the principle remains the same.

"And that, Cedric, is what I wanted to discuss with you."

Halfway through the professor's speech Sir Cedric's attitude had made an abrupt about-face. This looked like something he could use to the association's benefit. He paid close attention to Allier's description, memorizing key phrases for further interrogation later. However, the task at hand was to find out the professor's political leaning. He put on his "amazed scientist" expression.

"Why, Albert, it looks to me that you have made a major breakthrough! With the proper implementation you could easily win a Nobel physics award for this."

"I wouldn't go so far," Allier said modestly. "You have said the key words—proper implementation. Imagine what this invention could do in the wrong hands, or even if the information was made public."

"I see what you mean. Gangsters, mafia—they could easily make things messy for all of us. Even worse," Sir Cedric glanced at his colleague, "certain countries could… well, I don't even want to think about it."

"Again, you are taking simple ideas very far, my friend," the professor laughed. "I was only thinking about criminal elements…"

Sir Cedric decided to take the plunge. He talked about dangerous weaponry in the hands of tyrants, about the looming disaster of hundreds of millions dead in a global atomic war, and about what was being done to prevent it.

"You paint a very gloomy picture, Cedric," Allier said. "It is quite out of my grasp. I agree with your analysis, but I don't think anything can be done about it."

"How true. We, the regular citizens of the world, can do nothing but sit back and watch missiles with nuclear warheads rain down on us."

"That's a very pessimistic approach, don't you think? We mustn't lose hope. Perhaps something will pop up to save us."

"Hope is always a good thing, Albert. I've been told that our only *hope*—and I stress the word—is that these irresponsible tyrants lose their authority with their own people. As no democracy is going to act in suppressing the dictators, it is their own subjects who should overthrow them."

"My dear Cedric, today a subversive military takeover would never work. Maybe it would have a long time ago, but today it needs a rival government to provoke such a rebellion. And remember, even if you succeed you'll probably wind up with the same type of regime you're trying to overthrow."

"You're absolutely right! That is why my hypothesis lies in the fact that it is the people themselves that witness their leaders' downfall through shaming them, embarrassing them, showing them up as an 'emperor with no clothes'. Do you see where I am heading?"

The professor rubbed his beard.

"You have a point," he said. "If successful, such an action would deter atomic war, at least for a while. After all, a dictator is only human, isn't he? Just like we are. The difference is only in his megalomaniac ambition. But again, this needs very heavy preparatory work. Who could accomplish such a job?"

"I really couldn't say," Sir Cedric said carefully. "But as you can see, my opinions are similar to yours. I'll sniff around. If I get a whiff of anything, would you like me to inform you?"

"But of course! Every sane person *must* assist in diverting nuclear war."

Sir Cedric gave himself a mental pat on the shoulder. True, this was not full recruitment, but he had no doubt that this ripe fruit was ready to be picked. Now it was time to get access to Allier's invention.

"As to your laser discovery, Albert—perhaps you should experiment with additional types of explosives."

"Yes, I know," the professor said sorrowfully. "But I cannot continue these experiments in my laboratory. The university would never allow dangerous explosives within its compound. And as the pest control test was a failure, *oh yes, none of the pests in the field were affected at all*, I will not get the funding or the permission to repeat it. I was wondering …"

"… if in *my* laboratories …"

"… you could continue to …"

Sir Cedric burst out laughing.

"Of course—think no more about it!" Sir Cedric was elated. "My laboratories are privately owned and I can do there as I please. Just find a way to get the apparatus over to me in London."

Professor Albert Allier was no less jubilant.

"I shall send it to you first thing tomorrow morning. Together with an operations manual and specifications for further experiments."

"That would be excellent," Sir Cedric said.

"Thank you so much, my dear friend," the professor said, smiling from ear to ear. "You don't know how much this means to me. Please inform me of your results as soon as possible. I shall look forward to visiting London and reviewing them with you."

"You're most welcome!"

At this turn of events, Sir Cedric decided to go the whole hog and recruit Allier. Everything proceeded smoothly according to the "ten commandments," though the professor was hesitant and somewhat reserved. Sir Cedric attributed this fact to Allier's natural timidity, and he repeatedly assured him that he, the professor, would never need to take an active part in any stage of the association's endeavors.

"Your invention," Sir Cedric said, "is in itself a noble contribution to our efforts, which we shall never forget. And you may rest assured that *no one* outside the association will ever learn about this conversation. This secrecy will benefit us as well as you." He went on to further emphasize the need for the utmost confidentiality on the professor's part.

Sir Cedric had a funny feeling regarding Professor Albert Allier. On the way back to London, he mentally compared Allier's reaction to that of Rosetti in Milan. The latter was overflowing with enthusiasm, prepared to go out of his way to get things working. Allier, on the other hand, was hesitant and reserved throughout. *Different people react in different ways*, he consoled himself. *In time, Allier will discover that he is absolutely safe, and perhaps then he'll be less jittery. But I could not afford his invention to slip away—it is far too important for the association.*

## FOURTEEN

Neil Bennett was very much alive. Advanced in years, to be sure, but still spry and alert. He was tickled pink that Admiral Stone wanted to meet with him after all these years. A retired colonel himself, he enjoyed discussions with fellow servicemen. In his entire financial career he had met many high-ranking officers, but none of them was an admiral. Naturally, he agreed to the meeting, and he had his staff prepare the living room in his mansion in Bel Air with appropriate memorabilia that, in his opinion, would interest an admiral. There was the jet fighter he helped financing for the American Navy, and the trust fund for financing advanced studies for deserving cadets.

The association needed huge sums of money—several millions of dollars and probably more for running operations. The admiral had mentally built up a case that he intended to put before the millionaire—ten million would probably be more than enough, so his opening gambit would be for fifteen million.

The admiral usually detested transatlantic flights and felt quite grubby when he alighted. He freshened up at the airport terminal and took a cab to Bennett's estate.

The meeting itself went off in a friendly atmosphere. Drinks and snacks were abundant, and the admiral took his time admiring the framed photographs, shields, and trophies adorning every inch of wall space in Bennett's study and living room. Bennett took great pride in relating his achievements during his long life, and the admiral tried to counter with stories of his own exploits.

As planned, the admiral gradually brought the topic of conversation around to world affairs. He followed the ten rules step by step. He had prepared for a long argument—after all why should this very rich person want to help an enterprise such as this on the basis of just a verbal discussion? Therefore, he was rather surprised by the response he got.

Bennett stood up.

"Come, young man—*everybody* is young in comparison to me. Let's stroll outside in the garden."

They both walked in silence alongside blooming rosebushes and pools full of enormous goldfish.

"I prefer that none of my staff overhear what I have to say to you." The old man put a hand on the admiral's shoulder. "Look at me, Admiral Stone. I am ninety-five years old, even though I feel a young eighty. I am not fooling myself—I shall be dead, probably sooner than later. And before I die I want to leave a mark in this world. Oh, I know my name flies on many banners, and I'm honored on many plaques—perhaps they'll even issue a stamp with my picture on it. But that is not what I mean."

"It is *because* of your fame and fortune that I have contacted you," the admiral said.

"No matter. This is something *I* wish to do, and I have been racking my brains for the correct legacy I wish to leave to posterity. Note that I am not ashamed of the projects I have helped succeed during my lifetime. On the contrary—I am very proud that countless people have benefited, learned, and prospered as a result of my involvement. It would seem, admiral, that to want more would be as megalomaniac as the dictators you have described to me."

"I can't see how."

The old man halted in the path and turned to the admiral.

"I want to change history," he said simply. "I have, indeed, done a bit to improve a tiny part of my country. But what I really want is to change the course of human history. You see, dear Admiral Stone, I happen to agree with your statements concerning our global political situation. I believe that civilization deserves better than to be extinguished by fanatics with hydrogen bombs. Call me selfish if you like—I didn't get to where I am by being a spendthrift. But I want my acknowledged legacy to live on, even if I have to take part in subterfuge in order to ensure it."

"I understand," the admiral said softly.

"And I can afford it. You came to me in an attempt to find out which way my opinions on democracy and tyranny were leaning.

Now you know. But I have learned something, too. There is hope, there is a chance to *do* something about it. You have provided no evidence for me to believe you—just a very convincing argument."

"I can assure you …" the admiral began. The old man raised his hand.

"It doesn't really matter, Admiral Stone. *I* am the one who's gambling here. *I* am taking the risk. Either you are the world's greatest con artist—in which case you deserve to steal from me whatever you can—or you can truly confront the biggest threat this planet has ever known. And in *that* case, I want to be in on the game—even if my name remains unknown. And I'll contribute whatever is needed."

There was a long pause. The old man took the admiral by the elbow and steered him back toward the house.

"I am not going to ask you for the figure you had in mind. If I did, I'd have to ask you how you came to that number and how you intended to spend the money. So I'm going to give you a lump sum—no questions asked. And I'm going to continue believing you have not tricked me."

There was another pause. The admiral could not recall a time when he had been so lost for words.

The millionaire spoke.

"A hundred million dollars."

This time it was the admiral who stopped in his tracks. Bennett turned to him with a faint smile.

"You're not the first person to be dumbstruck when I spring a surprise. Believe me, this morning I had no idea that our conversation would wind up like this. So I'm a bit surprised as well."

"Mr. Bennett … I—"

"All I ask is that you get cracking as soon as you possibly can. As I said before, I can be selfish. I would very much like to see results from your actions before leaving this world. Our politicians, who assume to be 'statesmen,' are all insignificant pencil pushers. Every single one is wholly dependent on opinion polls. No good will ever come from them. I want you to count me on your team, even though I shall remain in the background. I see it as my job to keep you solvent, so that you can operate without any financial headaches that, admittedly, could be substantial. Do your stuff—I want to witness the downfall of the crazies!"

The admiral had swallowed and taken a deep breath.

"Please let me thank you on behalf of the team. Your extremely generous contribution will indeed liberate us from financial burdens. Now all we need to do is arrange the methods for the transfer of the funds."

The admiral told Bennett about his Vaduz account. They agreed that sums of no more than ten to twenty million dollars would periodically be transferred from the Hong Kong branch of one of Bennett's holding companies, thus largely concealing Bennett's personal involvement in the transactions. Admiral Stone would then move the funds to another account, thereby obliterating all traces of its origin.

Bennett and the admiral shook hands. The deal was done and all the necessary information was in place. As the admiral turned to leave, Bennett grasped him by the sleeve.

"Hurry, my friend! Show me results while I'm still alive." He winked.

C33O

Anne and Sir Cedric could hardly believe their ears as they listened to the admiral's report. They were assembled in Sir

Cedric's flat, and when the admiral had finished, there was a moment of shocked silence. Finally Anne spoke up.

"It seems that fate has destined us to succeed. We can now finance anything we need. Patrick, you deserve a medal like no other you have ever been awarded—perhaps we'll call it the Savior of Mankind Medal?"

The admiral was warmly congratulated and toasted.

"I'll probably deserve a smaller medal, Anne," Sir Cedric said. "I have succeeded in recruiting Professor Albert Allier, the irradiation genius. Here's what happened …" He related his conversation with the professor.

"We should receive the machine at my laboratory any day now," he concluded.

"Let's sum up our current situation," Anne said decisively. "First, I'd like to report that Martin and I met a few days ago and he has agreed to become our Operation Manager. Now let's take a look at what we have. The only tangible thing at the moment is Gustav Lemke's fertilizer, and we still need to test it. As we already have an Operations Manager and possibly a team for him to work with in a short while, *and* we shall soon have a fortune to back our expenses, we can plan this test for very soon. We have Emilio Rosetti's acoustic-electronic device, which should also be ready for testing before long. And, of course, Professor Allier's irradiation detonator should arrive any day, according to Sir Cedric. My friend Boulanger is preparing modifications in his satellite to suit our needs, but he's still waiting for instructions from us. Have I missed anything?"

Sir Cedric chuckled.

"You certainly have, my dear. Have you forgotten that I, too, am carrying out experiments on our behalf? I'm trying to produce a laser beam that will melt metal at a distance. I am also examining the option of increasing the beam's power and thereby—perhaps—penetrating heavily armored defenses, such as bunkers and maybe even nuclear reactors. Time will tell."

Anne couldn't help letting a little giggle escape her lips.

"Gentlemen, we're about to take off. Fasten your seat belts." The two men laughed and clapped their hands.

"I suggest," she continued, "that we invite Martin Cooper to our next meeting. First, you need to be introduced to our new board member. Second, there's a lot of planning we need to do with him. Things like which vehicles to use and where to conduct the fertilizer test. Third, we want to hear from him how he's done with his team and if we can make use of his underlings."

As they were preparing to adjourn the meeting Sir Cedric suddenly snapped his fingers.

"What an idiot I am!" he exclaimed. "This is the second time I've remembered someone only now. I should have considered Allier and Hoffman almost in the same thought! Oh dear, I *am* getting old...."

"What is it, Cedric?" Anne asked. "Who is Hoffman?"

"And I'm supposed to be our link to the scientific world ..." he muttered. "Shame on me. Anyhow," his voice brightened, "Conrad Hoffman lives and works in Vienna, and he was one of my brightest apprentices when I was still building up my career. He dropped a very promising laser research career with me in order to study nanotechnology. Today he is a senior researcher at the Vienna University of Technology. I know nothing about nanotechnology except that it deals with the extreme miniaturization of appliances and devices, and that this industry is expanding very, very rapidly. With your permission, I would like to pick his brains and see if he has anything we could make use of. And if so—to recruit him."

"Go ahead," Anne said, and the admiral nodded in agreement.

 CRBO

## Internet Newsflash

A number of terrorists were apprehended before they managed to carry out their mission, which was to blow up several car bombs in various civilian locations throughout the UK. They confessed that they were dispatched by Al Qaeda. Among them were citizens of Pakistan, Iraq, Jordan and even a few British-born Muslims. Subsequently, two medical students were also arrested in Glasgow. This proves that Al Qaeda finds its recruits not only—as many believe—among the poor and downtrodden, those who have nothing to lose, but also among the educated and established intelligentsia, who are just as prepared to blow themselves up for ideological motives.

## FIFTEEN

Sir Cedric was pleased that Conrad Hoffman could see him at such short notice. He had called him immediately after the last board meeting, and Conrad was delighted to hear from him. He was even happier when Sir Cedric informed him he would be in Vienna shortly. They had set up a luncheon date at a fashionable restaurant opposite the opera house. When they met, there was a lot of hugging and backslapping. Each blamed the other for not keeping in touch, amid jokes and memories of their common past.

The meal was excellent and the conversation seemed to drift naturally to world affairs—Sir Cedric was mildly surprised that his own incentive in that direction was almost nonexistent. In fact, it was Hoffman who peppered the discussion with sarcastic jibes at the international situation. Sir Cedric got a funny feeling that instead of being on a recruiting mission, he was being recruited by Hoffman.

"Just take a look at the American CIA," Hoffman was saying mockingly. "Have you seen their latest report? 'There is no danger that Iran is developing nuclear weapons!' Absolutely asinine!"

It didn't take Sir Cedric long to go through the recruiting steps. Conrad Hoffman was an easy catch.

"Well," Sir Cedric said. "I'm certainly very glad that we're in full accord regarding the necessity for action. Tell me, Conrad, how do you think nanotechnology could advance our cause?"

Hoffman pursed his lips and looked at the ceiling for a whole minute. Sir Cedric waited patiently. Finally, Hoffman straightened up and beckoned the waiter for another cognac.

"Our nanotechnology projects focus mainly on medical issues, and things are mostly still in their research stages. So I don't think I could be of any help there for the near future. However, I was thinking of something else entirely. You may recall that I began my scientific career as a microbiologist." Sir Cedric had totally forgotten this fact. "I have not given up my own research in that field, and I believe that what I'm working on right now may be of interest to you."

Sir Cedric was surprised. He had not expected this turn of events.

"Hold on there, Conrad," he said. "I thought I had explained earlier—we're not permitting violence or biochemical warfare of any kind. That includes bacteriological weapons."

"Take it easy, old friend," Hoffman said. "It's nothing like that at all. But I need some time to think this out. I'll call you when I've got something tangible for you."

They hugged each other again as they parted, promising to keep in touch.

# SIXTEEN

The exhibition was breathtaking. Anne admitted to herself how fortunate she was to be able to see masterpieces that would usually have required trips to Saint Petersburg, Moscow or New York. For a few months, Parisians would have the privilege of viewing these works of art not far from their homes. She had attended the opening ceremony, and patiently sat through speeches given by the Minister for Cultural Affairs, the Mayor of Paris, the curator of the museum, and other dignitaries. Then, free at last of her obligations of etiquette, she wandered around the museum, gazing with delight at works she was familiar with, but had never thought she would actually stand facing the original.

A Chetverikov bronze sculpture held her attention more than the others. You had to look at it just so in order to appreciate the work put into the three-dimensional figurine. As she stepped backward, she collided with a man standing slightly to her left and behind her.

"*Oh, pardon monsieur,*" she began, and then her eyes widened. "Mr. Dodson! Fancy meeting you here!"

The man was no less surprised than her.

"Professor Dupré, I'll be darned!" he cried.

Anne had met Andrew Dodson, the fabulously wealthy American businessman, a few times before, all very briefly, at various international conventions. Each time he had tried to get her alone, and each time he had failed. Not because Anne wished to avoid him—on the contrary, he was not the brash wolf type she was so used to politely reject. And he was also over eighty years old. It just turned out that way—either he or she was always in a rush to be somewhere else. So, save for a few introductory words exchanged hurriedly, they did not have a chance to really get friendly.

Anne was not superstitious. In fact, she was quite the opposite, pooh-poohing all accounts of bad luck omens, and lucky charms. Yet coincidences of the type that were happening to her lately— like meeting Andrew Dodson right now—quite bewildered her.

*I'll think about the mystical side of it later, she thought. Right now, I have another fresh candidate I need to recruit. His money could well be the financial fallback we'll need if anything goes wrong with Neil Bennett's support.*

They continued visiting the exhibits together. Neither of them, however, had their thoughts on the magnificent works of art they were looking at. They were both intensely interested in each other, although for different reasons. Dodson saw a fascinating woman he had long admired suddenly becoming available, possibly, for deeper acquaintanceship. Anne thought about recruiting him. They meandered through the museum barely mumbling a comment here or there, while regarding a still life or a landscape.

They had finished the exhibition's course and now stood at the exit gates of the museum. Neither wanted to part with the other and an embarrassing silence ensued. Dodson made an obvious effort and took the initiative.

"Umm, Professor Dupré, I hope you won't think me too bold, but I wonder if you would care to dine with me this evening."

Anne blessed him silently. If he had hesitated for one more second she would have broken the ice herself and invited him to dinner.

"That's very kind of you, Mr. Dodson. I'd be delighted. And please, forget the professor thing—I'm Anne to my friends."

"Great! And you can call me Andrew."

As they walked down the museum steps, a large black limousine drew up to the pavement and halted directly in front of them. The chauffeur sprang out and rushed to open the passenger's door. They got in, Dodson instructed the chauffeur to take them to "dinner—the usual place," and the limousine edged silently into the traffic.

It would be hard to estimate Andrew Dodson's age by his looks. He was over six feet tall, well tanned, and exuded health and energy, giving the impression of being twenty years younger than he actually was. As a young soldier in World War II, he fought under General Patton and saw a lot of action he would rather forget. After the war, he tried his hand at anything available—cab driving, laborer, copywriter—until he lit upon the vocation that would become his career: real estate brokerage. It didn't take long for the bright young man to understand how to *read* his clients and tune in to their thought processes. He gradually expanded his business, opening more and more branches, first in the US and later all over the planet. By sixty he had made a fortune and had raised a family and grandchildren. Since then he occupied himself with what he liked most—traveling, donating to various enterprises and charities, financing projects around the world, and just enjoying life.

He was a widower for over a decade but found no need to chase skirts. Anne attracted him for her personality and intelligence. He remembered the speech she had delivered on one of the international conferences he had attended—it had scintillated with brilliancies—and how much he had wanted to meet her and know her better. Here was the opportunity he was looking for. He considered himself very lucky.

Over dinner they talked about every imaginable topic, and Dodson confirmed his initial impression that he was in the company of a very remarkable woman. What she lacked in business acumen, she had in vast academic knowledge, of which he knew very little.

"I know what I like," he said stirring his fruit salad. "That art exhibition appealed to me aesthetically, though I couldn't tell impressionism from cubism. I suppose my home in New York has trash alongside masterpieces—I just buy what looks nice to me."

"You know, Andrew," Anne said, "this is just short of miraculous. Last week I was planning to attend a conference in New York in the fall. And I immediately associated this visit with looking you up and seeing if we couldn't finally get some time together. You know how we always seem to be out of time when we bump into each other accidentally. Now, suddenly, here you are, and I just happen to be free."

"Really! How fortunate." Dodson seemed genuinely pleased.

"There was also something particular I wanted to discuss with you. It concerns international affairs."

"There was a time when I had lady friends in several countries. I don't suppose you mean those kinds of affairs, do you?"

Anne grinned.

"I'm sure you could tell many a fascinating tale on that topic. No—I am quite serious. I think we are both aware of the shameful situation that Western democracies are in today. Some of them don't even have the sense to acknowledge this. The worst threats emanate from dictatorships with power-crazy tyrants at the helm."

"I'm listening," Dodson said.

"There are even those who say that if nothing is done about it, then in a year or two, no more than three, we'll be in the midst of a terrible nuclear war. In the last world war over fifty million people were killed. I believe you witnessed some of this first hand. This time, with nuclear warheads, 'first strike,' 'second strike,' missile-launching submarines, and all the rest, the estimate runs into the hundreds of millions of casualties."

"I think I get where you're heading—you needn't elaborate any further. You sympathize with 'those who say.' In fact, you would like some action. You have not explained to me *how* exactly you want to act, but I want you to know that even though I am eighty-five years old I am as fit as a fiddle, and I have not forgotten the craft of combat. So if you're looking for commando operations, let's say for doing away with those megalomaniacs, I'm your man. Count me in!"

Dodson sounded very determined, and Anne forced herself not to smile.

"Actually, I was thinking of something else," she said. She got him to swear to secrecy and then unveiled the basic principles of the association's ideology without mentioning names or revealing too many details.

"Our scientists are coming up with remarkable inventions. What we need now is more financing for the construction and testing of their devices. And we need it now, because if we don't manage to go into action within a year or two, it'll be too late. You'll forgive me for being so bold, but from the little I knew of you in the past, *and I know a bit more now*, you seemed to be the appropriate person to approach on this topic. I certainly did not visualize you crawling through mine fields with a machine gun, but I *was* hoping you could undertake to shoulder a lot of our expenses. Was I wrong?"

Dodson emptied his wine glass.

"How much are you talking about?"

"I'm not really sure. There's a list of things we need to do now and in the immediate future. Owning a small industrial workshop is high on this list. We also need to establish a couple of commercial businesses here and there, buy a few lorries and jeeps, purchase an executive jet—you see, it's hard for me to estimate the cost of these things, and the need for more stuff will probably crop up in the future. Our operations personnel will need to fly to far-off places, reside there under assumed names, pose as businessmen—I could go on and on."

Dodson closed his eyes and thought for a couple of minutes.

"I've made a rough estimate," he said finally. "The cost of buying a bankrupt plant, an executive plane, a few vehicles, etc., will be around two hundred million dollars, give or take a few million. I can transfer this amount to you within a few days. Let me know when you do a reassessment of your requirements—I'll add whatever is needed." Anne just nodded. "Anyway," he added with a wide grin, "I am rewarding you for preventing me from slogging through the mud with a submachine gun."

They lifted their wine glasses and clinked them.

"To success!" they both said together.

"Just how are such transactions carried out?" Anne asked. "I have no experience in such things. I mean, we wouldn't want anything to trace back to you...."

"That's my specialty, young lady!" Dodson said, smiling broadly. "Grandpa Dodson has done a lot of money shunting all over the world in his time."

"I'm truly overwhelmed, Andrew. Thank you so much. What will I have to do now?"

"Just have your guy who handles these things look me up in New York. I'll brief him with whatever's necessary, and you can sleep without another care in the world." He handed her his business card, which she left on the table. "What's his name? Or rather, what's the name I should expect?"

Anne was flustered—should she or shouldn't she reveal the real name? But she knew that these matters should not be delayed and that Dodson was expecting an immediate answer. She made a decision.

"His name is Martin Cooper and he's a relative of mine. You can trust him to the same extent you trust me."

They took another sip of wine. Dodson leaned forward and lowered his voice.

"You're running this show, aren't you? I mean, you're the boss?"

Anne's embarrassment grew. There was no escaping this unique, straightforward man.

"We're a board of three people, and my colleagues are very respectable gentlemen."

"No doubt. But I'm sure that they wait for *you* to make the decisions, right?"

Anne blushed and lowered her head. That was enough for the crafty old businessman.

"As you're the boss, you'll need to be familiar with at least the basics of monetary techniques. I shall instruct Martin to fly to Belize in Central America, where he is to register a new business. You had better prepare this new company's name in advance. Then he'll fly to the Cayman Islands and open a bank account for the Belize company. I'll transfer an initial deposit to this account— let's say ten million dollars—from Switzerland. Just to make sure everything's running smoothly. From then on, your man can transfer funds from Grand Cayman to another account, for instance in Vaduz, Liechtenstein. But you needn't bother yourself with the actual details—just be in touch with what's going on. I'll coach your Martin with everything he needs."

"Fascinating. I'll let you know when he'll arrive in New York."

"Call me at my office during working hours. Don't worry— I'm just a showpiece there nowadays and I have *plenty* of time to spare." He pointed at his card on the table. "You'll ask me how I am and I'll ask you when your next lecture will take place. The date and time you tell me will indicate when Martin will meet with me."

Anne listened attentively. *You always learn something,* she thought.

They drove to Anne's flat in Dodson's limousine. Before alighting, he squeezed her hand, kissed her on the forehead and said, "I wish you the best of luck!"

∞

This time Martin joined Sir Cedric and the admiral at Anne's flat, and she made the appropriate introductions. As she had already gone over Martin's background with the two elderly gentlemen, there was no need for any personal questions, but the admiral was genuinely interested in Martin's military career—inquiring into the units he served in, when he had joined the commandos and how long he had been in Iraq.

Then they got down to business. Anne reported on the recruitment of Andrew Dodson. She was aware that Sir Cedric and the admiral felt uncomfortable that this report was made in the presence of a person who was not a board member—namely Martin.

"Let me make myself perfectly clear—I needed to make a decision on the spot, and I did. Call it an operations decision if you will. Dodson needed to know the name of the contact person for the monetary shenanigans and I gave him Martin's. In any case," she paused and looked at each of the older men, "Martin will be leaving this meeting after we finish discussing the tasks he is directly involved in."

Sir Cedric and the admiral laughed out loud. This remarkable woman actually felt the need to explain her decisions to them. They had already resigned themselves to the fact that they *expected* surprises from her. In a matter of weeks she had brought about the founding of an association and the recruiting of scientists, establishing work procedures and finding financial funding. And all this out of the blue, as it was, just by exchanging ideas. She was a potent woman indeed—emanating power, intelligence and charm.

And now—more millions from this Dodson fellow. They took turns congratulating her.

All this while Martin sat silently to one side, listening carefully. He was deeply impressed by the esteem in which the two elderly gentlemen held Anne. *An admiral and a knighted scientist,* he mused. *They both seem very striking people. I know what it takes to rise in the ranks, and you don't get to be an admiral without some outstanding achievements. And getting the title of 'Sir' is nothing to be sneezed at, either. Quite an exciting trio we have here. Being offered the job of Operations Manager with them is an honor....*

"My apologies, Martin," Anne was saying, "for not consulting with you before giving your name, but I felt the need to strike while the iron was hot. And I had no one else to offer. This is no small task I'm asking of you, and it will enable us to get the money to begin our work. Do you think you could absent yourself from your duties at the gym for a few days so that you can hop around New York, Belize and Grand Cayman?"

Martin was amused by the way Anne manipulated things, and he smiled all the while she was addressing him. *I was right about her. My cousin is quite the smooth operator, first class. But that's just what is needed here. You can't afford to let naïve or slow people run a campaign of this magnitude.*

"No problem," he responded.

"Good. Well, then, let's tackle the topics we came here to discuss: preparing for field tests as soon as possible. I shall present the tasks as concisely as I can and then, Martin, we'd like to hear your comments.

"First we have the fertilizer that emits a gas that supposedly neutralizes vehicles passing over it. This has not been tested yet. We shall need a lorry or two and an accompanying vehicle. And we'll need a location for the test—some place where our secrecy will not be jeopardized.

"Next on our agenda, and we're hoping for positive results very shortly, is the detonation of explosive charges spread over a wide area. One of our scientists is developing an irradiation device to be operated from an aircraft. In this case the location is even more critical—we can't blow up a bunch of charges without drawing some adverse attention—and we may have a problem here.

"Then we have Sir Cedric's laser invention for immobilizing certain apparatuses, even if they're sheltered in bunkers. This also needs to be field-tested. Martin, as our Ops Manager and the most field experienced advisor, do you have any ideas on how to approach these topics?"

Martin was taken aback by the proliferation of devices under development. After a moment's thought he said:

"Let's take these in the order Anne presented them. The fertilizer—let's call it the 'vehicle fertilizer,' shall we—I see a few challenges here. I expect the effect is that the engine dies. So I'm asking—for how long? Will the vehicle be fully operable after that time? If not, would a simple fix—like replacing the carburetor—restore the vehicle to its former condition? Or is the entire engine irreparably damaged? Therefore, I suggest we perform the initial test in a closed environment—a garage would be best, but any warehouse or shed would probably do if we had the proper instruments and measuring tools. We'll learn just how much damage is done to the vehicle and how reparable it subsequently becomes. Only then can we conduct a test outdoors.

We'll have all the necessary replacement parts on hand so that we leave absolutely nothing in the testing area. Which brings us to the next question—where? It'll have to be somewhere very remote. We'll examine maps for suitable locations, and, after we have a few options, we'll visit these places to find out firsthand how appropriate they are."

"Bravo!" Admiral Stone muttered.

"As to the second test—remote detonation of charges—that one's a bit more complex and I need to study the case in depth before making a recommendation.

"I understand that my most urgent mission is to fly to the USA and get the funding for all this to happen. With your permission, I shall allocate subtasks to one of my team members, without specifying any revealing details. These will include finding large barren, uninhabited areas in Africa and Asia, or anywhere else, airline flights, distances, paths for off-road vehicles—I'll prepare a list with these and more, which I expect my man to follow and provide results. Upon my return to London, I shall review the results and prepare a report with recommendations for the association. However, I can safely say that we shall definitely need a building where we can conduct experiments with the vehicles and tinker about with accessories. And that means now!"

"Your trip has top priority," Anne said. "Which team member were you referring to?"

"George Graham fits the bill. He has talent and his loyalty is unshakeable. He is also my right-hand man at the gym.

If we ever purchase or hire a jet plane, he'll be the one to complement his flying knowledge to the higher level of flying jets. Oh dear, I'm afraid I'm doing what Anne has done—putting the cart before the horse: George hasn't been recruited yet …"

The other three looked questioningly at each other.

"But," Martin continued, "as I have already informed Anne, all my boys trust me implicitly and are eager for some action. I'm sure George will be happy to cooperate with us. And he won't know more than the absolutely necessary for checking out a list of items. Well?"

"This won't do at all," the admiral said. "If we intend to have your five-man team work for us, we need to formally recruit them according to our established rules. I'm prepared to brief Martin on this at some other time. I would also suggest that they needn't meet with anyone of us—apart from you, of course, Martin—unless absolutely necessary for the task at hand."

"Well, they *have* met me already," Anne said. "But, in principle, how does that sound to you, Martin?"

He nodded and got up.

"Will that be all? Good. Anne, and gentlemen—thank you," he said and picked up his jacket. "Good evening!" Martin left the flat.

The meeting was not over yet. The two remaining men discussed Martin's merits and both concluded that he was a valuable asset for the association.

"Let's get on, then," the admiral said. "I visited the lawyer handling my company in Vaduz. I browsed through the dormant file and announced that I was returning to international business. He congratulated me and wished me luck. I checked my bank account there and immediately put a call through to Neil Bennett, using the terminology we had agreed upon, informing him that he could begin the transfer of funds." After a slight pause the admiral added: "But it's a good thing we have an additional source of money. You never can tell … Bennett's age worries me. His donation is a personal gesture and will not oblige his heirs in any way … I think I should urge him to transfer more cash and in shorter periods of time."

Sir Cedric reported that his laboratory experiments were progressing as planned, and that he hoped his device would soon be ready for testing. "I believe that, at certain intensities, my beam could melt various metals—not only on the surface but deeper down as well. I am also toying with the idea of immobilizing a nuclear reactor with this beam, but that'll have to wait for the time being."

"Do you think you have enough specifications to send to Alfred Boulanger?" Anne asked. "You'll need to exchange data back and forth so that your device will not only fit into his satellite but also be controlled from the ground. I'll be your go-between."

Sir Cedric eyes widened.

"You know, Anne," he said, "I was so immersed in the development stages that I had completely forgotten how the device was to be launched. Thanks for reminding me. Oh, this is fantastic! I'll have the specs for you in a couple of days."

"Good," Anne said. "Now, weren't you expecting Allier's contraption to be delivered by now?"

"Indeed! I called him yesterday, and he told me he had just shipped it out by FedEx. I'll begin tests on it immediately it arrives."

"Didn't you mention a friend in Vienna?" the admiral asked.

Sir Cedric slapped his forehead.

"Silly me," he said. "Of course. Conrad Hoffman, the nanotechnologist. Very talented and extremely valuable. I met him and recruited him with no problems, though he hasn't come up with anything yet. I'm expecting him to call soon."

CR80

With the meeting over Anne felt she could relax. She removed her shoes and put on a pair of comfortable house slippers, prepared a snack in the kitchen, and settled in front of the television set to watch the news.

About half an hour later the thought suddenly struck her. *What's happening with Tanya? She hasn't called for over two weeks, perhaps even longer.* She picked up her phone, punched out Tanya's number, and after a few rings got her answering machine.

"Hey, Tanya, it's me. Haven't heard from you in a long time. What's going on with you? I'm beginning to miss you. Call me back when you get this." *Anyway, at this hour she's probably at the theatre.*

## *SEVENTEEN*

Next morning Anne paid special attention to her appearance. She acknowledged that it wasn't for the students in the lecture hall but for Martin. They had agreed to meet for lunch so that Anne could brief him in detail about his trip to New York, where he was to meet with Andrew Dodson.

Before leaving her flat, she tried calling Tanya again. There was still no answer. Anne decided to drop by her place on the way to the university. She took a taxi to Tanya's residence and went up to her apartment. She rang the bell and knocked loudly several times without getting a response. She tried the door and found it locked. *She's probably worn out from an action-filled night with one of her studs,* thought Anne. *Oh, well ... that's Tanya.* She went down to the waiting taxi and hurried to the university.

CB80

At the Bistro d'Etienne, Martin was already waiting when

Anne arrived. He got to his feet and they exchanged pecks on the cheek, as was their custom. They then sat opposite each other. Martin could not conceal his look of admiration, and Anne felt a bit embarrassed.

"I really must compliment you, Martin," she said hastily, "on your excellent performance last evening at the meeting. We were all very impressed."

Martin grinned, reached across the table, picked up her hand, and kissed it. Anne's eyes opened wide, and she blushed a beet red. Such a thing had not happened to her for many, many years. She had no idea how to respond. She was rescued by the arrival of Etienne, who took their order.

She got down to business as if nothing had happened. She described Dodson as a no-nonsense, energetic personality. Then she went through the details of the transaction setup.

"So now you'll book a ticket to New York. When you know at what time the flight lands we'll meet again and figure out the best time to set an appointment with Dodson. Then I'll call him and give him the particulars regarding 'my next lecture.'"

CB&D

Anne returned to her flat that afternoon, having completed her day's quota of lectures at the university before her meeting with Martin. She had barely put down her purse when the doorbell rang. This was quite irregular—the front door of her apartment building was kept locked, and visitors needed to buzz the intercom first, identify themselves, and then get permission to come up. *Perhaps it's the caretaker or one of the neighbors,* she thought. She peered through the peephole and saw an unfamiliar face of a young man. She quickly secured the chain latch on the door and opened it a crack. Two men stood outside. They were dressed in similar outfits—ties and overcoats—and the shorter one was obviously older than his companion.

Before she could ask what it was they wanted or how they got in, the older man flashed an open wallet at her and announced:

"*Police Judiciaire!* Are you Madame Dupré?"

Anne was surprised, but she nodded in assent.

"We'd like to ask you a few questions. May we come in?"

Anne's first thought was about the association, but she quickly dismissed it. After all, they had done nothing illegal—yet—and nothing that anyone knew could justify a visit by the police. So far she had never had any contact with the police. In fact, she had never even spoken to a policeman in her life. A feeling of slight queasiness churned in her stomach. But there was no choice—she let them in, offered them seats and seated herself opposite them.

"To what do I owe this honor?" she asked.

"I am *Inspecteur* Henri Marnier," said the older police officer. "This is my associate, Maurice Delgado. We believe you can help us in an investigation we are conducting."

"Really?"

"Do you know Mademoiselle Tanya Gerard?"

Anne grew tense.

"I'm her best friend. Is she in trouble?"

"We'll get to that in a minute. Please answer my questions first. When did you last see her?"

Anne didn't like this at all, and she was becoming worried.

"She was here about two weeks ago. I don't remember the exact date. She wanted to consult with me regarding an impending trip to Russia to direct a play ... She wasn't here for long. Or since."

"Was it customary in your relationship that she stay for just a short while? Did you quarrel?"

"We never quarreled. She was in a hurry because she had a new lover waiting for her."

"A lover?"

Anne gave a sad smile.

"Tanya is never without lovers—at least one at any given moment. This time she was in a hurry because her current lover was waiting for her impatiently in her flat."

"Do you happen to know who this lover is?"

Anne was getting more and more worried.

"No. Before she left she said he was a student named Lucien, about twenty years old, and that he was waiting for her in her apartment."

The two policemen exchanged glances.

"And then?"

"She hasn't called me since then. And I had no intention of interfering with her love life. Please remember, she is over forty, and boys in their twenties are not very … anyway, yesterday I wondered what could possibly keep her from calling me for so long, so I phoned her."

"You spoke with her yesterday?"

"No. She didn't answer the phone, and I left her a message to call me. It seemed pretty natural—she is usually at the theatre in the evenings. But this morning I paid a visit to her flat while on my way to the university. I rang and knocked several times, but there was no answer. So I assumed she was either in a deep sleep after a night of debauchery with her student lover, or that they had gone away for a while."

"Was there anything special about Mademoiselle Gerard when you last saw her? I mean her dress, her hairdo—was anything different or abnormal?"

"No. Well, I saw her new pendant for the first time that evening." Anne described the amulet as best she could.

Delgado flipped through a notebook he was holding.

"One of Ms. Gerard's neighbours tells us that she saw you leaving the flat this morning."

"What?!" Anne was stunned. "She must have been mistaken. I stood in front of a closed door, ringing and knocking loud enough to wake the entire building. The neighbor probably saw me when I had given up and was in the process of leaving. She probably assumed I had just come out of the apartment."

Anne felt a threatening chill enveloping her.

"Has something happened to her?" she asked in a low voice.

The inspector cleared his throat.

"Madame, Tanya Gerard is dead. She was murdered in her bed." Anne felt she was about to faint but kept her seat with an effort. Her face went ashen and she shut her eyes. The penny dropped.

"Are you suspecting me of murdering my best friend?"

"It may seem that way," the inspector said. "We also know that long ago she was engaged to be married to your now-deceased husband, and that you stole him away from her. In my book that is not the description of a 'best friend,' wouldn't you say?"

Anne felt the compulsion to slap this offensive policeman but she curbed the urge. She felt she needed a glass of water and a good lawyer. But for now she had to dispel these ugly allegations.

"Yes, she was a good friend of my late husband, Colonel Raoul Dupré. But her goal in life was the stage—she was married to the theatre. She never wanted to be tied down to one man—she wanted to be as free as a bird. You can confirm what I say with anyone who knew her. It was I who released her from any obligations toward Raoul and she was eternally grateful to me for that. We have been fast friends ever since."

Anne took a deep breath and pointed a finger at the inspector.

"Now *you* tell me—what happened? When? And why?"

"I am sorry to report to you that her throat was cut with a razor. Her body was discovered this morning after you left. The neighbor who saw you leave called the police and complained that there was something funny going on in the Gerard apartment. She said she heard loud knocking and when she looked out she saw you leaving in a hurry. Our people are currently checking out the apartment. That's all we have right now."

The inspector got to his feet, copied immediately by his associate.

"I must request you not to leave Paris until further notice," the inspector said. "Also, please visit my office tomorrow at any time you find convenient to be fingerprinted."

Anne was thoroughly shaken. Now she was regarded as a suspected criminal.

"Am I accused of murder?" she muttered.

"I did not say that, Madame. I said that an investigation was being conducted and that your presence may be required. Naturally, we shall need to compare all the fingerprints found at the scene of the crime to anybody who could have been there, which includes you. I trust you understand the circumstances we all find ourselves in. Thank you, Madame, and good day."

⚭

After the two police officers left, Anne stood dazed for a couple of moments. She felt she had to defend herself against criminal charges—had been forced to protest her innocence, and needed to prevent the besmirching of her name. She felt ashamed and sullied to the depths of her soul. She imagined herself losing her position at the university, her pictures in the newspapers under sensation-seeking headlines, the jeers of the public....

But now it finally hit her. Tanya was dead. Her best friend—murdered. She blamed herself for not encouraging her to travel to Moscow.

Anne had already undergone a traumatic experience in the past when her husband died. But it was different then. Raoul's illness had developed gradually, and at a certain stage it was clear that the end was near. She lived with that knowledge for several months, knowing there was nothing she could do about it. But Tanya? Her sweet, crazy friend, with all that special charm of hers, with her incredible love for life—that *she* should die so suddenly? And so horribly?

Anne began shuddering uncontrollably. She rushed into her bedroom, fell on the bed and wept as though her heart would break.

A while later, after she had calmed down somewhat and washed her face, she began thinking of what she should do. Her first decision was to keep this information from her colleagues at the association. Then she considered the possibility of engaging a lawyer. She dismissed this idea for tactical reasons—the police might interpret this as though she had something to hide and thereby enhance their suspicions.

Anne was also afraid that the investigation would interfere with her activities in the association. Right now, there wasn't much she could do about that. The press would be a real problem if and when they got wind of her involvement in the murder. However, she realized that at this stage the police were not divulging their activities on the topic. They needed discretion as long as they still hunted for the killer. If it was the young student lover that Tanya had described, they shouldn't have much trouble finding him. He probably left traces in her apartment, so they'll have evidence to prosecute him. Anne felt that, if the police caught him, they would leave her alone, and her name would not be dragged into the case.

Just the same, Anne felt the need to talk to someone about this turn of events. Someone to consult with, to share the burden. Her first thought was of Martin, currently her closest friend. He was smart, self-controlled, a cool and logical thinker. Yes, of course she knew Sir Cedric far longer, but right now she did not want to involve the association board in this matter. Martin was supposed to fly to New York soon, but she would still see him before he left—they had agreed to meet so that he could inform her of the flight plans and the Dodson meeting schedule. Excellent!

The thought of meeting with Martin relieved her somewhat. *But I mustn't call him from my home,* she thought. *Those policemen were so suspicious that they would probably misinterpret everything I do. I've got to think clearly. Perhaps a cold shower ....*

Anne walked slowly into the bathroom, undressed, and examined her naked body in the large mirror on the wall. Even with the morose thoughts still pounding in her brain, she found herself focusing on Martin again. Could this body of hers arouse passion in him? Her breasts were full and firm, her waist and hips still had those hourglass qualities, and her long legs had not lost their shapeliness. Although there were a few tiny wrinkles at the corners of her eyes, her face was of a much younger woman.

She got into the shower and turned on the cold water full blast. She gasped at the sudden drop in temperature, but then told herself that that was exactly what she needed. She hurriedly soaped and rinsed herself and then stepped out and wrapped an enormous beach towel around her body. She walked to her bed and lay on it still rubbing the towel over her body. When her hand reached her crotch she felt a long-distant, though familiar, thrill course through her veins.

She stopped the caressing and scolded herself. *My god, Annie, you* really *find the strangest times to get carried away.* She had never felt the urge to masturbate. And the few sexual encounters she had had since Raoul's death were of no consequence whatsoever. Why was it *now*, of all times, with Tanya's death so fresh in her mind, that sexual stimulation suddenly reappeared? And with Martin as the object?

She shook off the towel, got up, and still naked picked up her telephone. She recorded a new answerphone message: "I shall be away for a few days for personal reasons. Please do not leave messages. Thank you." Tomorrow morning she would visit the prefecture, get herself fingerprinted and then make her way to the university. She'd find an empty office and call Martin from there. If he wasn't at the gym she'd leave a message that she'd be expecting him for lunch at the restaurant—he'd know which one.

And what if the police got wind of this meeting? Anne had never found herself in such a surreal predicament. Well, if they questioned her about it she'd tell the truth—Martin was a relative, and she felt the need to tell him about the nightmare she was going through.

Anne had never met Tanya's family in Paris. She and Tanya hadn't discussed them much. She knew that Tanya's parents lived in Bretagne, in the northwest of France, and that Tanya hardly ever visited them. Once she had accompanied Tanya on one of those rare occasions. Tanya was an only child who became independent at a very early age, much to the dismay of her parents, who considered her wayward. Her few visits always ended in an explosive row, with Tanya exiting with a violent slam of the door. Anne did not remember the address—anyway, it was the police's job to notify them.

Anne then reconsidered the fact that she might be a suspect—anything was possible with "those retards." She would need witnesses to refute their charges. Like someone who could testify she had not been out of her flat the evening of the murder. And character witnesses as well, who could attest that she and Tanya had a very close and warm relationship.

And what about Sir Cedric and the admiral? All contact with them should be avoided, at least for the next few days. But when she *did* meet with them, should she inform them of the situation? They didn't even know Tanya existed. And if, heaven forbid, the case got to the newspapers and her name and picture, perhaps even as a suspect, were published for all to see—what then?


## EIGHTEEN

The next morning Anne dressed modestly, gulped down a cup of coffee and took a taxi to the prefecture. The taxi's radio had the news on, and one of the items mentioned was of the brutal murder of the well-known actress and stage director, Tanya Gerard, in her Paris apartment. The police were investigating. That was all. Anne let out a sigh of relief—perhaps she had gained another day of quiet.

She had her fingerprints taken, leaving her fingers smudged with ink. After cleaning them with a special lotion provided by a kind police officer, she made her way to the street. Wondering whether she could find the fortitude to stand in front of her students, she made a sudden resolution and, for the first time in her life, walked into a nearby bistro and downed a shot of cognac. A passing taxi then took her to the Sorbonne.

Before her first lecture, Anne found an empty office and immediately called the London gym. John answered the phone and identified her voice at once. No, Martin was not in. He had caught a morning flight to Paris to meet with her for lunch. He'd be away for three or four days. Was it something urgent? Anne replied that it could wait until their meeting and hung up. She felt much better now—good cognac and good news made excellent partners. Her first lecture of the day began with a beaming smile.

ॐ

Anne was particularly pleased to see Martin at lunchtime. Finally, after hours of worry and self-doubt, she could unload her burden to a friend, hear what he had to say and perhaps get a word of advice, too. Over lunch, Anne covered all the details of Martin's forthcoming trip to the US—she wanted to put these items behind her so that she could discuss Tanya with a mind free from distractions. Once she had all the necessary information for her call to Dodson later that day, she told Martin every little detail about the murder and the investigation.

"I called the gym from an empty office at the university— nobody could know about that. I'll do the same to call Dodson, or use a public telephone. Now, please tell me what you think of Tanya's case."

Martin listened all the while without any change in his attitude. He continued with his meal as if Anne was talking about the weather. When his plate was clean, he laid down his fork and knife, wiped his mouth with a napkin, carefully folded it and gently replaced it on the table. Then he began talking—more as if to himself than answering a question.

"If you have never been inside Tanya's apartment, the police will not find any of your fingerprints there. On the other hand, there will be a lot of Mister Lucien's fingerprints all over the place, as he spent a lot of time there. That, however, on its own, does not indicate that he is the murderer. Nevertheless, they will have to remove you from their list of suspects. In my opinion, when the police visited you at your apartment and interrogated you, they already knew you were not the killer. Their attitude and manner of speech, that feeling they induce in those they talk to as if they were suspects—that's routine police academy. 'Scare the interrogatee, make him believe he's a suspect and he'll spill his guts trying to clear himself.' And that's what they did to you. I don't believe you're being followed or that your phone's been tapped. One of the reasons is that they don't have enough manpower for such trivial tasks. I suggest you calm down and return to your normal life. If they *do* continue to pester you, you should tell them very clearly that you demand that your name not be made public, and that if through any action on their part you should lose your job, you would have no choice but to sue them in a civil court and demand compensation for a lifetime of salaries. Sometimes this puts them off. That's my diagnosis for now. We'll discuss this further when I return."

Anne felt as if a guardian angel had just made a revelation to her. With her confidence now restored, she felt she could face any adversary.

"You have no idea what a calming effect you've had on me. I'm so glad I met you before you left. Otherwise I'd remain in this nightmare for a few more days."

She wanted to add how much she admired his level-headedness and lucid thinking—in fact, how much she *really* liked him—but just then Etienne brought their dessert to the table and rescued her from being melodramatic.

When they parted, she bestowed a whole-hearted kiss on him leaving her cheek on his for several seconds.

CRBD

On her way home, Anne bought the latest edition of *Le Figaro*. Then she found a public telephone and settled the arrangements with Andrew Dodson in New York. Once home, she opened the newspaper and immediately found the article she was interested in.

The Préfecture de Police is still investigating the death of actress-director Tanya Gerard. Mlle. Gerard was murdered in her residence in rue Mozart two nights ago—her throat was savagely slashed with a man's razor. The door to her dressing room and the mirror opposite it were smashed. Bloodstains were found on shards of the mirror, and fingerprints were found on several articles in the apartment. The police have no doubt that Mlle. Gerard was murdered by a lover who resided with her at the time. It appears that the victim had locked herself in the dressing room during a fight with her lover, who subsequently broke down the door, dragged her to the bedroom and committed the crime.

The police suspect a man, allegedly a young student, who was staying at her apartment for some time recently. The public is requested to assist the police by submitting any information regarding the identity, whereabouts and/or the description of this man.

Anne put the newspaper down. Her name was not mentioned—that alone provided a modicum of relief. *They suspect a student—quite understandable, as it was I who told them about Lucien. He won't be hard to find—and if he's the killer, that'll be the end of the story. But what if it's not Lucien? It certainly isn't like Tanya to have only one lover for over two weeks. So let's take this a step further. Tanya's entire world was the theatre. Possibly the killer, student or otherwise, was an admirer of hers and used to hang around that area, either attending shows, visiting the dressing rooms, or waiting at the artists' entrance. Somebody might have seen him. I wonder if the police are thinking in this direction. Oh, well, I certainly don't want attention drawn to me—let the police do their job, they do it best anyway.*

## NINETEEN

The next morning Anne phoned the prefecture and was invited by Inspecteur Marnier to visit. As before, she dropped by on her way to the university. She was cordially received and offered a hot drink.

"*Alors, Professeur Dupré*, what can we do for you?" The inspector's manner was proper and polite—the total opposite of his earlier gruffness at her apartment.

"Well, I really don't know, inspector," Anne said. She felt she should have prepared something a bit more substantial to say. "I'm so upset about the murder of my dear friend. I suppose I just need to know if there were any developments in the investigation."

"We went over her apartment with a fine-tooth comb. There is no doubt that drugs were being used there, but Mme. Gerard's autopsy showed no sign of drug usage. Our killer is probably a heavy user of hard drugs. We have a partial description of someone who *could* be him from witnesses who saw Mme. Gerard in the company of a tall and blond young man. We're still checking this out. The interesting thing is that on the razor that killed her we found the fingerprints of *two* people."

Anne was hardly breathing.

The inspector leaned forward. "I really shouldn't be telling you all this, Professeur Dupré, as it is still under wraps. But I feel I need to compensate you somewhat for my behavior at your apartment a couple of days ago. For us it is just routine questioning, using routine techniques, so please don't judge me too harshly. You, personally, are not a suspect—neither have you ever been one. Your name will not be mentioned to the press or anywhere else. You are, of course, free to leave Paris at any time you desire. If we need you, we know how to request your presence."

"Thank you, Inspecteur, that is very kind of you."

"And I trust you will not repeat anything of what I have told you to anyone, *n'est-ce pas?*"

"Of course," Anne replied. "Can you tell me anything about the funeral arrangements?"

"Mademoiselle Gerard's family resides far from Paris. We are trying to coordinate something with them. When we have a date—I assume it will not take more than a week—I will make sure you are informed."

"*Merci bien, monsieur l'Inspecteur*," Anne said. "You have been very gracious."

The police officer smiled, got up, and held the door open for her. For a fleeting moment, Anne considered the possibility of suggesting that the police inquire around the theatre. But she dismissed the thought at once. *Who am I to give advice to the police? They'll poke fun at me, which will probably be worse than the treatment I got at my flat....*

In the taxi taking her to the university, Anne tried to put her thoughts in order.

*On the positive side we have exactly what Martin foresaw—I am not a suspect, and I am free to go where I please. On the other hand, I would expect the police to regard this case 'oh dear—Tanya is a* case *now!' with some more emphasis. I know they probably have other serious crimes to deal with—serial killers, rapists and God knows what else—but this, too, is a* murder. *I don't suppose there would be any harm in snooping a bit around the theatre, would there? It would be perfectly natural for me to associate with Tanya's friends and talk about her last days there—after all, I know some of them pretty well from the times Tanya and I used to meet at the theatre. Perhaps they would even reveal something about the blond man without my asking—if there were anything to talk about, these gossipy ladies would certainly say it.*

Anne made a mental note to schedule a visit to the theatre.

## *TWENTY*

Three days later, after Martin had returned from the US, Anne called a board meeting at her place. After the usual preliminaries, they began their reports.

"I have received Allier's irradiation device," Sir Cedric opened. "It resembles a mini-dishwasher. I have conducted all the tests I could in the lab, and they look fine. We now need to test it outdoors."

"That's good," Anne said. "We'll schedule a test as soon as possible. Martin?"

"Andrew Dodson is one of the smartest, talented and pragmatic people I have ever met. Not only did he coach me regarding where to go and what to do, he also went into minute detail describing the various persons I was about to meet. When he was through, I knew their character, their qualities, their emotions, and how to 'charm the pants off them.' Following that, everything went as smooth as silk. We should be getting the first deposit in a few days."

"Hear, hear," muttered Sir Cedric, but he was smiling broadly.

"Now let's talk about the field tests," Martin continued. "Before I left, I gave instructions to George Graham and John Carmichael. John was to find and lease the building we intended to use as our main lab-cum-workshop. He has experience in business transactions and easily gains the confidence of his partners in conversation. He came up with three possible options—in many aspects they resemble my gym."

"Where are these buildings," Sir Cedric inquired.

"One is not far from London. The two others are on the Paris periphery. I deliberated whether to search for purchase or lease options, and leasing won over. We may need to change our premises in a hurry if something unexpected occurs. The buildings are still being investigated."

"That will take care of the indoor testing," the admiral said. "What about areas for the open air tests? Was that George's task?"

"I'll get to George in a minute, admiral. No—that was the other task I'd assigned to John: finding a suitable location for our 'commando exercises.' It had to be deserted and remote but accessible to our vehicles. He has reported to me on two possible locations: one in Camargue in the south of France and the other in Scotland. We need to investigate both."

"And what do George and John know about us?" the admiral asked.

"Nothing. They know that *I* have tasks to fulfill and that they are helping me out. They know better than to ask prying questions. They were just happy to be doing something 'different.' It goes without saying that if I say 'task' or 'assignment,' without going into details, the implication is that something clandestine is in the works."

Anne sounded very pleased.

"Your man John has done a terrific job and in a very short time. I suppose one of us will need to accompany Martin to these locations—both buildings and open areas—and make decisions."

Admiral Stone raised his hand.

"It would seem that I have the most time available," he said. "I'll go."

Martin gave a curt nod.

"The more complex issue is the detonation of charges by irradiation from a plane. There were a number of ways to approach this task, and I must say George handled them thoroughly. He addressed the following issues: location for burying the charges, obtaining the various explosives, concocting a cover story for the team doing the work, method of smuggling the explosives into the country where the tests would take place, purchasing a plane and planning its official course."

Martin looked around, inviting questions. There were none.

"Here is what we have," he continued. "First, location for placing charges. Considering that we may have—in fact, we hope we'll have—multiple explosions, we cannot conduct our tests anywhere in Europe. Our safest area would be the Sahara desert, far away from *anybody*! And we need to select one out of the ten countries surrounding the Sahara."

"Which one have you selected, Martin?" Anne asked.

"Well, after checking and rechecking all aspects of security, tourism offerings, and vehicle accessibility in these countries, I recommend Tunisia as being most suitable. It caters to tourists. It has good land transport systems—I mean, roads leading everywhere and a reliable railway service—and there's no problem in renting a vehicle of any type there."

"Makes sense," Sir Cedric said. "How about obtaining the explosives?"

"That was the easiest part of the plan." Martin smiled. "Europe is rife with black market explosives. I know someone who can provide all we need, no questions asked."

"I'm still wondering," Sir Cedric mused, "what kind of excuse do we have for a group of people traipsing across the Tunisian desert with a load of highly irregular cargo? We'll certainly draw unwanted attention to ourselves, and perhaps even raise the suspicion of the authorities."

"Right you are, Sir Cedric. And I've given this matter much thought. Some of the options we've tossed around are: a cross-country jeep race, an archeological search, naturalists on a desert trek, and so forth."

"They all sound pretty good to me," Anne said.

"However," continued Martin, "the best option, in our opinion, is that we're a movie crew working on a film, and that we need a few scenes shot in the desert. The cinema and the people associated with it seem to have a magical effect on everyone you confront. They are accepted like royalty everywhere they go, including the bowing and scraping and the red carpet. Almost all of their requests are fulfilled by the local authorities, no matter how eccentric they may appear to be."

Anne smiled.

"Yes—I like that even better," she said. "How would we need to prepare for that?"

"Well," Martin said, "we'll need to register a movie company with an address here or in London—actually, anywhere would do—acquire the necessary movie gear and equipment, have a script of the movie we mean to shoot, and an actor or actress."

"I can envisage buying equipment," the admiral said. "But where do you hope to find a script and actors?"

Martin laughed.

"In fact movie scripts can be bought at a 'dime a dozen,' as our American friends would say. Any aspiring cinematographic student would be overjoyed to sell us his script for peanuts. Once we have all the rights to the script, we just modify it to suit our needs. As to the stars—well, any one of my lads could fill that role. The female star just has to look young and gorgeous. She wouldn't need to know exactly what we're doing, just be familiar with the script. If we actually *do* any real shooting and we have an audience watching us, she'll have to say a couple of lines. She'll need to come out with us to the desert only once, for the sake of the show. The rest of the time she'll be in one of the southern cities, or we could just send her home ahead of us."

"What did you mean—go to the desert only once?" the admiral asked. "How many times do you need for the experiment?"

"Here's the scenario the way I see it. Arrive at our base city, still to be established but probably near the desert, settle down at the hotel, and rent vehicles. First trek to desert—look for shooting location—which will in fact be a search for an area to place our charges. If we're lucky, we'll find such a place and bury our explosives. We'll shoot a scene or two with our star, and return to base. We can send her home now, if everything went smoothly. However, this step may need to be repeated as many times as necessary until we find a suitable spot for the test. Then we need to schedule the flyover with the irradiation gear—I'll get to that in a minute—while we're far away, probably at our hotel, and then we'll need at least one more desert trip to examine the results."

"Looks like a very sound plan to me," Anne said. "I suppose you already have the 'young and gorgeous star' on standby, don't you?"

"As a matter of fact, I do." Martin smiled again. "Only she doesn't know it yet. George Graham's sister is a 'drop-dead knockout,' if I may use another Americanism. I'm sure she'll be tickled pink by the idea. Anyway, if she turns out to be unsuitable we can easily find another."

Anne felt a twinge of annoyance that Martin could call another woman a 'drop-dead knockout.' She knew that she herself would never fit that description. Was that Martin's type?

"Now about the charges," Martin continued. "We need a way to bring them into our selected country. We think the best way would be to disguise them as tinned food—part of our provisions for the desert trip."

"And what kind of aircraft were you considering?" Anne asked.

"As you know, George is our aviation man. He poked around and recommended that the best plane for us would be a Dassault Falcon 900 EX, an executive jet. He was probably also intuitively preparing for future operations as well. Anyway, this aircraft can carry twelve passengers and fly eight thousand miles without refueling. It has a cargo area in the rear with in-flight access from the passenger cabin. It has an automatic pilot and a GPS navigation system, allowing the pilot to leave his seat during the flight—for instance, to access the cargo area. I won't bother you with additional technical details."

"How much will it cost?" Sir Cedric asked. "And how do you go about making such an acquisition? I mean, I don't suppose you just walk into a shop, browse around several models, and tell the salesman 'Could I take that one for spin, please?'"

"We'll leave that to George," Martin answered. "I've already said he comes from a very wealthy family, and a purchase such as this would not seem out of place. However, he will need to learn how to fly the jet, and I suggest he begins training immediately."

"You can tell him to go ahead," Anne said. "Agreed?" The others nodded.

"Now—Professor Allier's irradiating machine. We'll need—"

"It weighs about eighty-five kilograms," Sir Cedric said. "Shouldn't be a weight problem for a plane that can carry twelve passengers. The dishwasher comparison I gave earlier applies both to its size and shape. I have nicknamed it 'Excalibur.'"

"Thank you, Sir Cedric. Excalibur it is. At any rate, all this camouflaging—don't forget the charges in the food cans— will necessitate a well-equipped workshop. I'm talking about a computerized lathe, heavy and light welding apparatus, drills of all type, and so forth."

"I seem to recall," Admiral Stone said, "that civil aviation regulations call for all pilots to submit their flight course, including the destination airport, ahead of time. Is that correct?"

"Yes, admiral. The maps we've studied indicate that if we select a certain desert region in southwest Tunisia," Martin produced a map of North Africa and pointed to an X he had marked on it, "it would be directly on the flight route from Tunis, Tunisia's capital, to Lagos, the largest city in Nigeria and its main airport. It looks quite distant on the map, and the route crosses a few other countries, but the entire route is slightly less than two thousand miles—about a quarter of the maximum range of the aircraft. And from Lagos we could fly anywhere we pleased—Paris or London included."

"You haven't answered Sir Cedric's question, Martin," the admiral said. "How much will the plane cost?"

"About twenty million dollars. And I can assure you it will be used several times for future operations."

Sir Cedric laughed.

"I know I should be shocked and outraged at this exorbitant price," he said. "But for some reason I'm not. And not only because the money is coming out of somebody else's pocket. We have the money, or will pretty soon, and I regard the sum as a legitimate expense item."

"If we're agreed to the plan I have just described in detail," Martin continued, "I'll arrange a preliminary reconnaissance trip to Tunisia. One of you will need to come along. Then George will begin taking flying lessons on executive jets, and John will rent a building for our workshop."

"I'm still the one with the uncluttered agenda," the admiral said. "I'll join you in the trip to Tunisia."

"Just a minute, gentlemen," Anne said. "There's still something we need to clear up. I have met Martin's boys, or team, or whatever. Each one of them is an extraordinary and exceptional person. But, as Martin has already insinuated, it seems that they will be heavily involved in all the stages of what we're doing. Therefore, I believe we should not simply rely on their loyalty to Martin for keeping what they know secret. It is my opinion that they should all be recruited *immediately* according to our formal methods, like every other of our associates, and sworn to secrecy and loyalty regarding our cause. Even so, each one will know only what's relevant to his specific task."

"You have a point, Anne," the admiral said, while Sir Cedric nodded his assent. "What do you think, Martin?"

"Fine with me," Martin answered. "We've always been a team on missions. I could finalize the issue in one meeting with all five of them."

"And what if one of them declines or refuses?" Anne insisted.

"That," Martin said firmly, "is not an option. We have a sacred motto that, although not original, is very appropriate: One for all and all for one! Anne, are we adjourning this meeting?"

Anne waited for a second and, when no comments were heard, said simply, "Yes."

"Good," Martin said. "Admiral Stone, I shall call you in London to coordinate our visit to Scotland to investigate the fertilizer test location."

෨෨

## *News agencies—the Internet*

Copenhagen, Denmark—The Danish police have arrested eight Muslims last night in Valby. They were charged with belonging to the Al Qaeda organization and planning to plant a bomb somewhere in Copenhagen during the next forty-eight hours. The Chief of Police did not indicate the site of the intended bombing, but stated that this was the first time that the police had uncovered a direct connection between Al Qaeda and Denmark.

Sources in the USA have revealed that North Korea will remain on the list of countries that fund world terrorism. This was in response to a North Korean claim that she would be removed from the 'black list'.

## TWENTY-ONE

The date for Tanya's funeral was set for Sunday. Anne decided to attend, of course, but she also requested Martin to accompany her. He agreed willingly. It turned out to be the very day he returned from his trip to Scotland with Admiral Stone.

A large crowd had assembled for the funeral. There were Tanya's colleagues from the theatre, stagehands, the bohemian crowd, and several admirers—they all loved and respected Tanya's work, both as an actress and as a director. A number of columnists in the leading drama journals also attended. Anne approached the bereaved parents, who stood there with stony faces. She shook their hands silently and went on. Martin stood to one side and waited for Anne to join him.

Someone said a few words. Anne didn't know or care who he was. But she was deeply moved by his passionate description of Tanya's professional career as "a flower which a foul, criminal hand has so brutally plucked."

"If the police won't find that bastard, I certainly will!" Anne muttered to herself.

Martin overheard her words and they troubled him. He had already learned that his cousin didn't "just say things." What she thought and said shortly became action. The association was the most outstanding proof of that. If she had decided to find the killer of her friend, she'd go hunting for him. Martin was familiar with the uglier aspects of life—the underworld, the slums, the haunts of drug dealers, pimps and prostitutes, and other criminal elements. Anne only knew of the "nice" world—academics, diplomats, scientists, artists—where the rules were quite different. She wouldn't know the first thing about human scum. Her obstinacy and methodic approach to problems would necessarily lead her to the underworld. Once there, if she did not abide by the rules of the game, she would get hurt.

He suddenly found himself feeling responsible for her safety. Why? He knew she was very dear to him, and that he would never allow anything to harm her. So, instead of listening to the eulogies, he began preparing a plan of action. Should he try to talk her out of her resolution? He would probably fail. So—what else? Obviously—get her to confide in him so that he could keep an eye on her. He should get her to talk about Tanya, show interest in the police case, and discuss her opinions on everything concerning it. If he could have been in Paris continuously, he would be around her most of the time and be a kind of bodyguard to her. However, he knew that he would be constantly on the move—so scratch that option.

He needed to become her ally and share her thought and doubts. He wanted to be able to give her advice. She should get used to consulting with him before taking any action, or at least giving him prior notice.

Martin began implementing these ideas on the way back from the cemetery. He asked her how the police investigation was progressing, and she told him about her meeting with Inspecteur Marnier.

"I got the impression," she concluded, "that they were not really giving any priority to this case. So far, they've poked around only in the student community. I'm beginning to think there's more than a fair possibility that Tanya's murderer, this Lucien, is not a student but a hardened criminal—a drug dealer or addict whom nature has endowed with attractive features. He exploited this advantage to pose as a student and woo mature women. Some would be very flattered and would succumb to his charms. Remember, Tanya was past forty and was just this side of being a nymphomaniac. So I can easily picture her taking this fellow not only into her bed, but also providing him with a roof over his head, food and drink, and perhaps even a location for his drug business. Oh dear … I'm rambling…."

"No, not at all," Martin urged. "I happen to be thinking along the same lines. Please go on."

"Well," Anne continued hesitantly, "the way I see it, the killer found her somewhere, right? He must have seen her at the Théatre du Siècle Moderne or thereabouts. Tanya told me many stories about how and where she met men, and most of them were in the vicinity of the theatre, which makes sense because that's where she spent most of her time. So I guess this man hung around the theatre, marked her as a catch and found a way to meet her. Hell, Martin, what I mean to say is that it's quite impossible that nobody saw them or knew nothing about them. We're not living in a vacuum—and especially so in theatrical circles."

"Don't you think the police would take a similar approach?" Martin knew what Anne's answer would be before his question was asked. But he had to make sure he had played his last card trying to convince her.

"Quite frankly—no," Anne said. "They have their student suspect and that's where their efforts will focus. So, I intend to go to the theatre and snoop around. I'll probably get plenty of descriptions of men who were seen with Tanya—perhaps one will fit her description of Lucien, and I'll get a few more details. Maybe I'll discover how they met. And where they used to go."

*That was it*, thought Martin. *There's no point in trying to convince her that she was undertaking a stupid and dangerous task. Not to mention illegal—this could be considered as impeding a police investigation. She won't be swayed—she'll go ahead and do it no matter what. So best would be to be on her side, as it were, and have her share her plans with him.*

"That's probably the best approach, Annie," he said. "You've aroused my interest and curiosity. Like a thriller novel. I'd like to know how things proceed from here. And if you need any help, you can always count on me. Please, Annie—keep me up to date with what you're doing."

Anne felt encouraged by Martin's words. *I'm glad he's offered to assist me,* she thought. *Who knows—perhaps I'll actually need the help of a man like Martin during my investigation.*

## TWENTY-TWO

Back in London, Martin assembled his team after work hours and explained the essence of what the association was all about. He went through the recruitment procedure step by step in accordance with the admiral's instructions, though he knew that with these boys it was superfluous. It went off without a hitch, and the team of five unanimously and eagerly consented to cooperate by whatever means necessary.

ଔଛଠ

The association's successes seemed to pile up on each other. Both financial donations were deposited.

An empty warehouse on the outskirts of London was leased, and equipment was being purchased.

Martin and the admiral had found a vast isolated area in Scotland, with several access paths, which carried no traffic whatsoever during the night hours they were on watch. It was decided they would use this location for testing the fertilizer outdoors after completing the indoor tests.

They had also returned from a weeklong reconnaissance trip to Tunisia, where not only did they find suitable testing grounds in the Sahara desert for the irradiation experiment, but they had also thoroughly enjoyed themselves. They had observed that there was a wide variety of vehicles for rent in Tunisia. Martin suggested that the participants in the test team fly in with their movie gear and rent the necessary transport locally.

Negotiations for the purchase of an executive jet were under way.

Sir Cedric and Emilio Rosetti had set up a meeting in the near future to examine the latter's progress with the communications jammer.

The association's members all clearly felt that their visionary concepts, which not so long ago were mere ideas, were being put into practice. But the more practical things became, the more they felt concern about the moment when their plans would be implemented in the dictators' countries. That would be by far more difficult than finding the resources for the project. There would be real danger there. They would need to overcome problems such as entering the country—and with suspicious equipment and materials to boot. These countries, in particular, were more security-minded than others, and their border checks were very exacting. Stratagems would need to be devised. And then, after the operation, there was the need to exit the country safely.

They were all aware that they were now facing a series of complex debates and planning sessions in which they would be making critical decisions. They also had no doubt in their minds that Martin Cooper, with his vast military experience and his outstanding resourcefulness, would be of extreme value. They were now approaching the stage wherein, as they say, "operations will now lead the way."

◌ဆ◌

Emilio Rosetti paid Sir Cedric a visit in London. He brought a present with him—the most modern, state-of-the-art food processor, made by a leading German firm. At first, Sir Cedric was somewhat flustered, and his inquiring look seemed to ask "what in the world ..." But then he caught Rosetti's sly smile and he understood: the fiery Italian genius had built his acoustic-electronic device into the food processor.

"When you test it," Rosetti beamed, "you will notice that it may be set for a delay of up to twenty-four hours and also for the duration of its operation. All you need to do is to place it in a kitchen anywhere within a kilometer of your target, plug it into the power, making sure you have the right voltage, set the time and duration, and walk away. At the preset time, all electronic audio instruments inside the device's range—every radio and television broadcast, every line and cellular telephone, every public address system outdoors and indoors—will emit an ear-piercing shriek. The televisions picture will not be affected, but the sound will. This interference will stop after the duration period that you have set elapses. Even if the authorities begin a house-to-house search for the transmitter, they will never find it, as it is disguised as a normal household appliance."

Sir Cedric shook Rosetti's hand warmly.

"I can hardly wait to test it, Emilio," he gushed. "It seems too good to be true! I'd like to cover your expenses. You know, production, shipping, or—"

"Forget it, my friend!" the Italian boomed. "It's on the house! But please note—this is just a prototype. The device may be built into any other electric appliance, such as a radio or a baking oven. You might need a number of devices if you want to cover larger areas. Just let me know, and I'll try to provide you with what you need." He winked at Sir Cedric. "At no extra charge."

Sir Cedric thanked him profusely and promised to inform him of progress during testing. Before parting, they shook hands again and wished each other luck.

CREO

Perhaps there was truth in the old saying that success follows success. Conrad Hoffman, the Viennese nanotechnologist, called Sir Cedric saying he needed to show him something of interest, and that he could not say anything about it over the phone. Sir Cedric informed Anne that he was flying to Vienna on the first flight out.

Anne understood that something of importance was in the offing, but this was a realm in which she was a total ignoramus. She hoped she would be able to recognize the value of whatever it was if and when it was presented to her. No matter, the association had by now a number of tools that, if used wisely at the right time and at the right place, would certainly get significant results.

## TWENTY-THREE

Sir Cedric was so excited about what he had learned in Vienna that he requested a board meeting immediately. As Anne was the one most tied to a schedule, they decided to hold it in her flat in Paris.

When they had assembled, Sir Cedric produced a matchbox from his pocket. He opened it and shook out three green peas onto the palm of his hand.

"These peas are, in fact, capsules that dissolve in kerosene, petrol and diesel fuel. Each of these capsules contains millions of bacteria-like microorganisms that for years have been known to be 'consumers of fossil fuel.' They are mostly used to clean up oil spills, where they break up the oil into harmless material. Our friend in Vienna, Conrad Hoffman, is not only a nanotechnologist—he is also an expert in microbiology. And he has used his expertise in microbiology to bestow an additional attribute to these little rascals. One pea dropped into a fuel tanker lorry or reservoir will cause all the fuel contained in it to lose its combustive qualities.

In other words, that fuel will never drive another engine or motor. Friend Conrad has also provided me with a chart indicating how many peas are needed per various volumes of fuel."

"Very interesting," murmured the admiral.

"Yes, I find it quite fascinating," Sir Cedric went on. "Of course, I'll need to test the stuff in our new workshop. But how do we make use of this invention? Let's assume we find a sailor on an oil tanker and let's assume he'll actually dump a handful of these legumes into a couple of oil compartments. Now, when this tanker arrives at its destination the oil will be distributed throughout the country, and many private industries and quite a lot of civilian transportation will be heavily, and adversely, affected. That is *not* what we had in mind."

"I believe you have answered your own question, Cedric," the admiral said. "We do not recruit a sailor on board a tanker. Instead, we try to recruit someone who works on a military base, preferably one that is a fuel depot. Whether or not this is at all possible, if our target countries employ civilians in their military facilities—even only as sanitarians—well, there still remain many unanswered questions."

"And if it *is* feasible," Anne said, "then I suppose we should aim at central depots where chances are highest that the fuel will serve military parades and such. Or am I wrong, Patrick?"

"No, Anne, you're not," Admiral Stone said. "That certainly makes sense. I'll try to pry into some classified intelligence stuff and see if I can come up with something clearer on this topic for next time."

⊰⊱

The rented warehouse was registered as a workshop for the repair and maintenance of electric appliances. They nicknamed it "the cowshed." The proper furnishing and equipment were purchased—not only for the sake of a plausible cover but mainly to be used in the course of work called on by the association. It had a huge empty space in its center, and the various machines and tools were stored or stacked along the walls—most of them mobile on trolleys, tracks, or overhead beams.

Their first test was to immobilize an ancient, second-hand truck that John had bought. Some of the fertilizer was spread over the floor in the empty space and the truck was driven slowly over it. A few meters further, the engine sputtered and died. The truck was pushed into a work corner and the carburetor was dismantled, thoroughly cleaned, and replaced. The engine coughed into life immediately. Conclusion—fertilizer damage was local and temporary.

*Excellent*, thought Martin. *I can imagine a convoy crossing over a patch of fertilizer and halting. Suspicion will fall on the fuel—perhaps diluted with water. The carburetors will never be considered. One, perhaps—but several? Whoever heard of multiple carburetors conking out simultaneously? This will buy precious time!*

*Now we need to make the open-air test in Scotland. We'll take two lorries, just to double-check, and spare carburetors so that we needn't waste time cleaning up the damaged ones—we'll just replace them.*

Martin began delegating various tasks to his men. Bernard, who knew a couple of figures in the underworld, was assigned to the acquirement of explosives. He was instructed to get small amounts—not more than a kilogram or two—of as many different types that the market had to offer.

Spencer was familiar with vehicles. Martin requested him to buy a large, ten-ton truck and a closed jeep. Both needed to have replacement carburetors, and an additional carburetor was required for the truck they already had.

George Graham had already begun taking flight lessons on an executive jet. He was also assigned to buy a script from a film student—perhaps a cinema academy exercise. Martin asked him to browse through the script first to see if modifications, such as a setting in the desert, were easy, and if the script called for a young heroine. George smiled at this.

"If you're looking for an actress, I could ask my sister, Patricia. I think she'd be suitable. She's divorced now, you know."

Martin grinned.

"She's exactly whom I had in mind. I remember meeting her at one of our parties. If she's still the tall and glamorous blue-eyed blonde I saw then, she'll do just great."

CustomER

Bernard managed to get five different types of explosives— dynamite used for civilian purposes such as mining and quarrying, military charges, explosives used in mortar and artillery shells, explosive cartridges for propelling the shells, and a package of old-fashioned black gunpowder.

Next on his agenda was the purchase of supermarket-type food cans to contain the explosives. They had yet to figure out a method of doing so without leaving traces of tampering on the cans, and— of course—they had to be selective about the types of cans bought. For instance, food for babies or household pets was out. The cans they took with them had to make sense—they had to be suitable for a long trip into the desert.

Martin still had an item on his agenda that bothered him. Assuming that all the preparations worked out optimally, how were the cans of dummy food to be brought into the target country? Explosives would certainly be discovered at the airport control—perhaps they even had dogs that could sniff them out.

Conclusion—movie gear, food, and the jeep would have to be shipped by boat. The bogus cans would be at the bottom of a pile of bona fide cans and would escape detection. This would slightly complicate the timetable but would not be of significant hindrance. He could already imagine Philip and Patricia on the boat with the rest of the stuff, meeting up with the other team members with perhaps a day's difference in arrival. Then they would all head south.

Right now, however, Scotland was first on the list of tests. After that would come tests with the food processor.

## TWENTY-FOUR

On the dawn of Saturday, a convoy of three vehicles made its way north. The two trucks were driven by John Carmichael and Philip Brown, and Martin drove the jeep, with the admiral at his side. All vehicles had spare carburetors and a full range of mechanic's tools. A sack, half full with the fertilizer, lay in the back of the jeep.

It was over seven hundred kilometers to the test site. They had decided they would spend the night in Glasgow and leave early the next morning, so as to arrive at the site before noon. They stopped only once on their way, to eat something and refresh themselves.

Early on Sunday morning, after a two-hour journey, they arrived at a pastoral field. Not a single house or person had been in sight for the last half hour. There were no cultivated fields or woods anywhere nearby, and it seemed that civilization had overlooked this area since time began. They were certain they would not be interrupted by anyone here.

John and Philip were very curious regarding the identity of the "old man" who had joined them. However, Martin did not introduce him, and they knew better than to inquire.

The place Martin had chosen for the test was on a slight upward incline. The men used scoops to spread all the fertilizer they had along the dirt road, covering about fifty meters, while the vehicles waited further back. Martin and the admiral stood by the treated stretch of road, and then Martin signaled the trucks to move. They rumbled over the fertilizer—and about twenty meters into the treated area their engines died.

The admiral laughed and clapped Martin on the shoulder. The drivers put their vehicles into neutral gear and the trucks coasted back down to where the jeep was parked. This was necessary, as there was no point in replacing the carburetors while still in the "infected" area.

After replacing the damaged carburetors, they picked a few branches off nearby trees and, good citizens that they were, diligently swept the remnants of the fertilizer off the road so as not to damage any other vehicles that may pass that way. Then they headed back to London.

The entire round trip had taken them three days.

❀

Anne and Sir Cedric were updated by phone with just one word: "Success!" As pre-arranged, the admiral issued an order for fifteen sacks of the fertilizer to Gustav Lemke. These would be stored at the "cowshed."

It was now time for the acoustic tests with the food processor, nicknamed "Paganini." Martin described his plan to the team. They would find a small, remote township that had a couple of hotels and a disco club. Philip would take Paganini with him to one hotel while Bernard settled down in the other hotel. They would synchronize their watches, and at a given time, Philip would operate the device for exactly two minutes. His laptop computer would be tuned to a local radio station. Bernard would be at the bar of his hotel watching television. If there was a noticeable interference, Bernard would try to call John on his cellular phone and Philip would try to reach Martin on the hotel phone in his room. That way they could trace most of the effects of Paganini on the spot, whereas the disco club could be investigated a short while later.

CR80

At the same time, Anne had logged into the university's computer. She brought up the roster of students and requested a search of all those named Lucien who had registered during the past three years. She was presented with a list of several hundred candidates.

Anne honed down her query to those who had stopped their studies for whatever reason. She was convinced that even if Lucien was a student at one time, that he was not a student today. A drug addict could not possibly have finished his studies—he *had* to drop out at one stage or another. Furthermore, after committing a murder and knowing that the police had his description and fingerprints, he surely must have gone into hiding.

Anne focused on the dropouts. There were a few dozen of those, and Anne scanned the reasons for their quitting. Most had perfectly legitimate reasons, such as a prolonged illness, moving to another country, going into a family business, etc. Only three had no reason at all for quitting. Their surnames were: Dupond, Laval and Charpentier. *Now what?* She thought. *I have their addresses from the computer, but can I just go and barge in on them? I need to give this some more thought.*

CR80

That evening, Anne paid a visit to the Théatre du Siècle Moderne in the quartier de la République, where Tanya had worked. She knew a few people from the times she had visited Tanya there, because Tanya was *always* surrounded by friends and admirers. Though she didn't know most of them by name, they remembered her and were glad to talk about their mutual friend, who had met such a tragic fate.

Anne did not reveal what she was really searching for. Essentially, she was just reminiscing about the good times she had with Tanya and wanted to hear stories about her past from her close friends. She would disguise her queries in terms of: "I cannot understand what she could see in such a young boy," or "I'd give a lot to meet the chap face to face ... I wonder what he looked like."

Anne got descriptions. They all matched the police description. And one additional little detail that she couldn't have known before: one of Tanya's friends remembered that Tanya's companion had a red and blue tattoo on his left forearm—a snake or a lizard.

Anne had what she wanted now. She was searching for a tall, blond man in his early twenties, an ex-student with a red and blue tattoo of a snake or lizard on his left forearm and answering to the name of Lucien Dupond, Laval or Charpentier.

## TWENTY-FIVE

George Graham was now a qualified executive jet pilot. His next task was to purchase a suitable plane for the association.

At the same time, attempts were being made at the workshop to open and close tin cans without leaving traces of tampering. At first, the damaged cans were simply tossed into the garbage. But then the team became worried that if anyone saw these tins, suspicion would rise—why would someone first attempt to open them in an irregular manner, and then dispose them with their contents intact? They therefore decided to separate the tins from their contents—the latter could be dumped normally in plastic bags. The tins themselves, however, would have to be distributed in multiple, remote dumpsters.

It was a lot of hard work accompanied by frustrating failures. However, they finally hit on a method that worked. First, the labels were carefully steamed off the cans and laid out to dry. Then the tops of the tins were carefully cut off. The tins were then emptied and cleaned. An explosive charge, wrapped in a plastic bag, was placed inside, and the tin tops were resealed with by ultra-fine spot welding. The labels were then stuck back onto the tin, covering the cut. It wasn't perfect, but the tins could not be distinguished from genuine ones by sight, weight or touch.

Philip Brown went on the script-purchasing mission. It soon became evident that the supply greatly outweighed the demand. Thus, it didn't take him long to find a banal love story in which the girl and her current beau were being chased by her previous boyfriend. All it needed was for the couple to flee to the desert and continue the chase there. Philip couldn't have cared less regarding what happened next in the script. To the greenhorn author's astonishment, he was paid a thousand euros for the script. He also signed an affidavit transferring total ownership and copyright to the newly established film company: International Film Promoters— or IFP for short. This new company also had rented office space, phone and fax lines, business cards, letterheads, etc.—everything necessary for a bona fide outward appearance.

The team did not have the faintest notion of what equipment a film company worked with. Martin sent Spencer Partridge on a crash course on cinematography—mainly to familiarize himself with the professional jargon, and to get an idea of what gear was necessary and how to acquire it.

The trip to Tunisia was scheduled in just a couple of weeks, and the excitement was rising. George managed to buy the recommended aircraft, for IFP, with about as much trouble as he would have bought a car—of course, paying the entire price up front, without haggling, helped expedite the transaction. He tested the plane by flying it to Berlin, from there to Athens, and then back to Paris, its home base.

Martin found a solution for camouflaging "Excalibur," the irradiation machine, as an accessory of the jet, so as not to draw attention or suspicion. It was inserted into a container that normally would be used for the automatic developing of exposed film. The power to operate the machine would be provided directly from the jet's electric system.

Martin finished a few extra tasks he had on his agenda: he assigned John to join George on long flights—just to be on the safe side. Martin also took special pains to plan the exact timing between the completion of placing the charges in the desert and the jet's take-off from Tunis to Lagos. This meant that the aircraft should be on standby in Tunis a day or two earlier. Furthermore, Martin supervised the purchase of a satellite phone, with a large, chargeable battery—as they were preparing for a desert trek, this would not arouse suspicion.

CAEO

George contacted his sister by phone.

"Hi, Patty, how are things?"

"Boring as ever, George. Your call is like a ray of sunshine on a bleak morning."

"Well, maybe what I have to suggest to you will break that boredom. How would you like to star in a movie?"

"I'm listening," Patricia said carefully, not wanting to sound too eager.

"There's this old geezer with millions to burn. He's even more bored than you are, and he's decided to make a movie. He needs an actress for a short scene. If you apply for the part and get it, you'll have a wonderful trip to Tunisia and get paid for it."

"I won't do nude scenes ..."

"No, no," George said hurriedly. "It's not that kind of movie. Everything is in full costume."

"All right—I'll do it."

## *TWENTY-SIX*

Philip and Patricia boarded the ship in Marseilles with the jeep and all the rest of the movie and camping equipment. At the same time, Martin, Spencer, and Admiral Stone flew to Tunis on a regular commercial flight. They expected to meet the boat at the Tunis port two days later.

Meanwhile, they checked into a hotel and then went about being the perfect tourists. Tunis was a large and beautiful city, situated in a bay bearing the same name on the Mediterranean. If you included the suburbs, its population numbered around two million. They sauntered along Habib Bourguiba Avenue and Independence Square. They marveled at the sight of the nineteenth century Saint Vincent de Paul Cathedral, the magnificent seventeenth-century al-Zaytuna Mosque and the Bardo Museum.

The next day they rented an off-road vehicle—an *ORV*—and went to meet the ship at the Tunis port. The unloading was smooth and uneventful and a few hours later the reunited team was on its way south.

C8✷80

After an overnight stay at a very modest hostel in Gabes, the ORV with Martin, Spencer, and the admiral arrived at the designated test site, followed by the jeep with Philip, Patricia, and all their equipment. Though they had several hours of daylight left, they still had to stay there overnight to give credence to their cover story.

Patricia had not been told the real reasons behind the trip. Conversation in her vicinity was mainly about the film, Tunisia, and the weather. She found it strange that the film seemed so unimportant to the rest of the crew, but she didn't ask any questions. She and Philip spent a day going over the part of the script in which she participated, with Philip as her co-star, while the others went in search—so they told her—of a suitable location for shooting.

Martin led "the others" to the site that he and the admiral had picked during their reconnaissance trip. There they diligently buried ten charges, two of each type of explosive, approximately fifty meters apart from each other.

The location and type of each charge was accurately marked on a low-scale map and their GPS coordinates recorded in a table on Martin's laptop computer. Martin called George in Paris on the satellite phone and told him to be at the Tunis airport by tomorrow, arrange the details of his flight plan to Lagos with the authorities and be on standby starting at noon.

Then they set up camp to spend the night in the desert.

࿎

The morning hours were dedicated to the making of the movie. Spencer ran the camera and shouted "action" and "cut," and Philip and Patricia acted through the scene they had prepared. It was easy to satisfy the director, and they soon wrapped it up.

Martin supervised the dismantling of the campsite and the loading of the vehicles. When all was ready, he called George.

"You're in Tunis I assume," Martin said.

"Yes," George replied. "John and I are itching to get moving."

"Flight plan and other arrangements ready?"

"All shipshape."

"We're just about to move out. In exactly four hours from now I want you take off and go through the routine we've practiced. No changes in coordinates. Say hello to John for me."

"Right! We're all tanked up and we'll take off on time. Wish us all good luck!"

The two laden vehicles lumbered back north to Gabes. They arrived at their hotel tired and hungry. But, even after a hearty meal, the admiral had difficulty falling asleep. Had Excalibur operated properly? Had the charges gone off? How many of them? Would they need to repeat the experiment? Tossing and turning in his bed, he finally dozed off as dawn was breaking.

∽∾

After breakfast they all said goodbye to Patricia, who took a train back to Tunis and from there flew to London.

The team staged a bogus commotion at the hotel. It seemed that one of their film canisters was missing. As it couldn't be found at the hotel they needed to make the trip to the desert again, hoping it had survived the extreme weather conditions. No one at the hotel showed any signs of interest.

Back at the test site, they inspected every charge they had buried. All of them had detonated, except for the black gunpowder. The admiral was delighted, of course, as he saw yet another piece of the master plan jigsaw puzzle fall into place, and the gunpowder was the least important of all the explosives. Martin and his lads were also very pleased—they had been assigned a complicated task and had accomplished it successfully.

The return trip was routine. The men flew from Tunis to Paris, and from there to London. They took the exposed film canisters with them, because it seemed the natural thing to do. The jeep and equipment were shipped to Marseilles with instructions that they be forwarded to Paris by professional movers.

## TWENTY-SEVEN

There was some deliberation regarding the location for the acoustic test. The British Isles was a bit "too close to home" for Martin and his team. If a remote place in France were chosen, any hullabaloo resulting from either success or failure of the test would probably cause less trouble.

Paganini, the food processor—not a common piece of luggage—would have to be smuggled into a hotel. They found a large suitcase and buried the appliance among shirts and other articles of clothing. As planned, Philip and Bernard were given this assignment.

They chose a small township, named Auxerre, a hundred and sixty kilometers south of Paris, as their target site. It had about forty thousand inhabitants and did not boast of any major tourist attraction outside its picturesque architecture. Martin would have preferred a smaller town, but the chances of finding one—with two or more hotels that also had the required telephone and television facilities and a nearby disco club—were rather slim.

Philip and Bernard entered their hotels separately—if anyone tried to connect them, all he would find would be the proximity in the time of their registration and that each had registered for one night. But so had dozens of other travelers and tourists—in these and in other hotels. Bernard's hotel was adjacent to a nightclub which promised "dancing and girls every night."

Philip took Paganini into his room. Bernard watched television in the lobby of his hotel with a few other patrons. Back in London, Martin and John were waiting for phone calls. Philip set Paganini's timer to start at 11 p.m. and turn itself off two minutes later. People would be watching television all over the town and the nightclub would already have some customers dancing. He turned on his room TV to the news channel, and the portable FM radio he had brought with him was tuned to a dance program.

The news came on the television at exactly 11 p.m. The announcer reported on another Al Qaeda bombing in Iraq. Philip looked at Paganini anxiously—was there anything wrong with it?

Suddenly an earsplitting screech filled the room. The television screen still showed the commentator but his words were inaudible. Philip had to cover his ears as he rushed to the television set and turned it off. But the intolerable din continued. Philip remembered the radio and hastily turned it off, too. The room quieted—but from other rooms, and even outside, he heard the muted screech mingled by people yelling and cursing.

Philip picked up his room phone and it squawked loudly at him. He quickly replaced the receiver. He understood the delay in Paganini's operation—there was no way to synchronize its timer precisely with another clock, and it was about thirty seconds off. He made a mental note to report this.

Bernard tried using his cell phone to call John but encountered the same effect. He raced outside with some of the other guests who couldn't tolerate the noise, and watched the nightclub door. Sure enough, a stream of irritated customers ran out with their hands over their ears.

Exactly two minutes later the noise stopped, but things did not immediately go back to normal. Some people were still muttering profanities, others were shaking their heads, and still others were sighing in relief. Babies and children were heard crying, and some car alarms were set off. The only people smiling were Philip and Bernard.

Eventually things calmed down. Philip and Bernard collected impressions from their fellow hotel guests, and they all seemed to agree that this was a freak accident and that those responsible had managed to fix it and would probably lose their jobs tomorrow. The main thing was that their TV and their phones were now working properly.

Philip and Bernard called Martin and John, respectively, and made their reports.

Back in London, Martin—though pleased with Paganini's success—wanted to have it designed as something else. A food processor was well and good, and it did its job perfectly, but it wasn't applicable to every situation. Martin was hoping the inventor could be persuaded to modify the device into something that did not need to be operated within a room or a house. Something that could be left in the outskirts of a city or even tossed out of a light plane. And it would need to be miniaturized as well and disguised—not necessarily into a household appliance. He decided to raise this issue at the next board meeting.

ଓଃ୨୦

Anne saw no point in having a board meeting while the tests were being conducted in Tunisia and in Auxerre. She decided to continue her search for Tanya's killer. For no particular reason, she picked Lucien Dupond as her first choice—the sequence didn't matter anyway.

However, this was no simple matter. *Of course,* she thought, *I could visit the last address taken from the university's computer— somewhere along rue de Grenelle. He probably wouldn't be there, because if he were the killer, he wouldn't just sit around at a known address and wait to be picked up. And what will I say once I'm there? Why am I asking about him? If I'm offered to go indoors, should I agree or insist on staying outside? There's still a chance that the murderer would be there, and if he suspected I would turn him in, I could be in real danger. I could meet the same fate Tanya did. But wait—I have an idea!*

Anne rummaged around her apartment and found the clipboard she was looking for. Using her home computer, she printed out a list of fictitious names and personal particulars, which she then attached to the clipboard. Armed with a pencil, she could pose as a pollster. *Hello, I'm Christine from the university. I'm collecting information on students who quit their studies, and particularly why they'd quit. Were you subjected to adverse treatment by your teachers, or pestered by other students, or anything like that?*

Anne smiled at the image she had created for herself. It looked quite natural, and polls were common. She could do all the questioning while standing outside the house or flat—that's what pollsters usually do. *I really don't want to intrude ...*

Anne took a taxi and had the driver let her off a block away from her destination. She then walked slowly to Lucien Dupond's address and, taking a deep breath, rang the bell. Anne waited for two minutes and had almost decided to leave, when the door was opened from the inside by a fat, unkempt woman.

"*Qu'est que c'est?*" she asked rudely.

Anne recited the script she had prepared. The woman nodded in understanding and her features softened a bit.

"He doesn't want to study," she sighed. "He's just a fat, lazy good-for-nothing. He doesn't care that I've worked my fingers to the bone so that he could go to the university. All he does is loaf around, listening to that abominable music of his. I keep telling him 'if you don't move around you'll burst!' He weighs over a hundred kilograms. Perhaps you people could send a psychologist or therapist around? Maybe a professional could convince him?"

"So it is your opinion that he quit his studies out of laziness. Is that right?" Anne asked. "Could there have been another reason, perhaps? Maybe someone at the university hurt him? Or perhaps he was offended by one of the professors? It's very important for us to know, so that we can try to prevent future occurrences of the same."

"Why don't you talk to him yourself?" The woman raised her voice. "Lucien! Get your butt off the couch and come here. There's a lady from—"

"That won't be necessary," Anne interrupted. A fat, lazy boy was definitely *not* what she was looking for. "I am not authorized to interview the students—just to fill in this form. Thank you, Madame, you have been most helpful."

Anne turned on her heel and walked away.

## *TWENTY-EIGHT*

Martin was present, of course, at the next board meeting, which took place in Anne's apartment. He hadn't seen Anne for over two weeks, and he admitted to himself that he had missed her.

Anne had missed him, too. If she had met him somewhere else, without other people in attendance, she would have embraced him strongly and planted several kisses on him. *And he can take that any way he likes*, she thought. But in the current environment, they just shook hands warmly, like the others.

Admiral Stone was as pleased as punch. Despite his age and his retirement, he had taken part in a complex and interesting operation, and he was sure that its benefits were soon to come. He had marched in the desert along with the younger men, he had dug in the sand and buried tin cans—there was quite a lot to be proud of. He had also noticed how the others had looked at him admiringly, and he got well-deserved recognition at this board meeting as well. Could it be that Sir Cedric was a little envious?

The admiral described the operation concisely but left no detail out. He praised the other members of the team for a job done to perfection. It seemed that the association had come a long way, and it was now approaching the day when their plans would be realized.

Sir Cedric reported that his laser device would probably be ready for testing in a few days.

"Just imagine," he said. "You'd be able to point the beam in any direction—both horizontally and vertically. And the penetrating power—well, it looks like we'll have more than we expected ... And there's something else, too. Now that the Excalibur tests have proved successful, I think I should visit Professor Allier and report this to him. After all, it *was* his invention."

The others agreed.

Martin gave a brief account of the tests in Scotland and Auxerre, much to the satisfaction of his listeners.

"To conclude," he said, "I believe that Paganini could be even more effective in our future projects if it were much smaller. Sir Cedric, could you ask Signor Rosetti if he could miniaturize his invention for us?"

"I'll see what I can do," replied the old knight.

Then Martin raised the issue of the "fuel peas."

"We were too busy with the other tests to experiment with these," he said. "I'm still trying to work out how to run the tests. If we place a pellet into a barrel of petrol, how will we know its effect? Pour it into a car's fuel tank and see if it goes? And if it doesn't, what then? We might need to replace the fuel tank, the fuel hoses—perhaps even the motor."

"Let's take this step by step," Sir Cedric said. "I suggest that we prepare two items for the test: a regular paraffin lamp—you know, the old ones with a wick for lighting—and a small fuel-driven motor, like a battery-charging generator. We'll put some fuel into a container and then add a pellet to it. After waiting a few minutes, we'll put some of the treated fuel into the lamp and try to light it. If it lights up, that's that—the experiment has failed. But if it doesn't, we'll put the fuel into the generator. And now, if the generator doesn't start up either, we'll know that the 'peas' work! How does that sound to you?"

Martin confirmed the plan. It was obvious that he and his lads would be doing the testing.

"As to the fate of the motor," continued Sir Cedric, "I'll see if Conrad Hoffman has any ideas."

The meeting was adjourned, and Sir Cedric and the admiral departed. Martin remained seated. It was an awkward situation. Had they started the evening without company, they would no doubt have exchanged hugs and kisses. But the board meeting seemed to have affected the mood. They were finally together alone, and neither of them knew what the next step was going to be.

Anne sat helplessly opposite Martin. She didn't know what to say or what to do. It seemed that any initiative on her part would be grossly inappropriate.

More than anything, Martin wanted to take Anne into his arms and tell her how much he had missed her and wanted to be with her. But he, too, felt that anything he did would cause this delicate situation to collapse—the wrong way.

Finally, Anne cleared her throat.

"How about something hot to drink? And perhaps a bite as well? Some canapés, maybe?"

"Right!" Martin silently thanked her for breaking the hush. "I'll help you in the kitchen."

He followed her into the kitchen. Anne put on an apron, and then she took another from the closet and tied it around Martin's waist. As she reached behind him, he embraced her, held her close to him and kissed her full on the lips. She responded readily, and the kiss became a series of kisses—on the face, on the neck and on the lips again.

Martin held her out at arm's length and looked into her eyes.

"I think I've fallen in love with you," he said simply.

"I think it's happened to me, too," she answered.

It seemed they stood like that for hours. In actual fact, they shook themselves awake after a couple of minutes and addressed the issue of a snack. It didn't take long before the cold cuts, baguette slices, butter, and boiling tea were on the table.

The awkward feeling returned. They didn't look at each other, and no words were spoken. It was as if they were ashamed of doing something they shouldn't have. This time it was Martin who broke the ice.

"Did you continue with Tanya's case while I was away?" he asked.

Anne paused before answering. She remembered he had cautioned her—she could get burned if she played with fire. True, she had behaved quite irresponsibly. But she had an excellent cover story. She decided to tell him everything. Between bites of food, she described how she had approached one of the addresses she found by impersonating a pollster from the university.

"She asked me inside, but I refused," Anne concluded. "From the security point of view, I think I behaved properly."

Martin had listened silently. He seemed deeply attentive as he chewed slowly on his canapé. From time to time he took a sip of his tea, returning the cup noiselessly to its saucer so as not to interrupt Anne's flow of the story.

Anne waited, tense, for his reaction.

"Yes, Anne, you have acted properly," he began. "But, my dear lady, you must realize that you were lucky this time. Next time it could very well end up quite differently. And I sincerely hope there will not be a next time. Be honest with yourself, Anne—if you had met up with the murderer do you have any doubt that you would have been his next victim? Admittedly, you have proven yourself a true leader of a world-embracing operation. But that's by remote control—not hand-to-hand combat. You are not equipped to face a killer who may feel he has nothing to lose. He could, and probably would, drag you into his hideaway, done you in as he did Tanya, and nobody would know where you'd disappeared to or what had happened to you."

"You're probably right. Next time I'll have to think harder."

"No, Anne!" Martin was firm. "There will not be a next time! I love you, and I will not allow you to get hurt. Whatever next step you're planning, I want to be a part of that plan and be there to protect you."

"I wanted that, too. But you were away in Tunisia, and I couldn't consult with you. I just couldn't resist the urge."

Martin believed her sincerity. But it also meant she couldn't be left alone for too long, as she may get another 'urge.'

The snack was reduced to a few crumbs, and the tea was depleted. After taking the dishes back to the kitchen and cleaning them, they returned to sit facing each other in the living room.

More silent embarrassment.

Martin wanted to take Anne into his arms, but thought the timing was inappropriate. He couldn't just get up, walk over to her, bend down—no, that was grotesque. He wasn't thinking of sex. He couldn't picture himself leading Anne into the bedroom. Perhaps on a later occasion, at a more opportune moment....

*We're not teenagers,* Anne thought. *We can't just yield to our instincts. Hugging and kissing require the correct opportunity— like after being parted for a long time. Or the correct ambience— like when we kissed in the kitchen. No, we're two serious adults discussing a very unsavory issue. Not appropriate for hugs and kisses.*

For lack of a better option, Martin brought up an item he had been saving for the next board meeting.

"I think it isn't a good idea to have me as the sole signatory of our bank account," he blurted. "If anything happens to me, there'd be no way for you to withdraw the money."

"You're right," Anne said. "We should have thought about that earlier. That goes for the admiral's account as well. I'll bring this up at the next board meeting and you both can begin rectifying the situation."

Martin got up as if he was about to leave. Anne deliberated between inviting him to stay "a little longer" and accompanying him to the door.

"Well, we've talked enough," Martin said. "It's time to go."

Anne got up from the couch and joined him by the door. Martin held her hands gently and kissed her on the forehead.

"Next time," he said softly, "with your permission, I'd like to stay a little longer."

Anne smiled as she watched him walk down the stairs. This was one of the happiest days in her life. Yet, she was slightly disappointed that the evening hadn't taken a different turn. *I'm not a schoolgirl any longer,* she thought. *At my age, I should take a different view on life.* She paused while shutting the door. *And I* shall! *Tomorrow I'm going to have dates with a cosmetician and a hairdresser. And it's high time I get myself a new dress.*

⋘⋙

The Iranian president has announced that Iran has completed all the necessary stages in the development of nuclear power, and that his country may now consider itself as a member of the "nuclear club."

The Sunday Telegraph reports that diplomatic negotiations are doomed to failure, and that the Pentagon is planning a military strike against Iran's nuclear installations and bases aiding the Iraqi rebels.

At the assembly of the International Atomic Energy Agency in Vienna, the Iranian Prime Minister declared: "The Iranian nation is resolved to continue its progress to the highest levels of development and national might. We are not intimidated by the price of this achievement. We interpret all threats against us as weaknesses of our enemies."

Various sources report that North Korea has signed a treaty with the West in which she agrees to terminate her nuclear development. However, it was also reported that North Korea is currently selling nuclear technology and equipment to Syria, which could be "the initial steps leading toward nuclear weapons."

At the UN general Assembly, the French president has announced that his nation would act to exacerbate sanctions against Iran. However, he has made clear that France does not seek war with Iran.

## TWENTY-NINE

Sir Cedric dialed Conrad Hoffman's number from his office.

"My dear Cedric," boomed the Viennese scientist. "How good of you to call. I assume you have some initial impressions about the peas."

"Indeed I have," replied Sir Cedric. "Very valuable asset we have here. But there is still something I need to ask you—it will save us a lot of test time. Is the affected motor permanently out of commission or can it be repaired in some way?"

Hoffman laughed.

"That is the very first thing I asked myself when I realized that the pellets actually work. No, my friend—the motor is not even damaged, just temporarily neutralized. You need to drain the fuel tank. You may need to wait for some time until the tank, carburetor, and fuel hoses dry out. Or use compressed air to hasten the process."

"Conrad—our next dinner date is on me! Pick your favorite gourmet restaurant! Thanks a million."

## *THIRTY*

Admiral Stone hosted the next board meeting at his home in Brighton. Anne was delighted to leave the bustle of the city, if only for a few hours. On the other hand, she was eager to end the meeting as soon as possible so that she could join her parents and children for a long-awaited weekend together.

The topic under discussion was the political situation regarding Iran.

"Here's what we have," Anne said. "According to the press, and there seems to be mutual agreement about this, Iran is continuing her preparations for the production of nuclear weapons, and the West is preparing an attack on Iran."

"France still has its reservations," Sir Cedric reminded her.

"The way I see it, it doesn't matter whether or not there is a strike. It's a lose-lose situation both ways. If there *is* an attack, there will be very many casualties on both sides—Iran is bound to react with force. Perhaps just Israel will be the first target, as Saddam Hussein intended in the First Gulf War. But knowing how irrational they are, we shouldn't exclude other countries from being targeted as well. That would mean a complete failure for us, as we're working to eliminate casualties—or at least diminish them as much as possible. On the other hand, if these are just journalistic speculations, then nothing has changed in our position, except for the fact that time is running out!"

"So?" the admiral asked.

"So I propose we speed up our program. We need to prepare for action as early as possible."

"An American or Israeli strike against Iran—even if successful— will not wipe tyrannies off the face of the planet." The admiral's visage was very serious. "North Korea is backpedaling but it's only for tactical reasons—I have no doubt they will return to their old ways when they believe they can benefit from it. Al Qaeda is growing stronger by the week. South America is cultivating a new type of dictatorship. Therefore, I do not believe that our mission will end if there is such a strike. But I *do* agree that we should act quickly."

The admiral then reported that Gustav Lemke had called him the evening before.

"He sounded pretty excited. I asked him what it was all about, but he said that he needed to meet me in person. So I'm off to see him tomorrow."

"Anyone have anything else to report?" Anne asked. "Well, that's it, then. Thanks for taking advantage of my visit in London for this brief meeting." She got up, smiling.

As they were shaking hands with Admiral Stone on their way out, Martin steered Anne to one side.

"I hope I can offer you a lift to Reading. As we had such a short meeting, I hope you have a little extra time. There's this delightful Indian restaurant on the way, not far from here, in Cowfold, and I thought we might have lunch there, that is, if you like Indian food—my goodness, Anne, why am I babbling like a teenager?"

Anne's eyes shone as she laughed. This was certainly worth "postponing" her meeting with the children to the hour they had prearranged.

"I have a weakness for chicken vindaloo. All right, let's see how 'delightful' this place is."

"I see you like your dishes spicy. Just be careful you don't burn off the roof of your mouth."

Outside, they got into Martin's car and drove off. It had been a long time since Anne had been so at ease with herself. It was almost like the excitement of an anticipated childhood picnic. She joked and laughed with Martin during the drive, and they both arrived quite flushed at their destination.

Over lunch their conversation became serious. Anne wanted to discuss Tanya's case.

"I feel a kind of obligation toward Tanya," she said. "When Raoul, my husband, was dying, if it wasn't for Tanya I would have probably gone to pieces. Or a deep depression. He became ill while we were in London, and eventually, when it got worse, we had to return to Paris for his treatment. And indeed, he got the best possible treatment there. But they couldn't save him. Those were the hardest months of my life—raising the children under those circumstances is a nightmare. And what with the daily visits to the hospital—Martin, believe me, not only was I a physical wreck, I almost went out of mind! And who saved me? Tanya. She was direct, free—even shameless, I dare say. Here's an example: when we were outside the professor's office, the one treating Raoul, and we didn't have an appointment, I found I couldn't just walk in. I was afraid of rejection, afraid of the bad news, afraid of being scolded for barging in. But Tanya boldly marched into his office and a minute later he received me."

"I see," Martin said.

"She had a kind of agreeable arrogance about her," Anne continued. "She'd be firm and defiant, and yet you couldn't be cross with her—even if her motives were purely selfish."

"I certainly would have liked to meet her," Martin said.

"I loved her, but only now do I realize how much I loved her. I'm saying all this so that you'll understand why I'm so desperately concerned, even involved, in her murder case. I know I shall never find peace until the killer is brought to justice. I want him dead—but I acknowledge that a court of law will eventually decide what to do with him."

"I understand, Annie," Martin said softly and reached for her hand. "I offered you my help before, and that offer still stands."

Anne squeezed his hand.

"Thank you, Martin. I really appreciate it. But I feel I must hurry. Just please don't try to stop me—go along *with* me."

"That is my intention. What were you planning to do next?"

"Visit the next Lucien, of course. Lucien Charpentier. The address I have is on rue Cambronne, Montparnasse."

"And what cover were you preparing for yourself."

"Can you think of any reason why I shouldn't repeat the polltaker story?"

"No. I think it's quite acceptable. Now, Annie, I want you to have a relaxing weekend with you family. Why don't we meet in Paris early next week and have a look around the address you mentioned. Let's see what kind of house it is, if there are any back doors, which floor he lives on, and so forth. Then let's think about action."

She squeezed his hand again and the smile returned to her face.

 CRBO

Anne felt very refreshed after her stay in Reading. Her parents and her children were all in the best of health, and she managed to forget the convolutions in her life, resulting from her involvement with the association and the murder of Tanya.

She put the finishing touches on her pollster "disguise" and descended to the street holding her clipboard. As agreed, Martin was waiting for her in a taxi, and she gave the driver an address close to their real destination.

"It's best if you were not seen here twice," Martin said, after paying the taxi driver. "So I'll scout around first. Find yourself something to do, and I'll meet you here in a few minutes."

Anne breathed in the artistic atmosphere of Montparnasse. The last time she was here was years ago, with Raoul and the children, to visit the famous cemetery where Baudelaire, Sartre, de Beauvoir and Beckett were buried.

She decided to stroll to the nearest intersection and then walk back. If Martin returned, she would be in full sight. Meanwhile she could peek into the shop fronts and make believe she saw the literary giants who had frequented this area. She looked around— there was no missing the huge tower that dominated the skyline. *What would those authors have said about it?* she wondered. *And other patrons of this area: Zola, Picasso, Hemingway, Matisse, Modigliani? The list was endless. How different all that was from the present circumstances—now I'm on the trail of a murderer.* Anne felt herself growing increasingly impatient. *Perhaps I'm closer than I suspect. I must find out!*

Her thoughts were interrupted by the return of Martin.

"The house has a concierge," he said. "A remarkably disagreeable old crone. I inquired about the Lavoisiers, and she brusquely said there was no one there by that name. But through the main entrance I saw an open door to an inner courtyard. I couldn't see where that courtyard led, if anywhere. So I walked around the building, actually around the whole block, but I saw no other exit for Monsieur Charpentier's house. Just a line of closely packed houses."

"Thanks, Martin," Anne said. "I'm going in. Could you wait for me here, please?"

"Umm, Anne, maybe we should prepare a plan? I was thinking …"

"I can't wait any longer!" Anne was determined. "I must *do* something!"

Martin realized there was no stopping her.

"Very well. But promise me that you will not enter the apartment under *any* circumstances! I must insist on this, and you will insist on staying outside the door. If you see any signs that you are being coaxed or forced into the flat—*run!* Straight down the stairs. However, if you feel you have the time to explain a hurried departure, you can say that you've left a child alone downstairs or something like that. I'll be just outside the main entrance."

Anne took a deep breath, held her clipboard at the ready and rang the bell. The concierge buzzed her in.

"Bonjour, Madame," Anne said pleasantly. Martin was right— she *was* an old crone.

"What do you want?" barked the concierge. Martin was right again, she was a very *disagreeable* old crone.

"I'm from the university, and I'm taking a poll for them. Do you have a Charpentier family here? Their son, Lucien, was a student and he quit his studies without giving an explanation." Anne said all this in one breath so that the concierge could not brush her off with "third floor, second door to the left." Now the concierge was a party to her mission.

"Lucien Charpentier is dead," said the old woman. "He got sick and died."

"Good heavens!" exclaimed Anne. "When did this happen?"

"I can't remember," muttered the concierge. "Could be about six months ago."

Anne scribbled something on her clipboard and left. When Martin saw her reappear, he heaved a sigh of relief.

"He died half a year ago," Anne told him.

Inwardly, Martin was very pleased. He hoped that candidate number three would also turn out to be a wild goose chase and with that Anne would give up her insane chase after a killer.

"Too bad," he said. "Whom does that leave us with?"

"Just one name. Lucien Laval. I have his address at home. But I think I have had enough for today."

"Let's let it simmer for a couple of days, Anne. We may come up with a better cover, or a better escape plan, if one is called for. Keep in mind that, with two names eliminated, there's a good chance that the third could be our man. We need to be extra careful this time."

Even though Martin didn't really believe that the last candidate was the killer, he realized he had just made himself an accomplice to Anne's quest. He accompanied Anne back to her flat but—very reluctantly—refrained from going in with her.

"I simply *must* get back to London. My gym isn't getting the attention it deserves. Not only I, but the boys, too, are absent for long periods of time, mainly doing association-associated work."

He grinned at his feeble alliteration, and then became serious again. "I want you to promise me that you will make no attempt whatsoever to locate the killer without me. All right?"

Anne looked up at him and smiled.

"I promise," she said.

A quick kiss, and he left.

(3&0)

On the way to the airport, Martin was bothered by thoughts on his relationship with Anne. They both knew that love was blossoming between them, but it had not been consummated. *In other words*, he told himself, *we haven't had sex yet. Quite unlike any other woman I've met. True, the others were younger, but I bedded them all in no time at all. Anne, however, is no young virgin. She is a mature widow with two children and worthy of admiration and respect—because of her personality and because of what she represents socially. And because I love her deeply. Come on, Martin, admit it—why else would you want to protect her, to take care of her, to ... yes, hold her and kiss her and sleep with her, too. But that can wait—the right moment will arrive and then it will be ecstasy.* Martin surprised himself by discovering that no other women interested him now.

(3&0)

At the same time, Admiral Stone was visiting his friend Gustav Lemke in Hamburg. Lemke was exceptionally excited, as if he were preparing a surprise party. The admiral knew better than to ask questions. *Let the juvenile old guy have his fun*, he thought. Lemke took him to a brand-new restaurant that boasted an exceptionally varied menu and ordered for them both. Thus far, he had not given a clue about what the issue was all about, and the admiral was getting mildly curious.

Throughout the meal, they discussed almost every topic under the sun except their common dealings. The admiral began to wonder. *Is he trying to test my endurance before I snap and came out with a question? He has obviously discovered something new, but I really do not appreciate these kinds of games. Come on, Gustav—out with it!*

But the meal was magnificent. Trust Lemke to come up with the best of the best. Lemke beckoned the waiter to bring the schnapps.

"I got your order for fifteen additional sacks of the fertilizer," he said. *At last,* thought the admiral, *finally—our issue at hand!*

"Yes, indeed," the admiral said. "We hope we'll get them soon. By the way, Gustav, I must say that this was one of the finest meals I have ever had anywhere! My deepest thanks."

Lemke reached into his pocket and took out a pebble, about the size of a walnut. He placed it on the table in front of the admiral.

"Take it and examine it," he said.

The admiral turned the piece of gravel in his hand, shook it, tested its weight, held it to his ear—nothing. An ordinary pebble.

"Seems very commonplace to me," he said.

"A stone, *ja*? Just a stone. Like your name. You have no doubt?"

The admiral shrugged—there was a limit to how long he could play this game.

"This pebble," the German explained, "is actually a container made of a special plastic material. In it there is a paste that sublimates on exposure to air—it becomes a gas without becoming a liquid first. The gas is a soporific and a tranquilizer in one. Whoever inhales it gets a feeling of pleasant calm and a strong desire to sleep. Depending on the inhaler, the gas could act as a narcoleptic—the victim falls asleep involuntarily. The gas remains effective from six to twelve hours after exposure in locations without heavy winds or drafts. The effect on the inhaler could last from one to two days, again depending on the person and the amount inhaled."

"Well, well, well," said the admiral. "Camouflaged anesthetics."

"I can already sense the skepticism you and your associates will have toward this breakthrough. Frankly, when I was working on its development I was not thinking of dictators but of Al Qaeda. They are robots resembling humans only in shape. I always think of them as already being poisoned by a drug we cannot produce yet—the drug of fanaticism. My drug will act as an antidote to their drug."

"Indeed? I wonder how?" The admiral was genuinely curious now.

"We all know how hard it is to get to them—they're so hard to find, *nein*? However, some of them *are*, perhaps, accessible. We know that they train somewhere between Afghanistan and Pakistan. Now, if I guess correctly, you have access to secret intelligence reports that can narrow down these training areas to definite locations. You could spread these pebbles over that area."

"And how is the paste exposed," the admiral asked.

"Ah, yes! The paste is released to the atmosphere by melting the plastic container. This is done by dipping the pebbles into a liquid I have developed for that purpose. Once dipped, the pebbles start dissolving—and they continue dissolving even after the liquid has dried."

"Now that's an interesting approach," the admiral said. "Still, it would be quite cumbersome to take pebbles and liquid into the arena of action and then dip and spread, dip and spread—I can see our operators dropping with content smiles on their faces before getting anything substantial done. We'd have to wear gas masks—making the operation even more unwieldy."

"You are thinking faster than I can explain!" Lemke laughed. "There is no need to worry. You can *time* the beginning of the dissolving process by diluting my liquid, which I call the 'conditioner,' with ordinary tap water." Lemke produced a slim notebook, which he handed to the admiral. "Here, look. I have prepared a table that matches the amount of water necessary for each period of delay. You can delay the release of the gas by one to seven days—depending on the amount of water. With equal parts of conditioner and water, you get a delay of four days. Less water, less delay. And vice versa, of course—it's all in the table in the notebook."

The admiral shifted his gaze from the notebook to the pebble and thought furiously. *If this works, it could be a major breakthrough.*

"Just think," Lemke continued, his excitement mounting. "You prime these pebbles in the conditioner and then spread them where you think they'll be most effective. The crazies arrive for training and suddenly get very drowsy and drop off to sleep with big smiles on their faces. It could be very challenging for their commanders and trainers, except that they, too, would join Morpheus in dreamland. There's no limit to what can be done—use your imagination, my man!"

*He's right,* thought the admiral. *At the moment, I cannot think of how we could make use of these pebbles, but it most definitely has possibilities. How about if we got the gardener of one of the dictators to cooperate with us, and he would spread primed pebbles on the lawn where Mr. Tyrant has his tea and muffins. If this went on for a couple of weeks, everyone would be positive that the despot had lost his marbles. Oh, well ... nice thought, though.*

Admiral Stone went to great lengths to praise Lemke and his invention. He went into fantasies about how well this new development would be received by the association.

"I know that I don't need to urge you on. You are one of those rare people who not only look forward, they also *go* forward. Again, my heartiest congratulations. And any new invention of yours would be very welcome indeed."

Gustav Lemke was just made a very happy scientist.

## *THIRTY-ONE*

With the sense of urgency carried over from the previous board meeting, Anne requested a recap of what the association had ready—especially those inventions that were ready for immediate use. She ticked them off on her fingers:

"First, we have the fertilizer to halt vehicular convoys. Second, there's Excalibur, the irradiation machine that detonates explosives on the ground from an aircraft flying over. Third, we have Paganini, our acoustic communications disruptor. Now, we can add Lemke's pebbles and conditioner. And the fuel pellets that Hoffman mentioned. We haven't tested them yet, but I'm pretty sure they'll work. Martin, would you please see to it? We'll also need to think up ways to make use of these pebbles. All ideas welcome."

Sir Cedric stood up.

"You can add my laser machine to your list, Anne," he said pompously. I have completed my lab tests. Bottom line—it can melt most metals from afar as long as there is a direct line of sight. Most intervening non-metallic objects will not be affected, nor will they affect the laser beam. I am hoping that the machine will disable certain crucial metallic components in nuclear reactors, even if they are protected by thick layers of concrete. That still needs to be field-tested."

The old knight was smiling broadly. Anne was not smiling at all.

"Won't damaging a nuclear reactor have drastic ecological consequences?" she asked. "We all remember Chernobyl ..."

"No, Anne, we're not going that far. I am not talking about a nuclear explosion or a meltdown of the core. That would be beyond the power of my beam, as these locations are far more protected than the others. We have learned that in Iran the reactor is under several meters of concrete, over which about twenty meters of earth were amassed. My laser beam could not penetrate that."

"So what's the use?" the admiral asked.

"There are several other vital elements of the nuclear process that are not so heavily guarded. Take, for example, those centrifuges that Ahmadinejad is so proud of. My guess is that if they, or at least some of them, were neutralized, it would put a serious crimp in his plans."

"That's that, then," Anne declared. "We need to complete the outstanding tests as soon as possible, and then start preparing our real projects. If new inventions come along we'll test them, but meanwhile we're going to go for the real thing with what we have! For our next meeting, please all of you think of the most suitable target we could begin with, and what exactly you propose to do there. And when."

Martin reminded Anne about the signatory issue of the bank accounts. The admiral and Martin were assigned to arrange all the necessary paperwork.

∽৪৺

Sir Cedric and Professor Albert Allier had arranged to meet at the same brasserie where they had dined previously. Over their *choucroute garnie*, Sir Cedric praised the scientist for his brilliant invention.

"Your compliments make me blush," Allier said modestly.

"Not at all, my friend," boomed Sir Cedric. "Your device is the solution to several of the problems we were facing. I cannot think how I can thank you enough. We have tested your invention in the field recently. It works beautifully."

A look of slight concern flitted over the professor's face.

"May I inquire—what exactly did you mean when you said you performed a test in the field?"

"Just that, Albert. We irradiated various test charges and examined the detonations."

"Really? Where and when did you conduct these experiments?" Allier was beginning to become agitated.

"About two weeks ago in the Sahara desert. My dear Albert— you look upset! Are you feeling ill? Perhaps the wine ..."

"No, no." Professor Allier was frowning deeply, and he spoke slowly. "I am all right. What about the charges?"

"Four different types," Sir Cedric said, but his tone was addressed to the welfare of his colleague. "They were buried in the sand and they all detonated. Albert, you really—"

The transformation of the professor's features was profound. His face was livid with fury. He gritted his teeth, his cheeks changed color from red to purple, and his breath came in short gasps.

"How—dare—you!" he whispered, emphasizing each word. His brow was covered in perspiration, and he put two clenched fists on the table. "How *dare* you conduct an outdoor experiment without consulting me first!"

Sir Cedric's concern switched channels at lightning speed. Gone was the worry for Allier's health. Instead, he was facing outraged opposition to the association's program.

"My dear friend, calm yourself, please!" he said. "You'll do yourself damage. Didn't you send me the device with a specific request that I test it? Because your laboratories would not allow the tests done here? So what's the problem?"

The professor's gaze was ice cold.

"We did *not* agree that you conduct experiments outside your laboratories. You distinctly suggested that the tests would be made only there! I most certainly oppose your free and unauthorized usage of the irradiator in whatever environment you please— particularly not out in the open! You should have informed me of your intentions first, and I would have considered the pros and cons of permitting or forbidding your actions. As things stand, I must request you to return the device to me immediately!"

Sir Cedric was dumbfounded. This was a totally unexpected turn of events. And there didn't seem to be much he could do about it.

"Listen, Albert," he said, "I'm sure there's been a misunderstanding. We can work it out. If you would—"

"I'm sorry, Sir Cedric," Allier said bitingly. He had never used the "Sir" title before. "That won't do at all. It seems I cannot trust you. I must warn you that if I do not receive the machine within forty-eight hours I shall inform the authorities. And I shall tell them everything. Do you understand my meaning, Sir Cedric? *Everything!*"

Sir Cedric sat in silence. Inwardly he was fuming at this reversal of allegiance. But his features showed only humility and attempts at appeasement.

"Don't you think this is rather extreme, Albert?" he said soothingly. "I mean, obviously we did not go against your wishes intentionally or maliciously. I regret any blunder we may have made, but I'm sure—"

Professor Allier threw a fifty-euro note on the table and got up.

"Say no more, please. I will not associate with irresponsible adventurers who are likely to stir up additional international trouble. And the French government is strongly opposed to violence of all kinds. You may take that as a warning!"

Sir Cedric was now truly alarmed. He looked around at the other diners and was relieved to see nobody was paying them the slightest attention. Allier had suddenly become a threat to the association and would need to be dealt with by the severest of means. Right now, however, he needed to assuage the Frenchman's anger and buy some time. He was prepared to promise him anything—even lie through his teeth to achieve a reprieve of a few days.

"We have no desire to do anything contrary to our friends' wishes—that has always been our policy. Of course we shall consult with you before *any* future action regarding your device. Right now, it is on its way back from Africa. The moment it arrives, I shall notify you and have it shipped back to you immediately. It's a matter of a few days only. Could you spare us that time? I promise you we shall do nothing with it until you get it."

Professor Allier stood motionless for a long time as if preparing his next outburst. But he was apparently mollified by Sir Cedric's arguments.

"You have a week, then," he hissed through his beard. "If I don't get it by then, I go to the authorities."

He strode out of the brasserie. Sir Cedric yanked out his cellphone and dialed frantically.

## *THIRTY-TWO*

It was past 10 p.m. before Admiral Stone and Martin arrived at Anne's apartment. They had both dropped everything they had been doing in answer to Sir Cedric's call for an emergency meeting. Neither of them, nor Anne for that matter, was used to being summoned so hurriedly without an explanation. But Sir Cedric had mentioned "life or death," and that was enough.

Sir Cedric and Anne were waiting patiently. Anne had heard the bad news about Allier the minute Sir Cedric had arrived at her apartment, breathless and white as a sheet, and she became as disturbed as he. But by now, both of them had composed themselves and were ready to face the problem rationally and level-headedly.

Sir Cedric reported the events regarding Allier to the others.

"As you may recall," he concluded, "when we established our association we made a solemn decision that if any of our recruits were to turn coat and become a threat to us we would have to eliminate him. The rationale was that we are set to prevent a global holocaust, and that the life of one person attempting to hinder our cause was outweighed by the lives of millions who could be saved. I am afraid we are facing such a situation right now."

"Couldn't you have repeated our ideology to him?" asked the admiral.

"No, Patrick. This was a person who was listening only to himself."

A moment of silence ensued.

"I've been doing some thinking," Sir Cedric said finally. "I know Allier pretty well. I am not medically qualified, but it seems to me that this is a case of mental disturbance—I really cannot name it in any other terms. I have managed to get him to agree to postpone his plans for a week, but we must act quickly. He must be terminated, and I think I have come up with a manner to do so that would not incriminate us."

He had everyone's close attention.

"We should prepare a machine that closely resembles the original device we got from him. I shall explain to him that we made a few 'cosmetic' changes to make it look like an ordinary household appliance."

Sir Cedric took a deep breath.

"What then?" asked Martin, echoing everyone's thoughts.

"The machine we send will be booby-trapped. Two of Martin's lads will deliver it to Allier, unpack it, and make sure it's plugged into the electric outlet. Then they'll leave. When Allier touches it he'll be electrocuted to death."

The others remained silent, pondering over the details they had just heard, trying to find loopholes in Sir Cedric' tactics. This was a description of an execution.

"Martin," Anne said after a couple of minutes, "do you think any of your lads has the stomach to make the delivery?"

Sir Cedric interrupted.

"If not—I'll deliver it myself!"

Martin remained unruffled.

"My boys are not pansies. They've all participated in acts of violence far beyond what Sir Cedric has suggested—you don't want to know about them, believe me. They'll do it all right. Otherwise," he smiled at Sir Cedric, "you and I will deliver it together."

"What about the booby trap?" Admiral Stone asked.

"Bernard Webb knows a lot about electric circuitry. As a matter of fact, I have a smattering of knowledge on that subject myself. I'm sure we can buy an appliance that resembles Excalibur, and Bernard can rig it so that it will electrocute anyone who touches it."

Everybody was feeling dismal and distressed. They all knew this was a calculated, rational decision, and that the association's decision to implement it now was correct and proper. Nevertheless, this was a human life they were planning to take, and it went against their primal feelings of decency.

Admiral Stone noticed this and decided to address the issue.

"Killing a fellow human can fall into one of three categories," he said. "Manslaughter, murder, and execution. Manslaughter could be inadvertent or unintentional, as in an accident or a fight. Murder is always intentional and involves emotions such as love, hate or jealousy, or it is motivated by money or other material benefits. An execution is different. It is always decided upon by an authorized body, be it a court of law, a tribunal, the underground, or even the mafia. The executioner is not emotionally involved with the victim and usually doesn't even know who it is.

"This is what we have here and now. And that is how we all should see it. We have an enormous challenge—saving millions of lives—and anyone who stands in the way of the accomplishment of this creed should be eliminated. History is full of examples— and I'm sure Anne will back me up on this—of military leaders who have sacrificed individuals, even thousands, to save an entire nation."

"This is very hard for me," Anne murmured. "But it's got to be done. Right!" She raised her voice. "Martin, please get to work on the Excalibur replica—it should be ready in two days, latest three. When we have the … thing, Cedric, please call Allier and inform him of the expected date and time of the delivery. Tell him that the couriers will know nothing about their cargo, and that it would be better that he be alone when examining the device."

03☙

Three days later, the booby trap was prepared and camouflaged. The lab tests confirmed that when plugged into the mains, it would deliver four thousand volts at three amps through the body of the operator, stopping his heart instantly. It would then short-circuit itself and become harmless.

Sir Cedric called Professor Allier in Paris.

"My dear Albert," Sir Cedric found it hard to say the words, "I hope you have calmed down since our meeting."

"Yes, I have," Allier replied civilly. "But that doesn't change anything. You still have three more days to deliver my irradiation machine back to me."

"That is exactly the reason I called, Albert. It has returned and I am sending it to you by courier. I am paying them to have their Paris branch deliver it to you at your most convenient hour. When would that be?"

"I think around six in the evening would do, after work. Better still, six thirty. By then, everyone should have left. You realize, I am sure, that I have no interest in having anyone witnessing the arrival of the package. And, of course, I shall want to examine it."

Sir Cedric was delighted. Allier was making things so much easier for him. However, his tone of voice remained businesslike.

"Naturally, naturally. I shall request the couriers to unpack the device onto your desk, plug it into the electric outlet and leave. Is that all right with you?"

"I couldn't ask for more, I suppose. I appreciate your punctuality. When will they arrive?"

"How about tomorrow?"

"Fine."

"*Au revoir*, Albert," Sir Cedric said and hung up.

#### ☙

At exactly six thirty in the evening, two sturdy men in grey overalls and carrying a large cardboard box, arrived at Professor

Allier's office and knocked on the door. They had made sure that the corridors in the laboratory building were empty and that they had been seen by no one.

"*Entrez*," came a voice from inside.

They opened the door. Professor Allier was seated behind his desk, obviously anticipating their visit. One of the men glanced at a slip of paper in his hand.

"M. Allier?"

"Yes, it is I. Come in, please. Put the contents of the box on the table here."

The men removed a large device from the box and placed it directly in front of the professor. The object had retained most of the dishwasher shape that Allier had designed.

The two couriers were busy setting up the machine. One of them unraveled the electric power cable and plugged it into the electric socket as if it was an integral part of his duties. The other pushed a delivery order toward the professor.

"Sign here, please."

The professor signed and returned the slip.

"Thank you. You may leave now."

The two men left. The device on the table was positioned at an angle to Allier. He reached out to straighten it.

## THIRTY-THREE

It was nine o'clock in the morning. *Commissaire* Felix Duval of the *Police Judiciaire* took in the scene. He was standing near a large desk in the office of Professor Albert Allier, dean of the Department for Irradiation Research at the Paris University. The professor was seated behind his desk. His two charred hands were on the table, book ending an appliance that looked like a mini-dishwasher. An electric power cable ran from the dishwasher to the mains outlet in the wall. The professor's head was thrown back on the headrest of his comfortable chair and he appeared to be deep in thought. But he was dead.

Commissaire Duval was one of the most experienced and respected investigators on the force. His name had appeared more than once in the press as the solver of particularly tough cases. An hour earlier, while driving to his office, he had received the call from the dispatch center, and he changed his route accordingly.

It appeared that the cleaner had entered Allier's office without knocking, as she did every morning, expecting the room to be empty. She was surprised to see the professor at his desk and wished him a good morning. When she got no response from the man she had known for years to be a very polite gentleman, she looked at him again and suspected something may be wrong. She approached the professor with the intention of helping him, but then suddenly realized that he was dead. Her screams brought the guard on duty rushing to her side, and he was the one who called the police. Two police officers arrived and kept the other employees of the department, who had started to assemble, away from the arena. They then notified the *Police Judiciaire* and the commissaire was summoned.

He ordered one of them to use a handkerchief to unplug the power cord from the wall socket. He put in a call for "le Parquet"— the Prosecutor's Office—and looked around, taking mental notes of what he observed.

The office was tidy—it seemed that everything was where it ought to be. There were no signs of a fight or any other violence. Duval approached the table. All neat here, too. He bent forward and peered at the device between the professor's hands. *Possibly a dishwasher*, he thought. *The professor was probably handling it and got electrocuted. No matter—the autopsy would bring up the cause of death soon enough. What would the professor be doing with a dishwasher on his desk? Perhaps it was one of the inventions he was famous for. Leave that to the experts as well.*

The forensics team arrived and went about their business efficiently: gathering fingerprints, taking pictures, collecting every shred of suspicious evidence. They also took the device with them to the police laboratories. Duval stopped the coroner on his way out.

"What can you tell me, Alphonse?"

"Nasty business, Duval" he said. "Probably an accident. Don't get many deliberate electrocutions nowadays—though we'll need to prepare an official report on that. No doubt in my mind, however."

"Time of death?" Duval asked.

"My guess is between twelve and eighteen hours ago," the medical man said, and walked out.

*So he was here all night*, thought the commissaire. *I wonder if his family missed him.*

Two officers of Duval's staff took statements from all the occupants in the nearby offices.

CŚßð

Back in his office at 36, Quai des Orfèvres, Commissaire Duval summed up that morning's findings with his staff. Professor Allier was known to be a pleasant and friendly person. He was punctual, dedicated to his work, a quiet family man with nothing in his past to indicate anything out of the ordinary.

The press was beginning to assemble outside. Duval had already verified that Allier's widow had been notified, so he felt free to address the reporters. He raised his hands for silence.

"Ladies and gentlemen, you may report that Professor Allier died last night in his office. The police are investigating. That's all—I cannot give you any more information because I have no more information."

"Is it true that he was electrocuted?" a reporter shouted.

"That's what it looks like at present, but we are not certain yet. We need to examine all venues. Thank you." The commissaire returned to his office.

C3&O

That evening the printed press reported the professor's demise as luridly as they could—a new invention of his could possibly have electrocuted him—but they were fair enough to admit that this was all speculation. The news on radio and TV were even drier and made do with Commissaire Duval's statement only.

At the same time, Duval updated his two assistants with the latest information on the case.

"The autopsy has established that death was by electrocution. The lab examining the device reported that faulty internal wiring—we don't know yet whether it was deliberate or not—turned the contraption into a lethal hazard. There was nothing exceptional in Allier's actual presence in his office late last evening. One of his assistants related that the professor would sometimes remain alone in his office after hours, when everyone else had left—especially if there was something urgent that needed his attention. Nobody had ever seen the appliance that was on the professor's desk before today, and no one could say for sure what it was supposed to be. Nobody had even seen the device being delivered to the professor. In fact, for all they knew, it could have been in Allier's office for days or weeks, stored in a closet or cupboard, and the professor had chosen that particular evening to do something with it.

"The door to the professor's office was not locked. Only his fingerprints were on the machine. There is one item, however, that bothers me …"

His assistants remained silent.

"There were no fingerprints on the plug at the end of the power cord that was inserted into the power outlet on the wall. Not even Allier's. Why? There were no gloves found in the room. Could he have used his handkerchief or a rag or tissue to insert the plug? Why would he have done that? After all, he grasped the device with both hands uncovered and left fingerprints there. And no rags or tissues were found in the room or on the body, and Allier's handkerchief was neatly ironed and folded in his breast pocket— obviously unused."

"Commissaire," one of the assistants spoke up. "We know that Allier was a scientist through and through. He never concerned himself with anything else—no hobbies, no interest in politics, no parties—and we therefore know of no enemies he may have had. Which, with regard to the plug you have just mentioned—I cannot imagine anyone who *knew* that the device was dangerous would deliberately connect it to the electricity. It's just too far-fetched."

Duval stood up.

"I shall interview the widow at my earliest convenience."

CRECO

When Anne saw the reports on Allier's death, she became physically ill. She was overcome by nausea and vomiting. She lost her appetite.

She took tranquilizers. She went to bed with a book. Nothing worked. She tried to console herself with rational thinking: everything was well planned. There was no way the machine could be traced to the shop where it had been purchased—and it had been modified both externally and internally at the lab. They had taken great pains not to leave any fingerprints on the final product. Once the device was taken out of the cardboard box and placed on Allier's worktable, it had not been touched again. The box itself was removed by the couriers and destroyed. Could the police find anything—something they had overlooked?

*We had to do it. Otherwise, we couldn't continue with our work. It's all going to be okay.*

Anne knew she mustn't be weak. She went to the bathroom and threw up. She returned to the bedroom a bit shaky but actually feeling better.

*If only Martin were here! He's so smart and confident. He wouldn't let anything shift him off a logical course he had planned. He would take me in his arms and hold me tight. He would kiss me and I would open his shirt, and we would ...*

## *THIRTY-FOUR*

Martin opened the board meeting with a report on the tests of Hoffman's "fuel consuming peas" conducted at the "cowshed." The steps described earlier by Sir Cedric were followed meticulously. As a result, neither the generator nor the tested vehicle would run if fuel that was "treated" with a pea was used. There was no doubt now as to the effectiveness of Conrad Hoffman's pellets.

The admiral indeed had access to classified material, as insinuated by Gustav Lemke. He summed up his research:

"North Korea poses an accessibility problem. It has no tourism, and a businessman may acquire a visa only if the authorities happen to like what the foreigner is offering. In this case, there would be no point in establishing a straw company and using it as a cover. They check every application very thoroughly. If you really want to negotiate with them, you'll need to represent a large, well-known company. We could, of course, approach one of these large companies and propose that we represent them in North Korea. This would take a long time, I'm afraid—but it remains an option. Remember, however, that even a bona fide representative of a bona fide company will not be able to travel about freely. He will be housed in one of the deluxe hotels built by the government on an island in the middle of the river that flows through the capital, and he'd be able to leave that island only with special permission and an escort. Bottom line—using official methods will not get us anywhere in North Korea. If that is to be a target, we'll need to think of other methods."

"What other methods?" Sir Cedric asked. "Clandestinely by sea or air?"

"Or aided by smugglers," Martin added.

Sir Cedric's eyes opened wide and a smile flitted on his lips.

"Not a bad idea," he said. "But where do you find them?"

"You can always find smugglers," Martin said. "Especially in a country such as this. Anywhere you have hunger, smuggling becomes a thriving industry. If you like, I could take a short 'tour' with one of my lads along the border with South Korea. I can almost guarantee positive results."

Anne was worried. She had never expected one of the board members to undertake a dangerous mission such as this. Secretly, she was also very concerned for Martin's safety. But, as usual, her sense of responsibility brought her back to reality.

"I think it's an excellent idea!" she said. "If there aren't any objections, I move that we adopt this plan. But just a recon tour, and maybe making initial contact with a smuggler or two if possible. Nothing more—no operational missions, and no telling the smugglers what our real objectives are. After we hear the report we'll make a decision."

Admiral Stone was impatient to get back to his report.

"Iran," he said, "is a different kettle of fish altogether. Iran is a tourist country and there is no difficulty in getting an entrance visa. Hotels are well developed, you can rent a car and visit historical and archeological sites at your leisure. Security forces are very active, so you need to be cautious. A recon tour will be necessary here, too.

"Now, as to Al Qaeda and their training grounds—well, the border between Afghanistan and Pakistan is more than two thousand kilometers long! I think I might have located an area where they may have training camps. We could probably fly over this place—not during the day, they could shoot at us during daytime—and spread the 'gravel.' Dusk or dawn would be most suitable, I believe. We'll need to decide where the plane takes off and where it lands."

Mme. Allier was still in mourning. Commissaire Duval sat opposite her in her living room and waited until she had finished serving coffee and cookies.

"Madame, please allow me to convey my deepest condolences at the sudden passing away of your dear husband." The commissaire recited the words he had so often needed to say before. "We believe it was a work-related accident, but it is my public duty to investigate all other possibilities."

The red-eyed widow adjusted the hearing aid in her right ear, and tried to put on an apologetic smile.

"I don't hear so well, you know," she said.

The commissaire dismissed this with a smile of his own. He then repeated what he had just said, taking care to raise his voice slightly.

"Do you really think something criminal occurred?" Mme. Allier asked.

"I did not say that. But until we have the complete picture we must keep on investigating. And indeed, there are a few open items. So please permit me to ask you a few questions that may enlighten us in our inquiries."

"By all means. I shall be glad to be of assistance."

"Mme. Allier, was your late husband in good health?"

"Oh, yes! He was *never* ill."

"Was he particularly concerned with anything special lately? Was he working late more frequently than usual? Was he in good cheer? Or morose? Irate? Perhaps he was absent from home more than usual? In short—did you notice any change in his behavior?"

Mme. Allier furrowed her brow in thought.

"Now that you mention it," she said, "I recall that he lately always seemed to be in a hurry. Not that he was ever late for anything—not at all. He attended a few 'business lunches'—not a common event for Albert—and I even once entertained the notion that there may have been another woman. Of course, I dismissed the idea at once—after all, Albert's daily schedule had hardly changed."

"Do you have any idea about who those business lunches were with? One or more people?"

"I think he once mentioned a colleague from London. You know how these scientists love to exchange ideas."

"Do you happen to know who this colleague is?"

"I'm sorry, no. But perhaps he appears in Albert's telephone notebook."

Mme. Allier rose from her seat and picked up the notebook lying by the telephone. She handed it to Duval who began leafing through it.

"Here's a London entry," he said. "Norton, Sir Cedric." He glanced at her questioningly.

"Oh, yes! That's the one! I distinctly remember Albert mentioning his name regarding one of these 'lunches.'"

"Mme. Allier, do I have your permission to borrow this notebook for a day? I promise to return it to you by tomorrow."

"But of course, commissaire. It's no problem."

Duval asked a few more routine questions about family members. The widow answered to the best of her ability.

"And how about socializing, Madame?" he inquired. "Did you and your late husband meet with people, go to parties—you know?"

"Frankly, commissaire, we did not go out much. Albert simply *loved* music and the theatre. He had several subscriptions to concert series, and attended many of these events. I did not join him on those occasions—as you see, I have a hearing impairment. While he was out on one of his cultural evenings, I played bridge at the club nearby."

"Just one more question, if I may, Madame. Did your late husband have any enemies? Do you know of anyone who could have wanted him dead?"

"No, certainly not!" Mme. Allier was indignant. "He was loved and respected by everyone."

Commissaire Duval stood up.

"Thank you for your time, Mme. Allier. Again—my regrets. I shall have the notebook returned to you by tomorrow."

At the door he suddenly turned.

"Oh, by the way—did the professor have a life insurance policy?"

"Just what the university provides to all its employees," she replied. "I don't know of any other, private insurance policy—either for him or for me."

"Thank you again. With your permission I shall return if any more questions arise."

CK80

On the way back to his office, Duval weighed the pros and cons of verbally reporting his latest interview to the Examining Magistrate. *I think I'll skip it,* he thought. *Probably just a waste of time, anyway. He'd only say that nowadays scientists always exchange views, otherwise science wouldn't progress. I'll just make a regular entry in my written report ...*

## THIRTY-FIVE

Indeed, there was no progress in the Allier investigation. There was not a single shred of evidence that the death was premeditated. True, forensics had not managed to decipher the nature of the odd device that had caused the electrocution, but as it involved a scientist known for his innovative experiments, they eventually gave up the search. And Duval was not quite satisfied with the lack of explanations for the electric plug sans fingerprints and the unknown time and method of the device's delivery to Allier's office. But the Examining Magistrate ruled that there was no point in continuing the investigation and—given the evidence before him—death was caused by accident. Case closed.

Commissaire Duval did not agree with this ruling. He was convinced that Professor Allier had been murdered, although outwardly he concurred with the Examining Magistrate. *A man of my stature and experience should leave no stone unturned. I shall know no peace until I catch this murderer.* He therefore decided to continue the investigation on his own. He had Allier's telephone notebook photocopied and decided to begin with the 'business lunch associate.'"

## *THIRTY-SIX*

Loose ends were beginning to link together. Sir Cedric's laser was installed in Boulanger's satellite, and it could be aimed and operated from a console in Boulanger's office. Now they were waiting for a launch date, which mainly depended on weather conditions. The satellite's orbit was designed to fly over Iran and North Korea every one hundred and thirty-two minutes, at an altitude of three hundred and sixty kilometers.

The combined satellite-laser-projector was nicknamed "wasp." All the lab tests had been completed successfully, but simulation of the altitude distance was impossible. The intention was to disrupt the operation of a nuclear reactor, even by neutralizing external accessories only. If necessary, detonating depots containing explosives, shells and missiles, could also be attempted.

"Meanwhile," Martin said at the next board meeting, "we'll need to set up a test site. We need the exact coordinates of the targets in order for 'wasp' to succeed in its mission. Let's leave the discussion on that for later. There is another topic I would like to raise that we have not considered before. I believe it should be relatively simple to obstruct computer communications. My meager knowledge is just enough to advise that we should look into it. I wish I could show you how it's done—but I can't. Is anyone here an expert on the subject?"

All heads were shaken.

"I didn't think so. On the other hand," Martin continued, "there is an abundance of computer geeks out there who could probably do what we need in a few minutes' work. If they can break into the FBI data banks, they can do some underhanded stuff for us as well. I must warn you, though," Martin's face was grave, "this could be considered illegal by certain authorities."

Five seconds of silence. Then they all burst into laughter.

"You don't say!" roared Sir Cedric. "*We?* Doing something illegal?"

Martin grinned.

"Seriously, now," he said, "I suggest we all ask around and see if we can collar such a hacker, as they are called. If and when we find such a person, we'll recruit him, subject to this forum's approval. Agreed?"

Nods all around.

"One more thing," Anne said. "I'd like to set up the recon trip to the North Korean border. Martin, I believe you've made all the flight arrangements. So, to sum up: you and Spencer Partridge will pose as tourists. You'll take nothing with you that would indicate anything to the contrary. You'll arrive in South Korea and 'tour' the area along the border with North Korea. See if you can make contact with smuggler's who cross the border. We'll expect you back a week later with a full report. Any questions, anyone?"

There were none.

CB EO

The telephone in Sir Cedric's residence rang insistently. Sir Cedric ran out of the shower with a towel round his waist and picked up the receiver.

"Sir Cedric Norton speaking."

"Good day, sir." The voice had a refined, but definitely French, accent. "This is Commissaire Felix Duval of the Criminal

Investigations Department of the Paris Police."

Sir Cedric did some quick thinking. He knew that Allier's death had been reported in the French—and some of the British—press. He had closely followed the reports on the investigation, which were minimal, and he knew that the case was closed. Duval's name was familiar to him from these reports. Therefore, this call was an enigma.

"I apologize, Sir Cedric, for taking your valuable time. But I would be most grateful if you could assist me—even minutely."

Sir Cedric replied in a cool voice.

"How could a British citizen assist the French police, commissaire?"

"I am referring to the investigation into the death of Professor Albert Allier. I understand that you and he were professionally acquainted, and that you were in touch with him shortly before his demise. Perhaps you know of any other contacts the late professor may have had that could shed light on the mystery of his death."

Sir Cedric was frantically collecting his thoughts.

"I am quite aware, Sir Cedric, that I have no authority to interrogate a British citizen. The formal approach would be by putting in an application to Scotland Yard, who would then summon you … I thought that we could skip the unpleasant formalities as I only wished to ask you a simple question … you know … so I'm approaching you directly…. Naturally, you do not have to answer me at all."

*Why on earth is he so insistent?* Sir Cedric thought. *We both know the case has been closed. Better to let him think I don't know about that.*

"I quite understand," he said. "I have known Professor Allier for several years. We never worked on the same projects, but we did consult with each other from time to time, as scientists are wont to do. Occasionally we dined together. But what more can I tell you?"

"Do you know whether he had any contacts outside the academic world? Perhaps industrial concerns or other organizations? Or other scientists and just plain people with whom he had recent contact?"

"Over the years I have met a number of people who knew him. I cannot name anyone in particular, I'm afraid." Sir Cedric cleared his throat. "It is not my position to give you advice, commissaire, but I believe that in Paris you'll find many people who knew the professor far better than I did."

"You are absolutely right, Sir Cedric. But I have a number of points I need to clear up. For instance, the device that caused his death—nobody can explain what it is. And his wife claims that of late he had been overly excited and was absent from home more than usual."

"Indeed. And these are mysteries you want resolved. Well, all I can say is 'good luck,' commissaire."

"Thank you for your cooperation, sir. If you visit Paris, I would be delighted to invite you to a cup of coffee and we could discuss the professor at leisure. If you can afford the time, of course. Goodbye."

Sir Cedric put down the receiver but stood in thought, one hand on the telephone and the other still clutching the towel. *What was the* real *reason for Duval's call? He had spoken to the widow and probably got Allier's telephone book from her where my name appears. But what did he hope to get from this call? It's beyond me. Anne and the others must be informed about this. It's very unlikely that he has a tap on my phone, but just to be on the safe side I shall use a public phone. We need to assemble an urgent board meeting.*

⚜

Anne was troubled by what Sir Cedric had told her about the call by the French Police. She, too, had followed the press and she knew that Commissaire Duval was the officer in charge of the Allier investigation. When the association's members had all arrived, she opened the meeting.

"Gentlemen," she said nervously, "from now on we need to be doubly cautious. Even though none of us, barring Sir Cedric, have had any contact with Allier, we have no way of knowing how close Duval's investigations will take him. He might be capable of following Sir Cedric and eventually finding us."

"I don't think there is anything to worry about." Martin's voice was calm and soothing. "Sir Cedric is one of hundreds of people who probably had contact with Allier. Moreover, Sir Cedric's relationship with Allier is of a long-lasting friendship and scientific dialog. Even if they follow him right into this meeting of ours, they'll have to apologize and withdraw because they have nothing to ask us. Next—if they look for a transport company that delivered the device, they'll find nothing. There isn't such a company. I keep saying 'they,' but in actual fact there's only Duval—we know that the case is closed. His story about tying up loose ends is a fabrication—there's no such official procedure with a closed case. He may be conducting a private investigation of his own."

"Why on earth would he do that?" Anne asked.

"The only reason I can think of is that he has a clue or clues that his superiors rejected, which he thinks may be of importance. For instance, we took pains to leave the electric plug without fingerprints. I'm sure he noticed that, and perhaps he thinks it strange. Also, the machine itself does not really fit in with any scientific or industrial scheme. But we know that the Examining Magistrate has considered all this evidence, and that he ordered the case to be closed. So I suggest we forget this incident."

"Except me," Sir Cedric said.

"Correct, Sir Cedric, except you. Duval *did*, after all, get to you. But I think that if you just take a few precautions from now on, we won't run into any trouble."

## THIRTY-SEVEN

Martin studied North Korea through every source he found—publications, maps, Internet, press articles, etc. He requested Admiral Stone to provide him with data that might be less available to the public. They met in the admiral's office to iron out the details.

"I've done a little research of my own, Martin," the admiral said. "Even though politically the two Koreas were never a single entity, they are populated by the same people: same race, same language. In 1945, at the end of the Second World War, North Korea was occupied by the Soviet Union, and South Korea by the Americans. Two states were created: the North became communist, of course, and the South came under the American capitalistic influence. The population was also split between North and South. Families were torn apart, and many lost their land and possessions, remaining only with deep scars and bitter memories."

"Right you are, admiral," Martin grinned. "And here is what I found out. The population along the border between the two Koreas speaks the same language, and the contact between split families has never been severed. The political rift was deepened further by the 1950 war, which lasted three years, when the North was backed by Communist China and the South by the United Nations. So, we can expect that there are well-established routes across the border where people and goods travel … umm, unofficially. Furthermore, due to the immense impact of the Americans over the years, many of the populace speak English!"

It was the admiral's turn to grin.

"Off you go, then," he said. "Good luck."

"I'll have Spencer prepare the logistics," Martin said.

CB80

Some last details needed to be clarified before Martin and Spencer left for Seoul. At the board meeting at Anne's apartment, Anne made sure there were no misunderstandings.

"Martin, please repeat the nature of your mission."

Martin grinned.

"Sure. We are trying to find a way into North Korea in order to infiltrate at some later stage with personnel and/or equipment."

"What security measure are you taking?" the admiral asked.

"The utmost. We don't really know what opposition we're up against, so everything has to appear natural in accordance with tourist behavior."

"Dealing with smugglers," Sir Cedric said pompously, "is *not* a regular tourist activity."

"Correct," Martin said. "That will need extra special safety precautions. If we *do* meet up with smugglers, and we *do* get caught by the authorities—which I doubt, because they themselves probably benefit from this traffic—I'm pretty sure the smugglers will provide us with an alibi. The worst-case scenario is that we are stupid foreigners looking to make easy money. We pay a fine and leave the country. We won't be put in jail if no transaction takes place, and that is not our intention at the moment. Just investigation."

"How will we know if you're in trouble?" the admiral asked.

"We won't be." Martin grinned again. "However, I suggest that Anne and I keep in touch by telephone. All conversations will be normal as between a couple separated for a short while. Thus, we can discuss our health, the weather, flight schedules and the like. Nothing operative, of course."

"Are there any more questions?" Anne asked. "Well, thank you, gentlemen. Meeting adjourned."

Martin lingered in the kitchen while Sir Cedric and the admiral left. He wanted to have a more personal farewell from Anne. When the door had shut behind the two elderly Englishmen, he stepped forward and took Anne's hands in his.

"Umm, Anne, I'll be away for two or three weeks, and I—ahh—I didn't want to leave without giving you a goodbye kiss." He could feel his face turning red.

Anne smiled into his eyes, wrapped her arms around his neck and kissed him on the mouth.

"Don't go," she said softly. "Are you in a hurry to get anywhere?" He shook his head. "Then stay! I want to be alone with you."

In a flurry of joy, he picked her up by the waist and rained kisses on her face and throat. Anne glanced toward the bedroom— she just couldn't help herself. She hesitated a bit then indicated to Martin to put her down.

"Why don't we get something to eat," she said breathlessly, "And perhaps later we'll rest a bit."

Martin was relieved for the delay. He didn't know what to anticipate exactly. He, the ultimate ladies' man who could bed any female he wished, now had 'cold feet' when facing this extraordinary woman.

"Good idea," he said. "I've hardly eaten anything today. I could eat a horse."

Anne brought leftovers out of the refrigerator—sliced salami, a couple of cheeses, gherkins and half a bottle of merlot. They ate in the living room in silence, their eyes never leaving each other's faces.

"Silly me. I didn't fetch the biscuits," Anne said finally, when they had almost finished. "I'll get them now." From the kitchen she called, "Have you ever been anywhere beyond Iraq?"

"No."

Anne returned with the biscuits and took her seat.

"Personally, I have never been east of Athens," she said.

The chitchat continued for about half an hour. Then the food was all gone and the conversation died out. There was a minute of silence.

"You're ..." Anne whispered, "you're not going to leave now, are you?"

Martin's confidence was restored by this question, and he laughed out loud.

"Go and prepare yourself for bed. I'll join you when you're ready."

The ice was broken.

Anne had not felt so excited and stimulated in years. She went to the bathroom and changed into her sexiest negligee, sprayed a delicate perfume on herself and went to the bedroom. Martin had not prepared himself for an overnight stay and joined Anne wearing only his shorts. She was lying on her back on the bed, her arms tucked under her neck. Martin smiled at her and, without waiting for further encouragement, sat on the bed by her side. He leaned over her, laid his head on her chest and kissed her breasts through the fabric of her nightie. She gasped a short "wait," pushed him gently away and in one deft motion removed her pajama top. At the sight of her naked breasts, Martin could contain himself no longer. In a whirlwind rush, they were both naked and their bodies merged. Anne had never felt such passion since her days with Raoul—it was almost worth waiting all these years for it. She wanted it to go on and on.

When Martin awoke the next morning, he found himself alone in bed. He got up and found Anne preparing breakfast, complete with porridge, eggs and fried sausages. He was touched. Since childhood, nobody had ever prepared breakfast for him. He embraced her from behind and covered her neck with kisses.

Anne closed her eyes and absorbed his kisses as a sponge soaks up water, while a deep moan formed in her throat. *My life has changed overnight*, she thought. *I'm in love, and I have a lover.*

## THIRTY-EIGHT

"You're in particularly high spirits today, Martin."

Spencer Partridge and Martin Cooper were aboard the Korean Air flight to Seoul. Like many other tourists, they sat in economy class seats and sipped on soft drinks.

"Right," answered Martin. "I'd expect you to be, too. I find it quite exciting to visit a country for the first time."

They chatted and dozed intermittently until it was time for lunch. The petite stewardess suggested the airline's specialty, *bibim noodles*, which they both enjoyed.

"You know, Martin," Spencer said, "I love my job at the gym and range, but I am certainly glad for these opportunities to get away and do some operational work. I believe I speak for the others as well. We soldiers need a periodical change of pace— much like a car needs to have its oil changed regularly."

Martin knew all along that his boys were itching for action, just the same as he was. Otherwise, he would never have offered them the option of taking part in the association's activities.

Nevertheless, he was pleased to hear it come outright from one of his teammates.

*Hmm,* he thought. *The next time a trip like this is planned, it would look more 'natural' if a couple were to do the recon. I mean, a man and a woman. Look at the other passengers on this flight— I'd say that over three quarters of them are married couples or have a close boyfriend-girlfriend relationship. Perhaps a man and his mistress here and there. Spencer and I kind of stick out—two men traveling together. Let's consider this option for the trip to Iran.*

*Anne and I touring Iran—what a wonderful thought! Visiting the tourist sites, staying at luxury hotels, tasting the exotic dishes... FORGET IT! She'll be far too busy with the university and managing the association. Oh, well....*

They arrived at Seoul's Incheon International Airport at 10 p.m. local time, after a twelve-hour flight. Another hour was spent getting to their hotel, where Spencer had reserved two rooms. Both were dead tired and turned in for the night.

The next morning they met for breakfast.

"Slept well, I hope," Martin said.

"Like a baby," Spencer answered.

Martin laughed.

"Let's go over what we planned to do here. We must never forget that for all intents and purposes we are tourists. So, after breakfast we'll go to the desk and request to join a tour of the city."

"When we return," Spencer recited, "we'll book a tour taking us out of Seoul for tomorrow."

"Meanwhile," Martin continued, "we'll find out about renting a car and buy a detailed roadmap of South Korea. We'll probably get a map of Seoul on the city tour, but if not, we can pick one up at the desk. Starting on Sunday, we'll make preparations to take a car up to the North Korean border area."

## THIRTY-NINE

It had been two days since that glorious night with Martin. Anne was still tingling from the after-effects. She felt she had shed several years, become a young girl again, vibrant and full of energy. The first thing she did was go on a shopping spree, something she hadn't done for a long time. She visited the Galeries Lafayette and the boutiques of rue du Faubourg Saint-Honoré. She bought dresses and shoes that she did not need. She treated herself to an exorbitant meal of *plateau de fruits-de-mer* with dry wine. She took a taxi home, threw herself on the bed and relaxed into a satisfying nap.

When Anne awoke, it was already dark outside. She didn't feel like going out again, so she sprawled in front of the television set with a glass of orange juice and some crackers. She watched the news, and then a murder mystery began.

Anne sat bolt upright. Murder mystery! She was involved in one herself. She had neglected to follow up on her quest for Tanya's killer. Anne felt the guilt rising in her bosom. She had this uncontrollable urge to go out right now and continue her search.

*I know I promised Martin not to go alone, to consult him before taking action. But if Lucien Laval is the killer, he most certainly won't be at the address I have, waiting to be picked up. If I inquire about him there, all that could happen is that they'll tell me he has left, or perhaps not even answer me at all. That was probably true regarding the other two addresses I visited also—there never was any danger. So why take all these exaggerated precautions? And it certainly couldn't do any harm. Maybe I'll get a forwarding address, and then Martin and I could decide what to do. So there's no real reason why I should not inquire at Laval's address. It will just be some more information gathering. That's it then—I'm going there tomorrow.*

So here she was. Rue de l'Ourcq in the 19th Arrondissement— the address of Lucien Laval. She had dressed modestly, armed herself with the clipboard, had taken the metro to the Ourcq station and walked to the house, reciting to herself the pollster story.

Holding her breath, she rang the bell. She told the concierge that her business was with the Laval family and was buzzed in. She walked up two flights and was greeted by an elegantly dressed, elderly woman.

Before the woman could ask anything, Anne blurted out her story. She kept a lookout for anything suspicious, prepared to run down the stairs at the slightest provocation.

"I'm sorry," the woman said, when she had finished her introduction. "Lucien left the house a long time ago. He only shows up when he's broke and needs some cash. Even so, I haven't seen him for several weeks now. It pleases me greatly that the university is taken this kind of initiative. Please come in—perhaps I can help you find him."

Anne hesitated for a second. Then, despite all the alarms ringing in her brain, she entered the apartment.

"I really shouldn't, you know," Anne said apologetically. "I have a long list to cover. Perhaps just for a minute…."

Mme. Laval seated Anne in an armchair and brought lemonade from the kitchen. Then she, too, sat down and started to talk.

"Lucien is a good boy. While he was still studying at the university, he was industrious and diligent. Then he met this blonde floozy with the ponytail and everything changed. She has total control over him. He neglected his studies, frequently stayed out late, and demanded more money than his regular allowance from his father. My husband works as a cashier for the railway company—the SNCF—and earns a decent living. But we cannot afford Lucien's new extravaganzas. All we wanted is for our only child to get a good education. But this … this *tramp*," Mme. Laval's eyes burned with rage, "has ruined his life!"

"Do you think he's with her now?" Anne asked.

"I'm *sure* he's with her now!" the mother spat out.

"And has Lucien ever been mixed up with anything else besides this … woman? I mean, something—ahh—unsavory?"

"*Mon Dieu*, yes! He started taking drugs, thanks to that succubus of his. Listen, you've got to save him."

"That's what we're trying to do, Mme. Laval," Anne fibbed. "But for that I need your help in locating him."

Lucien's mother began sobbing quietly.

"I wish I knew," she said softly. "All I know is that this tart is seen occasionally on rue Saint-Denis. You may not be familiar with this, my dear, but rue Saint-Denis …"

"Yes, I know," Anne said, resting a hand on Mme. Laval's shoulder. This street was well known as one of Paris' famous red light districts.

"… And her name," continued the mother. "She is called Ninette. I doubt, however, if that is her real name."

"Could you give me the names of some of his friends? Perhaps they could help in locating him?"

"He had a number of friends. They kept walking in and out of here, but he never introduced me to any of them."

"Well, I guess that's all, Mme. Laval. I shall pass on this information and I hope the university will send someone who can assist your son. You have been of great help. Thank you very much."

On the way back to the metro station, Anne pondered on what she had recently learned. She was positive that the woman was perfectly frank with her. There was no sign that she was hiding anything. Anne was also convinced that Lucien's mother had no inkling that her son was connected to a crime in any way. Then again, perhaps she belonged to the type of people who don't read the newspapers or listen to the news.

Anne decided to wait for Martin's return. She certainly would not venture alone into a street full of prostitutes. That was *really* dangerous. But she was quite pleased with what she had achieved.

## *FORTY*

The first day in Seoul had passed uneventfully for Martin and Spencer. The hotel had provided first class Western service, including the Korean Times delivered early to the room, a well-prepared breakfast, and bookings for tours. Seoul was the habitat for ten million people, about half the entire population of South Korea. The tour of Seoul revealed an enormous city, divided in two by the Hangang River, with suburbs on the surrounding hills. These, they were informed, were built by the throngs of poor Koreans, who left their villages to seek their fortunes in the big city.

There were about twenty universities in Seoul. It was estimated that approximately a hundred and fifty thousand foreigners lived in the city—mostly Japanese and Chinese, but also some twelve thousand Americans.

Many citizens spoke English, though sometimes broken and funny-sounding, and their number decreased dramatically the further away you were from the city. After a few feeble attempts to get the hang of the language, Martin gave up. He and Spencer would have to make do in English and sign language if necessary.

He hoped that the smugglers, if and when they found any, would speak at least a little English.

Now, after two days of touring, they had rented a Hyundai and made their way north. They had prepared a cover story for their trip—the border between the Koreas was made famous by the press, and they wanted to see it with their own eyes. They passed through the townships of Uijeongbu and Tongduch'on, and they soon arrived at the first destination—the town of Ch'orwon.

Martin scouted while Spencer drove.

"Whoa, Spencer. There's something that looks like a food place. Let's go in and see what we can find."

Spencer parked the car, and they walked into a small restaurant. They sat at a table and ordered beers. The waiter, who was also the owner, spoke to them in English.

"You are Americans?"

"British, actually," Spencer replied.

The owner grinned broadly.

"We see very few Britishers here. Welcome! Are you here on business?"

"No," Martin laughed. An air of jollity encouraged conversation. "We're tourists. We wanted to see the famous 38th Parallel up close."

"Well, that's further up north," the proprietor said. "But the road will take you there. Once, before the division of the Koreas, this was one of the roads to the north. It leads all the way to Pyonggangup, the first town beyond the border. But you won't be able to go there. May I suggest that you drive up to the border, look around and return here for a first-rate genuine Korean lunch?"

The proprietor was short and pot-bellied, probably indicating his love for food. He had a constant smile on his face, which was a kind of fixture that people who serve other people acquire over the years. He had thin stubbly hair and was probably in his fifties.

"You honor us," Martin said. "We'd be glad to dine here." He was hoping to build a relationship of trust and friendship with this man—who knows when a local ally could become handy.

The trip to the border was very short. Beyond that point, the road and the fields on both its sides were blocked by huge chunks of concrete, enforced by barbed wire strung at shoulder height. Further on, they could see an ancient military outpost, a pillbox, manned by a short soldier in a Soviet uniform of the type seen only in movies nowadays.

Martin and Spencer got out of the car, strolled around, and waved a greeting at the North Korean soldier. They got no response, nor did they expect any. However, they refrained from taking pictures, as *that* may goad the 'Soviet' sentry to open fire. So they waved again, a friendly goodbye, got into the car and headed south again. On the way back, they stopped and dawdled away the time taking pictures, so as to arrive at the restaurant for noontime lunch.

At the restaurant, they were greeted by the owner as old friends. They introduced themselves by their first names. So did he.

"My name is Chou-Jiang-Ho but many foreigners find that difficult to pronounce. So they call me Charlie for short. You can call me Charlie, too."

There were a few other diners at the restaurant, all locals. They were all in a hurry to finish their meals and get back to work. Charlie served his foreigner guests various appetizers, most of them variant preparations of turnip, and it seemed that he wished to delay them until the others had left. Indeed, after the last diner had disappeared through the front door, Charlie served up fish, followed by meat, prepared in ways unfamiliar to the Englishmen, but which they found very tasty. Charlie, his smile unwavering, watched them as they ate.

"How about some tea?" Charlie suggested as they were finishing their meal.

"Just the thing," Spencer said. "Bring it on."

Charlie served the tea, and then sat down at their table. He leaned forward and his smile took on a shifty appearance.

"Just what are you looking for?"

"I beg your pardon?" Martin feigned indignation. "We told you, we're tourists."

The sly smile remained.

"Anyone coming to these parts is looking for something."

Martin's vast experience in working with people, together with his acute sense of judgment, convinced him that Charlie was neither hostile nor a threat. He gave a quick glance at Spencer and decided to test the proprietor.

"My office in London employs a very nice chap who came from this area many years ago. When he heard that we were planning a trip to Korea, he told us that he had a family on the northern side and that he wished us to transfer a sum of money to them. He also told us that he could not expect such a transfer to be done for free, and that he was willing to pay for it. We went to the border hoping to find somebody there to help us, but there was no one. Such a pity."

The smile on Charlie's face remained the same. He scratched his head and breathed heavily.

"Maybe," he said. "Maybe."

Martin looked him directly in the face.

"You are very guileless persons," Charlie said. "You say you want to do your colleague a favor and send money to his family. Right?"

"And you're trying to tell us that's impossible," Martin said. "Right?"

Charlie laughed so hard he had to hold onto the table to keep from falling off his chair.

"Everyone knows," he gasped, wiping his eyes with one of the napkins, "that this is the 'highway.' This is the main road for smuggling into North Korea. *Everything* passes through here: food, textiles, raw materials, currency, people—you name it. And you're telling me you want to 'help a friend'?" The loud, roaring laughter returned—wave after wave of belly-rolling cachinnation, the tears streaming from Charlie's eyes.

Martin and Spencer couldn't help themselves—the laughter was infectious. They joined in heartily, albeit with a certain degree of control and dignity. It took them all several seconds to calm down.

"So, Charlie," Martin said finally, "you have just met two naïve and ridiculous foreigners. Now please enlighten us—that is, if you weren't pulling our leg. *Is* there a way to send money into North Korea? How? Do we do it through you?"

The proprietor was suddenly serious. It was the first time they saw him without a smile.

"Oh, no, no, no. I'm just a restaurant owner. Everyone stops by my place to eat and I make a decent living. I don't need to undertake any additional adventures that, after all, *are* a bit hazardous. But I can introduce to someone who can help."

"Why would he meet with perfect strangers," Martin asked. "Wouldn't he be suspicious?"

"Suspicious of what? This has been a thriving business for over fifty years. Both sides, especially the North, realize that these ... er ... transactions are beneficial to all involved. The authorities over there are very severe in their control of the people, but they are well aware that they cannot clothe or feed them. Smuggling is the natural and necessary solution to the problem. Over the years it has become 'institutionalized,' so to speak."

"But doesn't Pyongyang take any action against smugglers." Spencer asked.

"The North Korean government, over there in the capital city, either doesn't know, or rather, doesn't *want* to know. They look the other way and allow some of their poverty-stricken citizens to survive the only way possible. Naturally, some of the officials have material gains as well—they get their cut of food, money, cigarettes, and so on—things that most other citizens there cannot afford. In *this* region, however, everybody knows, and nobody encounters any interference."

Martin and Spencer looked at each other.

"You needn't look so shocked." Charlie was laughing again. "Necessity sometimes leads to strange solutions. For fifty years, no one has disrupted this 'industry,' and smuggling privileges are bequeathed from father to son. Now ..." Charlie leaned forward, his eyes sparkling. "If you *really* want to send something up north, I'll arrange for you to meet the right person."

Martin nudged Spencer under the table to keep silent. His brain was working furiously. It seemed almost too easy—and that intimidated him. He knew that Spencer was working out the same arguments. Martin needed his confirmation for the decision he was about to make. Over the years in the army, Martin and his squadron had developed tiny signals to each other, and Martin hoped Spencer was on his toes.

He glanced at Spencer, his eyebrows ascending a fraction of a millimeter. Spencer responded with an almost imperceptible nod.

"All right, Charlie," Martin said. "When and where can we meet this fellow?"

"In the evening," Charlie said. "Always in the evening, and as late as possible. After the last of the diners has left."

"What, here? Come on, Charlie—you know we don't want your patrons to see us here."

"My house is right behind the restaurant. You will meet him there. Come, I will show you."

Charlie showed them out and led the way. Sure enough, a cozy cottage was located just behind the restaurant. Martin and Spencer followed Charlie into the house and admired the carpet-covered floors and the many photographic portraits hanging on the walls—probably relatives. Stylish furniture was tastefully placed in the living room. Charlie gave them a tour of the five rooms and introduced them to his wife. He sent a clear, unspoken message—*I have all I want and I don't need more.*

Back at the restaurant, Martin asked for the bill. Charlie rejected the request with a friendly gesture.

"You are my guests," he said. When he noticed that they were about to insist, he added:

"Listen, it's obvious that you did not come here to 'help a friend.' No matter, whatever you're after will end in a transaction with the man tonight. And I'll get my share from that, never fear. It will pay for your meal many times over, believe me." A soft laugh. "Come to my house at ten. He'll be there."

CSEO

At the same time, a board meeting was held at Anne's.

"No news from Martin and Spencer yet, I suppose," Sir Cedric said. "When are they supposed to return?"

"We didn't give him a time restriction," Anne replied. "They may need a couple of days to acclimatize and then some more time to find the contacts we're looking for. They've been away for only three days. I suppose they'll be back in a week or so."

"You don't believe they're in any danger, do you?" the admiral asked.

"Not really," Anne said. "They have clear instructions just to make contact without revealing our true intentions. There's no danger there. I think we needn't worry. I expect Martin will call sooner or later, and if there's nothing of importance to report, he'll just let us know when they're returning."

"That's it then," the admiral said briskly. "I would now like to draw your attention to one more test that we need to do—Lemke's 'gravel tranquilizers,' as I like to refer to them."

"Indeed," Sir Cedric stated. "What about them?"

"This is a bit more complex than our previous experiments. Let's say we strew them outside a remote village from a passing car. The villagers exposed to them will feel drowsy, tired, listless, whatever—and probably visit the local doctor or doctors. These will become aware of a collective phenomenon and alert the Health Ministry who may send in an investigation committee. Now, we do *not* want that to happen, right?"

"Very true," Sir Cedric muttered.

"And another thing," the admiral went on, "if the incident is not reported in the press or on the news, we'll have no way of knowing the experiment's effects. And we certainly cannot loiter around the village for days to observe the results."

After a few moments, Sir Cedric said:

"It seems that the experiment would need to be carried out on a hostile entity. That complicates matters considerably. And again, how do we get information about the results? Let's all consider this conundrum for a few days. When Martin returns we'll use his brainpower as well. By the way, Patrick, you'll have to inform

Herr Lemke that we need a supply of this gravel of his. Otherwise, we'll have nothing to experiment with."

⚬⚬⚬

Martin and Spencer returned to Seoul. While waiting in their hotel for dusk to fall, they rehearsed the anticipated meeting in Ch'orwon. It was understood that they would not reveal the real reason for their visit. But they had to find out exactly what the man they were about to meet could do for them. For instance, he would probably want to know what they wanted to smuggle across the border.

"Well, we've got to say *something*," Martin said. "Even if it's not very specific—like machines, or food, or chemicals."

"And we need to consider the packaging, too," Spencer said. "Will we be bringing crates or sacks or what?"

"Right you are. And, of course, we need a destination. We need to be very careful here. If the chap is anything like Charlie we won't be able to just invent stories."

There was a lengthy pause.

"All right," Martin said. "Let me bounce the following off you. We're here on a preliminary 'study tour,' as it were. We're checking just what the smuggling traffic will allow—what merchandise, where to, what size, what packaging, what frequency, and at what cost."

"Like maybe Pyongyang is off limits because of security reasons," Spencer said.

"That's right!" Martin was warming up to the idea. "If they insist on knowing who we are, we tell them we belong to an international aid drive funded by philanthropists in the West. We tell them that after we know the ins and outs of their methodology, we'll go back to England and arrange for the deliveries."

"If he's like Charlie, he'll smile from ear to ear and tell us it's a pile of bullshit."

"Then we play it by ear. Anything but tell him we intend to topple the North Korean government."

When it became dark, Martin and Spencer headed north again. At exactly ten o'clock, they knocked at Charlie's front door. They were greeted by his wife, who invited them in with a shy bow.

"Please sit down," she said in perfect English. "My husband will be here presently." Martin confirmed his previous impression that women spoke languages better than men. Their accent was better, too.

Two minutes later, Charlie entered the room accompanied by a thin man. He was taller than the average Korean, and his face was deeply tanned and wrinkled—typical for an outdoors person who spent a lot of time in the sun and wind.

"Gentlemen," Charlie said. "Meet Sing. At least, that's how he's known around here. Sing, these are the Englishmen I told you about—Martin and Spencer."

There were handshakes all around, and the foursome sat around a low table. Charlie's wife served them tea.

"Now, gentlemen," Sing said, his English was as good as Charlie's, "what can I do for you?"

Martin cleared his throat.

"I'll be quite frank with you," he said. "We represent an international drive to aid the oppressed and needy. You've probably heard of such organizations, so you'll know that some are public and official while others are private and avoid the headlines. Ours is one of those private ones. Our movement is funded by philanthropists, among them a few billionaires from Europe and the United States. They do not want their names to be made public in this altruistic enterprise. So that's where we come in. We need to know how deliveries may be made to the North Korean people using your good graces and your resourcefulness. You see, they are convinced that the official aid sent to the Pyongyang government ends up in the corrupt leadership's pockets, and that the people get nothing. If you can tell us what is feasible to take across we can plan the deliveries. And we also *must* know how the goods get to the needy."

Martin's eyes never left Sing's face as he spoke, but he could not see a flicker of any kind of reaction. There was a long silence. More tea was served by Charlie's wife.

"We transport anything and everything," Sing said finally. "Weight and size are of no matter. Yes, we can get to Pyongyang and to almost any other location in North Korea. But distribution is not our concern. We get an address and we deliver the merchandise— that's it. You'll bring us the goods, tell us where it goes, pay in advance and it will arrive there. You don't ask how we do it or who is involved on either side, and we don't inquire about you and your people. Everybody is happy and there aren't any problems."

Clear and succinct. Martin wanted to keep the conversation going.

"And how do you determine the price for your services?"

"Gut feeling," Sing said unhesitatingly. "We look at the size and shape and determine a figure. Then we raise this number if the package is particularly heavy or the destination is far or inaccessible."

Martin felt that these straightforward replies to his questions would very soon leave him with nothing more to ask. He needed additional, significant information to bring back to the association.

"May I ask you something unrelated to your occupation?" he said.

"As long as you don't pry *into* my occupation—certainly."

"Well," Martin said slowly. "I'm referring to you as an expert on the conditions on both sides of the border. I mentioned earlier that we had to know that our stuff reached those who needed it most, and you have clearly stated that that is something you do not handle. I was wondering," Martin smiled at Sing, "do you think that in, say … Pyongyang, there is a person or persons who would be prepared to undertake the distribution work?"

Sing's expression did not change.

"I mean for pay, of course." Martin continued rapidly. "Either as a part of the goods or in cash."

Sing dipped his head in thought, pinching the bridge of his nose with thumb and forefinger. He was obviously searching for the right words without over-revealing anything. Then he raised his head again. For the first time, Martin noted, the smile had disappeared.

"Anything is possible in a country overrun by corruption," he said quietly.

"And do you think this person could rent an apartment or a warehouse where the goods could be stored until distribution time?"

"Same answer as before." Sing's smile had returned.

"Forgive me, Sing, if my questions seem to compromise you. That is certainly not my intention—but I was sent here to obtain answers to these questions for our cause, and you are one of the key factors in our plans. I hope you understand that if I now returned to England and arrived here again a couple of weeks from today with, er … merchandise, I won't have an address to send it to, and I won't know if it will be taken care of the way we request. So, you see, I have a problem to solve while I am still here. For pay, of course. Can you help me?"

Sing shut his eyes and seemed to go into a trance. The only difference in his expression was the slight furrow in his brow. The smile remained unchanged. Finally, he reopened his eyes.

"I don't know what operation you're cooking up, Mr. Englishman, and I admit that your questions are difficult to answer. However," the smile turned into a wide grin, "my answer is yes, I can. But it will take time."

Spencer was highly entertained as he followed his boss' verbal maneuvering, but his face showed no emotion whatsoever.

"You appear to be a very resourceful man, Mr. Sing," Martin said warmly. "I think we shall enjoy working with you very much. How long do you think you'll need in order to find the person and the place in Pyongyang? Two weeks? Three? More?"

"Yes, three weeks should do it. You may return with the goods in three weeks. I do not know how much storage and distribution will cost—like I said, I don't handle these activities. I'll need to send out some of my men to snoop around. I may need to pay rent or 'service' fees. I shall need an advance of one thousand dollars, please."

Martin was surprised at the low amount Sing requested. Perhaps in North Korea this was considered a fortune. Keeping his poker face, Martin took out his wallet and counted out ten hundred-dollar bills, which he placed on the table. Sing picked them up without batting an eyelid and pocketed them. A handshake with Martin and Spencer closed the deal.

"We shall meet here in three weeks," Charlie said. "Sing and I will be waiting."

"Thank you both for your cooperation," Martin said. "It has been a pleasure."

⊰⊱

Charlie and Sing remained silent until the sound of the departing car faded into silence.

"What do you think?" Charlie asked in their native tongue. Neither of them was smiling now. Sing rubbed his chin.

"Do you suppose they're planning to establish a spy ring?" he responded.

"Not really. That's definitely *not* how you build a spy network. But I have a feeling that it's not what they say it is."

"So? Do we push ahead with their plan? If they return in three weeks, and they may not, we could always tell them that we failed to find a place or a person because of the danger involved— our accomplice could pay with his life. And that would be that. No refund, of course. As a matter of fact, we could say we had additional expenses and demand more money."

"Well, in my opinion," Charlie said carefully, "and you know you can rely on my intuition, these Englishmen don't have a clue. They're groping in the dark and they'll buy any story we give them. But I can smell a lot of money here if we cooperate with them. You can always back out if you don't like the way things are going ... they have nothing that binds you to them. So, in answer to your question, yes—I think we should go ahead with them."

Sing nodded.

ርଓ୫ଠ

In the car on the way back to Seoul, Martin exhaled as though he had been holding his breath for the past hour.

"I think we could say that our mission was accomplished," he said.

"And quite masterfully, too, I think," Spencer said. "There were moments when I thought we had arrived at the end of the line, but you always found the right words to bring the topic back to what interested us. And sometimes I thought the man would just get up and walk out on us. Fortunately, that didn't happen."

"Thank goodness. Listen, Spencer. When we get back to the hotel, make arrangements at the desk for flying back to London tomorrow, okay? I have a phone call to make."

"Consider it done."

Back at their hotel in Seoul, Martin called Anne from his room.

"Hello, darling!" Anne was genuinely excited to hear Martin's voice.

"Hello yourself, love," he replied. "I miss you terribly."

"Me, too. How's your trip going?"

"The place is far prettier than I expected. One more tour and we're headed for home."

"How are you managing with the language?

"Not much of a challenge. Almost everyone speaks English fluently. How are things with you?"

"You know—same old same old. There are a couple of letters for you."

"Bills, probably. They can wait."

"And how is the weather there? I hope it rained cats and dogs all the time, just because I'm not there with you."

"Sorry to disappoint you, love. Clear and sunny the whole time."

"Lucky you. Take care, darling." They both hung up.

## FORTY-ONE

When Martin and Spencer went down to the dining room for breakfast the next morning, there was a commotion by the front desk. People were talking to each other heatedly, and there was a lot of hand gesticulating.

"What's up?" Martin asked the desk clerk.

The latter smiled and handed Martin the morning newspaper in English. With Spencer reading over his shoulder, Martin read:

## ROH MOO-HYUN MEETS N. KOREAN LEADER

North and South Korea are on their way toward appeasement. The two leaders met in Pyongyang for a summit meeting. They discussed establishing peace between the two countries. South Korea would assist her Northern sister in matters of economy, tourism and other fields. The opening of the railway lines between the two Koreas was also discussed.

It is to be remembered that since the nineteen fifties, even though the war was officially over, a declaration to that effect has never been made. From the purely formal point of view, the two countries are still at war.

Martin and Spencer exchanged meaningful glances. This could mean that their efforts could have been in vain, and that smugglers would not need to be employed any longer.

"Congratulations!" Martin said to the desk clerk as he returned the newspaper. "It looks like you're on the way to unite North and South Korea into a single nation."

"Sir," replied the receptionist. "You are evidently new to these parts and unacquainted with local matters. Kim Jong-il is a crafty fox. He runs the cruelest dictatorship imaginable. He was never prepared to share his power with anyone else, let alone rescind it altogether. But he is in dire economic straits today, and has been for a long time. He is totally bankrupt. So now he wants to latch onto us and milk us for our money."

"So what does your president hope to achieve from this meeting?" Spencer asked.

"Frankly, I have no idea," the clerk grinned. "But I have no doubt that our president knows *exactly* who his counterpart is. I am willing to wager that after the meeting, everything will be as before over there—poverty, hunger, persecution and assassinations. So please, sir, do not congratulate me!"

⚬⚬⚬

Commissaire Duval visited the widow Allier once again. His lengthy experience with interrogation techniques proved that, given time, the human mind brings back memories of tiny details, seemingly unimportant. But when put together with other facts they sometimes serve to fill in an otherwise incomplete picture.

Mme. Allier received him warmly. She knew he was truly concerned with the solving of her husband's death, and she made every effort to assist him. They discussed various aspects of the case, when the commissaire suddenly asked:

"What did you usually talk about? I mean, like over dinner?"

Though surprised by his question, she did her best to answer.

"Nothing special, really," she said. "You know—current affairs, the house, the grandchildren ..."

"And his work? Did he ever discuss his work?"

"Commissaire, Albert's work was so scientific and professional, it was all way above my head. We had no common grounds regarding his work."

"I quite understand, Madame. I was not referring to the scientific aspect of his work. I was referring to his relationships with his fellow-workers. Was everything smooth in that regard? Did he ever tell you of a conflict he may have had with a colleague?

Perhaps even a quarrel? How about meetings with people outside his institution?"

Mme. Allier shook her head, smiling.

"I'm afraid I did not follow every little detail of his meetings and conversations, commissaire."

Duval leaned forward.

"Please try to remember," he said as respectfully as he could. "You told me he had meetings with a certain Englishman. Did he not say anything about the nature of this meeting?"

"I honestly do not believe this has any significance whatsoever to your case. But as you are so insistent—yes, I do remember a trivial incident. I once accused him of fabricating these scientific meetings, while in actuality he was partying somewhere. He became very annoyed and retorted: 'These are not pleasure lunches—we're discussing very important issues.' I replied, rather untactfully, I'm ashamed to confess: 'That's what they all say.' Then Albert got really angry, and he shouted: '*They* are all looking out for themselves. *We* are trying to save everyone.' And that's how the conversation ended."

"Was that all?" Duval inquired. "This was never discussed again?"

"Come to think of it, there was one more occasion. The next time he was off to see the Englishman, I said: 'You and your bloody Englishman!' Albert was furious! He yelled at me: 'That's damn right! My Englishman, and all the Englishmen, and all the Frenchmen and all the Europeans as well!' I remember now, while telling you this, that Albert was indeed very absorbed in something. Something was occupying his mind all the time. You know, I'm beginning to believe that he really may have been doing something outside his work at the university."

Commissaire Duval raised an eyebrow.

## *FORTY-TWO*

They had gathered at Anne's apartment and the report on Seoul was first on the agenda. Martin gave a detailed account on all that happened in South Korea. He ended by mentioning the meeting between the presidents of South and North Korea.

"The reception clerk at the hotel was of the opinion that this was a ruse by the North Korean president to upgrade his international position."

"I believe he was right," the admiral said. "Everything I've heard and read so far indicates that Kim Jong-il is desperate to improve North Korea's economic and political status so that he can prepare for the future. This does not necessarily mean that the *people's* condition will improve. I have no doubt that smuggling across the South Korean border will continue for a long time to come. It will remain the main artery through which basic necessities will be supplied."

"I think we are all in agreement on that," Anne said. "Martin and Spencer will return there for another survey in three weeks, as arranged with Sing, the Smuggler. I'd like to see a well-defined outline of this trip, please."

"Well," the admiral said, "I suggest that if our Singing friend comes up with any kind of positive results to Martin's requests, and, furthermore, shows indications of true cooperation, we should reveal to him that we're not an aid program at all, but that we're out to seriously damage the North Korean tyrant's public image."

Sir Cedric, startled, sat up straight.

"Why on earth would we want to reveal such a secret to a smuggler?" he remarked. "He could throw a wrench into the entire operation."

Martin spoke for the first time. Much as he had wanted to, he had avoided kissing Anne in front of the others, and so far had, with great difficulty, managed not to exchange looks with her any more than a normal friendship would allow.

"I think there is a lot of sense in what Admiral Stone has just suggested," he said. "If Sing is in tune with us, no pun intended, we will now have a very powerful ally. If not—we give him something very insignificant to smuggle across, pay him, and never see him again. However, if we *don't* tell him of at least the general nature of our activities, I'm sure he'll find out anyway—after all, we'll be delivering materials *and* operational instructions through his good graces. And if he thinks we're hiding something from him, we may find him a hindrance rather than a confederate."

Sir Cedric relaxed.

"Yes, I see now," he said.

"Thank you, Martin," the admiral said. "You've presented my case better than I could have done it myself. But I'd go even further. If, after revealing our purpose, our two faithful scouts see that he is still in a cooperative mood, they might test him with the notion that we're going to disrupt a public speech."

"I trust Martin and Spencer will employ the utmost caution before revealing anything," Anne said, her look lingering on Martin. "Many factors need to be examined on site, as they happen, not least the psychological attitude of the smugglers."

"And, of course," Sir Cedric said, "it all depends on the political atmosphere between the two Koreas. We may need to revise our plans if something dramatic happens during the next three weeks."

"Can we consider the Korea issue closed for tonight?" Anne was all business again. "Good. Now we need to discuss the testing of Lemke's anesthetic gravel. Come on, gentlemen—how do we do it?"

"I really have nothing better to suggest than to find a small village and test it there," Sir Cedric said. "I know we've deliberated and argued about the discomfort we may cause the inhabitants to experience, not to mention bringing down a governmental investigation, but I see no other way. So, I picked Donegan, a little village up in the Lake District. We'll need to learn the working habits of the local population and find the appropriate place to strew our gravel. We'll time it to work in two days, and on the third day we'll return to the place and see what effect it had."

"I don't like it," Sir Cedric muttered.

"Neither do I," the admiral snapped. "But unless you can think of something better, our only other option is not to test the gravel at all."

"I'm afraid that's it then," Anne said, and stood up. "We'll meet again to hammer out the details of the test in Donegan. Or maybe we could even do it by phone. Let's call it an evening for now, okay?"

The admiral and Sir Cedric filed out the door. The minute they had gone, Anne rushed into Martin's arms, and he covered her face with kisses. It had been a long parting for them both, and their passions were easily kindled. They made love on the sofa again and again, and night had fallen by the time their ardor was quenched.

Later, comfortable and satisfied, they sat holding hands in only their underwear, her head resting on his shoulder. Several minutes passed.

"So tell me," Anne said finally.

"I thought I had," he replied.

"That was reporting, silly, not telling. I want to know everything you saw, what the people are like, the food, the landscape ... the women, especially the young women ..."

Martin laughed.

"Forget about the women, Annie. They're relatively tiny compared to us, and they have those distinct oriental features, almost Mongolian. I know that many Western men find some of the Korean girls exceptionally beautiful—in fact, I saw a few myself—but they just don't do it for me. And the other stuff you mentioned is truly uninteresting. For the first two days, we were one hundred percent tourists and took in all the tours and sights they could throw at us. And that's more or less it. I was never any good at botany, so I can't tell you anything about the flora in Korea. There was no language problem as most of the population speaks English quite well, albeit with a heavy accent. The hotel served good food, with a mixed local and Western cuisine. Pretty good trip, overall. And you?"

"Me?"

Anne hesitated. Should she tell him about her visit to the Laval family? She preferred not to conceal anything from him—especially seeing that she needed him to be with her when she continued her investigations.

"I know you'll be mad at me for what I'm about to tell you, darling, but what's done cannot be undone."

Martin grew tense. He listened silently while Anne told him about her inner conflicts regarding the visit, and how she finally made up her mind to go ahead with it. He was horrified.

"Are you out of your mind?" he said, his eyes staring at her.

"Actually, I don't believe I am," Anne retorted, "considering the results I got out of Mme. Laval."

She told him of the conversation she had with Lucien Laval's mother. Martin paid close attention to what Anne said, and had to admit that the information she provided was a remarkable step forward. They had a substantial lead.

"You're a very naughty girl," he chided her. "Don't ever do that again!"

She put a finger in the corner of her mouth and pursed her lips in a mock pout.

"Are you going to punish me?"

In reply, he swept her into his arms, ripped off what little she was wearing and took her violently on the floor. She gasped, then clung to him and returned his thrusts eagerly, urging him on. When they both sank exhausted side by side, she said:

"Promise me you'll always punish me that way."

"I hope you'll find safer reasons for me to do so. Come to think of it, no reason at all is also a good reason." He kissed her lightly on the lips. She turned on her side to face him.

"When you return from your next trip to Korea," she said soberly, "we'll look for Ninette together. We'll dress up as residents of the neighborhood, and you can scout around and see how things are handled there."

"I don't want to leave you waiting for my return from Korea. Your impulses have a way of getting the better of you, even after you gave me your solemn promise. We shall go to Saint-Denis this week together, after I get updated on what's happening at the gym. But just a look-around, mind you. I mean it, Annie darling. No asking questions, and no attempting to find this hooker Ninette. That may come at a later stage. Is that quite understood?"

Anne nodded silently. *He really loves me*, she thought happily. *He wasn't as furious as I thought he would be.*

She got up, made a comical scene of being seen naked by a man, and prepared something to eat. In bed, they made gentle love again and fell asleep in each other's arms.

## *FORTY-THREE*

A sack load of gravel had arrived from Hamburg the day before. Martin had consigned John and Bernard to the task of testing its capabilities. They observed the region around the village of Donegan and noticed that most of the population, at one time or another, walked along the main road that passed through the village. This was where they planned to scatter the tranquilizing gravel.

The next step was the preparation of the liquid solution—the "conditioner," as it appeared on the instructions attached to the sack. Accordingly, they diluted the solution and dipped a few kilograms of stones into it. Their timing was such that the gas would be released in the early morning of the day after tomorrow.

After dark, when nobody was about, John and Bernard, equipped with the treated gravel, drove along the main road and spread the stones on both its sides. Now all they had to do was to return in three days and be inquisitive.

CR&CO

Commissaire Duval called up an old friend in Scotland Yard. He and Assistant Commissioner Neville MacLeod had known each other since Police Academy days, and remained in touch ever since—occasionally helping each other out informally on particularly tough cases.

"Neville, my dear friend, how are you?"

"Felix, is that you? It's been a long time since we last talked."

"True. And very sad. I must make it up to you soon. But Neville, I need your help again. I am working on an important case, and a British citizen just might be involved."

"Ah, Felix, Felix—you always call when you need something, never to socialize. And I miss your wife, Yvonne, sorely. So, tell me first when we can meet, and then I shall try to help you all I can. *Bien?*"

"You always made arguing so pleasant, Neville." Duval was getting impatient. "I promise you that when this case is solved we shall spend a weekend in London with you and Dorothy. And the sooner you can help me now, the sooner we'll be there!"

"Done! Now, what can I do for you? What is this case that involves a British citizen?"

"I have reason to suspect that this gentleman arrives from London to Paris almost every week and meets a certain person here. I do not know what the meeting is about—but I need to know whom he is meeting with in Paris. I have already spoken with him on the telephone, but he was not very cooperative. Do you understand?"

"There's not much to understand so far, old boy. What do you expect of me?"

"His name is Sir Cedric Norton." MacLeod gave a low whistle. "He is the head of Norlaser, a laser and electronics enterprise in London. I do not even have his description, but you probably do not need it.

"I know of him," MacLeod said. "Felix, my friend, you are skating on very thin ice here. I would like to caution you...."

"I know, I know," Duval said hastily. "Never fear, I do not intend to work up a scandal. I just need more information for my investigations."

"So? What exactly do you require?"

"I was wondering whether you could check with the London airports that have flights to Paris. And if you find his name on one of the passenger lists, could you alert me when he is expected to arrive here? That is all I ask."

"Is that really all, Felix? I know you too well. You wouldn't call me ..."

"All right, all right." Duval laughed. "You're still the wily fox you always were. Yes, I could make good use of his description as well. I admit this is a bit much to ask, so I might as well tell you that I'm investigating a murder case. Can you help me?"

"Felix, are you're telling me that Sir Cedric Norton is involved in a murder case in France?"

"No, Neville. I'm telling you that I am examining a murder case here, and that enhancing my knowledge of Sir Cedric Norton could serve me in this investigation. I repeat—can you help me?"

"I'll see what I can do."

"Thank you so much, Neville. I am counting on you."

## FORTY-FOUR

It had been three days since the gravel was put in place. John and Bernard returned to Donegan as the sun was setting. They went into a pub near the village square. The pubkeeper was slow in serving them their beers, and it was obvious that he was in poor health.

"Looks like you stayed up pretty late last night, eh?" Bernard commented jovially.

The pubkeeper leaned on the bar and tried not to slur his words too much.

"It's no joke, mister. Since the day before yesterday, some kind of disease has hit a great many of us."

"Really?" John said. "You've had an epidemic outburst?"

"Can't say for sure. We had a doctor come in but he says it isn't the flu, so we all got double doses of aspirin. He suspects water contamination and sent out samples to be tested in the lab."

"Yeah, that could be it," Bernard said. "That's why I drink only beer."

John used his elbow to nudge Bernard.

"Is water pollution the only suspect?"

"Well, he said that if the water was clean, he'd try to see if there were any heavy industries nearby. They sometimes 'emit noxious fumes,' those were his words, and the wind could have carried them here."

"Hey, bartender, you should be in bed until this blows over."

"Aye, that I shall. You'd best get out of here damn quick, too, mark my words."

John took out his wallet and paid for the drinks.

"Thanks for warning us. Take care."

Outside he and Bernard exchanged grins. The test had worked!

C820

The four board members assembled again at Sir Cedric's office in London. Anne had just completed a satisfying visit with her family in Reading. *It would have been so much nicer if Martin could have been there, too,* she thought, *but his backlog at the gym had prevented him. Anyway, he's here now.*

The report on the successful Donegan experiment with the gravel was delivered by Martin. Everyone seemed pleased by this.

"Which brings us to the Iranian topic," the admiral said. "The Western powers have failed to stop the Iranian leaders by threatening sanctions—no wonder, most of them are unfulfilled. We need to speed up our preparations in this direction. I suggest that Martin take a trip to Iran and look around. As this is a country open to tourism, a couple of travelers—I mean, a man and a woman—would look perfectly normal."

"Well," said Martin, "we don't have much of a choice, do we? Anne is the only woman around."

"I'd gladly go on that trip," Anne said, "but I'm afraid the timing is impossible. I'm in the middle of the semester exams and there's no way I can back out of them. We'll need another solution."

Anne was secretly pleased to see a look of disappointment on Martin's face.

"What about that girl we employed before, for our Tunisia trip," the admiral said. "George's sister. She did pretty well then."

"I assume," Anne said, "that she isn't stupid. You cannot sell her that movie story again. Patrick and Martin, you two know her best. What do you think? Can we recruit her into our ranks?"

"As far as I could tell," Admiral Stone said, "she is a bright, educated and experienced young lady who knows her way around. Sometimes I got the impression that she was observing us with a silent kind of irony, as if to say 'Come on, guys, do you take me for an idiot? I know damn well you're not making a movie!' I see it as a point in her favor that although she saw through us from the start, and could have embarrassed us with uncomfortable questions, she never let on and played her part to the hilt."

"I concur with everything we've heard from the admiral," Martin said. "It's true that I could make a survey of Iran without explaining anything to her. However, I would not feel as free as I would like when I investigate those particular locations that interest us specifically. I mean, like public squares and the adjoining streets and alleys. I'll be searching for places to plant acoustic devices and the like. And it's especially at those moments when I shall need her most as a cover. So if I do nothing irregular she'll wonder why I dragged her all the way to the Middle East, considering that no relationship developed between us while we were in Tunisia, *and* that she was aware that we were up to something at the time."

"Do we recruit her or not?" Anne said sharply.

"I vote yes," the admiral said.

"Let me talk this over with her brother, George," Martin said quietly. "If he's of the same mind we are, I'll recruit her according to our rules. She'll definitely be a valuable asset in future operations. Perhaps we should also consider letting George do the recruiting."

Anne would have preferred Martin not to be involved in the recruiting of a beautiful young woman. However, she understood that Martin would be spending a couple of 'romantic' weeks with her, so going through the motions of recruitment would be insignificant anyway. She joined the others who voted for Martin to do the recruiting.

"Very well," she said. "That's settled. Now—what are we hoping to achieve with this trip to Iran. Yes, I know it's still a bit early to plan, and that we have our third trip to Korea coming up shortly, but we can put a kind of framework on our goals, can't we—like we did for Korea? Martin? Admiral?"

"Offhand," Martin said, "I would say we need to know: a) the lay of the land, so to speak, b) border crossing procedures and security issues there, c) how tourists' bags and luggage are handled, d) how tourists are treated at the hotel, if there is any kind of noticeable surveillance, e) car rental procedures, f) if you can drive freely throughout the country, if there are roadblocks at sensitive locations, and if you can you cross from district to district without inspection. I'm sure there's more ..."

"Oh, there certainly is," the admiral said, smiling, "G) Can you use the telephone freely? Particularly for international calls? From your hotel? H) How widespread is the use of the Internet in the country? Can you access it from the hotel? From your room? And I was also thinking along the lines of: I) Can private aircraft fly into the country? And where are they allowed to land?"

"And don't forget," Sir Cedric said, "J) Where do public events take place? I mean, where does the president or the spiritual leader address the multitudes? What are the environs of this place? K) Can a foreigner rent a flat in the capital or anywhere else? How about in the area of public gathering I just mentioned?"

"That's good, Cedric," the admiral said admiringly. "I wasn't aware that you were a brilliant strategist, too." He turned back to the others. "Listen. I'll try to obtain maps and mark them with the sensitive locations we know, such as obvious military targets and nuclear installations. You'll have to stay away from these places."

"Quite a long list there, isn't it," Anne said. "And you'll have to be on your toes at all times, too, to pick up pointers for future operations that may come upon us. What will your cover stories be?"

"We'll stray from the truth as little as possible," Martin said. "I shall appear in my true identity as a fitness center owner. Patricia, or whoever it is that accompanies me, will be my fiancée. We'll book separate rooms, though—who knows, in the land of the ayatollahs they might frown upon an unmarried couple sharing a room."

Anne still didn't like the idea, but managed to curb her annoyance.


## FORTY-FIVE

Martin and Anne went for a tour of what was once the central marketplace of Paris—Les Halles. It had been partially torn down to provide space for the Centre Georges Pompidou, the modern arts and culture institution named after the late French president. The neighborhood may have changed since then, but the world's oldest profession had not. Tiny bars, cheap hotels, and ancient houses joined together in strings. And—of course—girls.

Girls in light miniskirts exposing their underwear. Push-up brassieres that force mammaries to overflow their confinement. Supposedly loitering in the hotel doorways, the prostitutes actually parade on the sidewalks. Men pass by without looking, ostensibly minding their own business, and suddenly one of them stops by one of the girls, a quick exchange of words, and they disappear into the nearest hotel. There are other men, too—they stand apart and watch. These are the *maquereaux*, or pimps.

Anne had tied a scarf around her hair and put on an enormous pair of dark glasses that concealed the upper part of her face. Martin had a Basque beret on his head and sunglasses on his nose. They strolled down the length of rue Saint-Denis, minding their own business in earnest. They did not wish to appear as tourists or even outsiders, so they did not carry cameras or expensive bags.

They walked into a bar, ordered two glasses of dry white wine, and drank it while standing at the bar, as was customary.

"Do you see now what you're up against?" Martin said. "Ladies do not walk around here alone—don't you dare try it."

"So what do you suggest?" Anne asked.

"Frankly, right now I have no idea what to do if and when we decide to look for your Lucien."

*That's not very encouraging*, thought Anne. *This street is very repulsive, even scary. I don't recall ever having been in such a place—the commotion, the half-naked girls, the men that feed this 'industry'—it's sickening!*

Anne removed her scarf and glasses.

"Let's go to a decent café," she said. "I need to get the taste of this locale out of my mouth."

While sipping coffee at the Café Beaubourg, with the grand view of the art center's façade, Martin realized that Anne must have undergone a mild shock. He regretted the discomfort he had caused her but hoped she would stay away from this neighborhood once and for all. Not without him in tow, at least.

CஐஇD

Commissaire Duval and Inspecteur Marnier arrived at Charles De Gaulle airport and waited by the gate through which Sir Cedric Norton was supposed to emerge. They were equipped with cell phones and could communicate directly with each other. Earlier, Duval had received Sir Cedric's flight particulars, along with his description and attire, from Assistant Commissioner MacLeod of Scotland Yard.

Duval had not informed the inspector who the target was or why he was to be followed. Marnier knew better than to ask—if the commissaire wished to share the information, he would have done so.

The passengers began to trickle out and then emerged in groups.

"There he is!" Duval said. "The elderly gentleman in the dark suit. Brown briefcase in his right hand, raincoat over his left arm."

"Got him!" Marnier replied. "Do you think he has a suitcase as well?"

"No, just the briefcase. Get a move on—he may go out and catch a taxi at any minute."

"On my way."

Commissaire Duval reevaluated the situation. Sometimes he wondered whether he was doing the right thing. After so many years on the Paris police force, he should know that there were paths you shouldn't stray away from. Why was he pursuing this case, anyway? To date, he had handled everything on his own— nobody else was involved. Now he had brought Inspecteur Marnier into the picture. This was *not* a good thing—not good at all!

Duval decided that, if the trailing of Sir Cedric resulted in nothing encouraging, he would give up the case. In fact, he was actually *hoping* for the case to terminate.

He started up the car and headed for his office. Halfway there, his telephone rang.

"Marnier here. The man went directly to the residence of Professeur Dupré."

"Do you know who she is?" Duval asked.

"She's the friend of the lady who got murdered some weeks ago. The Tania Gerard case—you're familiar with it, aren't you—it's still open and at a dead end."

"Is he still there now?"

"Yes."

"Good. Let me know where he goes from there."

Commissaire Duval was surprised. He *had* looked into the files of the Gerard murder case, but he was convinced that the Dupré woman had nothing to do with it. Marnier's recent information did nothing to change this belief. And yet … she knew the murdered woman, and now she's visited by a man who knew the deceased Allier. Could that mean anything? Not necessarily, but now he couldn't let go of the case. He had to find out if there was any connection between a British scientist from London and a British-born history professor from Paris.

Commissaire Duval decided he would have a chat with her.

## *FORTY-SIX*

They knew that it was rather uncommon for tourists to return to the same country within three weeks of their first visit. Martin prepared a cover story, which would serve them in case anyone challenged the reason for their revisit. He packed several brochures of his fitness gym and its equipment, and he did not intend to show them unless he actually needed a fallback. And if that was the case, he intended to visit local gyms and get interested with their equipment and fitness programs.

"What if there aren't any fitness gyms over there?" Spencer had asked.

"So much the better," Martin replied. "We'll be the first!"

They both laughed.

Their arrival had been preceded by a debate: whether or not to find a different hotel, where they wouldn't be recognized. They picked the same hotel mainly *because* they were known there and therefore less liable to be asked questions. Martin said, jokingly, "Have you ever heard of a hotel that asked its customers *why* they arrived or *why* they returned? We'll be taken for 'veterans' over there, and everything we do will seem natural to them."

Indeed, they had been graciously received by the management and were given two of the best rooms. Now, on the morning after their arrival, they rented a car and toured some of the area south of the capital. Not too much, however, as towards evening they intended to have dinner at Charlie's and meet with Sing.

Charlie was quite surprised to see them again.

"My good friends, Martin and Spencer," he called as he walked toward their car, a huge smile in his face. "Welcome back!"

They shook Charlie's hand vigorously.

"Come in, come in—have some dinner. How was your trip?"

"Just great!" They walked into the restaurant. "It's been three weeks since our previous visit. I hope Mr. Sing remembers that, and that he'll be here tonight."

"Of course, of course. Sing always keeps his promises. And now I see that you do, too."

Martin and Spencer enjoyed a sumptuous meal, while Charlie stopped by their table from time to time to exchange a few words with them.

"Tell us, Charlie," Spencer said. "Has there been any progress since the leaders of the two Koreas met?"

Charlie gave him a pitiful smile.

"It's been only three weeks, my friend," he said. "What did you expect could happen in such a short time? These kinds of changes could take months, even years."

At that moment, Sing walked in. Martin and Spencer began to rise, but he gestured to them to remain seated. He joined them at their table, and Charlie served him a drink. After the preliminary niceties, Charlie led them back to his house and they got down to business.

"I know you are anticipating responses to your questions," Sing said. "But before I answer you, I want to ask you something: Have there been any changes in your plans? Or do you still want to pursue the one you described to me three weeks ago?"

"Absolutely!" Martin said seriously. "Why do you ask?"

"It crossed my mind that after you learned about the intended meeting of the two Korean leaders, you may not be requiring my services any longer. You might have arrived at the conclusion that food and clothing need not be transported across the border by the likes of me—that this could now be done openly and officially. Normalization, you know ..." He glanced at Charlie.

"No, Mr. Sing, we did not entertain those thoughts at all. But what do *you* think about this?"

"Please call me Sing, like everyone else. Listen, I don't think—I *know!* If goods begin to flow across the border, *everything* will wind up with the supporters of the regime—the top leadership, the ministers, senior military officers, and a couple of thousand loyalists who form the basis for Kim Jong-il's dictatorship. The rest will continue to starve!"

"So you don't think you'll lose any of your business, eh?" Martin smiled.

"Not on your life!" Sing was dead serious. "You know, I often feel that we would all be better off if I *did* have a problem with smuggling. I'd have to find something else to do to make a living. But it would also mean that the nightmare over there was over! You are foreigners here. You live in an organized world. You have no idea what it means to have hundreds of thousands of families' lose their possessions, houses, land—everything has been confiscated or impounded."

"In the North," Charlie continued the narrative, "there is an acute problem of hunger. Millions are starving! Women go out to the fields to pick weeds so that they can give their babies something to eat. You see children on the streets with distended bellies. It is an indescribable horror!"

There was no doubting the man's sincerity. Martin saw this as a sign to forge ahead.

"Mr. Sing … I mean, Sing, let's get down to practical issues. For that, I see it my duty to modify the story I told you about us last time. It is true that we wish to smuggle goods into North Korea. But not food and clothes."

"Arms?" Sing asked.

"Not arms. Neither any other kind of war materials. We're not military, intelligence, or underground resistance."

"So what's left?" Charlie chuckled.

"I'll tell you. We are a circle of people who wish to topple dictators. Not only here. Everywhere."

"Really? How?" Sing usually listened in silence, but he could not resist the question.

"Not by force. Not by the use of weapons. By humiliating them."

Sing and Charlie looked at each other questioningly, as if saying 'what is this madman talking about?' Finally, Sing said:

"I have never heard of such a thing."

"Patience, Sing. I shall explain myself."

"I'm listening." But it was obvious that he was thinking it was a waste of time.

"We believe that if a leader is made a mockery in front of his people and his close supporters, his days are numbered. At least, *he* will lose some of his self-confidence—perhaps totally. He will begin to doubt his capability to carry out his megalomaniac ambitions."

"Very nice theory," Sing said. "Are you going to make his face turn blue on television?"

Martin smiled.

"You're getting the idea, though we have other methods in mind. A team of scientists is working on developing the resources to make things happen—similar to what you suggested. Let me give you an example. One of the most cherished occasions for these tyrants is to have a public appearance, where the people can 'adore' them. For a dictator this is a very important event, and they make sure that the population thinks the same way. Now, if we could disrupt his speech in a most embarrassing way— intersperse rude noises and eventually just turn the PA system into a horrendous screech—don't you think the crowd would flee from the square with their hands over their ears? And laugh at their leader for weeks to come? Don't you think his reputation, integrity, and general public image would be irreparably damaged?"

"Sounds like fantasy to me," Sing said.

"I'm glad. Because the impact will be so much greater when it actually happens. And let me tell you that when this acoustic 'fantasy,' as you call it, is accompanied by additional embarrassing events—the effect will be even more degrading!"

The two Koreans thought for a while in silence.

"You really believe that this could bring about his downfall?" Sing asked.

"Yes. And by using other means as well. It has a good chance of succeeding. Anyway, we think it's worth a try."

It was evident that Charlie and Sing were mulling over ideas that would never have occurred to them. These notions were strange, new, different—and yet, carried a certain logic with them.

"And now, Sing, please permit me to ask you if you and your men have found out anything for us."

It took a while before Sing responded.

"You have really astonished me," he said. "Something that happens very rarely, indeed. I did not expect anything like this. I thought that overthrowing tyrannical regimes was the job of governments and superpowers, not private enterprises and scientists. And I have many questions I wish to ask you. But first, I shall answer your request. Even though I doubted your credibility after our first meeting, I sent men to investigate the things you spoke of. Yes, there are people who will cooperate, even to the extent of endangering their lives. And hiding places for your … 'goods' can also be found. Now we need to be more specific about how things are going to take place. What else did you have in mind?"

"Sing, I have already informed you that I cannot reveal all the measures we're working on. But I shall give you another taste of what we can deploy so that you won't take us for reckless adventurers. We have a special material that looks like fertilizer. When spread, it emits a gas that can neutralize vehicle engines— they just die and cannot be activated until serviced in a special way. Now, can you imagine what that fertilizer can do to a convoy parading before the Great Leader? The tanks and the heavy lorries towing the missiles will all grind to a halt, while the dictator is heard hiccupping into his microphone. In time, you shall learn more, perhaps everything—after all, it's your men out there who will have to do the job. You will be shown all our techniques and how to operate the instruments. Have I answered your question?"

"You most certainly have! Tell me what you need, and we'll do the best we can."

"We shall need gardeners or groundkeepers who work in the public gardens—mainly the flower beds, lawns, and so forth—especially in the main squares of Pyongyang."

"That will not be a problem."

"They'll be the ones to spread the fertilizer."

"I gathered as much. Go on."

"We'll need apartments, shops, warehouses, restaurants—anywhere where we can deploy a small electronic device. Many of them. They will disrupt the PA system and other acoustic equipment. They may be placed anywhere within a kilometer of the parade itinerary, but they will still work.

Sing nodded.

"We need to know," Martin continued, "if there are any civilian employees inside military bases. I mean, personnel handling sanitation, gardening, kitchen duties, and so on. If so, could they be recruited, or could outsiders infiltrate into these bases? I'm referring only to bases within or nearby the city—where the parades would normally commence."

"I'll check," Sing said. "If there are any, I'll recruit them."

"We'll need to know the exact date and time of such a speech-parade event. And as far in advance as possible so that we'll have the time to complete all our preparations."

"This will take—"

"I expect you will have many expenses," Martin interrupted. "We shall cover them all. I shall give you an advance—that way you will not be delayed by lack of funding."

Martin withdrew a roll of bills from his pocket and carefully counted out five thousand dollars, which he placed on the table in front of Sing.

Sing hesitated for a second, then looked Martin straight in the eye, smiled, and pocketed the money.

"Good luck!" Martin smiled back.

The four men celebrated the conclusion of the deal by clicking their glasses in a toast. A round of handshaking followed. Sing needed about a month to complete his preparations, and they agreed to meet again at that time. Charlie gave Martin his home phone number so that the latter could inquire about the progress being made, and to set the precise date of the next meeting.

Martin and Spencer had further reason to celebrate. They had just completed another mission successfully.

CRITICAL

The most important item on the board meeting's agenda was, of course, Martin's report on the second trip to South Korea. They were assembled in Anne's flat in Paris, and the conversation was held while drinking tea and nibbling cookies.

Martin told them every detail of what happened, including all the questions that were asked and the conclusions they had come to.

"At our next visit there," he said, "they'll tell us if they have the manpower to run the operation. If so, we'll need to tell them about the gravel and the pellets, too. The only thing they'll remain ignorant about is Excalibur, the irradiation device, as it'll have no part in its functioning."

"Well done, Martin!" Anne said. "Please convey our appreciation to Spencer as well."

"Hear, hear," Sir Cedric said.

"Thank you, I shall," Martin said.

"Which leaves us about a month to have our tour in Iran. I suggest that Martin recruits his escort for the trip right away. All right with you, Martin?"

"Oh, yes. I'll need to contact her through her brother, George— I'm sure he knows how to locate her in London."

"About the Iran trip," Admiral Stone said, "if we operate in Korea first, the entire world will know what happened there during the pageant. I have no doubt that the Iranian president will immediately take steps to prevent something similar from happening in his country. I expect him to order his defense forces to raise their vigilance concerning factions hostile to his regime. He probably won't be able to instruct them *what* measures to take because, we hope, he won't have a clue as to how the events in Pyongyang came about. They may attribute the fiasco to North Korean ineptness, and consider themselves superior in this respect."

"What are you getting at, Patrick?" Sir Cedric said.

"Simply this. We need to be alert to the possibilities I have described. Therefore, we need to complete all our preparations in Iran before—and I emphasize *before*—taking action in Pyongyang."

"I get it," Martin said. "First prepare everything both in Korea *and* in Iran. Then, after carrying out our mission in one place, all we have to do is push the button, in a manner of speaking, to carry out the second mission. Without additional preparation."

"Precisely," the admiral said. He then added: "Of course, if any new inventions come along during that time, we'll consider deploying them."

"Well, I'd better get cracking," Martin said. "There's a lot for me to do—I must fly to London immediately, find and recruit the young lady, and book flight tickets to Tehran and hotel rooms there."

Anne was slightly disappointed. She had hoped Martin could stay for the night, but when duty calls … She nodded in assent.

CฦฦฦBD

After everyone had left, Anne prepared to retire for the night. She had just kicked off her shoes when the telephone rang.

"Professeur Dupré?"

"*Oui.*"

"This is Commissaire Felix Duval of the *Police Judiciaire*. May I have a few words with you?"

Anne was positive that she was about to hear some news about Tanya's case.

"Certainly," she said. "Anytime."

"Would it be too much of a bother if I came now?"

"No, that's quite all right. I'll be expecting you, then."

The commissaire arrived half an hour later. Anne led him to the living room, where he sat on the sofa. He politely declined the drink she offered.

"Mme. Dupré, you may have heard that I am in charge of the case of Tanya Gerard's murder. It has not been solved to date, and I am sorry that I cannot shed any more light on it."

Anne remained silent. Surely the commissaire had not come to tell her *that*.

"However, about a month ago, a scientist named Albert Allier was also murdered here in Paris. Are you familiar with that name?"

Anne felt the blood rushing to her head, and she turned her gaze to the side as if looking for something.

"I beg your pardon—what was the name again?" she asked.

"Professor Albert Allier." Duval stressed each word. "A specialist in electronic irradiation."

Anne shrugged.

"Perhaps on the radio or the television, or maybe the newspapers. Anyway, I don't know him. Why do you ask?"

"I just thought you *might* know him. It would help me in my investigation."

"But why ask me? There must be thousands of scientists and academicians in Paris, and it would be impossible to know them all."

"Yes, that's true. But both of you worked in the same university."

"I'm sorry, commissaire. It's a huge university, you know. I am not acquainted with everyone on the staff."

"I realize that, Professeur Dupré. But the late professor knew, and was in contact with, someone you *do* know."

The commissaire watched her face for any sign of alarm or recognition. There was none.

Anne felt as if she was on a torture rack, but did not let her emotions show. She waited in silence for him to continue.

"Sir Cedric Norton. He was in touch with Allier before the professor was murdered."

Anne made a supreme effort to curb her mounting anxiety and reveal nothing outwardly.

"Sir Cedric was a close friend of my husband's," she said quietly, "when he served at the London Embassy. We were ..."

"Yes, I know all about your late husband being an attaché there."

"In that case, you should also know that Sir Cedric considers himself a kind of guardian to me—as if he owed it to Raoul, my husband. Whenever he's in Paris on his business, he takes the time to call and pay his respects. The perfect gentleman. Sometimes he even brings me a present. But what has all this to do with your visit?"

Duval took a deep breath, and spoke slowly, as if to himself.

"A famous woman is murdered. You are questioned because you were a good friend of hers. Then a scientist is murdered, and *you* are acquainted with a man who had business with the victim a short time before his demise. Now, this may be totally insignificant—and yet, it *is* somewhat unusual, don't you think? Something that needs to be explained?"

Anne would have gladly thrown the vase on her desk at the commissaire's head.

"Monsieur le Commissaire," she said defiantly, "I am an academician—a researcher and lecturer in history. Research is my profession. Allow me to inform you that the deductions you are insinuating are far from scientific!'

Duval had an immediate response.

"Madame, police investigations are not similar to scientific or historical research."

"Indeed?" Anne said. "Then what do they resemble?"

"We deal with people, dead and alive, and with evidence collected at crime scenes. We compare fingerprints, gather cigarette butts, prepare lists of the victim's family and friends, the 'first circle.' Further out, in the 'second circle,' we interview acquaintances and friends of friends. As in your case, for example. It helps us put together the complete picture of what happened. I requested this interview with you without any knowledge connecting you with the murder. I was hoping, however, that you could help me get closer to my goal."

"And have I?"

"Not for the moment. But I would very much like to be able to contact you again in the future. Will that be all right with you?"

"Of course it's all right. Though I have no idea what good I can be to your investigations."

Anne showed the commissaire out. She stood pondering by the closed door:

*What an evening this turned out to be*, she thought. *Not only did Martin have to leave, he didn't even kiss me goodbye. And then* this *character shows up! How the devil does he know that Sir Cedric and I are acquainted? The last time Cedric and I met in public was in a restaurant, and that was before Tanya's murder. And before that, they didn't even know I existed. Yes, the commissaire called Sir Cedric—he probably found the number in Allier's phonebook. Therefore, it stands to reason that Cedric was followed here! And that could not have happened without the assistance of Scotland Yard. How else could Duval have known that Cedric was on his way to Paris? This is a complex and dangerous situation. The others should be alerted, and we can no longer meet at my place.*

She instinctively reached for the telephone … then stayed her hand. She had seen enough detective movies on television. What they do there is wait outside for the suspect to panic and rush blindly to other members of the crime ring, perhaps even the leader. They also have a tap on the suspect's phone. They find out whom she calls and eavesdrop on her conversations.

Anne's mind was racing. She needed to find a way to contact the others, tell them of the situation, and find alternate means of communications and places to meet. She made up her mind to call the admiral from a public phone, tell him everything, and have him inform Sir Cedric and Martin. She herself would be in London for the weekend and they could meet and discuss things there.

cs80

Commissaire Felix Duval sat in his car, smoking, thinking things over. He was not pleased with how the case was progressing, and he had a distinctly uncomfortable feeling about it. This was, after all, a case he was not ordered to solve. It was taking up valuable time, and it was getting nowhere. *Let's face it*, he said to himself, *that woman has nothing to do with the Allier case. And her British friend probably met with him on purely scientific issues. Marnier reported that when the Englishman left the Dupré apartment, he took a taxi to the LaserCorp offices in La Defense and stayed there for a few hours. And what kind of rivalry between them, or any other reason, could justify the professor's murder? Professional jealousy? Possibly, but surely not to the extent of murder!* He put out his cigarette, turned on the engine and said to no one in particular: "Check the electric 'killer machine' again! What in hell is it? Or what does it resemble, if it's been altered? Where was it purchased? Who bought it? When?"

CXEO

That same evening, Martin called George Graham on his cellphone from Heathrow Airport.

"Must be important," George said over a noisy background of a nightclub. "What's up?"

"Remember how well Patricia did on the trip we had together? Well, we'd like her to help us again on another trip. Do you think she'll agree?"

"I can't speak for her, of course. But I believe she enjoyed herself very much the last time. However, she's an independent young woman, and there's no telling how she'll respond. I think she'll comply, however."

"Do you know where I can find her?"

George laughed.

"I hope you're still in Paris, Martin. Because that's where she is."

Martin swore under his breath.

"Write this down," George continued, and he gave her telephone number and the name of the hotel she was staying in. "Good luck!"

"Thanks," Martin said, and hung up. "Damn!"

He looked at the number George had just dictated, and then dialed it. She was in. Delighted to meet with him. Tomorrow morning? Sure thing. Ten thirty. Where? Boulevard Saint-Germain, Café Latino. Fine. See you then. Bye.

"Double damn!" Martin turned to the ticket counter and bought a ticket back to Paris. The only one available was on an early morning flight that would barely bring him there in time for his date with Patricia.

## FORTY-SEVEN

Anne awoke with a headache after a restless, and almost sleepless, night. She took a couple of aspirins, showered and dressed, and felt just as miserable as before.

She took the metro and switched trains a couple of times, trying to make out if she was being followed. Far from home, at the Charles de Gaulle Etoile, Anne walked down the Champs-Elysées to the drugstore. There, she used a public phone and called the admiral in London. *At least*, she thought, *the police don't know about 'him'!*

Fortunately, the admiral was in.

"Patrick," Anne said breathlessly. "Something very serious has happened. We have got to meet."

"I understand you are quite agitated, Anne," he said. "Don't say anything now. Come to London at your earliest convenience and call me right away. I'll drop everything and meet with you."

"Thank you, Patrick. Thank you."

"Take care, now."

Satisfied that this crucial step was now over, Anne realized she hadn't had breakfast yet. She sat at one of the tables and had a coffee and croissant. It didn't take long for her to calm down. Her headache had disappeared and she felt ready to face the world again.

Anne had a lecture to deliver, and she took a taxi to the university. Feeling much more at ease now, she relaxed in the back seat of the taxi and watched the passersby. Traffic was heavy, and the taxi advanced slowly along Boulevard Saint-Germain, stopping frequently. Despite the hustle and bustle of the city, nobody was actually in an obvious hurry. There was the mother with her child just coming out of the department store. There was the delivery boy on his motor scooter, beating out the rhythm of an unheard song while waiting for the light to change. There was the sidewalk café, the patrons drinking and talking, some reading newspapers....

*What's that?!*

Martin! Yes, her Martin. He was seated at a table in the café! Opposite him sat a beautiful blonde young girl, and both were laughing heartily. Anne couldn't believe her eyes! Last night, Martin had said he was leaving immediately for London.

The taxi advanced. Anne turned her head and reconfirmed that what she had seen was not imaginary. She gasped. Apparently, she had held her breath for over a minute.

*Martin lied to me! He lied to me. He was in such a hurry to leave for 'London' he couldn't even kiss me goodbye—while in fact he was hurrying to meet this ... friend of his in Paris. Is she his lover, too? How many does he have? That laugh they were sharing—could it be that they were laughing at me? Was I the butt of their merriment? How he got into the pants of his naive and old cousin?*

Anne had never felt so insulted, so degraded, in her life. She felt an uncontrollable rage surge up inside her.

*Well, mister lover boy—you can just forget about your pushover cousin Annie. I am still considered your superior in the association, and there will be nothing beyond that between us again. And I certainly do not need you to find Tanya's killer. To think of you as my bodyguard—hah!*

For a moment, Anne lost her control. First Duval, now Martin—all too much, too close together. The tears welled in her eyes, and she choked an audible sob in mid breath.

She collected her wits as best she could, and leaned forward to the taxi driver.

"I've changed my mind," she said, and gave her home address.

The more Anne thought about the incident, the more ridiculous she felt. *I should have realized that a woman my age should not have romantic aspirations. A twenty-year-old girl could perhaps afford to have her feelings dashed now and then, but I can't! Having fun together for a while, a few nights of fabulous sex—oh, yes, I wouldn't want to miss those. But a real romance? Forget it! How could I have been so blind? They say it's never too late to learn. Boy, oh boy, how right they are!*

The taxi arrived, and Anne went up to her flat. She felt too humiliated to face anyone. She called the university and said she didn't feel well, canceled her lectures and requested they find a temporary substitute lecturer. She took another aspirin, and went to bed. Surprisingly, she managed to fall asleep.

Anne awoke in the late afternoon, covered in sweat. After a lengthy shower, she felt slightly better. She reached several conclusions while the water washed over her body, as if removing doubt, guilt and fear. She would spend a long weekend in Reading with her parents and children. Nothing would disturb her there. Later, from London she would contact Admiral Stone and tell him everything that had happened since this morning's conversation with him. As the admiral would not be pestered by the annoying French police, she would request him to take over the management of the association. Next Monday, she would return to Paris, released of all obligations—as if she had never had a relationship with Martin, and as if the police investigations did not concern her at all.

⋘⋙

Martin had arrived early. The Café Latino was already bustling with patrons and the only free table was on the sidewalk. He would have preferred not to be so exposed, and sit inside—but he took the only choice available. Patricia arrived at ten thirty on the button. Her outfit was very impressive, and many men swiveled their heads toward her. Martin made a mental note of her punctuality. In a city like Paris, he mused, in order to be punctual you need to arrive at your destination long before the appointed hour, wander around a bit, and then show up exactly on time. He didn't know if that was the procedure she had employed, but decided to find out at some later date. *There'll be ample time for that.*

Martin stood, shook her hand, helped her into a seat and ordered a café crème and croissant for both of them.

"The last time we met was in Tunisia, wasn't it?" Martin asked with a smile.

"Correct. And may I add that although it was a very pleasant trip, it was strange and made no sense. I'd even say it was silly."

Martin kept smiling. Patricia didn't know what to make of it, or why she was requested to meet with him.

The waiter served their order.

"Patricia, you're a smart and educated young lady, and we were all aware that you did not fall for the movie story we gave you. However, we kept playing our roles in accordance with the instructions we received before embarking on the trip. If there was no real necessity to reveal everything, we kept our exposure to the minimum. Well, today may be the day of revelation. It all depends on how our current conversation develops."

Martin added sugar to his coffee and waited for a response. Patricia just sat in silence, concentrating on her croissant as if she had nothing to say at the moment. Martin couldn't tell whether this was sheer indifference or a skillful act.

"In Tunisia," he went on, "we conducted a scientific experiment. For all the locals knew, we were a movie crew with an actress, and that's how we wanted it. We now need your help again. However, this time I'll explain what it's all about and then ask you if would like to comply."

Patricia was now interested.

"I'm listening," she said.

"Let's begin with the statement that the fate of the world is in danger. Dictators keep sprouting up, they threaten world peace, and the western democracies cannot cope with them." Martin described the association's ideology in detail.

"And how do you expect to achieve your aims, assuming it's at all possible?" Patricia asked.

"We believe it *is* possible. We have a number of top scientists working toward that goal, and a couple of very wealthy men who finance the entire operation. We already have a few devices that could seriously embarrass the most dangerous of tyrants."

"What," Patricia kept on asking, "are these mysterious measures by which you wish to humiliate dictators such as the Iranian president?"

"Well, as you're making an example of the Iranian president, you should know that there is strong opposition to him in his country. Even the religious leaders, who de facto run the country, are not pleased with his policies. They are quite aware of the dangers he might be inflicting on his country. So—sometimes just a little push can topple even a wrestling champion if he's teetering on the brink of an abyss. Now take North Korea. People there are starving. They need to rummage in the garbage to feed their children. The leader is a demagogue. Take away his oratory powers, and you may have finished him altogether."

"You still haven't told me *how* you're going to do it!" Patricia insisted.

"No, I haven't. That was deliberate." Martin smiled again. "First I need to know if you agree to help us in doing all the above. In other words—will you join us?"

Patricia still had questions.

"Do you really believe you can replace a regime without a war? Just by embarrassment?"

"Patricia, you are familiar with my military past. I'm sure you can put two and two together—if I am undertaking this mission, isn't that a definite sign that I believe it can be done?"

Patricia fell silent. She placed her elbows on the table and rested her head in her hands. Her eyes took on a faraway look, and then they closed gently as a faint smile came to her lips. You could almost read the deliberations she was going through just by observing her face.

She had filed for divorce three years ago because her husband wanted her to be a model housewife. That meant staying at home almost all of the time, shopping, cooking, and hosting his guests who bored her to tears. She just couldn't take any more! Since her divorce, she found she had changed. She was no longer the lively, happy-go-lucky girl she used to be before her marriage. She kept testing new fields of interest—sports, hikes, theatre, painting— but none had the appeal she was looking for. She really had trouble finding what to do with herself. Now here was an offer to participate in something that sounded as if it were very important. If nothing else, she'd be busy doing something useful. It could be exactly what she needed in order to extricate herself from the emptiness she was finding herself in. Just one more question.

"What would I have to do?"

"First, you'd have to commit yourself to total secrecy. Next, you'll be joining me on a mission commencing *now*! We're taking a tour of Iran. We'll be learning the local conditions in order to prepare plans for an operation later on. I suppose the trip will take us about a week. We will appear as an ordinary tourist couple. Between us, however, we shall maintain strict teamwork discipline."

"And if I agree?"

"Then you are committed. Not only for this trip, but you will have joined our association, with all that entails. And I shall reveal to you the means which we intend to deploy."

Patricia's features gradually became brighter, and her eyes sparkled.

"I agree to join you," she whispered.

"I am honestly very glad to hear that. You must never, ever, tell anyone of our conversation under *any* circumstances! This is a very solemn promise you are required to make—if word gets out, our operation will have to be cancelled, including what we have discussed just now. Can you promise?"

Patricia hesitated only slightly.

"Yes, Martin—I solemnly promise to keep everything secret!"

Martin leaned back and heaved a sigh of relief. He proposed they drink a toast, but Patricia declined, claiming it was too early. Instead, she requested examples of the methods used by the association. Martin's descriptions of Paganini and its anticipated effects had them laughing out loud. *What the hell*, she thought, *I might as well be a part of an exciting—possibly useful—adventure. Better than wandering around without a purpose.*

From this moment on, Martin and Patricia coordinated all the details of their impending trip. She got the task of planning the flights, booking them, organizing hotel rooms, tours, car rental—the lot. She even had to get the proper visas from the Iranian Embassy. Patricia felt a certain thrill of enjoyment in the hard work imposed on her. She hoped this thrill would go on and on.

## FORTY-EIGHT

Anne surprised her parents by arriving on a Thursday instead of the usual Friday. Her excuse was that she felt a bit tired and under the weather, and had taken a long weekend off. The family was delighted, naturally, especially the children who adored their mother. However, she specified that she'd need a couple of hours for some administrative chores—a few telephone calls, perhaps a social visit, but nothing more. She found her children in high spirits. They were about to finish the school term and were looking forward to the summer holidays.

CS&BD

The next day Anne took the train to London. While disembarking, though she knew she was being silly, she couldn't help looking back, trying to discover whether she was being followed. She entered a nearby mall and called the admiral from a public telephone.

"I'm at Paddington Station," Anne said when he answered. "Are you free?"

"Take a taxi down here right away," Admiral Stone said. "My secretary is on vacation and I'm all alone in the office."

Anne wandered around the shops for a while and then took a taxi giving the address of a hotel near the admiral's office. After walking from the hotel, she entered the huge lobby of the office building and joined the throngs of people entering and exiting.

This was ideal if anonymity was necessary—nobody could tell where anyone was going or where he or she came from. Anne had made the trip from Paddington in less than half an hour.

The admiral's office was on the sixth floor. She was warmly received and ushered into his private office, after he had carefully locked the front door. They sat on opposite sides of his large desk, sipping on drinks he had thoughtfully prepared, and Anne gave a detailed rendition of everything that happened with Commissaire Duval.

"I've given this much thought," she concluded. "I assume that Duval probably turned to Scotland Yard for help."

"But the case was closed," the admiral said. "We read it in the papers."

"Yes, it was. That's why I believe Duval has launched his own private crusade. He does that sometimes—the press is full of it. Mind you, Patrick, these are all speculations."

"They certainly are, Miss Sherlock Holmes. But they are also fascinating. Please do go on."

"He must have a friend in Scotland Yard. Through him, he knew of Sir Cedric's flight to Paris and probably also got his description. Duval waited for him at the airport and then trailed him to my apartment."

"That still does not justify harassing you. Rude as he is, that would be taking things a bit too far."

"Wait, Patrick, there's more. Just over a month ago, Tanya Gerard was murdered in Paris. It made headlines at the time—she was a famous actress and stage director. She was a very close friend of mine, and I was questioned by the police, along with all her family and friends. I was quickly dismissed as having nothing to do with the murder."

"And that was when you first met Duval?"

"No, just a minor official. But Duval was in charge of the case just the same."

"So?"

"Now, with the Allier case—closed or otherwise—also on Duval's agenda, he had the audacity to claim that as I was a friend of the murdered woman, and I was also a friend of a colleague of another 'murder victim,' there were grounds to question me again. I've told you the rest."

"What a bastard," the admiral muttered.

"Indeed. He requested 'my permission to have a talk with me again.' I told him he could do so any time. Now I am worried sick about what to do. Our safety, of course, comes first. And then— how can we stop this sonofabitch, pardon my French? I have deliberately refrained from contacting Sir Cedric and have come directly to you, as Duval knows nothing about you."

"Do you think you were followed here?"

"I took all the precautions I could on my way over—I'm pretty sure I was not followed. And another thing—I believe that now both Paris and London are 'out of bounds' for our meetings. There—I think that's everything. What's your opinion?"

Admiral Stone rose from his seat, went to the window and gazed in silence onto the London traffic for several minutes. When his thoughts had settled he turned back to Anne.

"There is no doubt in my mind that Duval is conducting his own private investigation. It is, however, no less dangerous than an official inquiry—perhaps even more. An official investigation is routine, a personal one is driven by ambition. Now, what could he possibly gain by interrogating you and by following Sir Cedric? Nothing, I believe. He can surmise and conjecture as much as he pleases, but that won't be enough to reopen the case. I think there is only one possible direction he could take, and that is the device itself. The police have it right now. We know from Martin that it is impossible to trace. So, dear lady, I believe you can set your worries aside. If he pesters you again, you may tell him exactly what you told him before."

"That's a relief," Anne sighed.

"As to stopping him," the admiral continued with a smile, "there may be methods. Short of eliminating him, of course. Why don't we discuss this at the next board meeting?"

"All right."

"Which brings us to our meeting location. You are absolutely right! We can take no chances. As you said—Paris and London are out of bounds from now on. Despite the discomfort it will cause us, we need to find somewhere outside France or England for our meetings. How about Amsterdam? I know of a very suitable office …"

Anne made a face.

"Amsterdam is a notorious drug center," she said. "Crime and prostitution are rife there as well. The police there are on constant alert. Personally, I prefer Brussels. It's closer to Paris and about the same distance from London as Paris is, so it shouldn't make much of a difference for you."

"Very well," the admiral said. "I shall consult with Sir Cedric and notify you."

"As you are the only 'unsullied' one of us three, it'll be up to you to notify Sir Cedric and Martin, and set up the next meeting in Brussels. I think it would be best to reserve a suite in a large hotel, where many people mill around most of the time. We could then all get to the suite without being noticed. Tuesdays are best for me, if possible." She stood up.

"Yes, sir!" the admiral said. "I mean, yes madam!"

They shook hands.

Anne took the train back to Reading in a much calmer mood. She'd be back home for tea, and she was bringing the children's favorite cookies with her.

CALL

## *NEWSFLASH*

The American president announced today that if measures were not taken against the Iranian nuclear program, a third world war would erupt. Iran, he said, is a threat to world peace. The American Secretary of State declared that the US would wait for the results of the diplomatic processes between the European Union and Iran, subsequent to which the US would decide upon its course of action.

On the other hand, the Russian president has met with his Iranian counterpart and has promised to continue his support for Iran's nuclear program. This has caused concern in the US, especially in view of the tension between the two powers due to the American intention of deploying missiles in Europe.

CALL

Admiral Stone, ever the proper naval officer, went immediately into action. He left his office and called Sir Cedric from a public telephone. They agreed to meet at their club, as was their wont for many years. If Sir Cedric were followed, he'd be seen entering his club. He would never be followed inside—everyone knew everybody, and a stranger's presence would not be tolerated.

Inside the club, after clinking their brandy snifters, Admiral Stone updated Sir Cedric with the most recent events.

"Following me?" Sir Cedric blustered. "It's an outrage! I shall notify the proper authorities. Such things just aren't done here!"

"I don't think you need go so far, my friend," responded the admiral. "Let the dust settle first. We'll just have to be more careful, that's all. I've consulted with Anne, and we propose to meet in Brussels next Tuesday."

"Wise choice." Sir Cedric had calmed down as quickly as he had flared up. "I shall never travel to Paris again. Where in Brussels do we meet?"

"I have booked a suite at the Sheraton Towers for Monday and Tuesday." He gave Sir Cedric the suite number. "I shall notify Anne and leave a message for Martin at the gym. We'll meet at eleven a.m. sharp on Tuesday morning. Each of us will arrive alone, linger a while in the lobby, and then come up to the suite. No one is to ask for me at the reception desk."

"Right!" Sir Cedric exclaimed, and finished his brandy.

CȘʬ

Martin wanted to inform Anne of his success in recruiting Patricia. He called her apartment but got no answer. What a disappointment—she must be busy. Well, he'd try later.

Meanwhile, he had preparations and packing to do for the trip to Iran. He and Patricia had set up a meeting that evening to compare notes. She informed him that they would need to visit the Iranian Consulate personally to apply for visas. On Fridays the consulate was closed—so they needed to wait over the weekend. She had also obtained a list of relevant round-trip flights, good tourist hotels in Tehran, prices, car rental agencies, and many other pertinent bits of information. All in all, once they had the visas they could leave at any time.

Martin called the gym and was informed by Spencer that he should contact "the guy who was with you in Tunisia." Consequently, the admiral told him of the meeting in Brussels, giving the exact time and location, with a further instruction of "don't ask for me at the desk—come straight up." But he disclosed no further information.

*That's odd*, Martin thought. *This is the first time that the admiral, not Anne, sets up the meeting. And outside France or England, yet. Could this possibly have anything to do with Anne's not answering the phone these past two days?*

## FORTY-NINE

The board had assembled in the admiral's suite. Martin was the only one who did not know what the meeting was about. He hoped he could see Anne, and that they could be together after the board meeting.

Anne related her story regarding Commissaire Duval's visit to her home. This was mainly for Martin's benefit, as he had to understand why they were now far more cautious about board meetings.

"Before we discuss current matters," Anne began, "I would like to pose the following questions: should we let Duval continue undisturbed in his quest to solve an officially closed case, or should we look for means to stop him?"

"Fortunately," the admiral said, "I have had a lot of time to think this over before arriving here. Let's examine a number of options—and then you can judge for yourselves. The simplest thing to do is to let him carry on as he pleases—we *know* he won't solve the case. Then I thought of notifying his superiors of the fact that he is still working on a case contrary to their ruling. *They* could then, possibly, stop him."

"But we couldn't be sure it worked," Anne said.

"Nothing in life is guaranteed, Anne," Sir Cedric chuckled. "I can guarantee that!"

"Please let me finish," the admiral said. "There's the possibility of sending him an anonymous letter, which we tailor to send him on a wild goose chase. This could be rather tricky, as the letter needs to be written by someone with a motive to 'assist' the commissaire … I haven't thought this one out completely yet."

"We could send him a threatening note, couldn't we?" Sir Cedric said, half-jokingly.

There was a short silence.

"I had considered that option as well," the admiral said. "A man like Duval has many enemies. He has put many law offenders behind bars and there would surely be a few who would be ready to … umm … dispose of him."

"Very true," Sir Cedric said. "Revenge is quite common in criminal circles."

"I refrained from suggesting this method because I believe it will serve as an excuse to reopen the case. Investigations may become even more intensive. We do not want that!"

"You could be right," Sir Cedric said.

"Well then, gentlemen," Anne said determinedly. "What do you propose we do?"

"I don't think that threatening him will work." Martin spoke for the first time. "Instead of keeping him away from us it might do the opposite—encourage him to get to the bottom of the case. In my opinion, the best way lies in informing his superiors, or the Investigating Magistrate who closed the case, that Duval is disobeying their ruling. The question now is how to do it? An anonymous letter to the authorities may backfire on us—suspicion may fall on Anne, as she was the one harassed by Duval."

"I suppose that goes for an anonymous phone call as well," Anne remarked.

"Do you have a suggestion?" Sir Cedric asked.

"How about an article in the press that hints at something like 'Professor Allier's murder to be solved soon. Commissaire Duval, who is still investigating the case, will soon reveal all.' I suppose we could get it worded better."

"Not such a bad idea," Sir Cedric said. "But how do you propose to leak this disinformation to the press?"

"That shouldn't be too hard," the admiral said. "Newspapers *love* anonymous letters, and they'll never reveal their sources—especially if they don't know who they are. However, any journalist worth his beans will want to know *why* the anonymous letter was sent. In other words, the letter should contain the motive for its dispatching. That's a bit tougher."

Another short silence.

"Very well, gentlemen," Anne said. "Would anyone like to summarize our discussion? No? Well, in the absence of a definite method, let's decide that for now we shall permit Commissaire Duval to follow whatever he's following. We're pretty sure he'll discover nothing. However, at the same time please think of a method we can use to halt his investigation. If an anonymous letter to the press is your solution, please draft up something that will also contain the reason for it being sent. Are we agreed?"

No one objected.

"Then let's continue with the issues at hand. The first operative task is Martin's trip to Iran. Martin, please report."

"I have recruited the girl—Patricia Welles, George Graham's sister—the same girl who posed as an actress for our 'movie' in Tunisia. She is financially secure, unemployed, and pleased at the opportunity to be of use to an important cause. I gave her the task of preparing everything for the Iran trip, and she performed outstandingly. In fact, all we are waiting for now is the green light from this board, and we'll be on our way. It could even be tomorrow."

"Any dissent?" Anne asked. "None. Good. You've got your green light, Martin. Let's get on to other matters now. I think we should have a stock on hand of the materials we have already tested—a few sacks of fertilizer and gravel, two or three kilograms of pellets, a couple of dozen acoustic disruptors, etc. Also, I think we should ask Mr. Rosetti if his device could be made smaller— much smaller. In fact, I dare say that the size of a cellular phone would be the *largest* option for us. So please, all of you, ask your inventors for a healthy amount of their stuff."

"Don't forget that they could be quite bulky to ship," Sir Cedric said.

"I know, Cedric, but it really doesn't matter. They all resemble normal, commercial materials. And they could be shipped quite innocently to our 'cowshed.'"

"Yes, that'll work," the admiral said. "Just don't forget to instruct your suppliers to utilize private shipping or delivery companies, and to leave the sender's particulars as vague as possible."

"I'll have a word along those lines with Boulanger regarding 'wasp,'" Anne said. "Now, there's another thing I wanted to bring up. We need to stay in contact with our generous financers. I'll talk to Dodson, and Patrick—please say hello to Mr. Neil Bennett."

"Right-ho!" the admiral said.

"Finally," Anne said. "I'd like to remind you all that we need to find a computer whiz, a hacker, who can penetrate into remote computers. Probe among your friends, neighbors, and relations— he's hiding out there somewhere.

"That's it, gentlemen. Due to Duval's interference, you may not contact me directly. At least, not until things clear up. I doubt very much that there's a tap on my telephone, but if Duval got assistance from Scotland Yard, he could just as easily have accomplices in Paris. We're taking no risks. The admiral here will take my place in administrative matters, and I will contact him only. From public phones, of course."

The meeting had taken about four hours. During this entire period, Martin had not managed to make eye contact with Anne. She appeared wholly immersed in the discussion. Her gaze would go around all those present—himself included—but it never lingered on him.

*She must be far more stressed than I imagined*, he convinced himself. *Duval's investigation must have strained her self-control to the limit. She is playing her role marvelously, despite the immense tension she must be experiencing. She wants to appear natural and businesslike.*

The meeting ended. Anne suggested they leave one by one at five-minute intervals, and that she would leave first. When it was Martin's turn, he half expected to find her waiting for him outside the hotel, but he realized she was following the rules all the way.

Disappointed and downhearted, he boarded the train to Paris and to the meeting with Patricia. They had to book a flight to Tehran.

C3&O

On the train to Paris, Martin couldn't help remembering that he and Anne had spent about four hours in the same room and had not exchanged a single word. Not even a glance. He would have liked to say goodbye to her before his trip, even just by phone, but she had forbidden anyone to call her. He was at a loss. For a moment, he thought he could override her ban with the excuse that he was a relative and therefore outside her ruling—he was calling as a cousin interested in how she was doing. But he quickly abandoned that idea—it would probably make her furious with him. *I'll try again when we get back from Iran*, her thought. *I hope that by then things will have returned to normal.*

But he was still bothered by Duval's private investigation. Martin tried to reconstruct every stage the device went through from the moment it was purchased. He shut his eyes and replayed the delivery scenario in his mind. It had gone off perfectly! No one saw the boys arrive or leave. It was a nuisance that that disagreeable French police officer decided to bother everyone who knew Allier, as he was probably pestering many Parisians, too. But that did not alter the fact that there *was* an investigation, and that Anne was on the list of people questioned.

He met with Patricia that same evening, and they booked a flight to Tehran on the next day.

ഗ൭ல

Meanwhile, Admiral Stone called Neil Bennett from his Brussels hotel suite.

"Hello, Admiral. I am pleased to hear your voice."

"I called you for three reasons," the admiral said. "First, to see how you were doing."

Bennett chuckled.

"All things considered, quite well, thank you."

"And second, to thank you once again for your generous donation, and to assure you that great advances have been made as a result."

"That's good to hear," the old man said. "I intended to transfer another sum this week. Do you remember what I specifically requested from you?"

"Yes, indeed, Mr. Bennett. That was my third point. You wanted to see results as soon as possible. It is my belief that you will not have to wait very long, though I cannot give you a definite date."

"Keep up the good work, admiral."

"My deepest thanks to you, and I speak on behalf of the team as well."

The admiral hung up. He considered calling Gustav Lemke as well, but thought the hour was too late—tomorrow would do fine.

CR80

Sir Cedric preferred to return to London. He took a taxi to the airport and boarded the first plane home. He'd call Rosetti and Hoffman in the morning. Damn that interfering French commissaire!

CR80

Anne wondered what she would say to Alfred Boulanger. She would have preferred to meet him face to face, and find out how Sir Cedric's laser could be tested from Boulanger's satellite. She understood absolutely nothing about this, and she needed a slow and detailed explanation from the inventor. She needed to call Dodson, too.

Anne suddenly felt very tired. It was all too much. She decided to spend the night in another hotel in Brussels, and call from there in the morning. Perhaps she would even think of where to meet Boulanger.

*As for you, Martin Cooper—you can go to hell!*

## FIFTY

The Air France flight landed at Mehrabad airport in Tehran. Martin and Patricia took a taxi to the Esteghlal Hotel, in the northern part of the city, where they had booked two adjacent rooms. In a country run by ayatollahs, where women walked around with veiled faces, they felt it would be better to stay in separate rooms, as they were not traveling as a married couple.

CR80

Sir Cedric decided to meet with Rosetti in Milan—the minia-turization of 'Paganini' was too sensitive a subject to be discussed over the phone. Their meeting began with a warm embrace.

"It's so good to see you again, Emilio," Sir Cedric said. "I wished to tell you personally what I said over the phone—that our tests with your invention went off beautifully!"

"*Bene, bene!*" Rosetti was beaming. "Tell me more."

"At first we were afraid that silencing all the communications in a large city would raise a public uproar. Perhaps even an official inquiry. So we chose somewhere less prominent. And—everything went exactly the way you said it would!"

"Did the television sets continue to operate?" Rosetti inquired eagerly.

Sir Cedric described the outcome of the tests. All audio devices had ceased to function, including the television speakers. And there was no public outcry when two minutes later everything returned to normal.

"The populace attributed the effect to freak weather conditions," Sir Cedric laughed.

"I am very pleased," Rosetti said. "Let's drink a toast to our success."

"Certainly, Emilio. But first, there is something I would like to ask you."

"*Si?*"

"I was wondering if the device could be made in smaller dimensions. You see, we will need many of them, and they will need to be transported to all kinds of locations—and some of these locations could be very ... er ... sensitive, if you know what I mean."

"When I first designed this device, *amico mio*, that was not one of my concerns. On the contrary—I thought that an ordinary-looking household appliance would raise the least suspicion. But now that you mention your preference, I can tell you that it would be no problem to make the device smaller—even to the size of a pack of cigarettes. It could be hidden in a shaving machine, a small camera …"

"A cellular phone?" Sir Cedric asked.

"Certainly! Anything you wish."

Sir Cedric was excited.

"That's wonderful!" he gushed. "It will be an enormous contribution to our cause! We won't need to search for rooms or shops to place the devices. Almost anywhere will do."

"I'll get to work on it. It shouldn't take long. I'll call you when it's ready."

"Umm, it would be better if I called you, Emilio. We're adopting stricter security measures. How about in a week? Two?"

"You are wise to be so cautious," the Italian said with a smile. "Let's say in ten days?"

The two friends parted with a handshake and another embrace.

⟐

Commissaire Duval was frustrated. He had sent Inspecteur Marnier to the flea market with photocopies of the 'murder weapon' with no results whatsoever. There seemed to be only one way to continue. On one hand, he knew how to manipulate his underlings without any concern about their own problems. On the other, he abhorred requesting the aid of friends and acquaintances. He had made an exception with MacLeod, at Scotland Yard, and felt very uncomfortable about it. Now he was forced to do so again. An old associate of his from high school days, Jules Racine, was an electronics engineer who owned a repair shop in the nineteenth arrondissement. There was no point in taking the photographs to him—he would need to examine the actual object. That wasn't going to be easy. There was a rigorous bureaucratic procedure for taking articles out of the police storerooms. But he would think of something.

## FIFTY-ONE

After a good night's rest, Martin and Patricia enjoyed a rich breakfast and immediately booked a tour of the city of Tehran.

On the bus, which departed half an hour later, they were joined by a few couples and an English-speaking guide. They visited the Royal Palace Museum in the buildings of the Central Bank of Iran, where the Iranian monarchy's treasures were on public display. These were so breathtakingly beautiful that Patricia doubted if there was anything like it in the whole world. They drove through the main streets of Tehran, noting especially the wide boulevard renamed from Pahlavi Street to Valiasr—a reference to the 12th Shi'ite Imam—Avenue. There was a wide difference between the modern and opulent north of the city and the ancient southern part, with its very different ambience. Black, the color of the "chador," the traditional garb worn by Iranian women that covered them from head to toe, was seen almost everywhere. Here and there, Martin and Patricia observed "decency" patrols who would occasionally detain a woman who may have accidentally allowed a stray hair to be visible. Sometimes these women were arrested.

The famous Tehran Bazaar was fascinating. Narrow alleys everywhere, stalls of all sizes overflowing with produce—jewelry, carpets, ceramics—and throngs of people pushing and shoving, seemingly living in a detached world, oblivious of anything happening outside the bazaar. Many of them spoke English. Martin and Patricia learned that Iran had two official armies, two navies and two air forces! Apparently, one set was the "traditional" national military force, while the other belonged to the "Revolutionary Guard"—originally created by the Ayatollah Khomeini to safeguard the revolution, but which, in time, took over the economy of the country. In fact, they learned in open disbelief, that there was even a *third* army—the people's army—which wore no uniforms and was meant to quash riots and demonstrations. Their guide overheard the tourists, and advised them to refrain from discussing these issues, especially in the bazaar....

The bus headed back north. On the way, they passed by the American Consulate compound. The bus did not stop, but it slowed down long enough for the guide to describe how the compound was conquered by the young revolutionary troops who converted it into the Iranian Revolution Museum. The guide stressed that this used to be the "nest of American espionage."

The tour ended in the Niavaran Palace, once home to the royal family. The new regime turned the palace into a tourist attraction, to send a message to the world of how corrupt the leadership was before the Islamic Revolution.

During the entire tour, Martin and Patricia had done their utmost to behave properly and correctly. Their attire was modest to the extreme, with covered arms and legs. And they took pains not to publicly display any affection between them.

Martin decided that in two or three days, after touring Shiraz and Isfahan, they would rent a car and, under their cover as tourists, look a bit more closely at one of the main squares in the city—the gigantic piazza at the end of Azadi Street.

CRSO

Retired Admiral Patrick Stone took his new position in the association very seriously indeed, as befitting a veteran who dedicated his entire life to the service of his country. Since taking over the reins from Anne, he had changed his priorities, putting items that did not need his immediate attention on a back burner. Now, the association occupied most of his time.

He was doubtful about the gravel—the pebbles would not be that practical on a paved area, such as streets or parade grounds. Fields, yes—and gardens and perhaps lawns, too. The Al Qaeda training areas did not concern him at the moment—he had never thought that the pebbles would be effective there.

And that went for the fertilizer as well! Prior to a military parade, they would doubtless sweep the itinerary clean—any fertilizer spread there would be removed!

*We need to improve our methods*, he thought.

He had set up a meeting with Gustav Lemke two days hence. That would not interfere with the association's schedule—Sir Cedric was on a trip to Italy, Martin was in Iran for at least a week, and Anne needed to remain in the background for now.

ജ്ഞ

Commissaire Duval prepared a formal document requesting an item from the police storerooms, supposedly in order to compare with another item. He then called his old classmate, Jules Racine. Forty-five minutes later, they were shaking hands in Racine's electronics laboratory.

"So, Felix," Racine said, obviously awed by the fame his old colleague had achieved. "It's been so many years, and neither of us has kept in touch. You said nothing of yourself over the phone. *Quel dommage.* So tell me now—do you have a family, or are you too busy creating headlines in all the newspapers? Here, let me get you a coffee."

"We can exchange domestic developments a little later, Jules," he said. "Right now I need your assistance in something very urgent."

"To be sure, to be sure! What can I do for the great commissaire?"

Duval plunked the box he was carrying on Racine's worktable. He opened it and took out the device.

"Take a look, Jules. Tell me what it is."

Racine sat at the table and observed the machine indifferently, turning it this way and that, looking underneath, and poking around with a screwdriver. He then folded his arms on his chest and gazed at the device for a couple of minutes.

"It reminds me of an ancient dishwasher," he said finally. "Some essential parts are missing. That doesn't mean a thing, however. What's it supposed to be?" He looked up at Duval.

Duval gave one of his rare smiles.

"That's what I came to you to find out," he said sweetly.

Racine scratched his chin, his eyes glued to the device.

"It doesn't have a motor, and it has no accessories that could do any tasks. It doesn't heat up and it cannot produce a sound. It certainly won't shine in the dark, and I doubt if any smell will come out of it when operated. It's not supposed to be moved about, and nothing I can see there will cause it to vibrate."

"So now we know a whole lot of what it is *not*!" Duval was getting impatient. "Can you tell me what it *is*?"

"It's nothing. It doesn't do anything. It could possibly be a reject by some novice electrician who was experimenting on it. You'd better watch out if you want to plug it into the electricity system. I noticed that the connections are faulty and could electrocute anyone who touches it. Where on earth did you find this?"

"Well, Jules, just *entre nous*, this device is involved in a case that is officially closed. However, I am not satisfied, if you understand my meaning."

"Oh, quite!" Racine was elated. Here was the master detective, about to reveal a professional secret. To *him*!

"This is the device that electrocuted and killed Professor Albert Allier some weeks ago. Do you remember the incident?"

"But of course! Everything I know I learned from him. What a wonderful man!"

"Nobody knows how this machine got on his desk. They say that he may have been developing something new, and that there was an accident. Case closed. What do *you* think?"

"You really want my opinion? All right, then. Professor Allier would never have made such a mistake. I mean, he would never have touched it. Safety was his number one priority at all times! He used to tell us students: 'Never forget that alongside all the blessings that electricity can bring us, it can also kill! *Always* check the connections before turning on an unknown appliance.' And I have followed that warning all my life." He pointed at the machine. "There is no way that this is something that the professor wished to develop. If it wasn't for the tragic results, I would have considered it a joke."

"I'd like this to be perfectly clear," Duval said. "It is your opinion that the late Professor Allier could never have used this device in the process of developing something new. Am I right?"

"*Absolument.*"

"Would it be reasonable to assume that someone had placed this thing on Allier's desk without his knowledge, and that he touched it accidentally? To remove it, perhaps?"

"It's possible. Did you find any fingerprints?"

"No. Excepting Allier's own hand prints, of course."

"What about the plug?" Racine picked up the plug and dangled the cord from his hand.

"Now there's a mystery. No fingerprints on the plug either. You understand, I hope, the significance of this." It wasn't a question.

"How about inside? Did you search for fingerprints *inside* the device? I'm asking because while building this thing, the insides—I mean, like this panel and this condenser—needed to be handled, too. Sometimes fingerprints are left there."

Commissaire Duval was aghast! The insides had almost definitely *not* been dusted for fingerprints. However, he did not allow his consternation to show.

"So," he said calmly, "from what you've seen here, would you say that Allier's death could have been a murder?"

"Judging only by the device's sole function—to electrocute—and the lack of fingerprints on the plug, I would say that murder is a strong possibility."

"That's what I thought, too. Well, Jules, my deepest thanks for your help."

Only then did the conversation resort to personal and domestic matters and, of course, coffee.

An hour later, Duval was back in his office. He hurriedly summoned Marnier and handed him the box with the device.

"Take this to the lab," he ordered, "and have them check everything in this machine's interior for fingerprints. Have them cut through the outside paneling, too, if necessary."

CR&O

Patricia and Martin were the epitome of correct and proper relationships. They spent the days together as model tourists, and parted to their rooms at night. Martin was always the perfect gentleman toward Patricia—friendly and affectionate. They talked about every possible topic under the sun, and discovered that they shared a passion for silent movies and Indian food. However, no other type of passion was involved. In Patricia's opinion, Martin was indeed an attractive man with many high qualifications to his credit, but he was the "boss," and work and play don't mix.

Besides, since her divorce she felt no real need for male company, although she supposed that someday she would.

As for Martin, the thought of hanky-panky with Patricia never even crossed his mind. He was too much in love with Anne for that.

## FIFTY-TWO

As usual, Gustav Lemke invited the admiral to a luscious meal at an exclusive restaurant. Sometimes the admiral believed that Lemke was trying to lull him into a false sense of security, whereupon he would pounce with an undeniable demand. But that had never happened—the food was excellent, his satisfied feeling was genuine, and Lemke was the model of hospitality.

"I would have spoiled that sumptuous meal if I had talked about business," the admiral said, hiding a faint burp. They were each holding a glass of red wine and enjoying a warm afterglow.

"*Ach, ja!*" Lemke responded. "That would have been a pity. But now is a good time, no?"

"Thank you, Gustav. There is something bothering me about the fertilizer and the gravel."

Lemke raised an attentive eyebrow.

"It would be hard to halt a military convoy driving on an asphalt road." The admiral continued describing his apprehensions.

Lemke looked disappointed. He pursed his lips and gazed into his wine glass. The admiral knew better than to disturb him—Lemke had, after all, proved himself to remarkable inventive talents.

Lemke seemed to suddenly wake up.

"I've been thinking about liquids," he said, half to himself. "A spray or sprinkler, perhaps. But liquids are too volatile—

they'll evaporate before being of any use. Maybe something more viscous. Or maybe something that leaves a thin dry film over the paved area. It will start sublimating only in the presence of petrol engines exhaust fumes. *Ja, ja*—that could work. Still just an idea, though. I've got to work on it—keep trying." Lemke raised his head, as if suddenly aware of the admiral's presence. "How much time do you have?"

Admiral Stone was already thinking along operational lines: how to sprinkle or spray a stretch of several kilometers a day or two before a parade. And perhaps a much shorter distance would suffice, as the leading vehicles would jam up the rest. But this was putting the cart before the horse.

"Take all the time you need," he said. "In any case, we cannot plan anything without your stuff on hand."

"I'll go at it right away! When I have something, I shall call you. No, wait! I remember you said not to call you. Very well. You call me, then. Shall we say … in ten days?"

"Indeed, we shall say!" the admiral said with a smile.

They clinked their glasses.

CRWD

School was out, and the Dupré children joined their mother on a visit to their paternal grandparents in the south of France. Anne felt a strong urge to get away from Paris and her everyday worries. Planning a meeting with Boulanger could wait until she returned.

For the children and the elder Duprés it was party time from beginning to end. Guy and Julie always enjoyed being spoiled by their father's parents. *Grand-mè*re cooked meals to die for, and *Grand-papa* took them on outings to country fairs and *petanque*—a form of boules—games.

Anne had a much-needed rest, loafing around, reading, strolling in the countryside, and avoiding thoughts of Paris. But human behavior does not always follow human desires. Every now and then, her thoughts would turn to the police investigation—and to Martin. She truly loved him. There was no denying that despite her jealousy, anger, and frustration, she still could not break away from that love. And now, resulting mostly from her own decisions, Martin was enjoying himself with another woman in a far-off country. Anne felt as if an anvil was pressing down on her chest.

## FIFTY-THREE

For two days, Martin and Patricia continued behaving like any other tourist couple. They took a long bus ride to Isfahan and stayed there overnight. The next day they flew to Shiraz and visited ancient Persepolis. In the short time at their disposal, there was no way they could actually cover everything these sites had to offer. However, like millions of tourists before them, they could now say they had "been there."

On the third day, they flew back to Tehran. They had enjoyed the outing immensely. Patricia was overwhelmed by the splendor of Persian antiquity and Iranian marketplaces, and had taken hundreds of pictures. Martin had purchased a golden pendant as a gift for Anne. Most importantly, they had established themselves to be bona fide tourists, doing what tourists do.

Now, back in Tehran, Martin and Patricia set out to do what they had come for. They rented a car and drove through the city. They chose the route to the airport that took them along the wide Azadi Street with the enormous Azadi Square at its end. This was where public gatherings would occur. Multitudes of citizens would assemble and listen to the oratory of the Iranian leaders. Martin paid close attention to all possibly relevant details: the distance from the square to the nearest buildings, the location of trees, bushes, lawns, hedges, sewer manholes—if they could even remotely serve a future operation at this site, these minutiae would not be forgotten. Using the odometer of his car, Martin measured the lengths of the piazza, and the most likely stretches of road before and after the square, where people would be gathered. At the same time, Patricia took as many pictures as she could.

On the last day of their trip, Martin and Patricia visited the Tehran Bazaar. This was the time to buy souvenirs and inexpensive knickknacks to give to one's friends. The rest of the time was spent packing and relaxing.

The next day, at the airport, Martin called the admiral and coordinated their communications schedule for after their return to London.

C3&0

The response from the lab was short and formal: fingerprints of two different persons were found on parts in the interior of the device that killed Professor Allier. None of these fingerprints were on file. On one hand, Commissaire Duval was glad that he had approached Jules Racine—his hunch had proved correct. On the other hand, there was no way he could discover to whom these fingerprints belonged. The owners of those prints weren't involved in any crime in France—of that much he was sure. So they could be foreigners, too. He couldn't very well turn to MacLeod at Scotland Yard again—there were limits, after all. But the thought of testing the fingerprints against those of Sir Cedric Norton had crossed his mind. *Ridiculous*, he thought, *a respectable gentleman like him would not be handling technical trifles such as these. And yet ....*

He decided to sleep on it.

## FIFTY-FOUR

The four board members convened at Admiral Stone's suite at the Sheraton Towers in Brussels. Their arrivals were spaced just minutes apart. Martin was the last to arrive. He found the others already seated in a semicircle, and he shook their hands one by one. Anne held out a limp hand and avoided looking into his eyes. Of course, he wouldn't dream of kissing her here. The admiral offered drinks all round.

"We have quite a number of topics on the agenda today," Anne began. "First, we'll hear Martin's report on his trip to Iran. Then Sir Cedric will tell us of his meeting with Rosetti. The admiral will inform us what's new in the field of fertilizer and gravel. And we'll revive the issue of the need for a hacker to invade targeted computers. We will not need another confirmation for Martin's next trip to Korea." She looked at him blankly. "When notification arrives, you'll take off ASAP." She gazed around the room again. "As for me, unfortunately I cannot report anything at all. Monsieur Boulanger is away on holiday. Martin, the floor is yours."

Martin briefly described the touristic side of the trip, and quickly came to the main point.

"The Azadi Square is a huge oval about four hundred by three hundred meters. With the surrounding ring road, the area is trebled. It, and the adjacent streets, can contain several hundred thousands of people. It is located outside the city—on the way to the airport—and therefore does not have many buildings nearby. We might face some difficulty in placing our acoustic Paganinis in place.

"The other thing that bothered me was how to get our stuff into the country. Subsequently we'll also need to store it, and find the people to do the necessary planting of whatever we bring in. Who will do the work?"

"By your tone," Sir Cedric said, "I'm sure you already have an answer."

"Well, perhaps just a suggestion. We noticed—and the tour guide confirmed this indirectly—that there is some criticism directed against the leadership. We can see it in the press, too. I thought we might try and meet up with Iranian emigrants in Europe."

"I suppose they *could* give us some more inside information," the admiral said.

"That's only part of it," Martin continued. "The main thing, I think, is that they may have connections with underground factions *inside* Iran. And those are the people who should 'do the work.'"

"Interesting concept," the admiral said. "Worthwhile considering."

"Do you totally exclude the possibility that we, as tourists, could do the job?" Sir Cedric asked. "After all, we're a bit more reliable, I should think."

"He's right, Martin," the admiral concurred. "How much of a difference would it make if *we* did it? Would we be so conspicuous? For instance, how are tourists treated at the passport control and luggage checking in Iran?"

"Quite normal. I couldn't see anything irregular about them. True, there are a handful of men who just loll around, watching other people go about their business. I really couldn't swear that these were security personnel, but that's the impression they gave me. However, foreigners stick out like the proverbial sore thumb. Their dress is in sharp contrast to the locals'—especially the local women, who are covered from head to toe in their tent-like chadors. A foreigner will always be noticed and eyes will always follow him or her."

It was clear to all that tourists would not be able to carry out an operational mission in Iran.

"Gentlemen," Anne said. "Let us all pick up on Martin's suggestion regarding the finding of Iranian expatriates. Each of us will try to get information on this topic. However, may I remind you, please, that no contact is to be established without this forum's specific approval."

Anne gestured toward Sir Cedric, who reported on his conversation with Rosetti.

"That's very good news, Sir Cedric," Martin said. "Significantly reducing the size of the acoustic devices will be a boon for us. Did he say when he'd be ready with them?"

"A couple of weeks. Knowing him he'll have several Paganinis ready by then!"

It was now the admiral's turn. All he had to say was that Lemke was working on another approach to the fertilizer and gravel problem.

"He agrees that the way his inventions are at the moment is not suitable for our purposes," the admiral concluded. "I hope we'll have results from him soon."

"Please follow that up, admiral," Anne said. "Now, what about our computer whiz?"

Sir Cedric shook his head. Martin shrugged.

"I have a grandson," the admiral said slowly. "He is seventeen years old, and has some knowledge of computers. As far as his parents—my son and his wife—are concerned, he spends *all* of his time by the computer. That alone, in their book, qualifies him as a freak. I cannot vouch for any of his capabilities, however. I'll try to see what he can contribute on hacker information."

"Good luck, admiral," Anne said, smiling.

The same departure ritual was now repeated. Anne reiterated that she was not to be contacted, and that all communications were to be delivered through the admiral. Again, she left first after instructing them to leave one by one.

And again, Martin couldn't find her when he got to the hotel's main doors. He wanted to see her, hold her, embrace and kiss her, give her the present he bought for her in Shiraz—and she was deliberately avoiding him. Why? Yes, he could very easily answer this question by breaking the rule she had imposed on them. He could just call her, and to hell with the ramifications. But military discipline overcame this urge, and with an effort, he restrained himself.

He decided to catch the next plane to London.

It couldn't be just the Allier investigation, Martin thought in the taxi on the way to the Brussels-Zaventem Airport. That's a dead end, and she knows it. And the association's progress is smooth enough—no worries there. So that leaves the Tanya murder case …

*My god!*

*She's going to do something on her own. She doesn't want me to interfere—perhaps even to stop her! But what is she planning? The only lead she had was …*

*MY GOD!!*

*She's going to rue Saint-Denis again! Alone!*

"Driver!" he shouted. "Forget the airport. Take me to the train station. Hurry!"

⊰⊱

Philip Brown was busy in London making the final preparations for Martin's next trip to Seoul. He had already registered a fictitious import-export business, Ascromex International Trade Ltd., in London, giving the 'cowshed's' address as its location. He opened a bank account for the new firm, and ordered stationery with a fancy letterhead. Now Martin would be able to instruct Charlie or Sing in Seoul to send orders for products to this company. The shipments would, therefore, be perfectly legitimate—even though their contents were legally questionable. From Seoul, however, it would be up to Sing to complete the delivery to North Korea.

⊰⊱

Martin's left the Gare du Nord railway station in Paris and took the metro to rue Saint-Denis. He sauntered down the brightly lit street with the dim doorways, trying to look like a potential customer. There were many other men doing exactly the same, so Martin did not feel so conspicuous.

"Why don't you come with me, *chéri?*"

A woman in her early thirties, in black netting stockings, short skirt, and heavy makeup had just linked her arm into his.

"Thank you, not tonight, mademoiselle. I am actually looking for Ninette." Martin was surprised at how easily he managed the conversation.

"Would that be *la grande Ninette?*"

"No. She's the blonde with the ponytail."

The woman pointed across the street.

"Perhaps in there," she said noncommittally, disengaged herself and walked away.

"Thank you," Martin murmured to her back, and approached the building. Three girls leaned against the doorway. None of them matched the description he had given. One of the girls detached herself from the group and walked toward him, smiling.

"Where's Ninette?" he asked her.

"She has a guest right now," she said. "But I'm available. How about it?"

Martin smiled back at her.

"Maybe some other time," he said. He made a note of the hotel's address and made his way back to the metro station.

*This is no place for Anne to come alone,* he thought. *Under* any *circumstances! I must find a way to prevent her.*

CRRED

Back at the London gym, Martin and Spencer Partridge began preparing for their third visit to South Korea. At the same time, Martin wanted to start the ball rolling concerning Iranian underground groups.

He had given the idea much thought. A couple roaming the Iranian restaurants of London would probably be the easiest way to begin. And Patricia would be just the girl to be half of that couple. He called her on her cellphone and set up a luncheon meeting at a London café.

There was still one thing to do before meeting Patricia. Martin called Bernard Webb and George Graham into his office.

"Lads," he said, "I need to find a computer hacker."

Bernard and George looked at each other. Another 'mysterious' assignment.

"Look," George said, "I'm pretty good with computers. Perhaps I could help. I once programmed—"

"Can you infiltrate into other computer systems?" Martin interrupted.

"Well, if they're protected, it would take some time."

"Thanks, George, but that's not good enough. I need someone who does this on a daily basis. Someone who can get through the toughest firewalls and security systems. Know anyone like that? Bernard?" They shook their heads. "Then find me someone. And soon."

CఇఠO

Martin took the subway into central London, where he was to meet Patricia. She was waiting for him, all smiles. Muffins and coffee were on the table.

"Good of you to come on such short notice," Martin said.

"Your offers always sound so enticing."

"Well, I hope you didn't find our last trip too tiring."

"Quite the contrary. Shiraz and Persepolis were somewhat grueling, but that didn't mean I didn't enjoy myself."

"I'd like you to do another task for us. Here in London."

"Oh, dear." Patricia acted out the disappointed schoolchild. "You're not sending me to bring penguins from the South Pole? Or a genuine Inca skull from Peru? I am truly devastated." She grinned.

Martin grinned back and took a bite of a muffin. He started to get up.

"Well, I'll just have to find someone else, then ..."

They both burst out laughing.

"Tell me about this London caper," Patricia said when they had calmed down.

"After our trip to Iran, we arrived at the conclusion that we could not do the job there ourselves. The risks involved in bringing our stuff into the country, distributing it and operating it, are just too high. We'll need local people to do these things."

"I thought you didn't know anyone there. Otherwise, we would have met them on our trip, wouldn't we?"

"You're right, we don't. But there are many Iranian émigrés in Europe—even here in London. Most of them oppose the current regime in Iran. And some of these opposers may actually be *doing* something about it."

"Like organizing underground movements?"

"Clever girl. And these organizations would probably have associates back in Iran."

"Makes sense," Patricia said.

"We want to make contact with these expatriates. Through them, we want to get the local Iranian underground—and believe me, it's there—to cooperate with us. As we do not employ warlike measures, there's a good chance we'll succeed."

"That's a tall order. How do you think I should go about it?"

"You won't be alone. We think it best if a couple visits places where Iranians tend to congregate. We cannot very well enter their mosques, but they *do* have restaurants open to the public, which are frequented by the Iranian populace. The couple would try to make friends, sympathize, strike up relationships—in short, build a stable contact."

"And then?"

"We'll play it by ear. You'll be gathering a lot of information, which we'll use to plan our next steps."

"Sounds all right. Who is to be my partner?"

Martin smiled.

"John Carmichael," he said, looking at her intently.

For the first time, Patricia looked startled, and she squirmed uncomfortably. She was not used to feeling awkward.

Patricia and John had been an item several years ago, before Malcolm Welles came into the picture and swept her off her feet. She had met John through her brother, George. They had a short, but torrid, affair, which was cut short by Malcolm's arrival and his dazzling charm. Malcolm was a mistake, of course, and her divorce soon after their marriage was an attempt to rectify this. But ever since then, she had avoided all contact with John, and George respected her embarrassment by not mentioning him. *Martin must have known*, she thought. *Nothing escapes him. Is he deliberately trying to get us together again?*

She made up her mind.

"All right," she said.

⋇

Commissaire Duval could not track Sir Cedric Norton in London. He had already used up all the hospitality that his friendship with Assistant Commissioner MacLeod would allow. Furthermore, he could not know when Sir Cedric arrived in Paris—dedicating huge resources to check all arrivals by air or by train would draw attention, something he wished to avoid at all costs.

But tracking Professeur Anne Dupré was another story. He had Inspecteur Marnier stake out her house and report where she went and whom she met. Thus, he discovered that she had made two train trips—one northbound and the other southbound, with her children.

To the south was a dead end—her late husband's parents lived there, and it was perfectly natural for her children to visit their grandparents. The northbound train, however, was an enigma. It passed through Belgium and the Netherlands, and she could have disembarked anywhere. Naturally, he could not order Marnier to follow her out of the country and find out her destination.

*Back to the good old days*, Duval thought. *I'll just have to follow her myself.*

He instructed Marnier to keep watch on the Professeur's house, to follow her to the train station, and to inform him the minute she did so. Duval's intention was to wait until she took a northbound train, then board it himself and note where she got off. If this occurred while still within France, there would be no problem in having her followed. And if she alighted in Brussels, for example, he would request immediate assistance of his Belgian colleagues in picking up a pursuit begun earlier in Paris.

Now all he had to do was wait for the opportunity.

⋇

Once again, Anne located an empty office at the university and used the phone on the desk to call Alfred Boulanger.

"My dear Anne! I thought you had forgotten me."

"Please forgive me, Alfred. I've been terribly busy. In fact, some of my busy time was discussing with my colleagues the possibilities your satellite affords."

"Yes. I was wondering what became of your plans."

"I'd like to talk about them with you."

"Could it wait for a few days, Anne? I have a three-day conference in Lyon starting tomorrow. After that, I'd be happy to—"

"You know what, Alfred? I'd be happy for a change in atmosphere. How about we meet in Lyon tomorrow, during you lunch break?"

Boulanger was delighted. They set up the location and the hour, and Anne left the office without being seen.

## FIFTY-FIVE

Martin Cooper and Spencer Partridge arrived in Seoul for the third time. During the flight, Spencer kept thinking of his good fortune in hooking up with Martin after being discharged from the army. Not only did he have a job with a decent income, he now also had these unexpected opportunities to visit far-off places and carry out exciting missions.

Martin thought of Anne. It had been weeks since they had been alone together. On two occasions, they had spent hours in conference with the board, and he had avoided looking her in the eyes because he felt she preferred not to meet his gaze. He thought of various excuses—the Allier investigation and Duval's audacity must surely have had an effect on the behavior of a woman as sensitive and fragile as Anne. But then, if that were the case, wouldn't finding solace in Martin's arms be the first option to take? But the decision had been made, and he felt sure it was the right one—he wouldn't call Anne until those issues had blown over. *That's it, then*, he thought. *Quit moping. You have a job to do.*

CS80

Inspecteur Marnier was fed up with the odd assignments delegated to him by Commissaire Duval. True, Duval was his superior, but Marnier had this growing suspicion that not all was as it appeared, and that the commissaire had ulterior motives behind his actions.

He had just followed Anne Dupré to the Gare de Lyon. He called Duval and reported.

"She's going south again," he said. "Probably meeting with her in-laws...."

The commissaire didn't like this at all. She was there with her children just a short while ago. It could certainly be that one of the elder Duprés had taken ill, but Duval was not one to dawdle when a quick decision needed to be made.

"Get on that train, Marnier," he ordered. "Make sure of where she goes. If you notice the slightest variation in her behavior, call me at once!"

The Inspecteur just barely managed to catch the train. He found a seat in the carriage behind the one carrying Anne, and at every stop he had to open the carriage door, lean out and make sure she hadn't got off.

To his surprise, she alighted at Lyon.

Marnier took care not to be seen by Anne as he followed her off the pier. Outside the station, he saw her get into a taxi. By the time he caught another one, Anne was out of sight. Frustrated, he called the commissaire.

Duval was furious by Marnier's report. He summoned the inspecteur back to the office in Paris. When he calmed down, the commissaire tried to work things out rationally. He still came up with no results. *I have nothing on her,* he thought. *In fact, I am probably doing her a great disservice. And yet ... I cannot quit now after investing so much effort. No, not yet. Something unexpected, extraordinary, should happen. Another murder, maybe, or an anonymous letter with a lead. Just a little bit more....*

CR80

Anne asked the taxi driver to drop her off at the Lyon City Hall. She walked directly to the ladies' rest room and waited inside a stall for three minutes. On exiting, no suspicious persons were in view. She left the building, got into a taxi, and requested to go to the Lyon Cathedral. Halfway there she informed the driver that she had forgotten something at City Hall and would he please take her back.

From within City Hall she looked out onto the street. No suspicious followers. If Inspecteur Marnier had followed her to Lyon, she would have seen him following her taxi to the cathedral. She then went to keep her appointment with Boulanger at the Place Bellecour.

The square was an immense rectangle, and Café Bellecour was neatly tucked onto one of its sides. It was relatively quiet despite being located in the center of the city. Alfred Boulanger rose to greet her with an outstretched hand and a smile. He had on a business suit, and a large conference badge—with his name emblazoned on it—was hanging from his neck. A briefcase was on the floor beside his chair.

"How are you, my dear? You look a bit tired. I know, train rides do that to me, too."

"I'm fine, Alfred, really. But you're right about the train ride. And how are you doing?"

"Fine, fine." He signaled the waitress and they ordered lunch.

"How is our satellite doing?" Anne asked.

"Better than you after a train ride," Boulanger joked. "It's up there in the sky, doing its commercial tasks to perfection. And it has its little extra something on board just waiting to be tested. A dry run, of course. We must be sure that the laser beam can be accurately aimed at any target. You realize, don't you, that our aiming apparatus is unique?"

"I was hoping you would explain that to me," Anne said with a smile.

"This is not a case of marking a target for a guided missile. We are not concerned with rockets and trajectories. We have our laser-beam generator *in* the satellite that, because of its distance, needs an extremely precise aiming mechanism."

"How precise is that?"

"You know, of course, that coordinates on the globe are measured in degrees, minutes and seconds. Well, one second of latitude is approximately equal to thirty meters. If the coordinates you provide me are accurate within a tenth of a second, I can guarantee a laser hit within five to ten meters, provided the target is within the hundred kilometer square view port of the satellite."

"That's ten thousand square kilometers. Very impressive, indeed. How do you aim the laser?"

"Through the control panel in my office. All the commands to the satellite, and laser beam, originate there."

"And how portable is this console of yours? I mean, could we have one and operate it ourselves from London or New York?"

Boulanger laughed.

"Actually, it's a pretty sophisticated computer that I use for all my other projects, too. I just added whatever was necessary to accommodate our little project as well. I'm sorry, Anne, but you would need a three-story building and two years' work, not to mention several million euros, to duplicate the console anywhere else."

"Just a thought." Anne smiled. "Please continue."

"Once I get the coordinates of the target, I feed them into the console. As the number of digits is quite large, maybe ten digits per coordinate, they need to be verified, in case a mistake has been made. One verification is by you or your representative. He or she will need to confirm the 'readback' of the coordinates, digit by digit. The second verification is for me—the location of the coordinates will show up on a map on my console."

"Why?"

"No offense, my dear, but I *must* be sure that your coordinates don't point to Paris or any other inhabited location on our planet. *You* could have given mistaken coordinates just as easily as I could enter them incorrectly. Both verifications need to comply with each other."

"You think of everything, don't you?" Anne was inwardly very pleased that she was in the presence of such a cautious man.

"I do my best," Boulanger said simply. "Mind you, I do not have all the answers yet. The aiming mechanism has not been tested, and the effect of the laser on the target is still unknown, though that part is none of my business."

"So now you want me to tell you where the experimental target is located, right?"

"However did you guess that?" Boulanger laughed. "Very well, here are our possibilities. Our satellite orbits the earth from southwest to northeast. It passes over the Sahara desert in southern Morocco, northern Mauritania, Algeria, Libya, northern Egypt, Iraq, Iran, Afghanistan, China, North Korea, northern Japan, the

Pacific Ocean, Central America, the southern Atlantic and back to Morocco. The entire cycle takes one hundred and thirty two minutes."

Anne did some quick figuring.

"That means that the satellite will be over the same spot about ten times a day," she said.

"That's right," Boulanger confirmed. He reached into his briefcase on the floor and took out a square envelope.

"This DVD contains all the technical information you need. Please do *not* allow it to fall into unauthorized hands. Not that they would make any sense of it—but just to be on the safe side. You can easily plot the orbit of the satellite on a map of the world. It also has a built-in formula that makes a two-way calculation: feed it coordinates and a date and you'll get back the precise hours the satellite will be above that location. And vice versa—feed it a date and time, and you'll get the coordinates of the location directly below the satellite. Pretty straightforward, actually."

"This really looks fantastic," Anne said enthusiastically. "I'll get my people to find some deserted place along the satellite's path to carry out the experiment. We shall need a couple of weeks for that, perhaps more. Why don't I call you in a week and let you know where things stand?"

"All I need are the exact GPS coordinates," Boulanger reminded her. "I'll do the rest."

Anne arrived at the Lyon railway station and called the admiral. They set up a meeting in London during the weekend.

## FIFTY-SIX

Martin and Spencer had a good night's sleep. Next morning they rented a car, drove around Seoul for a while and then made their way northward.

Charlie welcomed them warmly.

"Come in, come in," he urged, practically pushing them into the restaurant.

Once seated, Charlie placed cold beers in front of them.

"When do you think we'll be able to see Sing?" Martin asked.

"He'll be here for lunch," Charlie answered.

"That's good. Do you have any idea what the situation in North Korea is? I mean, in regard to our project?"

"All I can say is that there seems to be quite a healthy response over there. Sing will fill you in with all the details."

They whiled away the time discussing various topics. They didn't get very far when local politics were raised.

"South Korea is an industrialized nation with a flourishing economy," Charlie said. "One really cannot complain. On the other hand, the social front and the integrity of our leadership leave a lot to be desired. You noticed, I am sure, that nothing came of the meeting between the North and South Korean leaders—just as I predicted."

It was clear that Charlie felt uncomfortable criticizing his government. Martin and Spencer both knew that South Korea was one of the most corrupt nations on the planet. They quickly changed the topic.

Sing arrived, punctual as ever, with his usual smile from ear to ear. They toasted their reunion. Once again, Charlie led them into his house to continue their discussions.

"Let's get down to business, then," Martin said. "What can you tell us, Sing?"

"We've done quite a lot since last you were here," Sing said. "Most of the people we approached in North Korea responded enthusiastically."

"Great," Spencer said. "But what about those who responded negatively? They could expose us, couldn't they?"

"We thought about that. Before telling anyone anything of a revealing nature, we checked out his, or her, background. We use very stringent screening methods—take my word for it. You may rest assured that nobody who now knows anything will turn out to be an informer."

"And are any of your recruits in a position to be of operational assistance" Martin asked.

Sing smiled.

"Three of them are caretakers at the Pyongyang Municipality. Their job requires them to push wheelbarrows full of gardening materials and carry buckets of paint, pesticides or other liquids. They go all over the city, carrying out their regular maintenance duties. They have small sheds near the various parks and gardens where they can store their equipment."

"Sounds fantastic!" Martin grinned.

"I must warn you, however, that they informed me that the day before the parade, the entire route of the procession will be swept, hosed, and scrubbed so clean you could eat off it. Anything you want placed there will be completely washed away."

Martin expected that. He prayed Lemke's spray would solve this problem.

"I see," he said. "That probably negates the need for the fertilizer. What about military campsites?"

It seemed Sing's smile widened, though that was physically impossible.

"I was coming to that. Not far from Pyongyang there is a military base in which all the parade vehicles will be gathered—trucks, armor and low loaders to tow the missiles. They'll all arrive there a few days before the event."

"Did they see any fuel depots in this base?"

"Yes, they did. They saw several huge fuel reservoirs. However, they couldn't tell whether the vehicles were to be fueled from them, or that they arrived already tanked up."

"It seems, Sing, that the time has come to reveal to you another of our little tricks."

Martin described the fuel pellets, and enjoyed watching Sing's expression change from that of a bridegroom to one of amazement.

"So, Sing, we obviously need someone who could drop our little neutralizers into these reservoirs without raising suspicion."

Sing was beaming again.

"This is very good," he said. "I'll look into it."

"And the vehicles themselves could also be 'treated,'" Martin added. "One pellet in the fuel tank and the vehicle doesn't go anywhere."

"Good, good," Sing said. "Let us now fix up a more secure method of communications between us."

"It's already been done. We have a commercial company in London." Martin handed Sing a business card. "See? Name, address, phone, fax, email—all there. We'll set up an order together—you'll wish to purchase such and such an amount of merchandise (freely available on the market) that resembles our stuff. You'll prepare a Letter of Credit. We'll ship you the materials the same way all markets operate. Everything is aboveboard."

"Sounds all right to me," Sing said. "Charlie?"

Charlie nodded. He put down two business cards of his own on the table.

"We, too, have a legitimate trading company," he said. "All the details are on the card."

"There's one more thing," Martin said, pocketing one card and giving the other to Spencer. "Our tranquilizing gravel."

"Excuse me?" Charlie said.

"Huh?" Sing said.

Martin told them about the soporific effect of the gas when released from the pebbles. They listened in awe.

"We'll add that to the order. And the audio disruptors as well."

"That's quite a lot of sophisticated, unfamiliar stuff you're dumping on us," Sing said. "Flattering though your trust in us may be, we'll need some time to acquaint ourselves with the various items."

"We wouldn't have it any other way," Martin laughed. "I shall be here when the shipment arrives. You'll bring along your best men—those who can later teach others—and I shall train you all on each of the 'various items' you mentioned."

Charlie brought another round of beers.

"Time to make out the order," Martin said. "Charlie, you'll have it converted to the local legal format later. Let's see now ..."

They worked out an order for mosaic stones, that is to say, the tranquilizing gravel, and a sample of pea seeds—the fuel pellets.

"Leave out the acoustic disruptors. We'll add in a few as a bonus sample for your testing, with a request to return them to us if they do not meet your needs."

They agreed that phone calls could be made to Charlie's restaurant, and the Koreans could leave messages at the "cowshed."

க்ஜ்ஜ்

Anne rehearsed the preparations needed for the satellite test.

*First, find an uninhabited region on the path of the satellite's orbit. There may be many, so they'll need to be investigated for an abandoned building of some sort. Then we'll need to place a machine in this building, something with a motor that works—I suppose Cedric will want to know whether or not it runs properly after the test. Martin's boys can do all that. What else would we need to simulate a target? Ah, yes, a concrete ceiling.*

*Cedric will have to answer some questions, too—how tight is the laser beam from the distance of the satellite? How much separating concrete can it penetrate? How about other shielding materials, such as earth or lead. Does the motor have to run on fuel or is an electric motor just as vulnerable?*

*Oh, dear. This will probably be the most complicated experiment yet.*

## FIFTY-SEVEN

Patricia Welles came over to the gym to meet with John Carmichael, her old flame. John was waiting at the doorway and escorted her inside. She waved to the other members of the team, but as they were busy with customers, they just grinned and waved back.

"How are you doing, Pat?" John felt awkward in her presence. He had never stopped loving her. When Martin offered him the assignment with her, he had hesitated at first, cursed himself for being a fool, and then consented wholeheartedly.

Patricia was no less embarrassed. She knew she would be, but that didn't help much when the moment of truth came.

"I'm fine, Johnny. And you?" She was the only person he had allowed to call him by that name. She hoped he wouldn't resent it now.

"Can't complain," he said. He took a deep breath. "It's been a long time since I've been addressed by that name and not corrected its user."

"I was hoping you wouldn't mind," she said softly. "Now—what are we supposed to be doing on our mission?"

John shrugged his shoulders.

"I suppose Martin told you exactly what he told me. Make contact with Iranians in London. If we run into any trouble, contact the admiral—as Martin is away for about a week. So, in the words of the immortal Hercule Poirot, let us exercise our little grey cells."

"Do you know of any place where Iranians congregate?"

"Sorry, no. But we have a computer here—let's surf the Internet a bit."

They found Iranian associations, community centers, schools, bookshops—and restaurants. This seemed most attractive to them both.

"Let's not take one of the posh ones," John said. "It'll be harder to strike up a casual conversation there."

"So we're looking for a more down-to-earth type restaurant. Perhaps we could tell by the size of the advertisement?"

"Makes sense. But we're not limited to only one restaurant. Let's begin by visiting the one that is closest. Okay with you?"

The Bita "genuine Iranian food" restaurant was just ten minutes' walk away. It was quite large, with typical Iranian decorations on the walls. Blue was the dominant color throughout. Only one table was occupied: a couple eating dishes piled with a kind of steamy stew.

They walked to an empty table and sat down. A waiter materialized beside them instantly and laid two menus on the table.

"May I get you something to drink?" he asked.

"Beers for both of us," John said.

"Yes, sir. Would you like to taste our Iranian beer?"

"Certainly," Patricia said. "We're here for Iranian food, so we'll have Iranian beer to go with it. I assume it is non-alcoholic."

The waiter grinned.

"You are absolutely right, Miss. Perhaps the young lady learned this on a visit to Iran?"

Patricia turned to take a good look at him. He was tall and thin, with slick black hair and a weak chin. He resembled a droopy scarecrow in his Iranian waiter's uniform.

"As a matter of fact," she said, "I have just returned from a glorious trip to Iran. What a marvelous country."

"You are very lucky. Unfortunately, I cannot return there."

"Really?" Patricia eyes opened innocently. "Why not? Is there a problem?"

"It's a good place for tourists. But for an Iranian who does not bow his head, there could be great danger. I shall fetch your drinks now, and you will choose your lunch."

When he had left, Patricia leaned toward John.

"We probably won't have to look for them, "she whispered. "They'll come to us."

"Let's not jump the gun, Patty," John said. "Take it easy. Let's enjoy our meal first."

The menu offered dishes that Patricia remembered from the restaurants she had visited in Tehran. Then she had an idea.

"Let's ask the waiter to recommend a typical Iranian meal," she suggested.

"Right you are."

The waiter returned with the Iranian beer.

"What would you suggest for an authentic Iranian lunch?" John asked him.

The waiter smiled, somewhat embarrassed.

"You might not like it," he said.

"Nonsense," John insisted. "Just make sure it's authentic and tasty."

The waiter nodded and went to the kitchen. Fifteen minutes later, he returned with two plates, which he placed before them. He pointed to one.

"This is kebab koobideh. You won't find this in many places in London. It is our specialty. And *this* is our best stew, khoresht fesenjan. It has pomegranates in it, also rather rare on London."

Patricia had tasted other stews in Iran, but not this one. She found it delicious. The kebab and the side dishes were all familiar to her. They both enjoyed their lunch heartily. The waiter served them as if they were royalty.

Before asking for the bill, Patricia said:

"Well, what do you say? He could be our first recruit. At least as a yardstick to compare with other candidates."

"We'll leave him a large tip," John said. "When we return here, we'll be old friends, and we can pick up from there." He wiggled his finger in the air at the waiter for the bill.

Patricia smiled dazzlingly at the waiter as he laid the saucer with the bill and two sweets on the table.

"What's your name?"

"Farhad, Miss," he answered.

She held out her hand.

"My name is Patricia, and this is my friend John," she said.

He shook both their hands warmly.

"Do you work here every day?" Patricia asked. "We enjoyed our meal very much, and would like to return here. And we'd like *you* to recommend our meal to us."

"Every day except Friday."

"Evenings, too?"

"Yes. Afternoons and evenings."

They left an enormous tip and went outside. They both felt they had not wasted the association's money. This was a definite successful first attempt at making contact with an Iranian who didn't seem to like what was going on in Iran. Of course, they had other Iranian restaurants they had to try out, too.

⊗⊗⊘

Even though Anne knew that Commissaire Duval had no jurisdiction outside France, she still employed evasive measures on her way to the admiral's office in London. It was one of those weekends she visited her family in Reading, but the meeting with the admiral was imperative.

"Can you imagine that?" she told the admiral. "That blackguard, Duval, has even put a watch outside my house in Paris. I have lots of fun shaking him off, even when I'm on my way to the university."

"Have you considered that the commissaire may interpret your shenanigans as admitting that you have something to hide? That you're truly up to something illegal?"

Anne thought a bit.

"Frankly, no," she admitted. "Probably poor judgment on my part. I hope my behavior looked innocent and natural. But I *had* to take evasive action when I went to meet with Boulanger."

"Of course. That was different."

Anne gave Boulanger's DVD to the admiral. She described her initial plans for the experiment—the location along the orbit, the questions for Sir Cedric, the motor to be beamed, etc.

"We'll probably need to register another commercial company as our cover for the test. And it will be your job to supervise the team running it."

"I'll look into it. As you know, I have my sources of information. But I can tell you that a desert region will not be suitable because of the lack of buildings. And even if we did find one, we'd have a hard time explaining what we Westerners are doing there. We could, of course, make another movie. We'd still need to explain why we're putting a lorry or bulldozer into the building."

"So?"

"So be patient while I do my background research. It seems likely that we'll need to send out preliminary expeditions to the best candidate locations along Boulanger's itinerary. I'll consult with Martin—he should be back from Korea any day now."

"Well," Anne said, getting to her feet, "It's your baby now. I need to get to my children and parents, and catch up on my rest."

She felt relieved. Some of the onus of responsibility had been lifted off her shoulders.

CB&D

The children were upstairs in bed. Professor Cooper also felt he should retire early that evening. Anne and her mother chatted in the kitchen.

"You know, Annie," Mrs. Cooper said, "there's something I've been wanting to ask you for some time, now."

"No, mum, I'm not getting married again," Anne said lightheartedly. "Every few months you ask me the same question."

"And you always give me the same answer," her mother smiled. "But no, Annie. I wanted to ask something else. I'm worried about you."

Anne was on the alert immediately. Was she that transparent?

"Whatever makes you say that?" she asked.

"I'm your mother, Annie. Your being a grown woman with children does nothing to change that fact. You know as well as I do that mothers have an acute sensitivity about anything concerning their children. And I can clearly see that something has come over you. You're different from what you used to be, and you've told me nothing of your own volition. So I'm asking you outright— what's the matter with you?"

Anne made a feeble attempt to brush her mother off.

"It's nothing important, mum. I'm just tired …"

"Stop that, Annie. You don't fool me one bit. At first, I thought you were in love. Then I got the impression that it was something else. Am I wrong?"

Anne dropped her gaze. She couldn't hide anything from her mother.

"No, mum, you're very observant," she said. Then, as carefully as she could, she confessed. "I met someone. I stupidly thought that I had found happiness again. I was mistaken. It still smarts, mum, and I would rather not talk about it, if it's all the same to you."

There followed a long pause.

"And?" Mrs. Cooper prodded.

Anne was about to say "and nothing," but instead sighed and said:

"Yes, there's more. A pig-headed French police officer is giving me no rest. He believes that I am somehow involved in Tanya's murder. He has a detective outside my house who follows my every move. It's awful. Naturally, I look different, though I'm doing my utmost to ignore that aspect of my life."

Mrs. Cooper's face revealed that Anne's answer did not satisfy her, but she said nothing. There'd be time enough to catch up on this issue later.

"I think I'll go to bed now," Anne said, kissed her mother goodnight and went upstairs.

## FIFTY-EIGHT

Martin and Spencer had returned from Seoul, pleased with their achievements. Martin set up a meeting with the admiral, and they met in the latter's office. After toasting Martin's return with a shot of whisky, Admiral Stone listened carefully to his report.

"Spencer and I sincerely believe," Martin concluded, "that Sing is a loyal and trustworthy partner. Despite his being a smuggler, he is also a devoted patriot, and he would do anything to topple the North Korean tyrant."

Martin went on to describe the methods they employed for the shipping of the materials and the training of their use—which shouldn't take more than three or four days.

"Quite a nice job you did there," the admiral said admiringly. "Frankly, I believed it would take much longer. Have you seen John yet?"

"I got a very short report from him over the phone, on the Iranian dissidents' situation. I've fixed a debriefing meeting with him for tomorrow."

"We have a new mission on our hands now—testing 'wasp.' I mean Sir Cedric's laser beam inside Boulanger's satellite. It's orbiting us as we speak, and we need to set up an experiment to see that it works as designed."

"And *that*, if I remember correctly, is to neutralize machinery by beaming them with the laser. Preferably a nuclear reactor."

"Right. Boulanger met with Anne in Lyon and gave her this DVD with all the information we need on the satellite's orbit."

"Shouldn't pose much of a problem," Martin said, taking the envelope.

The admiral laughed.

"You'll change your mind when you look at the geography involved. We'll need to find a suitable location somewhere along a path several thousand kilometers long, crossing all of Africa and Asia."

Martin whistled.

"Let's assume for now that we have a suitable location," he said. "How do we simulate a nuclear reactor there?"

"Well, that's for Sir Cedric to advise. But I believe that if we have any kind of building it could serve as a bunker. We could add extra layers of concrete if Sir Cedric thinks it necessary."

"And the machinery itself?"

"Again—that's Sir Cedric's call. I think any old vehicle will do. As long as it runs. What we need to do now is plot out the itinerary of the satellite on the map. I'll get some up-to-date maps, geological data, and satellite photography from the admiralty. It'll be your team's job to find an isolated place along this path for the experiment."

"What do you want geological maps for?" Martin wondered.

"Who knows? They're available, and we might find something interesting there. Now go and get updated on the Iranian front. I'm off to the admiralty."

CR80

Anne's routine work continued as usual. All her activities with the association took place when she had no other academic obligations, such as lectures and exams. None of her university colleagues had the least suspicion that she was occupied with anything outside her normal, scholarly life. Yet this supplementary work amounted to just regular board meeting, two meetings with Boulanger, one with Dodson, and several hours of intense thinking.

Over the past weeks, she felt somewhat idle—the association's matters were now in the hands of the good Admiral Stone, and thanks to Duval's pestering, she was doing less of her regular routine. In retrospect, before becoming involved with the association and the police, *this* was her life! And she had not considered herself bored at the time—on the contrary, she thought she was a very busy woman.

Apparently, with the right incentive, you could do much more than you imagined you could. *And all this had started about a year ago with a simple challenge by a student in one of my classes.* It reminded her of a Till Eulenspiegel story in which a windborne feather hits the right place and pandemonium ensues.

Anne hadn't seen Inspecteur Marnier outside her house for a couple of days now. Had the commissaire concluded that she could not lead to the solution of his problem? Or that she wasn't worth the while and effort? Perhaps he had more important and urgent cases to attend? And did that mean she was off the hook? Could she now return to "active duty" with the association? Maybe that was exactly what that crafty Duval *wanted* her to think? So that he could apprehend her when her guard was down? Apprehend her for what? Did he think she would lead him to Allier's killer?

*What a lot of question!* she thought. *All speculations! Better wait a bit and see. But having 'nothing' to do is really tiresome.*

*Nothing? Tanya's murderer is still out there somewhere. The police have totally abandoned the case. The only lead I have is that the killer's girlfriend works in rue Saint-Denis. So, that's where I'm going, too. But I can't go looking like this—I have to dress differently. How about as a man? Forget it, everyone would see right through the disguise. How about an elderly woman: a lawyer or a social worker? Hmm, could work. Still, I need different clothes for the role. So—let's go shopping!*

A hop to the Galeries Lafayette took care of her needs. Back at home she surveyed her "harvest"—a grey suit with a skirt below the knees, a masculine shirt and tie, low-heeled leather shoes, glasses with thick, dark rims, a tough, plastic briefcase suitable for carrying under her armpit *very businesslike*, she thought, and, for security's sake, a stun gun.

Donning her new outfit, Anne looked at herself in the mirror. *Too new-looking*, she thought. She took off her shirt and skirt, deliberately crumpled them a bit, and put them on again. *There—that's better*. Next came a heavy layer of face cream, covered by lots of face powder—the way older women attempt to hide their wrinkles. She put on the glasses and faced the mirror again. *Not bad, not bad. The hair isn't okay, though*. Anne coiled her hair into a bun and used several hairpins to keep it in place. She slipped the stun gun into her waistband, where it would be concealed by the suit jacket.

Next, she transferred her cellular phone from her bag into a pocket of her jacket. Over her objections, Martin had bought one for her a few months ago. *You don't have to use it,* he had said. *I promise never to call you on it, either, or give anyone the number. But I insist you have a method of summoning assistance in an emergency. Here, look.* Martin coded it so that a long press on the digit 9 would dial the police. *That's all,* he said. *Keep it charged at night, and carry it with you wherever you go. I put it on silent, so you won't hear it if it rings. It would be a wrong number anyway.*

Anne summoned a taxi, stuck out her tongue at her image in the mirror, and went downstairs. As she was leaving the building, her next-door neighbor was making her way in. They both nodded to each other politely, as total strangers do under these circumstances, banal mutterings of "Madame," "Madame," and Anne was outside, rejoicing. Her disguise had worked!

Anne instructed the taxi driver to take her to Place Pompidou. As she walked toward the famous red-light district, her resolution began to falter. She bit her lip and forced herself to approach one of the dimly lit hotel doorways.

"Excuse me, where can I find Mademoiselle Ninette, please?" Anne asked the first girl she encountered. "The blonde?"

The prostitute looked her up and down scornfully.

"There," she said, and waved toward a hotel diagonally opposite the street.

With her heart in her mouth, Anne walked across the street in the direction of the hotel. She had no intention of going inside or of questioning anyone again. To keep up appearances she walked past the hotel, then hastened her steps, intent on leaving the area as fast as she could. But she had memorized the hotel's location.

At a nearby bar, she downed a glass of cognac to soothe her nerves. Then she took a taxi back home.

ೞ

John and Patricia visited three other Iranian restaurants. Though they exchanged a word or two with some of the waiters, they had never managed to strike up a conversation with any of the other diners. They decided to return to their first restaurant, Bita, where they already knew the waiter.

Farhad recognized them and welcomed them warmly. He led them to a table and set two menus on it.

"But perhaps you would like to trust me again with the dishes," he said. "Like last time."

"Oh, yes, indeed," said John. "Jolly good job you did then."

"I wonder," said Patricia, smiling at the waiter, "if you could clear something up for me, Farhad. I have already told you I was on a trip to Iran. However, I discovered there that people were not very open to conversation. Was I wrong? I mean, it seemed that they were only repeating things they were permitted to, and I never got an honest personal opinion about anything."

"You are very observant, Miss Patricia."

"We would like to invite you to dine with us on one of the evenings you're not working. Perhaps we could hear things from you that I couldn't hear in Iran?"

Farhad was embarrassed. He shifted his weight from one foot to the other.

"What could I possibly tell you? I haven't been to Iran for several years."

"Everything! The truth!"

He hesitated. His eyes darted around—Patricia couldn't tell whether he was looking for assistance or making sure he was not being overheard.

"You are very nice people," he said hoarsely, "and I am reluctant to refuse you. I am free only on Fridays. But I really don't think I can tell you anything more about Iran."

Patricia giggled.

"We don't want you to feel uncomfortable," she said. "We'll just ask questions. If you want to, you can answer them."

"All right," he said finally.

"Next Friday then," John boomed. "Now bring us your best meal, my friend."

## FIFTY-NINE

Martin and Admiral Stone met once again to finalize the details of the satellite experiment. This time they were joined by Sir

Cedric, who had earlier been given the outlines of Boulanger's specifications.

"What have you made of Boulanger's DVD?" the admiral asked.

"Very impressive," Martin responded. "I won't bore you with the technical details—I don't understand all of them myself. Basically, given accurate coordinates, he can aim Sir Cedric's laser to that location with amazing precision. When that target is 'in view'—about every two hours or a little more—Boulanger can activate the laser to shine on that location."

"Did you have enough data to find an area for the experiment?"

"Oh, more than enough. We've rejected anywhere east of the Red Sea—access is just too inconvenient. That leaves Africa. We have excluded all the countries with totalitarian regimes—their security measures are very tight and we would not be free to move about. That leaves only Morocco and Mauritania. Of these, Mauritania is far more attractive for our purposes. I have requested George to set up a five-day trip covering the northern area of that country. Naturally, if we find a suitable place sooner, we'll cancel the other visits."

"You've set your criteria wisely," Sir Cedric spoke for the first time that evening. "But you need to know more in order to make certain that you have the proper site."

"Yes, indeed, Sir Cedric," Martin said. "That is why we need your presence here. What, exactly, should we be looking for?"

"Keep in mind," Sir Cedric said, "that we are, in principle, attempting to simulate how we *think* a nuclear reactor could be built. It would probably be several meters underground, and enclosed in concrete. Access would be through a main tunnel, entering either horizontally from far away, or vertically through shafts drilled into the ground. There would be electrical systems, water systems, fuel systems, transportation systems, conveyance systems—almost anything you can think of to sustain uninterrupted work underground."

"Good thing we don't want to blow one up," muttered the admiral.

"That's the whole point," Sir Cedric said. "Neutralizing without blowing up! Most of these systems are there to afford mobility. Mobility is obtained by motors, whether fuel or electrically operated—we can dismiss wind and solar energy sources. The metallic mechanical moving parts of these motors are what my laser beams damage—or, at least, that's the idea."

"How on earth can we simulate an underground bunker?" the admiral mused.

There was a short silence.

"We'll need to find an abandoned building and try to extemporize as best we can," Martin offered.

"You may need to add additional shielding," Sir Cedric said. "Cover it with more concrete, for example."

"I'll need to think about it," Martin said. "What 'metallic mechanical moving parts' would be most suitable?"

"Oh, almost any old thing," Sir Cedric said. "Just have it large enough. A large car motor would be fine. Or a tractor. A windmill would do just as well, but you'd find it hard to pour concrete over it, eh?" He found his joke funny enough to laugh at it repeatedly.

"Anything else?" the admiral asked, rolling his eyes upward. "Good. Then we're adjourned."

⚜

Martin assembled all the scraps of information about Mauritania that he could get his hands on. The Internet, naturally, supplied volumes, but a lot was repetitive. Once he got the hang of what a tourist could expect—assisted by brochures from several travel agencies—he narrowed his scrutiny to the largest city in northern Mauritania: Zouérat. Right in the path of the satellite orbit. It was just over six hundred meters above sea level, and it was the capital of the iron-mining region. An active railroad connected Zouérat to Nouadhibou, the second largest city in Mauritania after its capital, Nouakchott, and also its largest port. This train, probably the longest in the world, sometimes it reached a length of three kilometers, carried iron ore from Zouérat and nearby Fdérik, to this port on the Atlantic Ocean. Two carriages on the train also carried passengers.

*Wait a minute! Mining areas! There had to be abandoned mine shafts in that area! They could easily be used to simulate underground bunkers for the satellite test. Sir Cedric needs to confirm this!*

*What's our cover story going to be? The movie business was quite successful in Tunisia. Well, we'll need a reconnaissance trip anyway....*

*As to the shipments to Seoul, we'll need to find a way to package the liquids they'll need there. There's the fertilizer, which should now be in liquid form, and there's the 'conditioner' stuff that the gravel has to be soaked in to make it operational. Bottles? Tins? Jerry cans? Under what label? I hope the answers arrive soon ...*

*And now—let's hear what John and Patricia have to report.*

CB&O

"What would you like to do until we have dinner at the Shiraz again?" John asked.

They had just had lunch at yet another Iranian restaurant. They kept a list of the eateries they had visited but had lost count by now. A few, like the Shiraz, they had deemed as worth a second visit.

Patricia hesitated.

"If you have nothing in particular scheduled," John continued, "we could take in a movie."

"I have a better idea," Patricia said. "Why don't we go up to my place, where we can rest comfortably until our evening 'assignment'?"

John was taken aback. He had not expected any signs of 'special treatment' from Patricia because of their common past. True, his feelings for her had not diminished, but he could not imagine her either reciprocating or deliberately trying to hurt his feelings. So far he had found her friendly, but absolutely 'proper' in all aspects.

He accepted her invitation, but not without some internal trepidation.

When they got to her flat, which, naturally, was not the one he was familiar with in the distant past, she tossed off her shoes and invited him to do the same.

"Make yourself at home," she said. "I'll make some coffee, and we can discuss a couple of angles of our project."

"Such as?"

"Such as what do we say to Farhad when we meet him on Friday?"

"And what do you suggest we say?"

"We cannot play hide-and-seek much longer. We've got say something to forward our mission."

"Depends on what that something is," John said.

"You're a big help." Patricia sound annoyed, but there was a glint of challenge in her eyes. "How about we tell him we are associated with a group of well-wishers who would like to assist the Iranian people."

John picked up the challenge easily.

"And if he says, for instance, that the Iranian people have no need for foreign assistance, and that conditions there are fabulous—then we ask him why he's here and not there."

Patricia's eyes now sparkled.

"And if he says that it is impossible to help the Iranian people? That the regime is powerful and brutal?"

"That's a horse of a different color. In fact, that's what we're hoping for."

"We could respond by saying that something should be done to weaken the leadership." Patricia was getting excited.

"And according to his reaction," John said calmly, although inside he was just as excited as she, "we could say something could be done! And perhaps more than just weakening the tyrants. Maybe actually bringing about their downfall!"

"And that we could help in that!" Patricia crowed triumphantly.

John smiled.

"Right. But let's not put the cart before the horse. Let's play it slowly …"

"You mention another cliché with horses and I'll feed you hay." She giggled. "I think I'll have a shower and stretch out for a while. Wake me when it's time to leave."

## SIXTY

Commissaire Duval arrived at the conclusion that Mme. Professeur Dupré was playing games with the police. It seemed she was taking unnecessary trips in all directions for the sole purpose of disconcerting him. It was quite clear to him that she had seen Marnier tailing her and had led him on a wild goose chase. *Well, if she can be so crafty,* he thought, *I can go one better.*

Duval arranged to take a few days off. He rented a closed van, and parked it overnight near Professeur Dupré's residence. He would come early next morning, leave his car parked a block away and stand watch from inside the van.

On the first day of his vigil, she left for the university.

On the second day, she left the house late and went shopping at the grocery store.

On the third day, a taxi pulled up to the house and took her to Gare du Nord. Duval followed them. When she got out of the taxi at the station, the commissaire forced the van onto the sidewalk, yanked out the keys, and hurried into the enormous building. *I'll handle the illegal parking later*, he thought. After Anne had bought her ticket, Duval elbowed his way to the cashier, brandished his badge of authority and demanded to know the destination of "the lady who was here a moment ago."

Brussels.

He bought a ticket. *So far so good. She's not going to play games with me.* Duval boarded the train.

Anne got off at the Brussels-Midi station, and took the metro downtown. Duval followed in her footsteps, a discrete distance behind. She alighted at the Central Station, and Duval watched her walk less than a hundred meters north and enter the Sheraton Towers Hotel.

He stood by a shop window, the entrance to the hotel in full view, and dialed the Brussels Police on his cellphone.

"Get me Commissaire Edouard Valentin," he told the switchboard.

After a short pause, he heard his colleague's voice.

"Valentin here."

"It's Felix Duval. Listen, I'm in Brussels following a suspect involved in a murder case. Could you please join me here—I'm opposite the Sheraton Towers Hotel. I can't explain over the phone. I'll fill you in when we meet. Hurry—it's urgent!"

"I'll be there," Valentin promised.

He was. Duval gave his host a brief summary of the investigation, emphasizing a possible meeting with an Englishman named Sir Cedric Norton. They entered the hotel cautiously, Duval covering most of his face with a newspaper. Anne was nowhere in sight.

While Duval browsed through a magazine rack, Valentin strolled over to the reception desk. The clerk was a familiar face.

"Hello, Henri. How are you?"

"Quite well, commissaire, thank you."

"Tell me, please—do you have any Englishmen in the hotel?"

"Surely you joke, commissaire. The hotel is overflowing with Englishmen."

"Ah, but I am interested in a particular Englishman. Does the name Sir Cedric Norton sound familiar to you?"

"I am terribly sorry, commissaire. But no—I would have certainly remembered such a name."

Valentin rejoined Duval and repeated what he had learned from the clerk.

"Perhaps," he joked, "she is having a clandestine affair with this English nobleman, and wishes to conceal it from her husband."

Duval brushed aside this theory, explaining to Valentin the connection between Anne Dupré, Sir Cedric Norton, and Albert Allier—who had died in Paris a few months earlier. And that Duval was sure he was murdered.

Duval and Valentin decided to wait for Anne to come out again. They walked into the hotel lobby and sat in easy chairs with a good view of the lifts. With nothing better to do, they browsed through magazines and kept a sharp eye open for Anne.

Three hours later, Anne emerged from one of the lifts. Duval scrunched low behind his magazine. Valentin stood up.

"Shall I have her followed?" he asked.

Duval pulled him down by the sleeve.

"No, Edouard. She's on her way back to Paris. I want to see if another familiar face comes out of those lifts. With a little luck we'll see the elusive Sir Cedric Norton."

Duval had hardly uttered those words when Sir Cedric stepped out of the lift.

"That's him!" Duval hissed. "That's Sir Cedric! If he's such a good friend of Mme. Dupré, the way both of them claim, then why does he have to meet her here in Brussels? He used to visit her regularly at her home in Paris until I began poking around. It appears I was right. Those two are up to something insidious."

"Well, shall I have *him* followed?"

"Futile. He's on his way to London. That's it, Edouard. I found out what I wanted—that they met here. Thanks to you and your help. I'm afraid, though, that this little episode will not be reported. You see, the Allier murder case is officially closed. I'm snooping of my own volition. I hope you'll forgive me for using you."

Valentin laughed.

"Come on, Felix. My wife and I are having you as our guest for lunch."

⊰⊱

At that very same board meeting, the most important item on the agenda was the satellite trial run.

"It looks like Mauritania is our best choice for a number of reasons," Martin said. "Point number one, the environs of the city in question, Zouérat, are very sparsely populated. We could roam around there pretty much as we please, as long as we don't go north, where the active mines are guarded. This brings me to point number two—the mines. I am pretty sure we can find abandoned mine shafts everywhere we look. Sir Cedric, am I right in assuming that mine shafts could substitute for underground bunkers?"

"Oh, admirably, my boy, admirably." Sir Cedric was duly impressed. "What a clever idea."

"Point number three—though in some ways Mauritania is somewhat backward, it has most the facilities that serve tourists. And point number four—I believe our cover story of making a movie might serve us well again here."

"Once we have the exact location," Anne said, "say, a mine shaft, we'll need to have its precise coordinates. I'll send them to Boulanger, who will, in turn, give us a number of alternatives of date and time for the experiment." She thought for a second. "If we adopt the movie cover, we'll need vehicles to transport the equipment. A lorry or a large van. It could also serve as a target for the test."

"Good idea," Martin said. "Of course we'll require another vehicle as well."

Admiral Stone reported on the next topic on the agenda.

"Our friend Gustav Lemke has informed me that he has succeeded in applying his fertilizer as a liquid spray. It can be used instead of, or in addition to, the regular fertilizer. It can be sprayed or sprinkled on a stretch of road, where if forms a very thin transparent film, just a fraction of a millimeter thick. However, it adheres very well to the road surface and cannot be washed, scrubbed, or even scraped off. It is activated by fumes given off by vehicles' engines—the material sublimates into a gas that enters the air intake and kills the engine."

"That's great," Martin said. "When you receive some of this fluid we shall test it. After that, we'll need to think about how to ship quantities of this stuff to Sing in Korea."

Sir Cedric then told the board about Rosetti.

"I am pleased to report that Emilio has managed to shrink Paganini and has installed it in an electric shaver, a cellular telephone, and a camera. This means we can transport it almost anywhere."

"Won't it show up on the X-ray machines at airports?" Anne asked.

"I asked Emilio the same question," Sir Cedric said. "The answer is yes. But not even an expert would be able to distinguish between Paganini and the genuine internal parts of these appliances."

Martin reported that John and Patricia had made contact with an Iranian who did not sympathize with the regime in his homeland. No further details were available and additional meetings were scheduled.

Martin kept a stern visage throughout the meeting, and did not make eye contact with Anne. As usual, she left first, followed by Sir Cedric and then himself. The admiral planned to stay in the suite overnight.

CB&O

John and Patricia took Farhad, with his consent, to a good French restaurant for dinner. After ordering, John deftly steered the conversation to the mission at hand.

"Well, Farhad, here we are—three people who have met by accident and seem to like each other. Every time that happens to me, it's as if a whole new world opens up to me. That is why I like to strike up new friendships. What do you think?"

"I admit it doesn't happen very frequently to me," Farhad said, a bit bashfully. "You see, we need to be careful about whom we make friends with."

John leaned forward.

"I'd like to discuss a couple of sensitive issues with you. So I'd rather prefer we kept this little discussion to ourselves. Are you all right with that?"

Farhad smiled.

"I'm all right."

"We belong to a group of people who don't like seeing other people oppressed. We don't belong to any party or political affiliation—just good citizens. But we do have good connections with very wealthy financiers who cover our expenses when necessary. We think there is no point in just handing money out— you can never reach all who need it. We believe that assisting an oppressed people is by changing the regime."

Farhad looked alarmed, and got to his feet.

"Please, Farhad, please." John did not lose his composure. "Let me finish. It's not at all what you think, I promise."

Farhad hesitated. He seemed torn between apprehension and curiosity.

"We are not revolutionaries," John went on rapidly. "Neither are we an 'underground resistance.' We do not have, or use, weapons or explosives." He paused. "Won't you please sit down again?"

Farhad said nothing, but slowly took his seat again, his eyes never leaving John's face.

"We think that a psychological approach will bring better results. If a dictator loses the faith and trust of his people, especially of his supporters, he could not possibly survive. We're looking for ways to embarrass the tyrant, to humiliate him in public, to make him look ridiculous in front of everyone. No one has ever thought of this." John peered intently at the Iranian. "Neither have you, by the look on your face."

Farhad remained silent.

"Don't you have anything to say, Farhad?" Patricia asked.

"I don't know what to say. You're saying very strange things. Why? Why are you telling me all this?"

"My words may seem very strange to *you*, Farhad," John said. "But others would take them very seriously. We won't be able to do anything without the assistance of Iranian citizens, whether in Iran or in exile."

"So?"

"So perhaps you know someone who *would* take our words seriously?"

Again, a hesitation followed by a resolution.

"Well, my older brother, Oumid, is always discussing current affairs, meets with people, has arguments with them."

"Could we meet him?" Patricia asked.

"Yes, I suppose so."

"When?"

"He and I live together. I could take you to him after the meal, if you wanted."

Patricia and John exchanged meaningful glances.

"Good idea," said John. "Let's have dinner."

After they had enjoyed a sumptuous meal, Patricia asked:

"Farhad, do you think your brother would be home by now?"

"It is very likely," Farhad said.

"Good," John said. "Let's have some coffee, and then we'll go."

"No, no." Farhad was smiling now. "You shall have coffee at my house."

CRWD

It turned out that Farhad's entire family populated "his house." The neighborhood was predominantly Iranian émigrés. Some of them were veteran Londoners by now, others were newer arrivals. The house itself was old, but the living quarters were large and comfortable. The lush couches and the carpets were the first to catch the eye.

"This is where we live," Farhad explained. "My father and mother, my grandmother, my brother Oumid and myself, and my younger sister Soraya."

Farhad's mother appeared from an adjacent room and offered soft drinks.

"Never mind, mother," Farhad said. "I promised them coffee. Is Oumid home?"

"He went to buy cigarettes." Farhad's mother smiled at the guests and made her way out. "He'll be right back."

"My father works late into the night," Farhad said. "He visits bars and restaurants and sells roses. In Iran, we owned a beautiful rose garden, and my father would tend it lovingly. But my father could not find a job here. He made contact with a local nursery and sells their roses. It doesn't pay well, but at least it's a living—he doesn't need anyone's help and his pride is intact."

Oumid arrived a short while later, and was duly introduced. He was about forty, plump, and with a white, soft face. He reminded Patricia of the shopkeeper in Shiraz who sold her a bracelet.

Oumid joined them at the table and Farhad told him, in a mixture of English and Farsi, the story of their guests' visit. His mother brought coffee, cold water, and an assortment of sweets.

Then it was John's turn to explain his presence. Oumid listened silently throughout.

"I hope everything is clear now," John said.

"No guns? No bombs?" Oumid said. "What can you hope to accomplish?"

John explained in broad lines how they planned to work and what the effects would be.

"It's all science. No one will get hurt. Isn't that worth a try?"

Oumid shut his eyes and sank into a deep reverie. The others waited patiently and made no sound. Patricia glanced at John and he acknowledged with a slight nod. Finally, Oumid straightened up and opened his eyes.

"What you have described has never been attempted before. I think no one has even *thought* about it before. So none of us—in fact, nobody anywhere—can foretell what the results will be."

"Let's assume," John pressed on, "just for argument's sake, that one isolated incident will not topple the dictator. But you must admit that there will be *some* sort of aftermath. The Iranian people—the whole world—will be abuzz about it. The press will have a field day! The despot will be much more careful about what he does in the future. And then, perhaps, we'll revert to phase two. We shan't be idle, you can imagine."

Oumid appeared nervous. He lit a cigarette with shaking hands.

"What can I say? Perhaps you should try it. But I don't see how I can help."

Patricia spoke for the first time since entering the Iranian house.

"We need people to place things, of the type we've mentioned, in certain places in Tehran. We cannot do this. We'll be watched at all times. Only men and women who live there—who do not draw attention to themselves—can do the job. In short," she drew a deep breath, "we need to contact someone in Tehran whom we can trust."

They waited some more time for Oumid to deliberate with himself.

"Listen. I believe you," he said finally. "But that is not enough. Personally, I know no one in Tehran who could help you. I hope you realize that I am now taking a great personal risk for you. I shall try to have someone meet with you, Mister John, alone—not you, Miss Patricia. Sorry. It will be up to you to interest this person the same way you've interested me."

"Very well," John said. "When?"

They set a meeting for later that night.

Outside, Patricia gave voice to mixed feelings.

"John, I don't really like us being separated on this mission. Oh, I know it can't be helped—that's the way they want it, and that's the way it's going to be."

"Look, Patty. I don't think you have anything to worry about. This is London, not Tehran, and we haven't done anything wrong. After the meeting, I'll call you at your flat. Okay?"

"Yes, do that. No matter how late it may be. I must know what went on there."

⚬❀⚬

## Steve's Blog, The Internet

This blogger has seen many diplomatic blunders in the past, but none as blatant as the recent agreement with the North Korean government. The North Koreans are undertaking the dismantling of their nuclear installations under the supervision of the International Atomic Energy Agency (IAEA). We, of course, are fully aware that nobody knows where all these installations are located, and that all we hear is hyperbole and diversion tactics. In return, North Korea will receive massive economic aid and support, without which the already catastrophic economic situation of the country will totally collapse. Your correspondent has heard reliable sources point out the weakness of the democracies in that they assist sworn enemies, allowing them to recover their strength. Don't they realize that when the troubles these dictatorships face today, troubles they themselves have wrought onto their own people, are resolved—when they get back on their feet again—that they will again turn against their benefactors? All this in the name of 'exalted humanitarian rights'. I ask you—what about our humanitarian rights?

The Iranian President, Ahmadinejad, has recently announced that Iran has three thousand centrifuges in continuous operation, and therefore Iran is now a nuclear power. Various intelligence agencies report that within a year Iran will have sufficient raw material to create one atomic bomb each year. Many nations have declared in reaction, that Iran is becoming a threat to them. Most of these declarations have come from Middle Eastern Arab nations. Western democracies, on the other hand, think they are doing their job by complaining that United Nations members are not enforcing the sanctions decided upon by the Security Council.

ᚲ₰ᚱ

Admiral Patrick Stone regularly visited his son to see his family. This time, however, he took special time to be with his grandson, Brian. Brian was a very bright seventeen-year-old, a model student, who spent every available minute at his computer.

Brian and his grandfather spent longer than usual in the lad's room. This, for the boy, was an exceptional gesture, and he was delighted at the opportunity for additional quality time with his grandfather, whom he adored. They sat opposite each other; Brian at the computer's keyboard.

"So tell me, Brian," the admiral said, "what do you do hours on end by the computer?"

"Come on, Grandpa," the lad said, "you use a computer yourself. You know its power."

"Oh, I just dabble with the mere basics, Brian. A document here, an email there—nothing serious."

"Don't you do any surfing on the Internet?"

"Not really, my boy. Why would I want to do that?"

"I can hardly believe it," Brian smirked. "Then again, I suppose that in your days you had underlings to dig up information for you."

"Correct. And I am not totally ignorant about the Internet. But not everyone can access everything, right? Take, for instance, reading the Pentagon files. I've heard it's been done."

Brian raised his eyebrows.

"I expect you know about such things, Grandpa, being an admiral and all. Probably more than I do."

"No, Brian. Of course I know *of* the break-ins, and how many times and what they found. What I don't know is how they did it."

"Neither do I, Grandpa."

The admiral winked.

"If you did, it would make you one of them, wouldn't it? No, I was wondering about the technique of going about such, umm … endeavors."

"Hacking, you mean?"

"Ah, yes, that's the term."

"It's a very interesting and quite dangerous occupation," Brian said carefully.

"I can imagine. How limited, from the geographical point of view, is the hacker?"

"No limit whatsoever. An experienced hacker can access any computer connected to the Internet. And that means worldwide."

"So, if I understand correctly, if the hacker can simulate the actions of a bona fide user, he can access that user's data. Right?"

"Yes, Grandpa. That's one of the ways—perhaps the easiest way. All you need is the user's password and you can do with his data whatever he can."

"And what are the other ways?"

"The equivalent of brute force. Hacking is mainly possible because of lax security. System administrators leave loopholes that the hacker uses to penetrate. The hacker uses tools—which, by the way, are available to everyone on the Internet—that 'sniff' out these loopholes. There are other methods as well. The tighter your security, the more up-to-date your protection, the harder it'll be for the hacker to get in."

"But not impossible," the admiral suggested.

"Nothing is impossible," Brian said modestly. "For the very secure systems, hackers usually write custom programs to break in."

"Won't the target *know* he's being, er … hacked?"

"Well, yes, if you don't use extra precautions in your program to conceal your penetration. No easy task, by all means."

"But not impossible," the admiral repeated. "Can you write such a program?"

Brian grinned up at him from the computer console.

"I was wondering when you'd come to that. You're going somewhere with this, Grandpa. Perhaps if you tell me the whole story I'd be able to help you."

"Can you?"

"Yes, Grandpa."

"How long would it take?"

There was a twinkle of amusement in Brian's eyes. He could not tell how serious his grandfather's questions were.

"Depending on the target, I'd say three to four months," he said.

"That's too long." the admiral muttered under his breath. But Brian heard him.

"I'll be straight with you, Grandpa. I've been occupied with this type of program for several months. So now I have a prototype program that needs only some outside parameters in order to run properly. Once I have a target, I could probably have the program ready in days instead of months, custom made for that specific target."

The admiral took a deep breath. He'd have to reveal a bit of his plans if he was to get anywhere.

"I know it's illegal," Brian went on, "but I haven't used the program yet. So I haven't broken any law so far. I'm telling you this because I sense that you have a problem that I could help in solving. Am I right?"

"It's tougher than you think, my boy. There's secrecy involved … oh, hell, let's go a bit further. It involves penetrating into the national security systems of a hostile country."

"That's not telling me much."

"You're aware, I'm sure, that as my grandson and a loyal British citizen, you are sworn not to reveal anything of our conversation this evening. Not to your parents, not to your friends—nobody!"

"That's what I thought," the lad said coolly.

The admiral had every reason to be proud of his grandson. He took the final plunge.

"Iran," he said. "Iranian War Ministry or the equivalent. Iranian Atomic Energy Commission or the equivalent. Iranian President's private correspondence and files."

"I'll see what I can do." The boy had not batted an eyelash.

"Her Majesty's government is not involved in this in any way. You are absolutely on your own. I am counting on you."

The enormity of the task was beginning to dawn on Brian Stone. His eyes glittered and his voice became a little hoarse.

"Thank you for your confidence in me, Grandpa," he said softly. "I'll try not to let you down. If and when I have results, I'll call you and tell you I've solved the puzzle. You can then tell me what to do next."

They got to their feet and stood facing each other. They embraced and then shook hands firmly, looking into each other's eyes. It was almost a ceremony.

C3⬥80

Patricia Welles waited impatiently for John to call. She had a bite to eat, listened to the Beatles' *Revolver*, and finally fell asleep on the sofa facing the television set, watching *Doctor Who*.

She woke up with a start at a particularly loud commercial touting the pleasures of touring the Caribbean Islands. It was two in the morning. John hadn't called. For a moment, she was alarmed, but she convinced herself that an intense argument might be going on. Perhaps John needed to go into great detail explaining their philosophy. *He just doesn't want to disturb me this late*, she thought. *He'll call first thing tomorrow.*

Patricia went to bed.

## SIXTY-ONE

But John didn't call the next morning either. When Patricia tried calling him, there was no answer. Now she was worried. She decided to wait another hour, and if John hadn't called by then, she'd take action.

The hour passed, and Patricia racked her brain—what was her best move now? Martin was away—no use trying to call him. Should she look for Farhad at the Bita restaurant and confront him with John's disappearance? Or go back to where he lives, and inquire there? *Better not just now*, she thought. *If I disappear too, nobody will know of our absence. Wait a minute! The old man on the Tunisia trip—what was his name? Patrick Stone! At least, as far as I recall, that is how he registered at the hotel.*

Patricia hunted through the telephone book feverishly. There he was—*adm. ret*. She let out a low whistle. She dialed, and a man answered the phone.

"Good day. Is this Admiral Stone?"

"It is. And who are you, please?"

"My name is Patricia Welles. We met on a trip to Africa. Admiral, I have an emergency on my hands and no one to turn to. Can you see me?"

The admiral was surprised. He knew she had teamed up with John Carmichael on the Iranian contact mission. If she saw fit to call him, there must be a special reason.

"Certainly, my dear. You may come to my office right away, if you like." He gave her his address.

An hour later, they were sitting face to face in the admiral's office. She related all that had happened the previous evening and expressed her concern regarding John's well-being. The admiral listened calmly, and did not seem overly worried.

"We have two addresses," he said, when she had finished. "The restaurant and his residence. I see no other resort but to approach Farhad and inquire. It's about lunchtime now, so he should be at work already. Stay where others can see you at all times. If he asks you to step somewhere secluded, such as an office or the kitchen— refuse. And if he knows nothing, you'll need to talk to his brother,

Oumid. He *must* have information—he is the last person we know to have seen John. I doubt he'll try anything untoward at his home, for fear of involving his family. Anyway, your main safety hatch is that you let them know that there are others who know exactly where you are and whom you are seeing. If you're really in a tight spot, say that if you don't make a call by a certain hour, the police will be alerted and they will raid the house. I suggest you go now, and clear up this issue. Call me whenever you can."

He gave her his home and cellular phone numbers.

CES80

Martin Cooper and Philip Brown arrived at Mauritania's capital, Nouakchott, on an Air France flight directly from Paris. They double-checked that they had everything they needed for the trip—passports and visas, of course, documents confirming their business as IFP—International Film Promoters—the script of the movie, including a scene in a mine shaft, and a satellite phone—in case there was no cellular phone coverage in Mauritania.

They had done their homework before leaving London. They now knew that the country's official name was The Islamic Republic of Mauritania, and that its population was around three million, that the capital, Nouakchott, had a population approaching two million, that the official language was the Hassaniya dialect of Arabic, but that French was also spoken—as the country was a French colony until 1960. They crammed up their knowledge on the currency, the ouguiya, on geography—mostly the Sahara desert—and on the economy, as most of the national income came from iron mining.

The oddest fact they learned was that slavery was still rife in Mauritania, though it was officially abolished in 1981. In fact, children were taught that being a slave was a religious obligation for being a good Muslim. Many still believed that, and remained slaves their entire lives. It was estimated that about thirty percent of the population were slaves. The government went to great lengths to deny this—it had banned the word "slave" from use by the media, and foreign journalists risked arrest and deportation for investigating the issue.

"Have you ever seen a slave in our life?" Philip whispered, as they took a rickety taxi to their hotel.

"Never," Martin whispered back. "And here they are in the thousands, roaming the streets. Amazing!"

"How can you distinguish between a slave and a free man?" Philip wondered.

"I don't know," Martin said.

⚭

Patricia returned to the Bita restaurant. Her determination had returned after her short talk with the admiral. Farhad was serving a customer. She went up to him.

"Farhad, I need to talk to you," she said quietly.

"I am terribly sorry, Miss Patricia," he whispered back. "As you can see, I am very busy right now."

"Please excuse yourself for a few minutes. We need to talk now."

The Iranian seemed not only nervous but distressed as well.

"Miss Patricia …" he began.

"*Now!*"

He could not withstand Patricia's staunchness. He made hand signals to the kitchen, and stepped outside with her. She got right to the point.

"Where is John?"

"Miss Patricia, I don't know what you're—"

"Farhad, last night your brother took John to meet someone. He has not returned since then. Where is he?"

"Miss Patricia, please. I have no idea whom Oumid knows or meets. He never—"

"Is he at home right now?"

"Actually no, Miss Patricia. He left this morning for Rome."

"Come on, Farhad. Something has happened to John, and I am very concerned. Please try to help me find him. Surely you know some of your brother's friends?"

Farhad grew pale. He spread his hands feebly, indicating helplessness.

"Farhad," she said softly. "I shall now go to your home and speak with your mother. Perhaps she can help me."

Farhad reacted as if struck by a snake.

"No, please!" he whispered hoarsely. "Miss Patricia, please do not talk with my mother. She is a very sick woman and should not be agitated. She knows nothing—believe me!"

Patricia shook her head and turned to leave.

"I have no choice," she said. "I have to!"

He grabbed her sleeve.

"Wait! Please! Let me think some more. Perhaps I shall remember something."

"Listen, Farhad," Patricia said as she shook off his hand. "I am not playing games. I shall have a light meal, and you will tax your brain and remember something useful. If by the time I am through you have not come up with anything, I shall go straight to your mother. Do we understand each other?"

Farhad nodded and reentered the restaurant. Patricia sat at one of the tables and asked Farhad to bring her a simple salad.

He ignored her request and plied her with dish after dish of tasty delicacies. It seemed he wished to prolong the meal to its utmost.

⋘⋙

Martin and Philip stowed their gear in their hotel rooms, and then went directly to see the desk clerk regarding how to get to Zouérat.

"Zouérat, eh? Are you in the iron or copper business?" he asked. His English was not perfect, but adequate. "Because if you are, you needn't go all the way to Zouérat. We have mining agencies here in Nouakchott."

"No," Philip said. "We represent a movie company. We need to find a shooting site. A few scenes occur in, and near, a mine."

Apparently, not many movies were made in Mauritania. The clerk's attitude became very friendly.

"I could book a flight to Zouérat for you. They leave twice a week. Or you could charter a light plane if you wish. I could book you a couple of hotel rooms."

"That would be very nice, thank you," Martin said. "Could you also book us a rented car? A lorry … er … truck or a van?"

"I'm afraid you'll have to do that after your arrival. I'm not sure they have car rentals there. It is a small city, after all."

"That's not so good," Philip muttered to Martin.

The clerk overheard him.

"May I make a suggestion?" he said. "I have a cousin in Zouérat who owns a garage. He may be able to help you. He belongs to a respected family in Zouérat and knows everyone."

Martin and Philip exchanged questioning glances.

"He could probably get you a vehicle for a short period of time," the clerk pressed on.

Martin shrugged.

"Might as well," he said. "We haven't come so far just to return empty-handed."

The clerk tore a slip of paper off a pad, scribbled on it and handed it to Martin.

"His name is Mahmoud Ould Salah, and this is his address. Ask about him at your hotel and you will be given directions. Everyone knows him."

"You have been most kind," Philip said. "Thank you very much."

"It has been my pleasure, sir. I will notify you when the next flight for Zouérat leaves."

CR&O

It so happened that a flight for Zouérat was scheduled for the next morning. They had no time to tour the capital, and, despite the 'attractions' in the brochure they found in their room, it didn't seem like they had missed much. There were a few mosques, a museum, and a seaport six kilometers away—not really a tourist's paradise. The clerk also informed them that he had reserved two rooms for them at the hotel in Zouérat.

Philip was apprehensive about car rental possibilities at their destination.

"I'm afraid we'll be wasting our time," he said. "It doesn't look like we'll find a car to rent."

"You can get anything if you pay enough," Martin reminded him.

"I know, I know. My concern is that there'll be no cars to rent around at all. It won't matter how much you can afford to pay."

"If we ever get into that predicament, we'll *buy* a car off someone at a price he could not possibly refuse."

CБ80

Commissaire Duval was frustrated, to say the least. He sat at his desk and reviewed the situation so far.

*Professor Albert Allier was murdered. That is, for me, a fact—though yet unproven. Fact—Sir Cedric Norton was an acquaintance of Allier. Another fact—Mme. Professeur Dupré and Sir Cedric Norton have a relationship that I have failed to identify yet. Open question: why did they meet earlier at her flat and now in Belgium? Secretly? Could it be an illicit love affair? Unlikely, but who knows?*

*Actually, I have neglected one possible angle of investigation. Envy! Allier's close colleagues were not questioned along this line because murder was not suspected. But perhaps one of them had felt that Allier had 'stolen' a scientific discovery of his? Perhaps Allier's worldwide reputation was at the expense of a lesser researcher who was never credited for his contribution?*

*There is a problem here, however. I cannot begin investigating French citizens, especially scientists and civil servants, without eliciting headlines in the press. It would be impossible to hide from my superiors. Yet ... perhaps a private conversation with one or two of Allier's close co-workers could get quiet results.*

The commissaire decided to search among his long list of acquaintances. There could be a scientist among them, someone who was close to Allier one way or another.

CБ80

Martin and Philip were the only Europeans on the flight to Zouérat. Obviously, the other passengers were better off than most of the population.

As it was still morning when they arrived, Martin and Philip went directly to their hotel, had a wash and something to eat in the hotel's modest dining room, and then went to see the manager. He spoke no English, but their French was adequate for conversation. They explained the purpose of their visit as seeking a location for shooting a movie.

"Most interesting," the manager said. It was obviously his first encounter with the movie world outside the cinema theatre.

"We were referred to a garage owner named Ould Salah," Martin said. "Could you please direct us to him?"

"Certainly," said the manager. "It's about ten minutes' walk from here." He took them to the hotel's entrance and pointed down the road eastward. "Just keep walking in that direction and you'll see his garage. You can't miss it."

Zouérat was more like a large village than a small town. It had about thirty thousand inhabitants. The streets were narrow and most of them were unpaved. The few people you could see walking about were mainly commoners—laborers, porters, vendors, and the like. Martin and Philip drew the attention of all, even though they were dressed in casual outfits.

Mahmoud Ould Salah's garage was an enormous courtyard surrounded by a stone wall. A large structure was built against one of the corners of the wall, serving as workshop, storage, and office. Another corner seemed to serve as storage, too, as it was walled with corrugated tin sheets. The entire courtyard was strewn with semi-dissembled cars, car parts, piles of old tires, barrels, tins, crates—almost anything imaginable.

As they approached the building, a man of about fifty emerged to greet them. He was a short and thin Berber, and he wore spotless, well-ironed blue dungarees. From afar, he greeted them in French:

"Welcome! Please enter my office."

They met and shook hands, and then followed him into the building. They entered a well-furnished office behind a wooden partition. A large desk was laden with files and papers. Behind it was an oversized swivel armchair, and in front were seats for customers or visitors. An ancient dial telephone stood on a small table by the desk.

"I am Mahmoud Ould Salah, at your service. Please be seated."

He went over to his armchair and clapped his hands. Instantly, a youth appeared and was instructed to serve tea.

"My cousin in Nouakchott informed me of your arrival," Ould Salah said. "What can I do for you?"

"My name is Martin Cooper," Martin said, "and this is my colleague, Philip Brown. We represent a London movie company. We're here concerning a movie we are planning. Your cousin is a very courteous and pleasant man, and we enjoyed making his acquaintance. He informed us that you were all-powerful in Zouérat. We were hoping you could help us on our quest."

Salah smiled.

"My family has been here for several generations," he said proudly. "It is true that I wield a lot of power here, as I am very well connected. If you ask for anything that exists here, I can probably get it for you. But if it is not here—well, that's where my powers end."

"We need a truck," Philip said.

"Yes, so my cousin informed me. There are several trucks and vans here, but they are all in use. There are no idle or unused vehicles in these parts. The owner depends on his vehicle to make his living. No vehicle—no work. I have a jeep, just outside. You would be doing me an honor if you would let me show you around Zouérat. I'm afraid, however, that I can do no more."

Tea was served along with local cookies. They sipped in silence.

"Mr. Ould Salah," Martin said finally, "allow me to tell you a bit about our movie. The plot is pretty standard—the hero chases the bad guy into a mine where he captures him. Zouérat is an excellent candidate for this scene—if we find a suitable abandoned mine."

Martin paused to make sure that Ould Salah understood.

"If you would be so kind as to let us use your jeep to scout the area, we will gladly compensate you for your trouble."

A glint of interest showed in Ould Salah's eyes.

"And," Martin continued, "if we *do* find a suitable location, we shall discuss the further possibility of using a truck to carry our equipment to the shooting site."

Salah smiled broadly.

"I can let you have my jeep and my driver," he said. "He will take you to places which may be suitable for you."

"I am very pleased to hear that," Martin said. "When do you think the jeep and the driver could be ready?"

"I will arrange everything by the time you finish your tea," Ould Salah said. He got up, walked into the courtyard and yelled: "Salim!" and returned to his seat in the office. A minute later, a young black man of about twenty entered. He was dressed in tattered overalls, and spoke in the local Arabic dialect:

"Yes, master."

Salah addressed him in French mixed with Arabic.

"Prepare the jeep and then take these gentlemen to the places I shall tell you."

"Yes, master," Salim said, and disappeared.

Salah turned to the Englishmen with a satisfied smile.

"You see? Even in Zouérat things can be arranged efficiently."

"We haven't discussed payment yet," Martin reminded him.

"Quite unimportant now," Ould Salah waved him off. "When you return, and if you're satisfied, you'll pay me whatever you think it was worth."

"That is very generous of you, Mr. Ould Salah," Martin said. "Unfortunately, this is the first time we have ever visited this region of the world, and we have no idea what an acceptable payment should be. So please throw us a ball-park figure so that we can get our bearings." Martin hoped he had worded his request as diplomatically as possible.

Ould Salah smiled again.

"This trip will be on me," he said. "Just give the boy a tip of three hundred ouguiyas. We'll talk again later."

Salim reappeared.

"The jeep is ready," he said.

Ould Salah gave him instructions what to show them, and the young man made some marks in a dirty notebook. Right outside the office door stood a large, shiny jeep with a bright orange stripe painted around it. Martin got in next to the driver and Philip sat in the back.

Salim was an excellent driver. He took them out of the city, and after about fifteen minutes of driving, he turned off onto a narrow dirt road that seemed to lead into the brown hills. A few kilometers later, Salim slowed down and turned right onto an almost imperceptible path. Turning around an immense rocky protrusion, they saw the entrance to a cave that, as they approached, turned out to be an abandoned mineshaft. Here and there were scraps from earlier days when work had been carried out—wooden shoring, metal piping and the like.

Salim brought the jeep to a halt in a cloud of dust, and they got out for a closer look. The mine's entrance was at the foot of a hill. The opening was about three meters wide and two and a half meters high, and it bored into the hill for several meters at the same level until it disappeared into the darkness. Right above the entrance to the mine, the earth was about a meter thick, but the steep incline of the hill made the thickness much larger as you entered into the mine.

Martin speculated the possibility of driving a van into the mine's entrance. He consulted with Philip in English.

"Looks all right to me," he said. "Sufficient 'shielding' of earth, I'd say."

"We couldn't get a large lorry into there," Philip said. "Not high enough. But I suppose any van could get in easily. Yes, this place looks suitable to me, too."

Martin made a note of the GPS coordinates directly at the mine's entrance and of three additional points outside the entrance in an approximate ten-meter semicircle. He would use them later to calibrate the precise coordinates given to Boulanger.

"Right," he said. "I think we're done here. We have a location, so we can call off the search for others. It has the ideal balance between closeness to the city and isolation from prying eyes. Let's get back now. I want to convince our host that anyone would sell their van to us if we give them the money for a brand new vehicle."

They instructed Salim to take them back.

Mahmoud Ould Salah identified the sound of his approaching jeep and awaited their arrival outside his office with a big smile on his face.

"What did I tell you?" he jabbered as he led Martin and Philip indoors. "You found a good mine, right? Of course. I told him where to take you. Come on in."

Philip handed the driver a couple of local banknotes and followed Martin into the office.

"You were right, Mr. Ould Salah," Martin grinned. "The place is suitable, it's nearby, and it didn't take long to find. So we're in a position to move forward now. We have a script, actors, a shooting site, and financial backing. All we need now is a vehicle to carry our equipment. A truck or a van would do fine."

"Mr. Martin, I would like to help you, but as I have already explained …"

"Time is money, Mr. Ould Salah. You were very helpful in saving us time finding the site. We need to press on. Now—I am proposing that any owner of an old van would be prepared to sell it to us for the price of a brand new van, the best on the market. Do you know of any such person?"

Salah's features seemed to be frozen.

"You, of course," Philip said, "would earn a broker's fee. You name the percentage. Doesn't that sound fair to you?"

It took a whole minute for Ould Salah's face to change.

"You have spoken wise words, sir," he said finally, "and they are probably true and factual in London. Your offer would be the normal form of transaction there. But this is Zouérat, Mauritania. A car owner here regards his vehicle as a member of his family. It serves him and earns his income—therefore, he treats it accordingly and becomes attached to it. If it breaks down, he will repair it again and again for years. But he will never sell it. A foreigner would probably find that hard to understand."

"But surely an attractive offer—" Martin began.

"I shall call a few of my friends who have vans that suit your needs. You can listen in on my conversation with them and judge for yourselves."

Martin and Philip remained silent. Ould Salah thumbed through his directory and dialed a number. He spoke mostly in French so that his guest could follow the dialog. It was evident that the party being called would not hear of any offer to buy his car. Ould Salah called three more people, and got the same result.

Salah put down the phone and leaned back in his seat. He shook his head slowly at the two Englishmen.

"I don't understand," Philip said. "It defies reason."

"Not really," Ould Salah said. "The second man I called spelled it out for me. If he sold his car, he would have to wait for at least two months before getting the new one. How will he make a living during these two months? Even if you compensate him for loss of income for that period, it won't do him any good—someone else will have taken his job by then. It is a very competitive and ruthless marketplace here, you know."

"This is a great disappointment for us," Martin said ruefully. "After finding everything matching so perfectly, we're now stumped for lack of a simple thing like a van."

Salah got up.

"Come with me," he said. "I would like to show you around my yard. It contains many interesting objects. Perhaps something may give you an idea."

Martin and Philip could not very well refuse. They were shown old, rusty parts of cars, the engine of a World War II fighter plane, an engineless tractor, tires of all types and sizes, and—inside the tin-walled storage space—a large generator on wheels.

"I used this old generator," Ould Salah explained, "before we were connected to the electric network. It hasn't worked for years. If I put a mechanic on it, it may be operational again in a day or two. Want a generator?"

Martin and Philip looked at each other. Ould Salah swept his hand across the courtyard.

"I could probably assemble a van from these loose parts here," he said. "Anything missing I could order from Nouakchott. Couldn't take more than a month or two. Want to wait that long for a van?"

The two Englishman did not want to embarrass their host, but they thought his offers were ridiculous.

"I'll sell you the generator for a very cheap price," Ould Salah went on. "I'll get it to work, add on some lighting equipment, tow it to your mine site, and it could provide you with the power to illuminate the inside of the mine. And I'll give you my jeep for a day or two to transport your movie gear."

"Your offer is very generous, Mr. Ould Salah," Martin said. "Unfortunately, it does not meet our needs. We will have to explore alternate venues."

"Pity," Ould Salah said. "I did my best to help you." He accompanied them to the entrance to the courtyard. "I shall get the generator to work, anyway. If you don't buy it, perhaps someone else will."

They shook hands, and Ould Salah gave Martin his business card.

"Call me if you change your mind," he said.

*I doubt it,* Martin thought, pocketing the card. They returned to the hotel and arranged to fly back to Nouakchott, and from there, back to London.

 C3❦80

Patricia finished her meal, asked for the bill, paid without leaving a tip and made for the door. Farhad caught up with her.

"Please!" His whisper was almost ferocious. "Give me another chance. I'll be going home at three and returning here at six. Come back here at six. I might have something to tell you then. All right?"

Patricia hesitated for a moment. Obviously, Farhad was cooking up something.

"Very well," she said. "But you had better have something to tell me! Otherwise, I'm going to make one hell of a scene!"

She left in a huff. *Perhaps I should not have agreed*, she pondered. *Maybe he was just buying time to make up a story.*

After turning the first corner, she called the admiral on her cellphone.

"Hello, admiral? It's Patricia. I've been to the restaurant."

"Did you see Farhad?" the admiral asked.

Patricia told him what had occurred.

"I don't think we have much choice," the admiral commented. "You'll go back there at six. Meanwhile, go to your flat and wait. Who knows, John might call you there after all."

But John did not call. At six, Patricia was back at the Bita restaurant.

Farhad was waiting for her. As she walked in, he led her into a quiet corner and made sure they were not being overheard.

"Mr. John will come tomorrow," he said in a low voice. "They are still busy with him and it will take until tomorrow. Then he will come back. I promise you that no harm will come to him. On my honor."

Patricia wasn't buying that.

"Farhad, you know me by now. I hope you do not consider me a fool." She looked the Iranian directly in the eyes. "You keep telling me that you know nothing. So how come you suddenly have this information regarding John returning tomorrow?"

Farhad remained with his mouth half open, as if restraining himself from saying anything incriminating.

"Your mother knows everything," she accused. "She knows where John is, doesn't she? Answer me!"

But Farhad bowed his head and said nothing.

Furious, Patricia stormed out and called the admiral again.

"You're probably right," the admiral said. "The mother is involved somehow and Farhad is protecting her. But we want them to cooperate with us, so we need to cooperate with them. Let's give them some credit; we'll wait until tomorrow and see what happens. I have a gut feeling that John is safe."

The admiral's soothing tone calmed Patricia's nerves. She went straight home and spent the night in a restless sleep.

## SIXTY-TWO

Retired Inspecteur Auguste Poulenc had invited two guests to dinner at his home. Actually, the idea originated with Commissaire Felix Duval after the latter discovered that his ex-colleague at the prefecture, Poulenc, was a close friend of one of the employees who worked with Professor Allier. Duval also learned that they frequently dined together at Poulenc's home, and easily got himself invited as well. Now Poulenc was introducing his guests to each other.

"Michel, this is Commissaire Felix Duval of the prefecture, where I used to work. Commissaire, this is Dr. Michel Alvarez, an old friend of mine. He works in the Paris University."

"Indeed," Duval said. "How interesting. Which department do you work in, Dr. Alvarez?"

"I'm in the Irradiation Research and Development department," Alvarez said. "It was in the news recently. You may have heard of it. Nasty accident."

"Ah, yes, I remember. An electrocution. Professor Allier, wasn't it?

"Correct. You have a good memory, commissaire."

"I need it in my profession. Did you know the professor?"

"Of course. He was my direct superior in the department. I was his right-hand man, so to speak."

"And who is your superior now?"

"Actually, no one." Alvarez smiled. "I am to be the new head of the department."

*That means a promotion*, Duval thought. *The job involves lectures and publications. He's looking at a professorship nomination. Oh, yes, that's motive enough for murder ...*

"Congratulations," Duval said. "Even though the circumstances were so regrettable."

"Enough shop talk, gentlemen," Poulenc interrupted. "Dinner will get cold if we do not commence at once."

Over wine and cheese, Duval reopened the issue.

"Dr. Alvarez, I hope you don't mind my prying. As a police investigator, I am intrigued by Professor Allier's death. May I ask your opinion on a couple of subjects?"

"Certainly, commissaire," Alvarez answered. "But I thought the case was closed."

"Yes, that is true. It was ruled as an accident, but I have reason to believe that this conclusion may not be accurate. Do *you* believe it was an accident, Dr. Alvarez?"

Alvarez shrugged.

"Who am I to argue with the law?" he said. "There was an inquiry and that was the verdict."

"I see. But what about the device on Allier's worktable? Nobody—and I assume you were asked about it together with the others—knew what it was. Could you try to give me a guess now, Dr. Alvarez?"

"I'm afraid not, commissaire." The wine kept Alvarez smiling all the while he was being questioned.

"I'll tell you something no one else knows. There were no fingerprints on the plug connecting the device to the mains. I know you're not a professional criminal investigator, but doesn't this fact seem odd to you?"

Alvarez thought for a moment.

"Well," he said, "it would make no sense for my good friend Allier to have wiped the plug after inserting it into the wall. So I would say someone else wiped the plug clean—perhaps even after the professor was electrocuted. So possibly there was someone else in the room with him at the time."

Duval was relentless.

"Countless criminal cases and detective novels indicate that you search for the murderer in the proximity of the victim. As we know that his family has no connection whatever to the case, we need to look within the department employees."

Alvarez frowned.

"Where are you heading, commissaire?" he asked.

"Oh, please don't be alarmed, Dr. Alvarez. I'm just trying to develop an academic theory, that's all. You don't mind, do you?"

"I see." The smile came back to Alvarez's face.

"I presume you know all the employees in the department. Who, in your opinion, would be interested in Professor Allier's demise?"

"You put me in a very delicate position, Commissaire Duval. It is not a simple thing to point the finger of suspicion at a coworker. Murder, yet. Of course, every organization has its internal rivalries, intrigues, and aspirations, etc. But from here to murder—that's a gigantic leap. To answer your question: no. I do not think anyone in the department would concoct, let alone carry out, such a plot. So I'm afraid you'll have to ask the classic question 'Who benefits from Allier's death?' to somewhere else."

They ended the dinner, congratulated Poulenc on an excellent evening, and parted company.

Duval was not satisfied by Alvarez's answers. *He was the only one who benefited from Allier's death*, he thought. *So far, nothing indicates that he could not have pulled off the murder himself. He was close to the crime arena, went about freely, nobody would question his authority or right to be anywhere ...*

*Perhaps I have been wasting too much time on the Dupré widow and her British friend? Perhaps I blinded myself from seeing other approaches to the case? The killer may well be in the department right now, enjoying the rewards of his crime.*

*Still—I should not jump to conclusions. Not again.*

CB&EO

The telephone rang in Patricia's flat at eight a.m.

"Patty?"

"John! Good lord, Johnny—are you all right? I was worried sick! What happened to you?"

"I'll be there in a few minutes, and I'll tell you everything. Prepare some coffee, please." He hung up.

Patricia called the admiral. He told her they should both be at his office at ten.

Half an hour later, John arrived. He and Patricia embraced and exchanged kisses on both cheeks.

"So tell me already," Patricia said. "Where did you disappear to?"

"They abducted me and interrogated me for twenty four hours, with occasional short intervals."

"But why? What did they want?"

"I had to convince them that I wasn't a British agent, or one of the Ayatollah provocateurs. I think I did pretty well. I hope that now they're ready to cooperate."

"Oh, I really hope so." Patricia's eyes were shining, and she pressed his hands in hers.

"Not so fast, Patty. It seems there's still an additional confirmation they need to get from someone higher up."

"The admiral is expecting us at ten. We'll hear all the gory details then. Drink your coffee and we'll leave."

"Mind if I have a wash up before we go?"

"There's a fresh towel under the sink." She smiled.

They took the subway and arrived at Admiral Stone's office on time.

"My dear boy, welcome back." Handshakes and backslapping were followed by an offer of drinks. "Frankly, we were somewhat concerned for your safety. Your disappearance was quite sudden. Perhaps we needed that, if only to remind us that we're not playing parlor games. Well, you're safe, sound, and healthy—that's the main thing. Now tell us what happened."

"Oumid told me that I had to meet one of their men who would take over responsibility. We set up a meeting in a public parking lot, and a closed commercial van picked me up. Oumid remained behind in the lot. The seat by the driver was occupied, so I sat in the back, between two heavyset men. I wasn't worried, because I knew they wanted me to meet someone who was waiting for me. It was quite a long drive, probably to one of London's suburbs. I can't tell which, because the only window in the van, the rear window, was covered by a blind. And there was a partition between the passengers and the driver, so I couldn't see out the front either.

"When the car finally stopped, my two burly neighbors exited first, and when I got out they grabbed me by the arms and led me into a small house. At this point, I realized that I was no longer free—that I was being held by force. But I decided not to resist. I was pushed into a large room that had one of its corners concealed behind a curtain. There were people behind it. I was seated facing the curtain and interrogated. I noticed that there were small holes in the fabric through which I was being observed. I guessed that they wanted to make sure that I was not sent by the British immigration authorities, or by the ayatollahs, as a provocateur."

"How did you come to this inference?" the admiral asked.

"It was quite obvious. First, they gave all my particulars to somebody to check out—to confirm my identity. I don't know what methods they used, but about fifteen minutes later they got the okay that I was who I claimed to be. Then they went into detailed questioning of my past—specifically regarding any connections I may have had with MI5, MI6 or Scotland Yard.

"While others checked out my responses, I was questioned about the ayatollahs. The fact that Patricia had recently been on a tour in Iran, and that I was working with her on this subject, raised their suspicions—I might have been using her to make contact with the Iranian regime. Or that perhaps she was recruited as their agent when she toured their country. My interrogators did not conceal the purpose of their questions, so it's not so hard to come up with the conclusions I did. I'm sure they did so deliberately— they wanted to prove to me that they were well connected and could check out any story I could throw at them, so I'd better tell the truth. I cooperated with them fully."

"And the bottom line is … ?" the admiral prompted.

"They are very methodical and industrious workers," John said. "I believe we're dealing with people we can trust. However, they want a final confirmation from someone in their leadership."

"And during all this time, didn't they give you anything to eat or drink?" Patricia asked.

"They certainly did—they were most courteous. Plentiful and tasty. But as I was under coercion, I didn't wholly enjoy the meals. But I'm not complaining—just stating facts."

"And then?" the admiral asked.

"This morning, when it was all over, it was still dark outside. They drove me to Trafalgar Square, told me to contact Oumid and sped away. I called Patricia, took a taxi to her place, and you know the rest."

The admiral leaned back in his chair, obviously relieved.

"No harm done," he said. "Carry on with your mission. I shall report to the board."

After they had left the admiral's office, John called Oumid and set up a meeting. Patricia was not at all surprised to learn that Oumid had not been in Rome.

CƆȣ੪Ɔ

## *From the Press—News Digest*

Iran's president, Mahmoud Ahmadinejad, publicly announced that Iran has developed centrifuges using a new technology that would greatly enhance the output of enriched uranium. Iran had thus become independent of other countries.

Two weeks later, the Iranians attempted to launch a 'spy' satellite into space. This was met with mixed reactions: the Iranians claimed a resounding success, while the West asserted that the launch had failed and the satellite had fallen into the ocean. Photographs of the satellite disintegrating in flight were presented to back up this claim.

CƆȣ੪Ɔ

John Carmichael brought Patricia along with him for the meeting with Oumid. The latter had obviously been briefed in preparation for this meeting.

"I can now tell you," he said, "that we have a figure of authority among us, a woman, who has ties with Iran. If you can manage to convince her, you'll have everything you need in Iran. I warn you, this is no easy task. She is highly educated, experienced and extremely clever. You won't pull the wool over her eyes."

"Convincing her is my responsibility," John said.

Oumid smiled.

"You cannot. She is of advanced age, married and very religious. She would never meet with a strange man, let alone in private. Only a woman may meet with her. You, Miss Patricia, would be that person."

Patricia recoiled. She considered herself a beginner in these matters and was sure she could not convince a powerful and suspicious leader to cooperate.

"I … I'm sorry," she said. "I think you need someone more experienced than myself."

"That's all right, Patricia," John said. He remembered Anne Dupré, who had formed the ideology of the association. "We have the lady to do the job—I'll just have to arrange it with her. But tell me, Oumid, why does a religious lady such as your leader object to the regime in Iran?"

"She expresses what we all think," Oumid said seriously. "Those people over there are not true Muslims. They have abused Islam to gain power and oppress the populace. They are religious fanatics—totally without conscience. True Islam is a good and humane religion, full of brotherly love. Mohammed has ordered us to respect women and to provide for them as they deserve. The ayatollahs degrade women and make them their slaves. As for the economic and political aspects, they are ruining the country. Iran is an international pariah and the Iranian people are tyrannized. Yes, our leader is a devout Muslim, but an enemy of the Iranian government. I hope I have made myself clear."

"You certainly have," Patricia said. John nodded.

"When do you think the meeting could be arranged?" John asked.

"I assume it will take about two days for our leader to be assured of the meeting with you and to prepare herself for it," Oumid said.

John realized that he had to report again to the admiral, as Martin had not yet returned from Mauritania. The admiral, in turn, had to finalize the meeting with Anne Dupré.

"So let's settle for about three or four days from now," he suggested.

"Fine," Oumid said, and they parted as good friends.

John and Patricia went to a nearby café. Over coffee, John called the admiral and reported on the meeting with Oumid.

"Sounds good," the admiral said. "I will need to call Anne over from Paris. It may take two or three days."

"That's what I told Oumid," John said. "When you know exactly when Anne will arrive, I'll call him and set up the meeting."

"I think that went pretty well, all things considered," John said.

"I think you were magnificent," Patricia said. She laid her hand on his.

"Let's celebrate!" John ordered two whiskies. They had a toast while looking deeply into each other's eyes, still holding hands.

"You know, Pat," John said suddenly, "I think you're more beautiful today than when I dated you years ago."

Patricia couldn't believe she was actually blushing. She gripped his hand tighter and then let go.

"Who is this Anne woman?" she asked. "You mentioned her on the phone just now."

"She's Martin's cousin. I don't know her personally, though we've met a couple of times." John described Anne as best he could as the founder of the association and its main ideologist.

"Sounds like a formidable woman," Patricia remarked. "If she's half of what you said, she's ideal for the meeting with our Iranian torchbearer."

⋙⋘

The admiral left his office and took a taxi to Tottenham Court Road, where he called Anne from a public booth.

"How are you doing, Anne?"

"Fine, thanks. And you?"

"Same here. Listen—I have a complimentary invitation to that symposium you were interested in. It starts the day after tomorrow and will run for two days. I'll save the invitation for you if you can get here in time—otherwise, I'll very reluctantly have to take Margaret. What do you say?"

"I'd be delighted. I'm always happy to get to London. Thanks for thinking of me. I can be there tomorrow evening."

"My pleasure. See you then."

## SIXTY-THREE

Commissaire Duval decided to dig a little deeper into the doings of Dr. Michel Alvarez. As taking the direct approach was his custom, Duval called him and set up an appointment for the next day. Now the commissaire sat facing the new head of the Irradiation Department in his office at the university.

"I'll come straight to the point, Dr. Alvarez," Duval said. "Please tell me of your relationship with Professor Allier."

"I'm afraid there isn't much to relate," replied Alvarez. "We worked together for five years. We solved complex problems, some of which were of international significance. I won't list them now—everything is on file or in the computer databases. I can positively state that Professor Allier and I were always on the most cordial of terms—even friendly. You can verify that with other employees in the department. I cannot recall a single occasion in which we had a dispute. Well, there was one exception, I suppose, when he offered me to join some kind of organization or society with the intent of saving the world. I thought it was a crackpot idea."

The commissaire's forehead twitched almost imperceptibly.

"Really?" he said. "What else did he say about this organization?"

"I'm surprised you're interested, commissaire," Alvarez said. "It has nothing to do with our topic of discussion."

Duval made a dismissing motion with his hand.

"You never can tell," he said. "Anything can become important in an investigation. Sometimes a speck of dust can solve a crime."

"Like I said, it sounded too bizarre to me, and I did not attempt to understand his explanations. I listened out of courtesy toward my superior. He spoke about dictatorships, and how weak Western democracies were, and how science could save the world."

"What did you say to him?"

"I commented that this kind of enterprise didn't stand a chance. No sane scientist would risk his career on such a dubious venture. That's why we have governments, armies, budgets, etc."

"And his response?" Duval was getting impatient.

"He said that governments don't do a thing against tyrants, but that his association had contacts with scientists all over

Europe, each offering some kind of unconventional contribution. I answered that I didn't believe in that kind of nonsense and that I would not take part in any illegal activity, that we had families to support and that he should forget about such fantasies."

"Did that make him angry?"

"On the contrary. He mused in silence for a bit, and then said I was probably right. He never brought up the topic again, but it seemed that from that day he was worried. And absent minded. He remained this way until the day of his death. Funny—it just occurred to me now that the device on his desk might have had something to do with that cause he talked about."

The commissaire thanked Alvarez and took his leave. He recalled that Allier's widow had implied that during his last weeks, her husband had been worried and absent-minded.

*It seems*, he thought, *that there's an international conspiracy that recruits scientists who develop secret inventions to fight totalitarian regimes clandestinely. Or something like that. And, so far, I know they have collaborators in France, England, and Belgium—doubtless, other countries are also involved. This is a very serious and severe situation. Of course, it does not prove they had anything to do with Allier's murder. But if I take this story to the prefecture, they'll think I've lost my marbles and probably transfer me somewhere where I wouldn't be a bother. Worse, they may force me into early retirement.*

*On the other hand, I cannot rule out that Alvarez fabricated the entire conspiracy story in order to throw me off the scent. There is nothing to contradict the theory that Alvarez committed the murder himself. For all I know, he could be a serial killer, responsible for several unsolved murders in our files. I'll need to find evidence to corroborate this hypothesis.*

⊗⊗⊗

It was still morning when Anne walked into Admiral Stone's office. The admiral updated her with all the details that John and Patricia had gathered, and why her presence was now essential.

"How come such a religious woman opposes the ayatollahs?" Anne asked.

The admiral gave her Oumid's answer. Anne nodded.

"I'll do my best," she said. "I would, however, like to have a chat with John and Patricia first."

"I've requested John Carmichael to come here. I don't remember if you've met him before."

"I have. I haven't met Patricia, though I know she was with you in Tunisia and with Martin in Iran. George Graham's sister, isn't she?"

"Correct. Fantastic girl. She and John used to be a close couple several years ago. And it looks to me that their romance is reviving." The admiral winked, and switched smoothly to another topic. "Look, Anne, I've called for a board meeting here, tomorrow evening at six. I want everyone to hear your report on your interview with the Iranian woman."

Anne's eyes widened.

"I thought we'd agreed that London—"

"... was out of bounds. We did. But I've given this much thought. It's been a long time now, and I believe that if you're in any danger at all of being followed, it's in Paris and nowhere else. I know the Scotland Yard's methods and I know their mentality—your commissaire could have used the aid of his colleague here once or twice, but that's it. Not any more than that."

There was a knock on the door, and the admiral ushered John in. Anne immediately recognized the tall, handsome man she had met on her visit to the fitness gym.

"Hello, John," Anne smiled as she shook his hand. "Nice to see you again."

"Likewise." He grinned back at her. "Good morning, admiral."

"Is everything set up?" the admiral asked.

"Patricia is waiting for us in the lobby of the Hilton Hotel. We'll call Oumid from there, and he'll lead us to the woman in charge."

"Good luck," the admiral said, and saw them out.

Anne and John took a taxi to the Hilton. Patricia rose to greet them as they entered.

Anne was thunderstruck! This was the same gorgeous blonde-haired woman she had seen with Martin in the café in Paris! Anne felt slightly dizzy and felt the need for a couple of seconds to pull herself together. She feigned correcting something with her shoes and sat in the nearest chair to do so. She then took a deep breath, pasted a warm smile on her face, and rose to greet Patricia with her hand outstretched.

"Hello, Patricia. We finally meet. I've heard such a lot about you."

"Hello, Anne. And I of you," Patricia answered. "I understand you're Martin's cousin."

They continued to chat. John left them to call Oumid.

"Before meeting with the Iranians," Anne said, "I'd like to hear some more about the ones you have met."

"They're two brothers. Farhad, the younger one, is a waiter in a restaurant we dined at. He's a nice chap, though rather timid. We think he's not directly involved in what the Iranian group is doing—more like a go-between. The other brother, Oumid, whom we're about to meet, is one of the activists. And we're sure their mother is an activist, too. We visited their house."

"I'd like you to be with me during the meeting," Anne said, "if they'll permit it."

Patricia was quite taken with Anne. She knew that Anne was a senior academician and very talented. Now she saw that Anne was also a striking figure of a woman with a charming personality. Being offered to join Anne at the meeting was indeed a compliment.

"I'd be glad to," Patricia said. "It would be a wonderful opportunity to hear the ideology coming directly from you."

John returned.

"All set," he said. "I have the directions where to meet Oumid."

"In a minute," Anne said. "Please sit down. I think I have all the necessary information from the admiral, but I'd like to hear all that happened from you two as well."

She listened carefully as they told her of their various attempts to contact Iranians, of the success with Farhad, and mainly what their personal impressions were of what happened to them. Anne was particularly interested in the period that John was in their custody.

"Could you identify any of them if you saw them again?" Anne asked.

"Only the bodyguards, who were not even present during the interrogation. The others were concealed behind the curtain."

Anne thought for a second.

"It seems they are not aggressive. Good. Let's go, then," she said.

John stopped a passing taxi and gave Oumid's address. Oumid was waiting on the pavement, and when the taxi stopped, he joined them inside. He gave instructions to the driver, and then let John introduce Anne to him.

At their destination, they all got out, but John requested the driver to wait a couple of minutes.

"Mr. John, I'm afraid this is as far as you go," Oumid said. He then addressed the women. "Our leader is Mrs. Leila Bahtyar. She belongs to a very respectable family from the days of the Shah. You two ladies will accompany me, and I shall introduce you to her husband. Please follow me."

"I'll wait for you at the Hilton," John said, and reentered the taxi.

Oumid led Anne and Patricia into a modern, multi-storied building. They took the elevator to the eighth floor, where Oumid rang the bell on one of the doors. It was opened by a girl, probably a maid, who ushered them into a spacious, typically Iranian, living room. The floor was covered in lush carpets, the armchairs and couch were of expensive leather, and the tea tables were hand-carved teak. Anne sat on a couch, while Patricia browsed through the pictures and ornaments on the wall.

An elderly man entered the room about a minute later. He was short, about seventy, with sparse white hair, but with the ramrod posture of a military colonel.

"I am Omar Bahtyar," he introduced himself in flawless English. "Leila Bahtyar's husband. Welcome to our home. Please come this way."

Anne got up and was about to introduce herself, too, when she saw Oumid shake his head, and gesture with his hand to follow the man. She nodded to Patricia and let Omar lead them along a corridor, where he knocked on one of the doors. He then opened it and signaled the two women to enter.

It was like a smaller living room, resplendent with lush carpeting, furniture, and ornaments. On one side of the room a very fat woman sat on a couch, almost filling in both seats. She was dressed completely in black, her head was covered with a black shawl, underneath which was another shawl that covered her forehead down to her eyebrows. Anne and Patricia approached her and they shook hands.

"Please sit here opposite me," Leila Bahtyar said. Her English accent was in stark contrast to her appearance—she could have been an Oxford English professor. "I was told you are interested in what's happening in Iran today. How may I assist you?"

"Thank you for receiving us, Mrs. Bahtyar," Anne said. "We are very honored. I shall get directly to the point. We believe that Iran, just like any other nation led by a despot, is a threat to its surroundings and to the world."

"So do I, my dear," Mrs. Bahtyar said. "But what can you do that powers such as the United States and the European Union cannot?"

Anne took a deep breath and made full use of her oratory skills, honed to an art from years of lecturing on history.

"The reason Western democracies do nothing concerning dictatorships is that they *cannot* do anything. Therein lies the root of the problem. And why can't they? Ironically, because the democratic system forces the leadership to put their own political survival *before* their own country's benefit. Their main concern is to be re-elected to office. And their voters want peace, quiet and comfort. History has proven again and again that democracies enter wars only with the support of the majority of voters." Anne went on to describe the casualty statistics of both world wars, and the horrifying forecast of a possible nuclear war in the future. She paused to let the Iranian leader contemplate the picture she had presented. Then she pressed on.

"We want to prevent those horrors from happening," Anne said softly. "But let's concentrate on Iran, now. The current regime is openly and deliberately provoking the rest of the world, and adamantly defying it in its continuing research into nuclear weaponry. Sooner or later this *must* erupt, and the ensuing conflagration will cause innumerable casualties of Iranian soldiers and civilians, immeasurable suffering on the entire population, and probably the collapse of the whole nation."

Anne waited for a response. Patricia's mouth was slightly open in awe.

Mrs. Bahtyar had listened silently with lowered eyes. Now she opened them and her eyes bore deep in to Anne's.

"And how," she asked, "do you propose to stop the dictators?"

"We are a small group of academicians and scientists. We eschew all violence, even in our countermeasures against tyranny. Our aim is to damage the dictator's reputation, to humiliate him in front of his own people, and to cause him to doubt and even abandon his megalomaniac dreams."

A faint smile played on the face of the fat woman.

"Please go on," she said.

"Without going into technicalities, I'll try to depict to you a possible scenario resulting from our work. Imagine, please, your national holiday. Your president is facing hundreds of thousands of his people in the main parade grounds, and the world press is aiming cameras and microphones at him to catch every word and gesture. He opens his mouth to speak …" Anne paused for effect, "… and out comes a horrendous shriek! Magnified a thousand fold by the public address system. Caught on hundreds of millions of television sets. Heard by as many millions over the radio.

"But that is just the beginning. It is followed by the infantry parade going off course, armored and missile-towing vehicles stalling, earsplitting screeches from all acoustic speakers drowning out any other sound…. Mrs. Bahtyar, do you suppose any dictator could survive such a debacle? Do you not agree that his prestige would be irreparably discredited? If by some miracle he remains sane or has not been deposed by his own people, do you not believe that he would be extremely careful in calculating his future steps?"

"And you can cause all these things to happen?"

"Yes, we can," Anne said simply. "As I mentioned earlier, we have scientists working for us, and each has contributed inventions to help us on our cause. On the other hand, we cannot make use of them in Iran without cooperation from the inside."

Mrs. Bahtyar ignored Anne's hint.

"Tell me about these inventions," she said.

"Tiny acoustic devices disrupt all wired and wireless communications. A special chemical emits a gas that stops vehicles. Another causes large groups of people, like a soldiers in a military parade, to languish in apathy and forget what they were supposed to do. And we have more devices under development."

Mrs. Bahtyar listened attentively and nodded her head from time to time.

"I see," she said. "You are engaged in preparing measures no one has ever thought of before. I must remind you, however, that, in Iran, tyranny is enforced differently than in other countries such as Libya and North Korea, where just one individual wields all the power. The Iranian president is subject to the religious authorities headed by the Ayatollah Ali Khamenei. Any action you intend to take must also take him into account."

Anne was not prepared for this, but she plunged ahead.

"We have thought of this, and our teams are preparing plans of action. At the same time, any suggestions you and your followers could make would be most welcome. As I have said, we need your help—I would not be here otherwise."

"What do you expect of me?" the fat woman asked.

"Our people have visited Iran as tourists. They have concluded that foreigners could not operate there—only the local populace could get away with what we're planning. We need to send objects and materials to accomplish these plans. We need an address, a company or an importer, who could place a legitimate order for legitimate goods that would pass the customs without any problems. We would send our stuff inside the bona fide packaging."

"Let us assume you have managed to deliver the goods. Then what?"

"That's the second thing we need. People who could distribute the stuff at the right time, to the right locations, and in the right dosages."

"Is there anything else?"

"No, Mrs. Bahtyar," Anne said simply. "That is all the help we request from you, if it's not too much."

Anne and Patricia waited several minutes while the Iranian matriarch sat with her eyes closed, thinking about what she had heard. Finally, she raised her face to her visitors.

"I shall help you. But first I must consult with those who will be doing the job. I hope to connect you in a day or two with the person who will follow through. Oumid will notify you."

"We are very much in your debt, Mrs. Bahtyar," Anne said. "Thank you." She and Patricia stood up. At that moment the door opened and Omar Bahtyar appeared to escort them through the corridor.

When they reached the living room, Oumid joined them and took them down to the street. He hailed a taxi for them, and then went back into the building.

Patricia seemed to be in a daze.

"That was absolutely amazing!" she said. "The way you handled the conversation … it's … I'm …"

Anne laughed.

"Thanks, Patricia," she said. "I 'orate' for a living, you know."

"Did you notice how the old man came in the second we got up? Do you think she signaled him with a special pushbutton? Or maybe he was watching us through a peephole by the door?"

"Perhaps. It shows that we're dealing with a well-organized group."

The taxi brought them to the Hilton Hotel, where John was waiting on tenterhooks. Anne called the admiral to inform him that everything had gone smoothly.

She then left the hotel, took the first available taxi and gave the address of the admiral's office. Her heart had not stopped pounding since she had first laid eyes on Patricia a few hours earlier. A couple of times during the interview with Mrs. Bahtyar, she thought she was about to faint. Now she was alone for the first time since then. She took several deep breaths.

*It was she! Martin was recruiting Patricia when I saw them together in Paris. And I thought he was philandering. I couldn't have been more wrong! And now, I have wronged Martin terribly. Oh, god—I wish I could climb into a hole in the ground and pull it shut over me. How can I face Martin again? How can I face* anyone *again?*

CﬆⱭ

Admiral Stone had hardly put down the phone when it rang again. It was his grandson, Brian. This was quite unusual—Brian had never called him before, so there were probably interesting news.

"Hello, Grandpa," Brian said. "I've solved your puzzle."

"Indeed?" said the admiral, a bit surprised. "Excellent. I had no doubt you could do it, my boy, but I honestly believed it would take you longer. I'd be delighted if you showed it to me."

"Can you come over now?"

"I'll come as soon as I can, Brian." The board meeting came first.

"Hurry. I'm dying to show this to you."

CﬆⱭ

Martin had arrived from Mauritania the evening before. He had called the admiral, reported the failure of the mission, and he now took part in the board meeting at the admiral's office. Anne watched him, her heart pounding, but he didn't give her more than a casual glance of recognition.

There were five topics on the agenda: the Iranian contacts, the Mauritania trip, hacking into the Iranian military computers, using Excalibur, the irradiation beam, and the vehicle-stopping fluid.

The admiral described all that had happened with John and Patricia until the meeting between Anne and Mrs. Bahtyar. Anne then took over and told the forum about the contents of that meeting.

Sir Cedric and Martin listened intently to every word.

"What now?" Sir Cedric asked.

"John has already met with Oumid," Anne said, "and the latter will set up a meeting with the Iranian contact. It will be up to Martin now to lead this mission and arrange for the transfer of the goods and the training of their activists. And we need to take heed of Mrs. Bahtyar's warning: we might have to consider the simultaneous 'offensive' against the other members of the Iranian leadership."

"We'll give it some thought," the admiral said. "Now let's hear about Mauritania from Martin."

Martin glumly told them about the flight to Nouakchott and the trip from there to Zouérat, Ould Salah, the mine, the lack of vehicles, Ould Salah's jeep, and his offer to loan it to them, and the generator.

"The mine is ideally located," Martin concluded. "We have its accurate GPS coordinates, but they're useless if we can't get a car into it. I'm sorry—but this mission has been a flop."

There was a short silence.

"Maybe not," Sir Cedric said slowly. "After all, weren't we the people who invented 'if you can't beat 'em, join 'em'? Let's be a bit more flexible, shall we? Your garage man made a proposition we should take advantage of. He's prepared to sell you a working generator, tow it to the mine site and let you have his jeep for a couple of days. So why don't we forget the lorry-slash-van option and use the generator instead? Stick it into the mine, and we'll have my laser beam work on it. As a matter of fact, I even prefer the generator to the lorry—the engine is more massive."

Martin was dumbfounded. Then he got to his feet.

"Sir Cedric, I salute you!" he said. "I bow my head in shame for not having thought of that myself." He turned to the others, and his voice was excited. "It could work! Ould Salah requested me to call him if there was a change of plans so that he could sell me that generator. He gave me his business card. It's a bit too late to call him now, but I'll do that first thing tomorrow morning."

"You'll need to plan your return visit right after handling the Iranian contacts," Anne said. She forced her voice to remain calm.

"You'll be faking the actual filming this time, won't you?" the admiral said. "So you'll need a second 'actor'—you know, one to chase and the other to be chased. Who did you think of taking along?"

"Bernard Webb," Martin said, sitting down again. "He speaks excellent French."

"Let me have the mine coordinates," Anne said to Martin. "I'll give them to Boulanger, and he'll let us know the exact timings to expect the satellite to pass there on any given date."

"This time you'll have the movie gear with you," the admiral said. "And the satellite phone. If the beam fails to stop the generator, or misses it altogether, we'll attempt the experiment again while you're still there."

"However, Martin," Sir Cedric butted in, "if the generator *is* halted by the laser, I would appreciate it if you could bring me samples of the damaged parts." Martin nodded. "And furthermore, if what's left of the generator looks visibly suspicious, I suggest you douse it with fuel and set light to it."

"I shall," Martin promised.

"And now," the admiral said, with a sheepish grin on his face, "I'd like to report that my grandson, Brian, has hacked into one of the Iranian top security computer systems." At the babble of comments from the other participants, he raised his hand. "That's all I know. I found out about it only an hour ago and I have no further details. But if Brian says he's done it, then I believe him."

"How do you propose we use this ... this invasion?" Anne asked.

"Right now all I can say is that we can cause a hell of a mess, wherever we penetrate. But if our timing and our target are right, meaning during the grand rally, it could intensify the confusion considerably."

"And now," Anne continued, "we need to talk about Excalibur— our irradiation beam that detonates explosives—and it's a matter of principle. When we established our association, we laid down some ground rules—one of which was that we would not use weapons against people. We want to cause consternation, disrupt communications, and so forth—and not harm the population. All our devices, excluding Excalibur, follow this philosophy. With Excalibur, there is a very good chance that the explosion following its use on a military depot will cause severe casualties among the personnel in the vicinity—perhaps even civilians. It would be like bombing from the air. It would be an act of war!"

There was a long silence.

"Anne, gentlemen," Admiral Stone said finally, "I thought we had covered this a long time ago. Perhaps we had not said the words outright, perhaps we just implied them. But let us make no mistake about this—and I shall explicitly say what our charter, if we had ever written it out, would have contained as a major clause. Our very existence as an association is based on the premise that democratic powers do not act the way they should to keep world peace. If they had, there would be no need for our association. And what was it we expected them to do? Act! Bomb! Destroy!" The admiral took a deep breath. "Our assumption was that by the democracies' non-action, hundreds of millions of people would die. But if they *did* act, there would also be casualties. Thousands—perhaps hundreds of thousands. And what do *we* propose? Irradiate explosives depots in military camps in order to eliminate them, and to wag a warning finger in the dictators' faces saying: 'Watch it! You're out of line!' Yes, it is quite possible that there'll be some soldiers and civilians near these depots. Is that a valid enough reason for us *not* to act?"

"Hear, hear," Sir Cedric said.

"You're quite right, admiral," Martin said.

Anne listened throughout with her head bowed. Then she sighed deeply, as if battling with her conscience. A moment later, she looked up.

"So be it, then," she said. "However, there is still something bothering me. Our success in Tunisia rather prevented us from thinking a bit deeper into this. Can anyone tell me how we're going to irradiate military bases in North Korea? Our plane will be shot down almost instantly. As to Iran, we could probably fly there under a suitable cover, but I can't imagine what that cover could be. Besides, on rally day I suppose all civilian flights will be suspended. Ideas anyone?"

"Why don't we try an unmanned aircraft?" Sir Cedric asked. "I know nothing about these things, except that I know they exist. Make sense to anyone?"

Martin got to his feet, his eyes shining.

"Sir Cedric, you're outdoing yourself this evening!" he said. "In my army days, I've had some contact with UAVs and RPVs. I think it's worth—"

"With what?" Anne and Sir Cedric asked together.

"Unmanned Aerial Vehicles and Remote Piloted Vehicles. We'll need to do some research on them, but in principle I think Sir Cedric has hit the nail on the head. I'll charge George with finding out availability and range versus payload." He sat down.

"And price," the admiral added.

"We'll need to consider how to modify the remote control so that we can activate Excalibur from afar," Sir Cedric said. "And, like the generator, in case we won't be able to bring it back, there needs to be a self-destruct mechanism integrated into the … flying thing."

"Right," Martin said. "Let's discuss this again after I've collected more information."

Sir Cedric stood up.

"I would like to report now on the tests George Graham, Spencer Partridge, and myself conducted on the new fluid developed by Gustav Lemke," he said. "We received a couple of large bottles of the stuff from him about a week ago. We drove north—in two cars, of course—and repeated our old experiment with the fertilizer. We used a gardener's watering can to sprinkle the stuff on the road. We got the same successful results as with the fertilizer! If we could get a municipal water tanker to do the sprinkling, even on just a short stretch of road, it'll be a triumph."

"So, do you think it could replace the fertilizer?" Anne asked.

"Not really. I think they should be used in tandem—some places, mainly roads, would be sprinkled, and others, such as parks and lawns near the parade itinerary, would be … umm, fertilized. It would heighten the effect!"

"You're right, Cedric," the admiral said. "Furthermore, taking into account what Mrs. Bahtyar advised, gardens surrounding the religious leadership in Iran should be considered as target areas, too. It wouldn't hurt to reduce the ayatollahs' mental facilities for a few hours of the day by spreading some of our gravel there. Provided, of course, that we can get hold of gardeners who work around those places. Martin, perhaps you could make this issue one of the topics you discuss with your Iranian contact."

"This all sounds fine in theory," Anne said. "However, I have a feeling that it won't be enough. We have to continue developing new methods to meet the threats facing us."

૭૪૦

The moment the board meeting was over, Martin hastily left the admiral's office. He couldn't stand the ache in his chest any longer. He had been snubbed by Anne for too long, and being in her presence during the meeting actually had him in physical pain. He got into his sports car, turned off his cell phone and began driving north—he had no destination in mind, just to get away as far as possible and let his frustration settle down.

When Anne saw Martin leave in such a hurry, she politely excused herself and went after him. There were only a few people in the lobby of the office building, but Martin was nowhere in sight. She returned to the admiral's office, where Sir Cedric was already putting on his jacket.

"There you are," the admiral said. "I was rather surprised you left without taking your purse and coat."

"Did I?" Anne said, now genuinely flustered. "Well, I'm back now. Do me a favor, please, Patrick. Call Martin on his cellphone. I need to talk to him."

The admiral looked at Sir Cedric quizzically, and dialed Martin's number.

"There's no answer," the admiral said after a while.

Anne tried to compose herself.

"I suppose it can wait. Well, I'm off to Paris now. We'll keep in touch." She collected her purse and coat and left the office.

∽⧣∾

On her way to Paris, Anne went over what had happened.

*I'm behaving like a teenager! I can hardly believe it, but I am! I was deliberately avoiding any direct contact with Martin during the meeting, and yet—when he left so abruptly—I just couldn't let it remain hanging in the air. And if I had caught up with him, I would have died! I don't think I could have faced him. But I had to try.*

*How could I have been so stupid? I saw him with a pretty girl in a café and immediately jumped to conclusions. And my subsequent behavior toward him is inexcusable! I shall never be able to explain it to him, and he'll never be able to forgive me.*

Anne straightened her shoulders and dialed Martin's cellphone number. On the last digit, her nerve failed, and she hung up.

*Oh my god, I can't do it! I just can't do it! Oh, Martin, my darling—please call me!*

∽⧣∾

The next morning, Anne discovered that Inspecteur Marnier had not returned to his usual post. *Perhaps Duval has given up on me,* she thought. *They may have finally concluded that they're wasting their time on me. Let's see if it stays that way. Meanwhile, we remain cautious.*

## *SIXTY-FOUR*

Oumid had made all the arrangements. The contact man was named Shahram, and through John, Martin was notified that the meeting was to take place at Oumid's house.

Martin, John, and Shahram sat alone in one of the rooms. The Iranian was about sixty, tall, and distinguished looking—Martin could picture him as a high-ranking ex-army officer. After the opening formalities, Martin described the means and methods that the association had developed and that they intended to deploy in Iran. That is, all save for Excalibur and the "wasp."

"The tasks you require," Shahram said, "are relatively simple, and we have no lack of people in Iran to do them. They are prepared to sacrifice their lives for freedom, but you do not even ask them to endanger themselves. Yes, we have gardeners, garbage collectors, sanitations workers, and employees at military bases. They will eagerly carry out these missions. Shipping is no problem either. If you could deliver all your stuff to our warehouse near London, we'll take care of the rest. We have all the legal formalities worked out, and a lot of experience in implementing them."

"I am very pleased to hear this," Martin said. "Shahram, I travel a great deal, and I won't always be available in London. John, here, will take my place in my absence."

Shahram nodded toward John, and they exchanged telephone numbers.

"John, please arrange for the goods to get to the warehouse. Take George to help you. Now, Shahram, we still need to train your people. How do you propose we go about it?"

"Our head of instruction will be at your service. If you can train him, he will pass on what he learned to others in Tehran in the best possible way."

⊂⊃⊂⊃

While John made the necessary arrangements with Shahram, Martin was busy preparing for the return visit to Mauritania. He called Mahmoud Ould Salah.

"Hello there, Mr. Ould Salah. It's Martin Cooper from London. How are you?"

"Ah, yes, Mr. Martin," Ould Salah answered. "How can I be of service?"

"Do you remember the generator you showed us? I was wondering whether it was operational now."

"Indeed it is, Mr. Martin. I began working on it the day after you left, as I said I would. Two days later it was purring like a kitten."

"I hope none of *my* cats purr like that," Martin laughed. "Listen, Mr. Ould Salah, I would like to take you up on your offer of using your generator. Of course, I expect you to sell it to me at the special price you talked about."

"No problem. It's yours." Ould Salah sounded very pleased. "When will you arrive?"

"In three or four days. Please have it fully fueled."

"It will look like new, my friend. Fuel in the tank, air in the tires, and a fresh coat of paint. All okay?"

"All okay, Mr. Ould Salah. À bientôt."

CRED

When the board decided to continue with the Mauritania experiment, Martin had forgotten to give Anne the GPS coordinates of the mine's entrance. Anne was then to deliver them to Boulanger. Martin could not call Anne now—there was still a strict restriction on calling her directly.

He called the admiral.

"Admiral, I am texting you the coordinates of the mine. I will need a table of all the days until the end of next week with the precise times the satellite will be over the mine for each day. And please, ask Boulanger to be ready with a twelve hours' advance notice to 'press the button.' I also think that Sir Cedric would like to be informed of the proceedings in real time."

"Call me back before you leave," the admiral said. "I'll update you on the situation."

 C3&O 

Martin worked on completing the preparations for the trip. The movie gear and satellite phone were tested and packed. So was a toolbox, in order to remove parts of the generator. Bernard Webb was to join Philip and him on this trip as the second 'actor' for the movie.

They were fortunate that so far no one had ever questioned their presence anywhere. But this might not always be the case, and they needed to have effective cover stories. It was very likely that if the word got out that a movie was being shot near Zouérat, a horde of busybodies would converge on them. This could possibly be the first occasion in which anyone in that region had ever been close to a film crew, and it would definitely prevent them from carrying out their experiment. The questions were no problem. "We're doing a couple of action and scenery shots here, and we'll handle the rest back at the studio," would be the usual answer. No, what was really needed was a way to keep the inquisitive crowds far back. With that in mind, Martin packed a few hundred meters of rope and red ribbon, intending to cordon off the mine area from prying onlookers.

## SIXTY-FIVE

By the time Martin, Philip, and Bernard got to Zouérat, they were pretty much dead on their feet. Carrying all the extra gear took its toll, and they all needed a well-earned rest after a sleepless night, before resuming their mission. They stumbled into their rooms at the hotel and roused themselves around noon.

After lunch, they walked to Ould Salah's garage. Their arrival was a major event by Ould Salah's standards, and after the welcomes and Bernard's introduction, they were invited inside for tea.

"Thank you for the warm welcome," Martin said. "We would like to start work early tomorrow morning. Therefore, we'd like to tow the generator to the mine today. May we see it, please?"

Ould Salah smiled and beckoned them to the open window. Outside stood a shiny generator that looked as if it had just left the shop.

"Does it—" Bernard began.

"Salim!" Ould Salah yelled through the window. The boy dashed to the generator and pressed the starter button. The machine roared into life, and a pilot light shone brightly.

They watched the generator operate for a while. Ould Salah made a gesture, and Salim cut the engine. Ould Salah turned to his guests, beaming.

"How much do you want for it?" Martin smiled.

"Twenty thousand ouguiyas," Ould Salah grinned. "That's five hundred dollars."

Martin counted out the banknotes, and they shook hands to close the deal. He also asked Ould Salah for stakes or metal poles to cordon off the "filming area."

Ould Salah was a very efficient man. Everything they wanted was available. The generator was hitched to the back of the jeep, and Salim gathered stakes from around the yard and placed them in the jeep.

"Actually, Mr. Ould Salah," Martin said as diplomatically as he could, "we won't be depriving you of Salim tomorrow. We can drive the jeep to the mine ourselves."

The garage owner shook his head.

"Now is the time you'll need him most," he said. "He'll help with the generator, put up the stakes, and perform any task you ask him to do. And tomorrow you have the jeep for the entire day."

"We are truly grateful. But this time we're talking business. I shall pay for the boy's work and for renting the jeep. That's for today's work and for tomorrow. And perhaps we'll need an extra day as well."

Ould Salah gave him a paternal smile.

"We have settled on an agreement," he said. "So be it. You shall pay me a hundred dollars for every day you use the jeep. That includes the boy's work today."

Salim drove them to the mine's entrance. The three Englishmen got off and watched as the boy skillfully backed the generator into the mine. They applauded his driving abilities, and Martin handed him a ten-dollar bill. Salim froze for a moment, then bowed low and kissed Martin's hand.

While Salim was busy pounding in the stakes with a large mallet he had brought along, Philip asked Martin:

"Do you think Salim is a slave?"

"I suppose he is. But we'll never know for sure unless we ask Ould Salah, and I, for one, don't intend to."

The site was ready an hour later. They drove back to the garage, and left Salim there. Martin asked Ould Salah whether they could take the jeep to the hotel, as they needed to get up very early the next day.

"You rented it," Ould Salah said. "It's yours to do with as you please."

Back at the hotel, Martin consulted the chart Boulanger had supplied. They could begin the tests at five seventeen in the morning. After that, every one hundred and thirty two minutes would provide another opportunity for a test. He picked up the satellite phone and called the admiral.

"Everything is ready," Martin said. "We begin filming tomorrow at zero-five-seventeen."

After lunch, they bought a couple of fire extinguishers at a nearby hardware store. They decided to retire early, in anticipation of a hard day's work on the morrow. Martin requested the receptionist for a wake-up call at four a.m., but just to be sure, they all set their alarm watches to that time, too.

03&80

At their meeting earlier that morning, John and Shahram had agreed how they would get prepared for their training program. Accordingly, John had rented a commercial van in which the goods and equipment were to be delivered to the Iranians. He and George had just loaded the last carton into the van and now went over their checklist.

"Fertilizer and gravel?" George called.

"Three sacks each," John answered.

"Conditioner fluid for the gravel?"

"One carton containing a dozen cans labeled 'conditioner.'"

"Fertilizer activation fluid?"

"Three twenty-liter jerry cans labeled 'flower-bed fertilizer.'"

"Fuel pellets?"

"One carton containing fifty bags of pellets labeled 'dehydrated peas.'"

"Paganini?"

"One carton containing twenty miniaturized acoustic disruptors disguised as electric shavers." These had arrived just the day before from Italy.

"That's it, then," George said, as he closed the van's back door. "Off you go."

John drove the van to Daisy Lane, just off Hurlingham Park, where he met Shahram. John got out of the van and Shahram replaced him in the driver's seat.

"It's a nice day," John said. "I'll take a stroll in the park until you return."

"You can take my car for the next hour, until I return," Shahram said.

"That's all right, Shahram. Thanks, anyway."

"Okay. I'll give you a buzz on your cellphone as I approach."

John enjoyed his walk. Teams were playing football and basketball amid a lot of yelling and laughter. He knew that Shahram was driving the van to the Iranian secret warehouse, where all the goods were to be unloaded.

Forty-five minutes later John's phone rang.

"I'm ten minutes away from where we met," Shahram said. "Meet you there."

Shahram arrived very punctually.

"Did everything go smoothly?" John asked as he and Shahram switched places again.

"Oh, quite," the Iranian responded. "Now we have to wait until Mr. Martin returns so we can commence training."

"I'll let you know," John promised, and drove off to return the van.

CR80

## *Press Summary*

There are clear indications that Western democracy leaders, diplomats, and even the press, seem to say one thing (probably for public consumption), while their actions indicate the opposite. The United States is a prime example—their rhetoric of a tough stand against Iran's nuclear program is contradicted by the relaxing of the sanctions against Iran. The Turkish president has even declared that Iran had the right to develop nuclear capabilities for peaceful purposes.

The president of North Korea has announced the festivities to take place soon, in which the country's military power will be exposed for the world to see. Political sources state that he desperately needs such an imposing fete in order to raise the morale of his own people, which had been sorely deflated since he agreed (at least publicly) to curb his country's nuclear weaponry development, and began to dismantle nuclear installations. There is no doubt that the rally that he plans will show off his pièce de résistance—the long-range ballistic missiles.

Worldwide press reports indicate that for the past two years the International Atomic Energy Agency (IAEA) has known that Iran had finalized designs for manufacturing nuclear warheads. During a routine visit at that time, these sketches were shown but were concealed immediately thereafter. Since then, Iran has adamantly refused to reveal these documents again. Now that international pressure to substantially increase sanctions is rising, Iran has submitted these plans to the IAEA in Vienna. They 'explained' that they had obtained these designs 'by accident' together with other goods they had bought on the 'free market'. The Iranians were thereby hoping to tone down the demands for increased sanctions against them. They were supported by Russia and China, who oppose sanctions against Iran. As a result, the Iranian president issued a demand for an American apology to the Iranian people for libeling them. The latest Iranian move is seen as a blatant ploy to gain the time they need in order to achieve their goal of nuclear weaponry with the least interference possible.

CRBO

Martin and his companions left for the mine at half past four in the morning. It was still dark. They had laden the jeep with the movie gear, lighting equipment, work tools, and gloves, flashlights, a jerry can of petrol, the satellite telephone, sandwiches, soft drinks, and a thermos of coffee. Twenty minutes later, they arrived at the mine.

They shone their flashlights on the generator. It was in exactly the same condition it was when they left it—nothing had been stolen. It fired up on their third attempt and ran smoothly.

"Philip," Martin directed, "string up the rope on those stakes, please. Bernard, put the movie equipment into position facing the mine entrance." He himself began placing the red ribbons along the roped-off perimeter of their site. He then uncoiled a cable from the generator and plugged it into a lamp, just for appearance sake, in case anyone inquisitive enough—perhaps even Ould Salah himself—wanted to pay a visit.

As five a.m. grew near, they drove the jeep to a distance of about fifty meters from the mine. As dawn broke, it began to get brighter. They settled down with their sandwiches and drinks and watched the mine entrance closely. Their tension mounted. Five seventeen a.m. came and passed—nothing happened. The only sound was the distant clatter of the generator.

Suddenly they heard a sharp crack! The sound of a pistol shot in the open air. Nothing changed in the mine entrance, and they heard the generator chugging along merrily.

"There!" Philip shouted, and pointed to the right of the mine. A small puff of dust rose some twenty meters from the entrance.

When the trio got there, they saw a little crater, about forty centimeters across and thirty centimeters deep. A tiny depression at the bottom of the crater indicated that the hole had gone much deeper, but had apparently collapsed on itself. There was no doubt that the laser beam had hit here!

There was an obvious discrepancy in calibration! The experiment had to be repeated, and the discrepancy accounted for and corrected.

"Bernard, turn off the generator!" Martin yelled as he ran back to the jeep. "Philip, get the GPS coordinates of that hole in the ground."

Martin quickly dialed the admiral's number.

"Yes, hello?" The admiral's voice was groggy. He had evidently been sleeping. The time in London was the same as in Zouérat.

"Good morning, admiral," Martin said cheerily. "Is everything okay over there?" If the experiment had been a success, he would have said "Good to hear your voice."

The admiral knew at once that Martin wanted to tell him more.

"Oh, fine, fine," he said. "You didn't call me at this unholy hour to ask me how I was, did you?"

"No, of course not. My apologies, admiral. We've found a wonderful spot for an angle shot."

"Oh, really?" The admiral sat on the edge of his bed and turned on his reading lamp. He groped in the drawer for a notebook and a pencil. "Do you have the coordinates?"

Philip was racing back to the jeep with the GPS system in his hand.

"Right here, admiral." Martin took the device from Philip. He added twenty degrees to the latitude and longitude and rattled off the numbers into the phone. The resulting coordinates fell somewhere in the Mediterranean west of Sardinia, but he knew the admiral would subtract twenty degrees before alerting Boulanger via Anne.

"Got it," the admiral said. "Was the timing accurate?"

"Just a few seconds off," Martin answered. "Nothing to worry about."

"When are you going to resume filming?"

Martin did some quick mental calculation. The admiral needed to call Anne from somewhere outside his office. Then Anne had to find a different phone to call Boulanger. These could all involve traveling, at least for a short distance. Five hours should do it.

"We'll skip two scenes and prepare for the third on the agenda. Shouldn't take long."

"Good luck," the admiral said, and hung up. Martin would wait for two more passes of the satellite and be ready for the test on the third. Boulanger had just over six hours to press the activation button again—in fact, he was waiting for instructions. The admiral left the office to phone Anne.

According to Boulanger's chart, the third satellite pass would occur at eleven fifty-three a.m. Five minutes before that time Bernard started the generator again. It ran smoothly at the first attempt, which the team took as a good omen. Once again, they took up their watchful position by the jeep.

At twelve seconds past eleven fifty-three they saw flames darting out of the mine's entrance followed immediately by a loud explosion. Rocks and dust burst out of the mine, obscuring visibility for several minutes. The generator was silent.

The trio approached the mine's entrance cautiously, Philip and Bernard holding the fire extinguishers at the ready. They could feel the heat emanating from the generator, though the flames had died down. They noticed a small perforation in the cowling of the generator, and that its edges showed evidence of melting.

Martin grinned at the other two.

"We'll have to wait for it to cool down," he said, "but I think there's no doubt that we have a success on our hands."

There was a round of backslapping as they walked back to the jeep. Martin called the admiral again.

"Admiral Stone speaking."

"Good morning again, admiral," Martin said, just as cheerily as before. "Good to hear your voice."

"Good to hear yours, too," the admiral responded. "Is there anything you want?"

"Just a welcoming party for us when we return. I think the producer will like the footage we're bringing with us." The producer was, of course, Sir Cedric.

"Excellent. Hope to see you soon."

An hour later, the generator had cooled down sufficiently for them to approach it and complete their mission. It was apparent that the blast and flames they saw were the result of the fuel tank exploding. Fragments were strewn around the mineshaft. They put on their work gloves and began working. The cowl could not be removed by unfastening the clips that held it to the body of the generator, so they had to break through it with a hammer and a chisel. They found a mess there. Metal had melted and flowed partway down the sides. The ceramic part of the spark plugs had disintegrated into a white powder. The pistons and valves were almost unrecognizable. It seemed that the laser beam had penetrated the earth above the mine effortlessly but had spent all its energy on the metallic object it had encountered. Martin looked for an exit hole of the laser beam, but the bottom of the generator was intact.

They collected the dissembled samples and the powder from the generator and placed them in the jeep.

"We have what we need now," Martin said. "Let's burn the remains of the generator now to remove all evidence of our experiment. We'll tell Ould Salah that we're through filming and that the generator unfortunately caught fire just as we were finishing. How sad." He grinned.

They poured the petrol in the jerry can over the generator and set it alight. When the fire died down and nothing could indicate that this was not a normal accident, they used their fire extinguishers to give the impression that they had tried to control the fire. Then they pulled up the stakes and ropes and tossed them into the mine.

"Let's go home, lads," Martin said.

## SIXTY-SIX

The order from Seoul for supplies had arrived. Sing had signed a commercial order from a legitimate Korean importing firm. Martin instructed Philip and Bernard to prepare the delivery, and to make sure it looked like a bunch of ordinary commercial packages. They were to be sent the regular way, via a customs broker, to Seoul. It would probably take a couple of weeks to get to Sing. Only after Sing had confirmed their arrival would Martin plan his next visit to South Korea in order to train Sing's people in their use.

So, for now, Martin concentrated on training the Iranian representative. The apartment of one of the Iranian group was selected as the training arena. A sample of every item of the earlier delivery was brought from the warehouse by Shahram. It turned out that they were well organized. The Iranians were not a crowd of unruly immigrants—instead, they were a unified and disciplined community. They had their own authoritative institutions, and quite a number of other resources such as apartments, vehicles, and warehouses. That was all Martin could see—and he was impressed. There was probably more under the surface, which was kept secret. They were highly motivated, and it looked like they were even prepared for casualties in pursuit of the liberation of their country from the tyrants.

Martin and John avoided ideological discussions with them. It seemed that when Mrs. Bahtyar made a decision, everyone obeyed orders and asked no questions. Nothing could have fitted the association more.

ଓଃ୫ଠ

Admiral Stone rummaged through the admiralty's map collection, looking specifically for military bases in North Korea and Iran. Satellite imagery now covered every centimeter of the earth's land surface, and concealing what you did not want the satellite to observe became an art of camouflage. You needed intelligence reports to place a base accurately on the map, and hoped that the satellite image would confirm it. Sometimes you had to backtrack through images a couple of years back in order to see the bases, as they were being constructed in deep craters gouged into the earth. Then they could disappear underground as, in one Iranian case, everything was enclosed in concrete and buried under about twenty meters of soil. A grove was planted on the area and no satellite photography could now detect a strategic installation at that location.

There were about forty such Iranian installations on the intelligence maps. Only two of them were buried as described. The others were more or less at ground level and were vulnerable to Excalibur and the "wasp." They could be targeted immediately after the rally or at any other date—the board would have to decide on that.

ଓଃ୫ଠ

Martin met Shahram that evening. Shahram led the way to the "training" apartment.

"You're going to meet Jack," he said. "Our training officer."

"Jack?" Martin wondered.

Shahram grinned.

"You know us all by our real names," he said, "because we all live here. For various reasons, we cannot go back to Iran. But Jack *will* be going to Iran. Therefore, he is known only by his nickname. Even I don't know his real name."

A few minutes later Jack arrived. He was a short man in his thirties, with a swarthy complexion and big black eyes. Martin would have taken him for a merchant at a carpet shop in Tehran— he would never have considered him a revolutionary.

"It is a pleasure to make your acquaintance, Mr. Martin," Jack said with a heavy oriental accent. "I have only a very sketchy outline of what we are about to do here, so if you don't mind, please start at the very beginning."

They took seats besides a small worktable. Shahram joined them and listened attentively.

Martin explained the association's ideology. Then he described the various means and methods they were hoping to employ in achieving the association's goals—namely, publicly humiliating the Iranian leadership.

Then came the stage of "hands on" training. One by one, Martin demonstrated the devices, and then watched as Jack practiced the motions until he caught on fully. After all the different pieces of equipment in the warehouse were accounted for, Martin challenged Jack.

"Right, Jack! Now—*teach me* to use these things."

At first, Jack looked alarmed, but then a grin spread over his face.

"You are very thorough," he said. "That's good!"

Jack went through the teaching course as if he himself had invented the devices.

"You're very good," Martin said. "I'm sure all your pupils will understand your tutoring easily."

"I had an excellent teacher," Jack said.

After that, Martin and Jack discussed likely locations for placing the gravel and acoustic disruptors, and also the timing of their operation. It took several hours, but in the end, Martin was firmly convinced that his "apprentice" did very well indeed. The association would have a talented operative inside Iran very soon, along with the equipment and devices he needed to do the job.

"Once you've taught your people in Tehran," Martin said, "please let me know that you're ready. Please remember that any action needs to be coordinated with us first. Oumid knows how to contact us. You can also ask us questions the same way."

"I would like to express my deepest gratitude," Jack said as he pressed Martin's hand warmly, "for the opportunity you have provided us to embarrass our leadership. I promise that when the time comes, you will find us prepared to do our best for the success of the operation."

CBEO

The next board meeting was held in Brussels, at the Metropole Hotel. The admiral had switched hotels as a matter of routine caution. Despite the fact that Anne had not observed Inspecteur Marnier near her home for quite some time now, she employed all her evasion techniques on the way to the train station. She hoped there would be time to have a talk with Martin before the meeting began.

Martin, however, was late.

"Well," Admiral Stone said, "something must have held him up. He would have called if he were seriously delayed. Let's begin …"

Just then the doorbell buzzed.

"Sorry I'm late," Martin announced as he took off his jacket. "Traffic jam."

"You're just in time," Sir Cedric said, "to deliver your reports."

Martin ignored Anne completely, though she desperately tried to catch his eye.

"The 'wasp' test in Mauritania was a smashing success, on all counts. In fact, I found it quite surprising that it took just one calibration correction to hit the bull's eye. The beam penetrated about two meters of earth and through most of the body of the generator."

"Martin brought me samples of the remains of the generator," Sir Cedric said. "I'm studying them now. At first glance, it seems that the beam carries immense power, and can do intensive damage to metal, especially to engines. That seems to be the case with ceramic components as well, which just crumbled away."

"You should have been there," Martin grinned. "You would have danced a jig."

"I have no doubt," Sir Cedric grinned back, "that if this beam hits any working installation, that installation will immediately cease from functioning. In fact, damage will be done even if the machine isn't turned on." He glanced at Anne. "I trust Professor Boulanger was informed of the success of the experiment."

Anne nodded.

"Good. When I complete my tests, we shall send him the results."

"Right!" the admiral said. "Martin, how is the Iranian training going?"

Martin described Jack, the training, and the communication method via Oumid and Patricia. He then went on to inform the board of how the shipment to Sing in South Korea was handled.

"We are now waiting for confirmation of receipt from Sing," Martin concluded. "I assume it'll take a few days. Training can commence thereafter."

"Do you actually *need* Spencer Partridge to go along with you?" Sir Cedric inquired.

"He's wonderful company," Martin answered, "but I can deal with the training on my own. Like I did with Jack. And as we're in a friendly environment in Korea, Spencer's security backup will not be necessary now."

"Agreed, then?" the admiral asked. There were no dissenters. "Martin goes to Korea alone. Now, Martin, what about information on those unmanned flying vehicles?"

"George is working on it," Martin said. "I hope that by the time I get back from Seoul I'll have all the details."

"Our experiments were successful," Anne said. Even when she spoke, Martin did not look at her. "The goods have been delivered to their destinations, and we're almost ready for action. However, I have a feeling that we were so busy with North Korea and Iran, that we have neglected other targets, mainly South America and Al Qaeda. I think we should start gathering data on them as well."

A short discussion followed. It ended with the resolutions that Sir Cedric would take a private vacation in South America for about two weeks. During this time, he would try to get the "touch and feel" of what was going on there, especially in Venezuela, where a new type of dictator was emerging. At about the same time, Admiral Stone would pay a visit to Pakistan—after having carefully studied all intelligence reports he could find—and poke around, trying to add to his knowledge base.

"This raises a problem," Sir Cedric said. "Who is to be in charge here when both the admiral and myself will be absent? Anne still cannot be contacted."

"And I'll be in Korea part of that time," Martin grunted.

"It looks like we won't be meeting again for about three weeks," Sir Cedric continued. "What if Martin needs Anne's confirmation or assistance for something?"

Anne looked hopefully at Martin, but he was watching Sir Cedric.

"What do you suggest?" Martin asked.

"How about this," Sir Cedric said. "If an emergency arises in which Anne simply *must* be involved, you'll call her from some public place and offer carpet cleaning services. Or leave a message on her answerphone. You will then wait for her to call you back at the gym, from a public phone as well."

"No problem," Martin said. "Are we done?"

"I think so," the admiral said.

"I'm off then," Martin said. He grabbed his jacket and left the suite in a rush.

಄಄

On the express train back to Paris, Anne tried to put her thoughts in order. She had hardly said anything at the meeting…. She was too focused on Martin. It was obvious now that he was deliberately avoiding her. She couldn't really blame him—she had caused it herself. And she couldn't leave the meeting and run after him— she'd done that once before in London, and it nearly exposed her.

*He has the opportunity to call me now,* she thought. *But I don't think he will. I've offended him so deeply. Even if an emergency arose, he would probably prefer to wait for the admiral's return instead of calling me. God, I love him so, and now I've entangled both of us in this unholy mess.*

*DAMN! How could I do such a stupid thing to myself?*

CG80

"Hey there," Martin said, as he walked into George Grahams's cubicle. "Our delivery to Korea has arrived safely, and I'll be off to Seoul in a couple of days. But I'd like to talk to you before I go. How are you progressing with your investigations on the unmanned planes?"

It was a quiet day, and Spencer was handling the only customer at the gym. George put down the manual he had been reading and straightened in his chair.

"Well, Coop," he said, "I have some facts, and I have some questions still left open."

"Start with the facts," Martin said, and sat down opposite him.

"All right. First—Iran is a country where private aviation is permitted, if you have a valid enough reason. I suppose that with the right cover story, this could be arranged. You wouldn't need a pilotless aircraft. However, North Korea is a totally different kettle of fish. If you took a manned plane into their airspace, you would definitely be intercepted, and probably shot down, by their MIGs, Therefore, an unmanned aircraft makes sense for this country."

"Won't it be shot down, too?" Martin asked.

"Could be, but it would probably take longer. The aircraft is smaller and harder to detect. It could complete a number of missions before being shot down. And we won't lose a pilot!"

"Where can we obtain such a vehicle?"

"I haven't got that far yet, Coop. I'm still studying the market."

"You said you had questions as well," Martin reminded.

"Yes," George said. "Let's assume we *have* a UAV. Where will we launch it from? And how do we get it to wherever it's going to be launched from? Small as it is compared to executive planes, it still could have a wingspan of up to twelve meters. Only those models can carry a payload of eighty-five kilograms, about the weight of Excalibur. The UAV's bulk also includes a fuselage and tail. All this takes space—lots of it."

"Can't we find a model you can take apart and reassemble?"

"That was the first thing that crossed my mind, Coop. But, no—at least, I haven't seen such an option on the market yet."

Martin got up and looked out of the window.

"Doesn't that seem odd to you?" he asked.

"Not really," George replied. "You see, UAV's are made in several countries, but mostly for military purposes. The deployment of these aircraft for non-military use is quite limited—fire control, police supervision, monitoring natural disasters, etc. Private usage is far less widespread."

"I see. And I admit that the usages you mentioned don't actually require that the plane be taken apart for transport. We'll need to address this problem soon."

"There's more. Eventually we'll need to approach a supplier. And we'll need a story. What kind of reason could a commercial company provide for purchasing a UAV?"

Martin thought for a while.

"I don't know," he said at last. "We'll need to work on that, too."

George grinned.

"I'm surprised at you, Coop," he said. "You've used the same story successfully on two different occasions. Why not again?"

Martin turned from the window with wide eyes. He, too, broke into a wide grin. As he left the cubicle, he slapped George on the back.

"Good work. Keep it up."

## SIXTY-SEVEN

It had been a lonely flight. For the first time, Martin did not have a partner at his side. Worse, all he could think of was Anne. If Spencer or Philip were there, they could have discussed their plans.

*Fool that I was. I thought we had such a great thing going. If she had just told me it was all over, it would have hurt—but I would have understood. Was it something I said or did? For the millionth time—I can't remember anything that would even cause embarrassment, let alone the cold-shoulder she gives me. Just like that—I am suddenly a total stranger. I can't look at her at meetings, and I certainly shall not approach her of my own volition.*

At his hotel in Seoul, it did not get any better. He tried to focus on the upcoming meeting with Sing. He hoped the people he would meet spoke English. Otherwise, Sing would have to translate.

After a night of troubled sleep, Martin forced himself to return to earth and get on with the job. He called Charlie and set up a luncheon date with Sing. Then he rented a car and drove north to Charlie's restaurant.

Charlie took him to his house, where Sing was already waiting. They had a round of handshaking and "good to see you's," and then settled down to lunch, which Charlie brought over from the restaurant.

"Everything arrived safely," Sing said, while chewing a mouthful of rice and shrimps. "No problems with the customs. It is already located at the place where we will do our training."

"And the, umm … students?" Martin asked.

Sing smiled craftily.

"They are here, already," he said. "They will carry out the operation in Pyongyang. We shall start work tomorrow morning in Charlie's storeroom."

Martin was very pleased. As there was nothing further to discuss regarding the training, he decided to talk about current politics.

"I was wondering what the citizens of North Korea are thinking today. You know, after the dismantling of the nuclear reactor in exchange for economic aid from the West."

"The apparent dismantling," Sing corrected. "Everyone in the know will tell you that the stories are all hogwash. In the North, and here as well, they all know that plutonium production is continuing in several places unknown to the West. Just like in Iran."

"Do you really believe," Martin pressed on, "that in the US they don't know this? Or that they don't understand what's going on?"

"There are those who say that the US knows, but prefers to claim diplomatic successes."

"But why?"

"Because North Korea doesn't bother them in the least, with or without the bomb. Anyway, the North Korean people will continue to starve—all the economic aid goes to the leadership, and what they don't pocket for themselves will go toward developing nuclear weapons."

They set up the timetable for the next day, and Martin returned to Seoul.

⊂ℑ୭

Martin met his "pupils" the next day. To his surprise, he found two men and three women. It was hard to tell their ages, but Martin assumed they were all under thirty. Not one of them spoke English, and Sing appointed himself translator.

"Usually it is the women who are more talented and industrious," Sing explained. "They are also often quite braver when in a tight spot. But these boys here will do just fine, too."

Sing introduced each of the trainees by a code name, which Martin didn't even try to put to memory.

"Each of them will be a team leader," Sing said. "They will teach other activists, and then they will supervise the operations."

Martin started with the association's credo, and then went over all the details of the devices and materials, as he had earlier in London with the Iranian, Jack. Each of them not only went over the operation aspect of all the gear, but also practiced how to teach others to do the same. Martin found them to be a group of very intelligent, dexterous and quick-learning pupils.

Charlie brought in food and drink for everyone, just as they completed the course of familiarization with all the equipment. The youngsters laughed and chattered, and Martin felt a bit self-conscious for being left out of their conversation. He asked Sing what they were talking about.

"You don't want to know the details," Sing laughed. "It seems the girls have taken a fancy to you, and the boys are poking fun at them for it."

Practical training was now over. Martin spread a large, blank sheet of paper on a table.

"Ask them," he requested Sing, "to draw a sketch of the area where the grand rally will take place. Have them include the nearby vicinity as well."

One of the Koreans drew a beautiful urban layout of a large square, flanked by houses and side streets.

"Now ask them to describe, on the chart, how they will make use of what they have learned today."

Sing translated, and there was a short silence of concentration. Then they all began jabbering at once, pointing fingers, and some wrote down notes. Five minutes later, Sing managed to translate two different plans of operation, while the trainees held their breath, waiting for Martin's approval.

"They say," Sing said, "that these are only draft outlines, and that after they scout the arena, they will fill in details and combine them into one plan."

Martin smiled and clapped his hands at them in applause. They applauded back at him, all smiling broadly.

Martin raised his hands for silence. He produced a map of North Korea, spread it on the table, and although he was talking to Sing, his gaze was on the five trainees.

"Ask them if they can mark this map with military positions of the North Korean armed forces and air bases," he said. He knew he was taking a risk here—this request was pure espionage. On the other hand, he was facing the precise forum from which to collect this type of information. One or two military targets for the "wasp" or Excalibur would do it.

To Martin's delight, they eagerly marked over a dozen sites on the map—bases, airfields, and at least three that they claimed were of a nuclear nature.

It was approaching suppertime, and Charlie served them all a meal. Martin wrapped up the day's work with a short ideological speech, which repeated some of his earlier opening remarks. This time he got several nods of agreement whenever Sing finished translating a sentence.

Nothing to do now, but wait for the big event.

ᢏᢒᣝ

Commissaire Felix Duval was still in a quandary regarding Allier's demise. Suspicions were everywhere, but there was no evidence to support them. The connections Allier had with Sir Cedric Norton and—perhaps—with Mme. Professeur Dupré, were flimsy to say the least. He could never make a case out of that alone.

Two possibilities existed: either Dr. Michel Alvarez killed his superior in order to step into his shoes, or that vague organization did away with one of its members. Then, of course, that same organization existed only by evidence of what Alvarez said—very possibly a tactic to divert attention from himself. Alvarez had most of the necessary attributes that a classic killer required: motive and opportunity. The method, however, left a lot to be filled in. Still, it was a better beginning than the alternative—he would not be laughed out of the prefecture if he presented the case this way.

But he needed more evidence. He needed to talk to more of the employees of the Irradiation Institute, but he could not do so officially—this was, after all, a closed case. If Alvarez were not a suspect, Duval would have asked him to find colleagues to interview. But, of course, Alvarez should never know that others were being questioned about him.

Commissaire Duval needed more time to think.

## SIXTY-EIGHT

When Anne left her flat, she found an envelope in her mailbox. There was no stamp and there was no address—just her name in handwritten block letters. *Strange*, she thought. *And suspicious.*

She opened the envelope, and took out a folded page. With mounting horror, she read the block letters:

I KNOW EVERYTHING! YOU WILL PAY ME HALF A MILLION EUROS IN CASH TO KEEP SILENT! YOUR ASSOCIATION HAS 48 HOURS TO COLLECT THE MONEY. MY NEXT LETTER WILL CONTAIN INSTRUCTIONS FOR ITS DELIVERY. I KNOW THAT YOU CANNOT CONTACT THE POLICE. DO NOT TRY TO EVADE THIS DEMAND—IT WILL LEAVE ME NO CHOICE BUT TO PUBLISH WHAT I KNOW. CONSIDER YOURSELF WARNED!

Anne gaped at the letter and read it through once again. Her first thoughts were, naturally, as to the identity of the writer. She knew everyone who knew about the association. Furthermore, she also knew those who had never heard of Anne Dupré—Lemke, Rosetti, Bennett, and Hoffman. Martin and his gang were above suspicion, and so was Patricia Welles. So, who could know so much about the association, including where she lived?

Anne raced back to her home. She called the university and fed them a story about a sudden illness in the family. She then ordered a taxi to take her to Gare du Nord, forgetting all her evasion tactics. At the railway station, she frantically called Admiral Stone in London and informed him she had to see him, and that she was arriving on the next Chunnel train.

It was still morning when Anne rushed into the admiral's office and handed him the letter. He read it twice without the slightest revelation of emotion.

"I want to call Sir Cedric and Martin here immediately," he said. Anne nodded.

Admiral Stone picked up his phone and summoned the two men to his office. They were to drop everything and arrive as soon as they possibly could. While waiting for them to arrive, the admiral brought Anne a drink, which she downed unceremoniously. They tried to figure out how the information could have leaked to someone "outside," as it was inconceivable that someone "inside" could be the perpetrator.

Less than an hour later, they were joined by Sir Cedric and Martin. Martin was surprised to see Anne there, but he quickly averted his gaze. It was all Anne could do not to burst into tears.

The information came as a shock to them. They quickly agreed that it couldn't be an insider, and the list of known "outsiders" was faultless.

"So let's look at the 'periphery,'" Martin suggested.

"What do you mean by that?" Sir Cedric asked.

"We've been in contact with many people outside the association besides our scientific and financial collaborators. Various suppliers and vendors, the people who rented us the 'cowshed' and the offices for the film company, and so forth. And, of course, the Iranians. Perhaps one of them put two and two together and came up with conclusions."

"So let's think about people that we have encountered!" the admiral said.

Sir Cedric shook his head.

"None of them know of Anne," he said, "except for Mrs. Bahtyar, her husband and Oumid. I doubt they are suspects. Still, maybe preparing such a list—with all the possible contacts we have made—could possibly narrow us down to a suspect or two."

"Which leads me to suggest that in the future we should refrain from introducing ourselves by our real names when going about the association's business. We can always hide behind a bogus company name and address."

"We don't have the time!" Anne blurted out. "Almost half a day has already passed since this posting, and we need to pay up in less than forty hours! Do we pay or not? And if we do, we need to get the money. You can't pick up half a million euro at the teller's at the bank."

"We don't have much choice, then, do we?" the admiral said. "We'll pay, but just in order to buy time. I'm positive that the blackmailer will come back with a demand for more."

"That depends," Sir Cedric said. "If he's a big time operator, you are probably right. But if he's just small fry, he could suffice with the half million and disappear forever. Just the same, we have to be prepared for the worst. Anyway, we need to get the money now."

"I'll call the bank now," the admiral said. "It'll be ready by tomorrow morning."

Martin raised a hand.

"The note was delivered in Paris," he said. "I think it quite likely that the blackmailer will want the delivery site to be in Paris, too. Two of my boys and I could wait in hiding at that location for the bastard. We'll try to apprehend the fellow, but if we can't do that, perhaps we could identify him, or take his picture. Maybe follow him."

"It's a good idea," the admiral said, "but very dangerous. If he catches wind of what you're doing he could take the money *and* publish what he knows about us."

"That's a risk we're taking anyway," Martin argued. "Let me work something out."

"Who is going to make the actual delivery of the money?" Anne asked.

"It pains me to say," the admiral said seriously, "that you are the only one to do the job. All we know right now is that he knows you personally. Despite his allegations, we cannot be sure that he knows anyone else of us."

Anne inwardly trembled at the thought. But none of her feelings showed outwardly.

"You're right," she said. "I'll do it."

Martin felt a surge of apprehension at the danger Anne was putting herself into. While he was still battling with his emotions, he heard the admiral speaking to him.

"Martin," the admiral was saying, "Anne will call you on your cellphone the minute she gets further information from the blackmailer. From that moment on you will be in constant communication. I have thought over your surveillance suggestion, and I am prepared to authorize it under the condition that whatever happens, your primary concern is for Anne's safety—even if it means losing the blackmailer and the money. Am I clear?"

"Yes, sir," Martin said solemnly. "I promise."

"Good! I don't think he'll choose the daytime for the transaction," the admiral continued. "So we possibly have until tomorrow evening. I'll notify the bank right now, and collect the money tomorrow morning. I suppose a large briefcase would hold the sum required. Anne, I shall fly to Paris and bring the briefcase to your flat—don't worry, I'll have a disguise on.

"Any questions? Right, we're adjourned. Anne has to get back to Paris today. Martin, please stay—I want to hear what you're 'working out' on this plan of yours. But first, I need to call my bank manager."

ଓଞ୍ଚ

Anne went downstairs to check her mail at eight in the morning. There was nothing. She returned to her apartment and called the university saying that the crisis was not yet over and she had to be absent for another day. She tried peeking through the window, from behind the curtains, but the nearest she could observe was the other side of the street—anyone approaching on her side would be invisible to her.

The tension was nerve-wracking. She paced about, tried to drink some coffee, but she was getting increasingly nervous. After about an hour, she went down again. Still no mail.

At eleven a.m. the intercom buzzed. Anne jumped at the sudden sound, and answered it immediately.

"Yes?"

A strange voice answered.

"Open please. Supermarket delivery."

Of course, she had not put an order to the supermarket. This was the blackmailer, notifying her of the new message he was leaving. She buzzed him in, intending to go down a few minutes later to pick up his letter.

The doorbell rang. Anne was aghast. He dared come up to her apartment! But she had no choice, and opened the door. There stood a deliveryman in long grey overalls, a visored cap covering most of his upper face, with a large carton on his shoulder. He walked right in without waiting for an invitation.

"This is for you, Madame," he said, setting the carton on the table.

Anne recognized the admiral then. He removed the cap, and she was so relieved that she went up to him and kissed him on both cheeks.

"That was very clever," she said.

The admiral leaned against the table and wheezed. It was a heavy load, and he was not a young man any more. Anne offered him a drink and let him rest a bit.

"There's half a million euros in there," he said when he had caught his breath. "It's pretty hefty. You cannot take it in the carton. Do you have a large bag with two handles?" Anne did not respond—instead, she went into her bedroom and returned a minute later with a large blue traveling bag with two red carrying handles.

"That'll do fine," the admiral said. "A bit conspicuous, but never mind. Help me move the money into it."

After completing the transfer, the admiral put on his cap again and left. His plan to deliver the money to Anne could not have gone off more smoothly. His bank in London had provided the cash that morning, and he packed it into a briefcase. He then flew to Paris and, at the airport, booked a hotel room and rented a car.

He requested the bellhop to find him a large cardboard box, and bring it to his room. When it arrived, the admiral moved the money into it. He then took the lift down to his car in the parking lot under the hotel, put the carton into it and drove the car to Anne's neighborhood, parking a couple of blocks away from her home. There he quickly changed into his deliveryman disguise.

Now that the transfer was completed, the admiral walked back toward the rented car. He turned into a side street, stood inside one of the doorways, and removed a large plastic bag from one of his pockets. He then took off his overalls and stuffed them, with the cap, into the bag. He continued walking, looking like a normal pedestrian, and dumped the bag into the nearest trash bin. Finally, he arrived at his car and drove back to his hotel, where he intended to be close to the action, and in constant communication with Martin!

In the afternoon, Anne found an envelope, identical to the first, in the mail. This time she took it upstairs before opening it. In the same block letters, it said:

TODAY, 5 P.M. CAFÉ DUPOND, RUE DE PRESBOURG. BRING THE MONEY. GO DOWN TO THE TOILET AND THE PHONE BOOTHS. WAIT BY THE LEFTMOST TELEPHONE. WHEN IT RINGS, GO INTO THE BOOTH AND ANSWER IT. YOU SHALL THEN GET ADDITIONAL INSTRUCTIONS. IF THE BOOTH IS OCCUPIED, WAIT PATIENTLY UNTIL IT IS FREE. AN ATTEMPT TO DO ANYTHING ELSE WILL RESULT IN EXPOSURE.

Anne's hands shook. Cold sweat covered her body. She knew she had to call Martin. She had tried once before, and failed for lack of nerve. Now there were no excuses. *God, what he must think of me!* she thought.

With trembling fingers, she tried to key Martin's number into her cellphone. It was the first time she had ever used it, and it took a couple of attempts before she succeeded.

"Yes? Anne?" she heard Martin's voice.

"I … I got another letter." Anne's voice was shaking as well. She read the letter to Martin.

There was a short pause.

"I'll look up this place," Martin said. "I'll try to find somewhere to observe …"

"That won't be possible," Anne interrupted. "I know where the café is. The street makes a loop around half of the Étoile—the Charles de Gaulle Square. There is nowhere to park and visibility is also very limited."

"Not good," Martin muttered. "You'll be alone, and we won't be able to see you inside the café. Well, we'll have to improvise something else, then. After getting the instructions by phone, leave the café and walk slowly. It may buy us some time to work something out."

"All right, I will. And Martin …"

"Yes?"

*I love you!* she wanted to say. *I made a mistake. Come back to me!* But the words wouldn't come out.

"Anne?" Martin was saying. "Is there anything else?"

"No, no," Anne whispered, and clicked the cellphone shut. She leaned on the bag of money, her eyes shut tight. A tear trickled down her cheek. Then she went to wash her face and reset her makeup.

Martin felt a surge of mixed emotions. Annoyance was the most prominent—Anne was treating him as an ordinary team member, not anyone special. And concern—concern for Anne's safety. Despite her disgraceful behavior toward him, he would have much preferred to take the phone call himself, down near the toilets of Café Dupond.

Martin called the admiral.

"Sitting in the café is out of the question," Martin said. "We're only assuming he knows only Anne. But if he recognizes one of us there, that will be the end of the story."

"Not good," the admiral repeated Martin's words.

"As there is no parking along the street, I thought I'd fake a breakdown and raise the bonnet of my car. But it's the oldest trick in the book, and if the blackmailer *does* come along, he'll be sure to notice me."

"Don't use a car, then," the admiral said. "Try to find somewhere to observe the café while on foot. Follow Anne when she walks out. The blackmailer will probably be calling from somewhere else, so have your car on standby as near as you can."

CB&O

Anne got out of the taxi in front of the Café Dupond at five minutes to five p.m. She entered the café, stood by the bar, and ordered a glass of white wine. After drinking it and paying, she took the bag and went downstairs. There were three telephone booths—beyond the leftmost were the toilets.

There was no one in sight. Anne began to perspire again, and she found breathing an effort.

"Shut your eyes!" a gruff, male voice commanded her.

Anne obeyed. She felt the bag being snatched roughly out of her hand. Anne opened her eyes, and briefly saw a man running up the stairs. In that split second, she saw a yellow raincoat, and possibly a woman's blonde wig.

*He fooled us,* she thought. *He was waiting in the toilet!*

Anne was still afraid to go upstairs. She made urgent use of one of the toilet stalls, and composed herself to face the world again. She had just experienced the most frightening event in her life.

Anne staggered out of the café as if drunk. She walked slowly, using the wall with one hand for support. Martin saw her come out without the bag. No one else had left the café before Anne.

*He tricked us!* Martin thought. *He must have found another exit.*

He continued to follow Anne carefully, and Philip was not far behind him. It wasn't long before she hailed a cruising taxi and drove off. Martin immediately called the admiral, and reported what he had witnessed.

"Come to my hotel at once," the admiral said. "Anne will probably call you shortly, and I want us to be together then."

"I'll be over right after we check the café's interior," Martin said and hung up.

Martin was just entering the admiral's hotel room when his cellular phone rang.

"It … it was awful," Anne stammered. "I'm still shaking."

"Are you all right?" Martin asked.

"Yes, I'll be fine," Anne said. "Martin, I …"

But Martin had already handed his phone to the admiral.

"It's Patrick, Anne," he said. "Are you in need of any attention, my dear?"

"I … no, I'm fine. Hello, Patrick."

"Tell me what happened."

"He … he was waiting for me in the toilets. He grabbed the bag and ran. I didn't … I couldn't …"

"Take it easy, my dear," the admiral said in a paternal voice. "You're safe now. Try to relax. Do you think you could manage a train trip to Brussels?"

"Yes … I'll be there."

"Six o'clock then, Anne. I'll summon Sir Cedric, too. Get some rest on the train."

CঙৣৎO

At the emergency board meeting that evening in Brussels, the entire blackmailing episode, and their failure to get the faintest lead to its solution, were the first topics on the agenda.

"Philip and I followed Anne until she got into a taxi," Martin said. "We then returned to the Café Dupond and discovered a back entrance. I peeked outside and saw a small yard with access for the dustcart through an alley at the back. Our man pulled off a neat trick, there."

"We must now always keep in mind," Sir Cedric said, "that from now on we should consider ourselves exposed. This mystery man knows about us, and we are at his mercy. I think we should reconsider the entire issue."

"Indeed, I have," the admiral said softly. "I've been trying to put myself in the blackmailer's shoes. I'd be thinking something like: 'What do I gain by exposing these people? So maybe they'll be arrested—why should I care? On the contrary, as long as they are free and active, they'll continue to be a target for more blackmail. If I expose them, I'll be killing the goose that lays the golden eggs.'"

"That's all well and fine," Sir Cedric spluttered. "But *we* cannot tolerate being blackmailed!"

"I agree. But judging by this blackmailer's conduct—the notes, the café, the disguise –my gut feeling is that he is really just small fry. Half a million euros must be a fortune for him. So I'm not very concerned about exposure. I expect him to make another demand, eventually, possibly for an even larger sum, but, by then, I'm hoping we will have either accomplished our missions, or found a way to thwart him, or both!"

"Rather expensive, isn't it?" Martin said.

"Consider the alternatives," the admiral said simply.

The admiral's words had a soothing effect on the foursome. As there was no more to be said on the blackmail issue, they proceeded with the agenda despite the bitter taste they still carried with them.

They discussed some of the recent statements by heads of state worldwide. Apparently, Iran was not preparing a nuclear arsenal, and couldn't do so even if she wanted to. Some press reports claimed that this was known to the US for over five years.

The association referred again to the Iranian president's call to the US to apologize for libeling the Iranian people to the effect that they were building nuclear weapons.

"The Persians have a long history," Sir Cedric smiled sadly, "of being the most wily merchants in the world. There has never been a case in which they have not outwitted their innocent Western customers. And it's working today, too. They played the game of standing their ground, not permitting IAEA inspectors to investigate their nuclear installations—thus creating pressure with which the West doesn't know how to cope. And their little stratagem with the 'accidental' sketches. It's pitiful!"

"According to my sources," the admiral said, "and I needn't remind you that this information is strictly confidential, the Iranians are forging full steam ahead with military nuclear development. They want the bomb—no doubt of it. But they needed to buy time to build their underground installations, and they gained this time by their various methods of artifice and trickery. Now that they have probably completed the concealing of the bulk of their activities, they'll allow inspectors a 'free hand' in checking anything they liked."

"That *really* puts the West in a rather stupid light, doesn't it?" Sir Cedric said.

"Actually, no," the admiral said. "I believe that the West has not been bamboozled, and that they are well aware of what I have just told you. But for tactical reasons, they pretend to believe the Iranian promises. At the same time, they're preparing for the worst. At least, I hope they are."

"As far as we're concerned," Anne said, "it means we need to finalize our preparations. We need to act as soon as possible. I suggest we now hear about training in Korea, and then more facts about pilotless flying objects."

*I couldn't even say his name,* she moaned silently. *I know I cannot take much more of this agony.*

Outwardly, her voice indicated that she had regained total control of herself, and that the traumatic events of a few hours ago were now just unpleasant memories.

Martin glanced at Anne sharply, regarding her rather rude choice of words. Her face was already downcast and studying the glass in her hand. He turned, deliberately addressing the other two men, and described the training sessions with Sing and his team.

"I gave the map with the military base markings to the admiral on the day I returned," Martin concluded.

"Weren't you afraid they might construe this as spying?" Sir Cedric asked.

"Yes, I was. But I had prepared an excuse—if challenged, I would 'clarify' that I only intended to know of the bases from where the parades were supposed to leave."

"Very clever," Sir Cedric said, nodding his head.

"Now," the admiral said. "Is there any progress regarding the unmanned planes?"

Martin had debriefed George earlier, and had the information at his fingertips.

"There are quite a few manufacturers of UAVs," he said, and repeated the uses that George had told him. "Some of them can fly as high as twenty thousand feet and remain airborne up to fifteen hours without refueling. All of them are radio-remote-controlled from the ground. And nearly all of them are equipped with cameras, also operated by remote control."

"How much can they carry?" Sir Cedric asked.

"That depends on the model. Our Excalibur weighs eighty-five kilograms, so George looked into models that could carry more. A certain Swiss company could possibly provide the solution."

"We have to find a justification for buying a UAV," muttered the admiral.

"Yes, of course," Martin said. "George realized he'd need to tell a story to the company from which we make the purchase. We don't qualify for the regular civilian usages I mentioned—firefighting, border patrolling, etc.—but we can definitely reuse our old cover story—movie making! I challenge you to find a defect in that!"

They smiled at each other.

"Point taken, Martin," the admiral said. "It will be an adequate cover."

"George did, however, raise two questions to which I had no answer," Martin continued. "Where do we launch the UAV from, and how do we get it to wherever that location may be?"

"Oh, that shouldn't be too hard … ," Sir Cedric said, and started mumbling alternatives to himself.

"Let's see now ..." muttered the admiral, and sank into silent thought.

Anne, too, furrowed her brow in contemplation.

Two minutes later, the admiral broke the silence.

"I'm sorry," he said. "I can't come up with anything. This looks like a tougher nut to crack than I imagined. Why don't we all—"

"Boat," Anne said.

"I beg your pardon?" Sir Cedric exclaimed.

"We can transport the plane on a boat," Anne repeated. "They carry huge containers and stuff, don't they? Why not a UAV?"

Admiral Stone stared at her.

"Why, Anne," he said, "I do believe you're absolutely right! Though a yacht would be more suitable for our purposes. We could calculate the dimensions of the yacht in accordance to the size of the UAV. Martin, could we take this plane apart and ship it in pieces?"

Martin shook his head.

"I already inquired," he said.

"So it'll have to be a bigger yacht," the admiral continued.

"Just how much should such a yacht cost?" Sir Cedric asked.

"Well," the admiral said, "it's been some time since I last dabbled in these things, but I can tell you that for our purposes—that is, a boat that can travel thousands of kilometers and be self-sufficient for several weeks—it would probably cost several million dollars, perhaps as much as twenty million, depending on size and age."

"As far as I know," Martin said. "UAVs need a runway to take off from. So we can perhaps transport a UAV, at enormous expense, to wherever we want, but we still don't know how to launch it once we're there."

"I'm a sailor, Martin," the admiral said, "not an aviator."

"No offence, admiral," Martin said. "But off the cuff, I would suggest that when the yacht approaches as near as possible by sea, the UAV will have to be taken ashore. A land vehicle would tow it and the control panel to a runway, and the launching would occur there."

"Do you think your friends could find such a runway in South Korea close enough to the border?" Sir Cedric asked.

"Stop, please!" Anne requested. "This is getting us nowhere. Launching may be difficult, but I think it's feasible. Let's stick with what we *know* for the moment, shall we? And by that I mean Admiral Stone's nautical expertise."

"Thank you, Anne," the admiral said. "There are a few additional things I think you should be aware of. A yacht of the size we're talking about needs a crew—a qualified captain, a mechanic, a cook, and some deckhands. Recruiting these personnel would be an operation unto itself."

"We might restrict ourselves to recruiting just one or two," Anne said with a smile.

"And how do you figure that?" the admiral asked.

"With all due respect," Anne's smile remained on her lips, "could a retired admiral be qualified to sail a yacht?"

They all laughed, not least the admiral.

"I don't know of any mechanic among us," Anne continued, "but we have deckhands and, I believe, more than one cook. Remember, we'll be a movie crew as well. So, we have our actress, Patricia, who did so well in Tunisia and Iran. There's George, her brother, who'll be our aviation expert—he'll operate the UAV when the time comes. Then there are George's four colleagues: John, Bernard, Philip, and Spencer. With our illustrious captain here, that's seven crewmembers. So all you need to recruit is one seaworthy mechanic!" Anne looked around her triumphantly.

"You know," the admiral smiled softly, "that just might work."

Sir Cedric clapped his hands in glee. Martin nodded to himself, still not looking at Anne.

"Would it be too presumptuous, Patrick," Anne continued, "to request you to handle the yacht issue? It would look like a very natural quest for an admiral, and your knowledge of the subject is certainly the most extensive."

The admiral smiled and nodded.

"I doubt we'll find a yacht large enough to contain the twelve-meter wingspan of a UAV," he said. "And we're certainly not going to leave it exposed on deck. Let's ask George to find one with folding, or detachable, wings. If none are available, we may need to modify an existing model or have a new one built for us, no matter how much it costs."

"What about recruiting a mechanic?" Martin asked.

"I'll poke around and get some recommendations. Then I'll interview the candidates regarding their qualifications. I'll then refer them to you to screen ideologically, and see if they're fit for our association."

"Well, then," Anne said, "I suggest that Cedric leave right away for his South American tour, and you, Patrick, will visit Pakistan after you've found a suitable yacht and candidates for a ship's mechanic. Agreed?"

It was unanimous.

"Good" Anne said. "We'll continue meeting this way, even though I have not observed anyone following me for some time. Before the admiral leaves, we'll find another way to keep things under control in his absence. We'll leave, as usual, one by one."

Anne left the suite and went down to the lobby. Her heart was pounding savagely. She stood by the newsstand for a couple of minutes, willing her emotions into a lull.

*This time I'll catch Martin and explain everything. But I need to calm down first. Deep breaths, now. I think I had better sit down and wait for him to descend. Is he going to forgive me? Or brush me off forever? There he is!*

Martin came out of the elevator and walked briskly to the exit.

*Now! Catch up with him now! Call him!*

Anne couldn't move. She sat as if paralyzed, and watched Martin disappear through the revolving doors. With an immense effort, she wrenched herself up and ran after him. She was just in time to see the taxi he had entered drive off.

Numb with disappointment, she took the next taxi to the railway station.

*I can't believe myself. Am I really that weak? Is this the way I'll live my life now—trying all the time, but not trying enough? Day after day of self-imposed wretchedness? I'm losing Martin, the man I love with all my heart, and it's just because I lack the courage to face him? Professor Anne Dupré, you deserve all the misery you have!*

## SIXTY-NINE

Commissaire Duval combed through the list of employees at the Irradiation Department. He compared the list to the pile of statements deposited by these employees to the investigating policemen. There was a single discrepancy: Jean-Paul Valensi, an elderly archive clerk about to retire, had not been questioned. Duval memorized the number written next to Valensi's name.

In his car, while driving toward the university, Duval dialed Valensi's number.

"Archives, Valensi," crackled a dry voice at the other end.

"Ah, Monsieur Valensi," Duval said in his warmest tone of voice. "This is Commissaire Felix Duval of the prefecture. I wonder if I may trouble you for a few minutes."

"Why, certainly, commissaire. It would be an honor."

"Well, it's lunch time now. Why don't we meet and talk things over with a little bite to eat, then? If you're not too busy, we could meet at the bistro La Concorde, across the street from the department. I could be there in ten minutes."

"I'll have to ask—"

"Good. I'll see you there, then." Duval was quite sure that nobody would miss an old archive clerk for an hour.

Duval had, in fact, already arrived at the bistro during the conversation. He parked, went in, and seated himself at a table. His hunch was correct. A few minutes later, a stooped man with thinning hair stood in the doorway and peered around at the diners. Duval stood up and waved his hand. The stooped man smiled, and made his way to the table. They shook hands and sat down.

"What will you have," Duval asked graciously as the waiter hovered by for their order.

"I have to watch my diet," Valensi snickered. "Doctor's orders. I'll have a salade du chef, please."

"Make that two," Duval told the waiter, "and two glasses of beaujolais."

"Now, Monsieur Valensi," Duval said, after the waiter had scampered off, "I need to talk to you about the Allier case." He continued to describe those portions of the case that were relevant to the questions he was about to ask.

"So you see, Monsieur Valensi, this is not a police investigation. Rather, I am trying to tie loose ends in order to get a complete picture. Any information you could give me would be most appreciated."

"I quite understand," Valensi said.

"What can you tell me about the device on Professor Allier's desk, the one that probably caused his death."

"I don't know anything about that, Monsieur le commissaire. But I can tell you that on the day before the professor's demise, I saw Dr. Alvarez carrying a large carton into Professor Allier's office."

*Eureka!* Duval thought, but his face revealed noting.

"Do you remember what time this was?" he asked.

"Of course. It was a few minutes before everyone went home."

"Why didn't you tell this to any of the investigators after the professor's body was found?"

"I wasn't asked," Valensi said defensively. "I wasn't even questioned."

"How could that be, Monsieur Valensi? My team interrogated all the employees that day."

"Ah, yes. I found out about that later. I wasn't in that morning—I had a day's authorized leave, as I had a doctor's appointment." Valensi was almost apologetic.

*My inspectors didn't bother to check if everyone was accounted for*, Duval thought. *Sometimes you can't trust anyone!*

"Thank you very much for your time, Monsieur Valensi," Duval said warmly. "Would you be prepared to testify if requested?"

"Certainly."

Commissaire Duval, gratified at what he had learned, ordered a rich dessert for them both.

CB❧SO

The commissaire considered rebuking his inspectors for not fulfilling their duty, but decided not to attract attention. He knew that Inspecteur Marnier and his immediate team members were aware of his continued prying into the Allier affair—they had no secrets amongst themselves—but as long as they pretended that they knew nothing, he preferred to "let sleeping dogs lie."

Alvarez, who had meanwhile been awarded the coveted professorship, was now the prime suspect. Duval visited him in what was once Allier's office.

"Congratulations, Professor Alvarez," he said, "on your new position. And your professorship as well."

"Thank you, commissaire," Alvarez said. "Now, what was so urgent?"

"Professor Alvarez, a witness claims to have seen you enter this office the day before Professor Allier's death. He said you were carrying a large carton. Would you explain that to me, please?"

Alvarez stared at Duval. He went deathly pale when he realized the enormity of what the commissaire was implying. He quickly recovered and got up from his desk, walked to the large wall closet in the back of the room, and opened a side door. He took out a large carton box, which he placed on the desk in front of the commissaire.

"Commissaire Duval," Alvarez said, "this is the carton. I had just arrived from Rome that afternoon. Three days before, Professor Allier requested me to bring him a 'genuine Italian espresso machine.' Which I did. I couldn't go right into Allier's office because he was busy with some people. After they had left, I brought it in to him. He thanked me, paid me, and placed the box into that closet without even opening it."

The box was indeed still sealed. Alvarez opened it carefully, and showed the contents to Duval—a brand-new, shiny espresso machine in its original plastic wrapping.

Commissaire Duval was stunned. This time he had guessed wrong, and it was hard to acknowledge. Perhaps Alvarez brought in the box *after* the murder, to provide himself with an alibi in case he was seen with the other carton—the one with the killing device? Did his investigators notice this box when they searched the office? He couldn't remember anything of the kind in the reports.

The silence was getting to be too long. His theories were too far-fetched. He had to say something to Alvarez—perhaps even apologize. What an embarrassment!

"I find your explanation quite satisfactory, Professor," he said at last. "There are a few more issues I need to clear up. I may yet call on you again, with your permission. Meanwhile, I thank you for your cooperation."

"That's quite all right," Alvarez said. "Now that you've reminded me of the package, I must take it to the widow. It's hers, after all. *Au revoir, commissaire.*"

When Duval was back in his car, he strapped on his safety belt but did not switch on the ignition. Too many thoughts chased each other in his head. *I should change course again. There's still a lot to learn about that secret organization. It seems less of a trumped up story, as Alvarez has now gained credibility. I cannot use Marnier any longer –enough is enough. So it seems I'll put an end to the surveillance of Professeur Dupré's house, because I certainly shall not stand watch there. Should I ask Neville of Scotland Yard to check into the doings of Sir Cedric Norton? Absolutely not! I've overreached his hospitality as it is. Not to mention that I haven't the slightest shred of evidence against Norton. Once again—I need to sleep on it ...*

❦

Later that afternoon, Inspecteur Marnier entered Duval's office with a file he had just prepared. Duval looked up from his computer as Marnier put the file down on the desk.

"By the way, Marnier," Duval said, "remember the old Allier case? Do you happen to recall if you found a sealed box in one of the closets in his office?"

"Absolutely," Marnier responded unhesitatingly. "It was an Italian espresso machine, still in its original packaging."

"Did you check the contents?"

"Not much point, was there? The electrocuting device was right there on the desk. Is there a problem?"

"No, no," Duval said, with a wave of his hand. "I just happened to think of it."

૭૪૪૭

While Sir Cedric Norton was beginning his South American tour, Admiral Stone hunted for a yacht suitable for carrying a UAV. After several inquiries, he focused his efforts on a four-year-old, hardly used, yacht he had discovered in Brighton. She was a hundred-and-fifty-five-footer, capable of twenty-five knots, with two diesel engines and nine double cabins.

In his mind, the admiral already saw how the crew would fit—the master cabin would be for him, of course, then one for the mechanic, one for Patricia, one for George, one for Philip and Bernard, and one for John and Spencer. The three other cabins would need to be combined to provide space for the UAV, after its wings had been either removed or folded.

The price was eighteen million pounds, more than the admiral had expected. But it would do the job—the distance to the Yellow Sea near North Korea would be about twenty-two thousand kilometers. The round trip would be twice as much. Taking into account stops along the way for fuel, supplies, etc., the voyage would take about two months.

This meant they had to leave at least a month before the grand event in order to be there on time.

Under the pretence of doing a favor for a friend, the admiral instructed his secretary to find suitable candidates for a qualified ship's mechanic. It would take several days, but once he had narrowed their number down to the five or six most likely, he would let Martin take over and find the one with the "correct" frame of mind, and recruit him into the association.

Only then could he begin preparing for the trip to Pakistan.

❦

The association's cover company, International Film Promoters, began negotiations for the purchase of the yacht. John Carmichael, as the company's CEO, gave the owners a down payment of half a million pounds, but it was agreed that the final purchase would occur later, "after certain modifications were planned." The idea was, of course, to first find a UAV that would fit into the yacht, after combining three cabins. This was George Graham's job.

Martin and the rest of the team returned to intensive work at the fitness gym, which had been neglected somewhat during the past weeks. Patricia Welles joined in the effort—not only was she interested in the work, but also because her assistance was sorely needed in the absence of John and George.

## *SEVENTY*

The admiral had begun his Pakistani tour. Sir Cedric was still in South America. Anne was back on her regular schedule at the university in Paris. The search for a UAV was still on. The remaining team members ran the gym smoothly.

Martin interviewed four candidates, sent to him earlier by the admiral, for the position of ship's mechanic. Only one of them showed interest in world affairs, and his views happily matched the association's ideology. However, he requested a postponement of negotiations for a week, as he wished to visit his family after a two-month absence on his last cruise. Martin had no objection to this—the UAV had not been found, the yacht had not been purchased, and the candidate's return would just about coincide with the admiral's.

෨෮

Anne considered this new phase in the developments as a vacation from the association. In many ways, it was a relief to return to the academic world. Mainly because it helped in taking her mind off Martin. She reviewed her lectures and found she could update them with fresh material. Most of her time was spent at the university or at home, reading or listening to classical music.

But alone in bed she could not push away the memory of Martin. Guilt washed over her. Why couldn't she face him? Or even call him? Why was it so imperative for *him* to make the first move? Especially as *she* was the one who had placed them both in this ridiculous situation?

What would she do if a UAV was found and a decision needed to be made? Martin would call her—that's how it was arranged. What would she tell him? Wait for the admiral? Make use of the opportunity to meet him face to face? Perhaps at the university cafeteria, where they could have a "chance" meeting?

*I DON'T KNOW!* she wailed internally. *Please, please, Martin—call me and say you want to clear up our issues. It's the only way! I know it's my fault, but I can't take the next step, no matter how necessary it is. Just like I got nowhere with Tanya's murder ...*

Tanya!

The memory of Martin was briefly overshadowed by the thought of Tanya Gerard and her grisly fate. Anne sat up in bed. She glanced at the clock—ten-thirty p.m.

It's not too late. In fact, things are only beginning to stir in rue Saint-Denis at about this time. I could go there again....

Anne got up and went to her wardrobe. The "elderly lady" outfit hung there like a ripe fruit ready to be plucked. She reached out her hand, then slammed the wardrobe shut, turned around, and leaned against it, panting heavily.

I must be out of my mind. I must check with the police first—perhaps they've found something.

∞∞∞

The next day Anne called Commissaire Felix Duval at the prefecture.

"Good morning, Madame," Duval said cheerily. "How can I be of assistance?"

"I wished to inquire, commissaire," Anne said, "whether anything new has come up regarding the murder of my good friend, the stage director Tanya Gerard."

"Professeur Dupré, we are not in the habit of disclosing the details of our investigations to the public. But since we're old friends, I can tell you, off the record, that there is nothing new regarding this case. Like other homicides, they usually demand a great deal of patience."

Anne made an effort not to openly accuse him of incompetence. Her own inquiries had brought her almost to the killer's doorstep, whereas the police, with all its resources, were floundering aimlessly. Or worse, doing absolutely nothing! She adopted the "concerned citizen" approach.

"Does the commissaire expect anything to happen in the near future? I mean, do you think it wise if I call again in a few days? Perhaps...."

"I am sorry, Madame," Duval interrupted. "This is not a matter of days. May I suggest you wait patiently, just like the rest of us? If any developments occur, I can promise you that you'll know from the press sooner than from me."

"But commissaire," Anne insisted, "I was her closest friend. As her family is rather distant, don't you agree that I should know before the press?"

"I cannot promise anything, Madame. I shall do my best. Au revoir." He hung up.

Anne was furious. True, she was withholding evidence from the police—she thought she knew who the killer was and where he was hiding. On the other hand, if she was wrong and alerted the police, it might end up in a false arrest, and she would be in deep trouble.

☙❧

For the past several days, George had been busy hunting for the right kind of UAV. After examining several models, he decided to take a shot at the Swiss company, UAV-Suisse, which he had checked out earlier. He set up an interview with their London representative.

"My company is seriously considering the model you showed me," George said, when they met. "However, we have to be sure of a few details first. As I have informed you the first time we met, my company has special demands of the UAV we purchase. The movie we're making calls for launching it from a boat or a yacht. Therefore, two things need to happen: first, the wings need to be detachable, or foldable, in order to fit on the boat, and second, a solution needs to be given to the problem of the runway needed for takeoff and landing."

The information George already had was that it could carry two hundred and fifty kilograms—far more than was needed for Excalibur. No problem there. Neither was there a problem regarding the operator's console—about the size of a desktop computer. However, the wingspan of the model offered by UAV-Suisse was twelve meters—much too wide. If something could be done about this, it could fit into the yacht. But the main problem was that the UAV also needed a two-hundred-meter runway for take-off. George had no answer for that.

"Mr. Graham," the agent said, "have you considered an unmanned helicopter? I would think that would be ideal for launching from a boat. The rotors fold down for storage, and you don't need more than four times the aircraft's footprint for takeoff and landing."

George was taken aback. It sounded like an excellent idea, and it hadn't occurred to anyone heretofore.

"Yes, it does sound attractive," he said. "Could you tell me how it compares to the regular UAV we've been discussing?"

"Well, besides the obvious advantages of vertical takeoff and landing, we should also look into payload and maneuverability. The smaller models can carry up to fifty kilograms and are relatively agile in the air. The heavier models are bulky, can carry two jeeps, but they are slower and less maneuverable. Also, their range cannot exceed two hundred kilometers."

George made some mental calculations. It didn't add up to something advantageous.

"I'd like to think these options over later," he said. "Could you please provide me with any write-ups you may have on these helicopters."

"Certainly," the agent said, and handed George a pre-prepared sales dossier.

"I'd still like to know," George said, "about the UAV wings issue and the runway."

"Well, let's take each item separately. Removing the wings and reassembling them—that's not impossible. It's been done with warplanes in the past. About the runway—we could fix a rocket or jet booster on the undercarriage of the UAV. We'd also install a launching ramp on the boat."

"How much would that cost?"

"These modifications would probably double the price of the UAV."

"Well, you've got the UAV flying. How do we get it to land?"

"Not on the boat, I'm afraid. You either put it down on land or lose it."

"Thank you," George said. "You have given me much food for thought."

CRECO

Upon Admiral Stone's return from Pakistan, he convened the board at his office in London. He explained that he no longer saw London as "out of bounds," but reluctantly agreed that meetings could alternate between London and Brussels.

Sir Cedric had returned a day earlier, and was also eager to report.

Anne and Martin found themselves in an impasse—on one hand, Anne was dying for Martin to initiate the renewal of their relationship, as she was physically unable to take that step. On the other hand, Martin was so upset by Anne's past and present behavior toward him that he deliberately avoided all contact with her.

After reporting on the conditions he found in Pakistan, the admiral focused on Al Qaeda.

"I managed to get a little information on Al Qaeda," he said. "I have many acquaintances from my official job years ago. I also flaunted my rank quite openly, which opened the doors to many formal events with high-ranking officials. I didn't learn much, I'm afraid. It seems that Al Qaeda troops train near the Afghanistani border, just east of Kabul. True, this is only a small portion of the two-thousand-kilometer border with Afghanistan, but it is still a few hundred kilometers long. And we have no specific location pinpointed in this area. So, we'll need to fill in the missing information from official intelligence sources here. If I find anything up-to-date and relevant, I could probably make use of what I learned in Pakistan and get a plan ready."

"So it wasn't a total waste of time, then," Anne said.

"No, I believe not. I got a feeling for the country, and if I get my hands on intelligence files, I shall probably be able to make a lot of sense of them. Cedric, your turn now."

"Thank you, Patrick," Sir Cedric said. "I visited three South American countries: Peru, Columbia, and Venezuela. They are trying to form a kind of coalition with Cuba and other South American countries against the US."

"Have you concluded anything regarding our involvement there?" Anne asked.

"Nothing is urgent at the moment, so there's no need to go into details. We just need to be alert, as developments may occur suddenly and without warning. Anyway, the Venezuelan leader just loves to give public speeches, and I think we're pretty well prepared to handle that aspect."

"Martin?" the admiral said.

"I examined the yacht that the admiral recommended. It's beautiful and it's suitable. There'll be extra expenses to combine three of the cabins, and also to install a crane on deck for loading and unloading the UAV—probably a few hundred thousand pounds."

Martin went on to describe the properties of the UAV, including the issue of detachable wings, jet engine addition, and launching ramp.

"We were advised by UAV-Suisse to shoot the UAV scenes close to shore so that we could retrieve the aircraft by landing it on land."

"That won't do at all," Sir Cedric said. "Land here means enemy territory, and there'll be stuff on that plane that we don't want to fall into *anybody's* hands, let alone the enemy."

"UAV-Suisse offered us a vertical take-off and landing aircraft—an unmanned helicopter. George and I went over all the specifications. Yes, we could launch it from the yacht and get it to land there, too—but it will be slow and would not get very far before being shot down."

"Couldn't we have the UAV open a parachute as it approached the yacht?" Anne asked. "It would not need a long runway then."

"Interesting," the admiral said, "but impractical, I'm afraid. Remember that using a parachute is actually a slowed down free fall. Even a live parachutist would find it almost impossible to land *exactly* on the right spot on a rolling yacht. A parachute's descent is pretty fast. We could never get an unmanned device to be that accurate."

"Well," Martin said, "at the moment it looks like we're going to have to crash the UAV into the ocean on its return from the mission."

It was also resolved that the purchase of the yacht, and its modifications, would begin at once—John Carmichael would be assigned to that task. The modified UAV was also authorized, and George Graham would be given the green light to close the deal.

"We'll need to test the entire maritime exercise," the admiral said. "I can see us having the yacht and the UAV ready in about a month's time. By then, Martin, I hope the ship's mechanic will be recruited and indoctrinated. The entire team will then take an ocean voyage for a few days to get an idea of what the real mission would feel like—the actual voyage will take about two months, there and back. We'll test the UAV launching from the yacht, but unless we have an alternative solution, we'll perform that test close to shore, and land it there."

"Well, here's an idea for an alternative solution," Anne said. "It occurred to me when Martin mentioned crashing the plane into the sea." She looked at him, but he did not turn toward her. "I thought, why crash it? Lots of planes manage to land on water because they're equipped with those water-ski things instead of wheels. Why couldn't our UAV thing have them, too? It would be unharmed, and we could use it again."

Sir Cedric and the admiral gaped at her. Martin began to smile.

"You know, Anne," the admiral said with a broad grin, "the disadvantage of working with you is that sometimes you make me feel so stupid! Yes, of course—a seaplane. Or a sea UAV, in our case. It takes care of the launching as well—no need for a ramp or a jet booster. Just unload it into the water with the crane, and there you are!"

"Chapeau, Anne!" Sir Cedric said. "That was brilliant. Wasn't it, Martin?"

Anne felt herself blushing, and she looked sideways at Martin. He wasn't facing her, but she could see his smile and the nodding of his head.

"Oh, quite," he said, and the tone of his voice indicated that he meant it.

"I believe that is all," the admiral said. "I'll call you for our next meeting. Meanwhile there is a lot of work to be done. I want to draw up an initial checklist of everything we have to do. Then build a timetable with dates and hours. We need to time our

GLOBAL CONSPIRACY by DAVID SHOMRON

cruising speed, the time to assemble the UAV's wings, lower it into the sea, test the range and speed of the UAV, and practice landing it close to the yacht. And probably a million things more. Martin, please, stay a bit and help me out with this."

## *SEVENTY-ONE*

Martin had three urgent tasks to complete. First, and most urgent, was the purchase of the UAV, so that work on the necessary modifications could begin. Second was the acquisition of the yacht, which also needed internal changes. And third, the recruitment of Olaf Gunnarson, the candidate for ship's mechanic, who should have returned by now from his vacation in his homeland of Norway.

Martin joined George when he next met with the UAV-Suisse agent. Martin was presented as the president of the movie company IFP.

"So good to meet you," Martin said amicably. "Let me say right away that if we can overcome the technical modifications we require of the UAV, I intend to finalize the deal at this meeting."

Four hours later, they seemed to have come to an understanding.

"Here is a rundown of your requirements and our undertaking," the agent said. "Correct me where I'm wrong. You want our model UAV-III to be converted into a hydroplane, or seaplane as you called it. If I may add a personal note, I think it's an excellent idea and I shall recommend adding it to our catalog. Floats on struts will be installed alongside the current wheel undercarriage—thus enabling sea *and* land launching and landing. Furthermore, you require the wings to be detachable. Am I right?"

"I believe you are," Martin said. "Now, we're running a very tight schedule. How long will these modifications take?"

"Once you have purchased the vehicle, and paid an advance on the modifications, I would say two weeks would do it. Three, tops."

"I can assure you that the formalities will be over within the next fifteen minutes. May I request that the finished product be shipped in a container to the yacht marina in Nice, France? We'll pay for the shipping, of course."

"Done!" The agent opened his briefcase and withdrew a sheaf of papers. "I took the liberty of preparing the documents ahead of time. All we need to do is fill in the blanks."

 CallEnd

Buying the yacht was a far easier process, and John handled it without a hitch. A certified check changed hands, and the Mimosa, flying a Panamanian flag, became the property of International Film Promoters. Now, it had to be sailed from Brighton to Nice, where not only would it pick up the UAV but also have the internal alterations made. But first, the ship's mechanic needed to be recruited. Martin set up an appointment with him for that afternoon.

Olaf Gunnarson was forty-five, short, and tanned. His face was lined with the outcome of twenty years of seafaring, and an unlit meerschaum never left his mouth. His three last jobs were as ship's mechanic on millionaires' yachts, and they were the easiest of his career. The downside was that these jobs were short-lived— either the owners gave up the idea of luxury cruises or they went bankrupt. This was what had happened to his last employer a month ago, and Olaf was very eager to get this job.

Over beers in one of Chelsea's pubs, Martin began provoking Olaf's political leaning, which he already knew to be anti-dictatorial. This time, Martin adopted the role of a "leave the East to solve their problems—we have enough of our own" sympathizer. He wondered how far Olaf could be goaded before his need for a job overcame his ideology. To Martin's surprise, Olaf didn't budge an inch.

"I don't know where you're headed, Mr. Cooper, sir," Olaf said, "but I believe I would find it very difficult to work alongside someone holding your views of the international situation. I've turned down job offers based on these grounds before and, reluctant as I am, I'm prepared to do so again."

"Let me tell you where I'm headed, Olaf," Martin said. "I bought the Mimosa to have a good life and a good time. I intend to make friends with world leaders like Ahmadinejad and others, because I seek the glory of the limelight. I shall need your expertise in keeping the boat ship-shape so that my guests will have the smoothest sails of their lives. And I shall pay you more than you usually earn, I can promise that."

"I am sorry, Mr. Cooper, sir," Olaf said, getting up. "I shall have to decline your offer, with all due respect. I feel it would be an offense to my upbringing, and I would not wish to be in a position where I could possibly offend anyone else, mainly my employer."

"Sit down, Olaf, please," Martin said with a huge grin.

The recruitment process was short and decisive. Olaf was thrilled at the opportunity of joining the association's enterprise. So Nice was the first destination? Fine, he knew the Côte d'Azur like the back of his hand. When do we leave?

"Hold on, Olaf," Martin laughed. "Not so fast. Let's discuss your wages. And let's arrange our means of communication."

ନ୍ଦ୍ର

The team had begun the waiting period. The shipments to Pyongyang via Seoul had arrived and had been distributed. The same held for Tehran. Their first operational target was set: North Korea, during the revolution day ceremonies, about three months away.

The North Korean reports presented to the world gave contradicting statements almost every week. Sometimes they complied with "Western pressure" and were "planning to dismantle" their nuclear installations. At other times the reports told of abandoning their agreements with the West and proceeding with their nuclear development "as planned." As a result, it was proposed that the operation in North Korea be postponed.

Martin did not take part in the next board meeting in Brussels. He was far too busy with the logistics of the preparations for D-day. However, in his absence, the proposal was strongly opposed.

"Never!" the admiral stated flatly. "That North Korean bastard wants some breathing space. There is no doubt in my mind, and I believe this is shared by most political and military analysts, that he is continuing nuclear development regardless of what appears in the press. That nuclear plant in Syria—you don't suppose that was one of the items he intended to shut down, if the Israelis hadn't bombed it, do you? You can bet your life that if he succeeds in calming down international fears, he will use the time to finish the making of the bomb. The operation *must* proceed as planned! Take him down a couple of notches. Get him where he'll be personally humiliated! Make him *really* change his strategy!"

CうそD

Three weeks later, the UAV was ready. UAV-Suisse's headquarters and main assembly plants were in Zug, conveniently located near Lake Zug. Now, in the presence of the vice-president of the company, the engineering department was proudly showing off their product to the "executives" of International Film Promoters. Even the London representative had arrived for the occasion.

While still on the lake's shore, the UAV-Suisse engineers demonstrated the techniques of removing and assembling the wings. Then, with the aircraft fully assembled, it was lowered on a ramp into the water. The two floats held the UAV afloat, bobbing slightly on the ripples of the lake.

One of the technicians approached Martin and George.

"My name is Caspar," he said. "Please follow me."

He led them to the rear of a van, in which the operating console was located. It resembled a computer, with a flat monitor, keyboard, and joystick. A short antenna rose from the van's roof. George sat beside the technician in the van, while Martin observed closely from outside.

*Where's the mouse?* George wondered.

"We turn on the console thus," Caspar said. He pressed a button and the monitor lit up with an array of menus and commands. "Now, we start up the motor." He pointed at a command on the screen with his finger. Thirty meters away, on the lake, the UAV's motor hummed into life.

One by one, Caspar demonstrated the gamut of functions the UAV could do. George found that flying the UAV was even simpler than flying a real plane. He learned the use of the simulated throttle by dragging a finger on the touch screen, and control of pitch, roll, and yaw by using the joystick. He learned to taxi the aircraft on the water, take off, climb, bank, dive, and touch down again on the water. Everything the UAV's controls sensed appeared on windows on the screen. This included anything observed by two onboard video cameras, which could be pointed in all directions around the aircraft.

"You're very good," Caspar grinned at George. "However, just in case you need it—or get bored—the operator's manual is in the drawer under the console."

Caspar and George eventually landed the UAV on the lake and had it roll on its wheels onto shore. There they cut the motor.

There was a lot of handshaking and backslapping. Martin and George were genuinely pleased. The vice-president invited them back to UAV-Suisse headquarters in Zug. The financial transaction was closed, papers signed, ownership transferred, and the aircraft company promised to ship the UAV to Nice immediately.

Martin and George flew back to London.

CB80

The admiral took over the handling of the yacht, and they set out on their initial familiarization cruise from Brighton to Nice. He was delighted with Olaf Gunnarson, who proved to be an excellent seaman and mechanic. The other crewmembers consisted of Patricia, John, Philip, Spencer, and Bernard. George would join them later, as he had to fly the executive jet, with Excalibur on it, to Nice.

They sailed at an unhurried pace, allowing the inexperienced landlubbers to acquaint themselves with life on the open sea. They passed through the Straits of Gibraltar, and moored at the Quai Papacino, in Nice, three days after they had set out.

The next week was dedicated to the yacht's modifications, which were carried out by the dockyard's building and maintenance crew. Admiral Stone was a strict taskmaster and would tolerate no dillydallying, which the workers soon learned to appreciate. He knew the exact dimensions he wanted, and how the deck needed to be opened in order for the UAV to be placed inside the yacht and taken out of it. The crane was fitted outside the deck opening and tested for its reach, both deep into the newly created storage for the UAV, and over the side to deposit it into—and later collect it from—the water.

CB80

Back in London, Martin put the finishing touches to the preparations. Communications with the yacht would be kept open at all times to the IFP number at the "cowshed." Martin hired a manpower company who supplied three office temps to man the telephone in continuous shifts. Their job was to take messages and deliver them verbatim to Martin when he inquired from time to time. If the caller indicated there was an emergency, they were to alert Martin immediately. Naturally, all conversations were to refer strictly to the movie industry. Mission success would be declared by the media—mission failure would be met with silence. Only on the way back would the yacht's position and condition be reported in.

George prepared the executive jet, with Excalibur still installed, for the flight to Nice.

Cぽび

The UAV arrived from Zug the day after work began on the yacht. The next day, George flew the jet into the Nice airport. With the help of the ground crew, he transferred Excalibur into a rented van. Upon joining his comrades in the yacht, he quickly got their assistance in transferring Excalibur into the UAV. Using the user manual, George switched the wiring of one of the video cameras to Excalibur, enabling him to operate the irradiation beam from the UAV's console.

Now that they were expecting no one else to join them, the team set about their preparations for the final test. They watched anxiously as the UAV was lifted from the van and lowered gently into the storage space in the yacht, where it fit easily. The deck was closed snugly above it.

With George now on board, they set sail into the Mediterranean. They practiced the transfer of the UAV from the hold into the water, and George went through his set of maneuvers. After he landed the aircraft by the Mimosa, they carefully loaded it back into its place inside the yacht.

Pleased with the results, the admiral reported to London that they were now ready to "film." They returned to Nice and stocked up on food, drink and fuel. Pyongyang's grand event was just five weeks away and they wanted to be in the vicinity several days beforehand. So, they needed to set out now.

## SEVENTY-TWO

Four weeks later, the yacht cast anchor near Seokmo, one of the many small islands off the South Korean western coastline, yet near enough to North Korea. The tiny island, only a few kilometers across, had not much more to offer than magnificent sunsets and salt farms. Admiral Stone felt they could safely use the island as a temporary base.

The admiral looked once again at the map spread out on his work desk. Three military bases were marked, courtesy of Sing's trainees. The plan was to approach the North Korean shore on D-day, remain just outside their territorial waters in the Yellow Sea, and launch the UAV. While the aircraft described a large, clockwise arc over the North Korean military bases, the yacht would proceed south at full speed. George would guide the UAV and operate Excalibur at the appropriate moments. If the plane wasn't shot down during its flight, George would land it by the Mimosa while safely at sea, far from the target arena. If the UAV *was* shot down, it would take the North Koreans time to locate it. By then it would have self-destructed, and it would take them even more time to derive that it was launched from the sea. By then, the admiral hoped, they would be safe once again in Seokmo.

CRRO

*This cannot continue any longer!* Despite himself, Martin could not get Anne and her behavior out of his mind. Now, with his teammates on the yacht, he had some time to come to grips with his absurd situation with Anne.

*Yes, she snubbed me. And it hurt. Very much. Why? At first I thought it was the police investigation and the shadow they put on her. That would be enough to make anybody's behavior erratic. But that was long ago. She isn't being followed today. She herself admitted that.*

*Secrecy and security? Bah! She has found solutions to far tougher problems, and she could surely find several for this little issue.*

*What does that leave us? All I can think of is stress—of the most intense degree imaginable! And I don't think she's getting any help in that direction from anyone, least of all from me. I think she isn't even aware that she's under such extreme stress. Unchecked, she could be going downhill all the time, and sooner or later she'll hit bottom, and then all hell will break loose.*

*There's only one way to stop that from happening. The time has come, Martin old boy, to save her. Forget your hurt feelings, swallow your pride, and confront her face to face first thing tomorrow morning. You'll actually be doing her a service!*

Martin took the first Chunnel train to Paris. There was no point in telephoning. She might refuse to see him, and he was not prepared to take "no" for an answer. He arrived past midnight, checked into the nearest hotel, leaving instructions at the desk to have a rented car waiting for him in the morning.

Martin knew the times Anne left for the university. He also knew she walked to work. He would wait for her outside her home, and talk to her when she came out. Much better than going up to her apartment. They *had* to talk rationally out there in the street—Anne wasn't the one to make a scene in public.

∞

It was still morning when the telephone rang on Commissaire Duval's desk. He picked up the receiver.

"Duval," he said.

"It's Anne Dupré. I'm sorry to bother you, commissaire, but I'm frantic with worry. Tanya's killer is still on the loose, and I wondered whether ..."

"Madame," Duval said sternly, "I must ask you to stop calling me on this topic. You must trust me when I say you'll be the first to know if anything develops. I sincerely hope that I shall not be getting any further calls from you. Au revoir, Madame!"

Duval slammed down the receiver. But his hand remained on the telephone as his thoughts were jolted by the abrupt exchange with Anne Dupré.

*She's right, Felix, and you know it,* he upbraided himself. *You've been so obsessed with the Allier case that you've neglected your other duties.*

As if on cue, there was a knock on the door. Inspecteur Marnier poked in his head.

"May I have a couple of minutes of your time, commissaire?" he asked timidly.

Duval found this intrusion unwelcome, but he did not have a ready excuse to send Marnier away. His computer was off, and his desk was clear of documents.

"Yes, of course," Duval said, forcing himself to smile. "Come in, Marnier. Sit down. Now, what's this all about?"

Marnier squirmed in his seat.

"This ... this is not easy for me at all," he stammered. "I'm afraid you may not like what I have to say."

"Come, come, Marnier," Duval said patronizingly. "You have nothing to worry about. Out with it!"

"I happened to pass by the office of *Monsieur le Directeur*. He was in conversation with the Chief Prosecutor. Commissaire, please believe me—I am not in the habit of eavesdropping, but I heard them mention your name, and my curiosity grew. So I continued listening."

Marnier searched his superior's face for a signal to go on. There it was.

"In the Directeur's words," continued Marnier, "'Lately, I've noticed that Duval seems to be floating on some distant planet. Some say he's doing some private investigations on his own.'"

"And?" Duval prodded.

"And then the Directeur's secretary showed up with a stack of files, and I had to move on."

"Thank you, Marnier. Thank you very much. You did the right thing by telling me this. Forewarned is forearmed."

Marnier left, and Duval leaned both elbows on his desk. He bowed his head and breathed heavily.

*I am destroying my illustrious career with my own two hands*, he thought. *I am the famous Commissaire Felix Duval, who could solve any puzzle, whose picture appeared in the press at least every two weeks—and* that *is how my superiors talk about me!*

He rose from his desk and walked over to the wall cabinet. From within he took out a bottle of cognac and poured himself a stiff swig.

*But I* have *to go on! My hunches were never wrong in the past. And too many loose ends are still floating around. However, I'll need to tone it down. Quite a lot, in fact. Marnier and his team will never hear of the Allier case again. My superiors will once again see their brightest star shine again, solving difficult crimes. But, Professor Allier, rest in peace—I will find your killer!*

CRBD

Anne felt physically abused. Commissaire Duval had brushed her off so rudely, that it was clear to her now that the police would do nothing to apprehend Tanya's murderer. Therefore, it was up to her to take action now!

In half an hour, Anne was ready. She had on the "elderly lady" outfit, heavy makeup on her face, and her chestnut hair rolled into a bun. The dark glasses went on her nose, the stun gun got tucked into her belt, and her cellular phone, with the speed dial set for the police, went into her trouser pocket.

Anne definitely approved of what she saw in the mirror. She went to the phone and dialed for a taxi.

ೞ

## Radio broadcast

World press is abuzz with reports that North Korea has begun reactivating the nuclear reactors that were shut down for several months as a result of an agreement signed with the West. According to reliable sources, this reversal in attitude stems from the USA's refusal to delete North Korea from the list of countries supporting terrorism.

ೞ

Martin sat in his rented car a few meters away from the entrance to Anne's residence. He was half an hour early, he knew, but it was safer that way—he did not want to miss her. The car radio was playing softly, and his eyes never left the main doorway.

A taxi pulled up at the entrance. *If Anne's taking a taxi, I'll need to follow her and catch her somewhere else to have our conversation.* Martin started his car in anticipation. An elderly woman came out of the house, entered the taxi and drove off. Martin relaxed.

Then he sat up straight.

*Wait! That posture. That walk. Too familiar. Could it be … ? My god, it's Anne! In disguise! What the hell is she up to?*

Martin followed the taxi. His mind was churning in search of an explanation. He knew that there was no constellation on the association's agenda that required a disguise. And at this hour in the morning it was highly unlikely that Anne was going to a fancy dress ball.

The penny finally dropped when the taxi stopped at exactly the same corner of rue Saint-Denis where he and Anne had, a few months earlier, searched together for Ninette.

*That crazy woman! She's going after the killer! Alone!*

*Go after her! Stop her!*

*Park now! Nowhere to do so! There—an alley. No entry. Park illegally. Hell with the fine!*

*Run back to rue Saint-Denis. Anne is nowhere in sight. Run up the street and look around. Hell—this isn't rue Saint-Denis.*

*Damn and double damn! I'm losing precious time!*

*Ask someone for directions.*

೦ᔓ৪ಂ

Anne paid the taxi driver and started hesitantly down the now familiar street. Her mouth was dry, and her breath came in short gasps—yes, she was definitely frightened. But her sense of duty urged her on. Nobody else would do the job, so it was up to her. She had no idea what she would say or do if and when she faced the killer. Secretly, she hoped he wouldn't be there—nothing would happen, and her chase would end. She had no more leads.

Yes—that would be her final decision! Let that sonofabitch Duval go on with his lies—he would hear from her no more.

Anne arrived at the hotel. Several prostitutes were bunched in the doorway. They did not approve of strange women on their turf.

"What do you want here, Madame?"

"No young men here for you, grandma!"

Anne pushed her way through wordlessly, and went up a rickety flight of stairs. A maid, carrying some soiled bed sheets, looked at her in astonishment.

"Who are you looking for, Madame?" she asked.

Anne tried to compose herself as best she could.

"Ninette," she replied.

The maid shrugged.

"She's upstairs in her attic studio."

Anne reflected that this must be Ninette's residence as well as her place of "business." *Of course*, she thought, *how else could she afford to host a man for so long?*

Anne walked up six more flights. At the top landing she paused to catch her breath. She faced a short corridor with three doors. Taking a deep breath, she knocked gently on the nearest door. No answer. She waited a few moments, and then knocked on the second door. It opened a crack, and a young woman with yellow hair collected in a ponytail peered out at her.

"*Qu'est-ce que c'est?*"

Anne silently put her foot in the door.

"Hello, Ninette," she said with a motherly smile. "It's me, remember?"

Ninette's face was a picture of confusion. Anne took advantage of this, and pushed her way through the door. The room was sparsely furnished, with faded curtains on the single window. But Anne had no time to take in the décor.

Ninette was backing away, and Anne slowly advanced on her, leaving the door behind her ajar.

"Where is he?" Anne asked with a hint of menace. But she had no idea how to continue. She saw a closed door to her left and immediately assumed that Tanya's killer was behind it.

"Tell Lucien," Anne said in a flash of inspiration, "that his mother sent me."

Ninette's eyes were wide open, and Anne noticed a touch of fear in them. She realized that Ninette was fully aware of the penalty for harboring someone wanted by the police.

Anne moved left toward the door. In a flash, Ninette stood before it, arms splayed.

"You're not going in there," she said defiantly.

Anne pushed her aside. She threw open the door, her heart thumping wildly. It was the bathroom cum toilet. A tall, young man in torn jeans and an undershirt stood by the shower curtain. Despite his magnificent physique, he seemed cowed and submissive.

*It's him!* an internal voice screamed at her. *This is the man who cut Tanya's throat!*

The man was gazing at her with terrified blue eyes. He raised his hands as if to protect himself. Anne noticed a red and blue tattoo on his arm.

"What do you want, Madame?" he muttered. Then he added: "How did you find me?"

Now it was Anne's turn to be confused. Instead of a monstrous murderer, she was facing a trembling, terrified boy. He didn't look dangerous at all. Ninette, standing behind her, could be a larger threat if she decided to use violence to protect her lover.

Anne stepped back so that they were both in view.

"Your mother sent me, Lucien," she said rapidly. "She wants you to continue with your studies."

Lucien lowered his hands.

"You're not from the police?" he asked.

"Why did you do it?" Anne asked softly, ignoring his question. "Why did you kill Tanya Gerard?"

Lucien walked slowly into the room and slumped onto the tattered sofa.

"He didn't do it," Ninette said, and hurried to Lucien's side.

"Oh, really?" Anne said half mockingly. "Then why is he hiding from the police?"

Lucien sighed deeply.

"I'm hiding from the killer," he said, his voice barely audible. "I saw what happened, and he knows that I saw him. If he finds me, I'm dead." Lucien's voice rose a little. "But yes, I am also hiding from the police. They won't believe my story, and I'll be charged with murder. My fingerprints were all over Tanya's flat."

Anne was thunderstruck. Lucien's story was plausible enough to be believed. These revelations threw the entire case into a new perspective.

"So if it wasn't you, who did it?" she asked.

"I … I can't tell you," he mumbled. Then he quickly changed the subject. "How did you find my mother?"

"I was a close friend of Tanya's," Anne said. "She told me about you. I wanted to find out what really happened." She added bitterly: "I tried the police. They are incompetent and ineffectual."

Ninette wriggled nervously next to Lucien. She obviously disliked talk about his previous lover. But she didn't interrupt.

Lucien examined Anne's face closely.

"I know you," he said slowly. "You're disguised, but I know you. Tanya told me about you, and I've seen the two of you together. You're a history professor."

"Yes," Anne said simply.

"Why the ..." Lucien waved his hand at Anne's face and clothes, "... the deception?"

Anne removed her glasses and pushed them into her jacket.

"That wasn't because of you," she said. "That was for the benefit of the girls downstairs."

"What do the police know?" Ninette asked in concern.

"Nothing," Anne said. "Like I said, they are very incompetent. I found out everything by myself." She looked steadily at Lucien. "I still want to know who the killer is."

Lucien went ashen. He shook his head violently. Ninette hugged him closely.

"He can't tell you!" she cried. "He wouldn't even tell me! It's too dangerous!"

"No, no," Lucien mumbled. "If I tell, he'll find me. He'll kill me. He'll kill me, just like he killed her. I'm dead. He's insane." He kept on muttering incoherently.

CRWD

Martin finally located the hotel. Anne was not in sight—she must have gone up already. He barged through the girls in the doorway, and raced noisily up the stairs, four at a time. The maid came out of one of the rooms and noticed him. She understood at once, raised six fingers and nodded upward. Martin nodded back, and pounded up the six flights. He saw a door slightly open and rushed in.

The sight Martin saw was quite different from what he had expected. Anne was standing in the middle of the room, facing a sofa on which a young man and a blonde girl were huddled. Obviously, these were Lucien and Ninette, and Anne seemed to be having no trouble with them at all. All three looked at him in shock.

Martin was embarrassed by his unnecessarily turbulent entrance.

"Are you all right?" he asked Anne.

"I'm fine," Anne murmured. Her astonishment at his sudden appearance was quickly replaced by relief. She had been at a loss regarding how to continue with this unfortunate couple, but now Martin had given her a way out. The frustration of the past several weeks disappeared in a flash—as if a balloon had burst.

"This is my friend, Tony," she told the pair on the sofa, blurting out the first name that came into her head. "Tony, I'd like you to meet Ninette and Lucien. Lucien claims he is not Tanya's killer, but that he knows who is. He won't reveal his name for fear of being killed himself."

Martin quickly assessed the situation. He had intended to apologize for crashing into the room so unceremoniously, but considering Anne's words, he now changed his tactics. He pulled up a chair with its back facing Lucien and straddled it, trying to give an impression of official authority.

"Now listen carefully, young man," he said. "You are, and shall remain, a first degree murder suspect. We know who you are and where to find you. Unless you give us the name of the killer, we'll have no choice but to inform the police of what we know. They'll prefer to use you as a scapegoat, you'll get the guillotine, and the killer will go scot-free."

Panic overcame Lucien. His muscles tightened, and for a moment it looked like he was about to make a lunge for Martin. Martin tensed, but Ninette threw herself on Lucien.

"Don't be foolish, *chéri*," she whispered. "Hear him out."

"Very sensible, Ninette," Martin said, relaxing. "Thank you. Now, on the other hand, we have the means to catch the bastard. I can also promise you that until we do, we will not reveal anything about you to anyone. After we get the killer, we will provide you with the best legal assistance against the possible charge of withholding information from the police. Make a choice now!"

Lucien's eyes were rolling about the room. A few drops of saliva formed at the corners of his mouth.

"He'll kill me," he hissed. "Don't you understand? He'll kill—"

"He won't be able to touch you from his prison cell, where he'll spend the rest of his life," Martin said.

"He has friends," Lucien whispered, still panicky. "They were together in the war and they do everything together."

"And how do you know that?"

"That's what he said. Listen, I lived with Tanya for over two months, and she introduced him to me. I know everything about him. She was a bit anxious that he might be jealous, as he has a fiery temper, so she presented me as her cousin. He knows my name, and that I am, or was, a student."

"About his friends," Martin prompted.

"I'm coming to that." Lucien seemed a little calmer, now that he had begun to talk. "He would appear every now and then at Tanya's without notifying her. He would force her to have sex with him, even against her will. He would abuse her physically—brutally in fact. And then he'd leave. Tanya wanted to get rid of him, but didn't know how. She was really scared of him."

"Did you actually witness this behavior?" Anne asked.

"If Tanya knew ahead of time that he was expected, she'd toss me out of her flat. But if he arrived suddenly without any warning, she'd shove me into her dressing room and lock me inside. He never went in there—'too effeminate for his taste' he claimed. There was just enough space there to sit comfortably in private opposite the mirror. However, I could stand on the chair and observe what went on in the room through the transom above the door."

"And what did you see?" Anne pressed on.

"What do you think I saw?" Lucien said bitterly. "I saw him ravishing my girlfriend. I saw him brutalize her. I saw her suffering under his hands. He could stay for hours, and when Tanya finally let me out, I was so cramped, all my muscles were aching. And she was usually in pretty bad shape herself."

"He tortured her for hours on end?" Anne was aghast.

"Not always. Actually, these attacks of violence did not take long. They usually happened around the sex act. The rest of the time he was rather civil as long as she 'behaved.' Which meant doing everything he demanded of her. And they did have some lengthy conversations during his periods of calm."

"Which is when you learned about his friends," Martin said.

"Yes. He used to brag about his heroics during the war in Iraq. He even gave her a golden oriental medallion, saying it brought good luck."

"So why did he kill her?" Martin asked.

"That night he showed up drunk. Unannounced. I was in my regular hiding place. He bragged about removing jewelry and other 'mementos' from dead Iraqi soldiers. For his 'collection,' he said. Tanya lost control, screamed at him that he was a beast, and said she'd inform the police. He went berserk, grabbed my razor from the dresser, and slaughtered her like a chicken. He then yanked the medallion off her neck and put it in his pocket."

"And why do you think he knows you witnessed this?"

"Because he found me there," Lucien raised his voice. "How else? I was so overcome by what I had just seen that I fell off the chair. I was about to vomit my guts out. He heard the noise I made, and rammed the dressing room door so hard that it broke, and he hit his head on the mirror, smashing it. For a few seconds he was dazed, and that saved my life. I managed to run out of the dressing room and made a rush out of the flat. He followed me to the door screaming 'I know who you are. I'll get you. You're dead!' only he used much more colorful language. He could have caught up with me, but he was so covered in blood that he probably did not want to be seen in the corridor." Lucien took a deep breath. "That scene will haunt me for the rest of my life. His face—"

"No. His name. What is his name?" Martin asked very intensely.

Lucien hesitated.

"I'm dead anyway," he whispered hoarsely. "Bernard Webb. Didn't I mention he was an Englishman? His name is Bernard Webb." He stood up, shook his fists at the ceiling and screamed: "Come and get me, Bernard."

Anne looked at Martin, horrified. Martin clamped his lips shut, indicating to her not to say anything. Ninette was having a hard time calming down Lucien.

"Feeling all right now, Lucien?" Martin asked softly. "I realize what a strain this must be on your nerves. You have my solemn word that none of us—and I know I speak for Ninette, too—will breathe a word about anything you said here." Ninette nodded silently.

"Now let's finish this nasty business as quickly as possible," Martin continued. "Do you know whereabouts in England this Bernard Webb lives?"

"I know he lives in London," Lucien said dully.

"Anything more specific? Where in London?"

Lucien shook his head.

"What does he do? Where does he work? Think, Lucien. We need to pinpoint this character."

"I think he has something to do with sports," Lucien said.

"What did he say about his military service?"

"He fought in the Gulf War in 1991. He said he was a commando officer."

Martin stood up.

"Very well, Lucien," he said. "You're safe here. Sit tight and wait for news about this Webb fellow."

"He has friends," Lucien insisted. "If I ever leave this place, they'll find me and avenge him."

"I wouldn't be too sure about that, Lucien. A maniac like him won't have many friends. I believe it was just another of his boasts."

Lucien glanced at Ninette, and she nodded.

"What do you want me to do?" he asked.

"Just sit tight here. When we catch Webb, he'll stand trial and you shall testify against him. Then you'll be a free man again."

Lucien covered his face and remained that way for a couple of minutes without moving. No one said a word. Then he dropped his hands and looked directly at Martin.

"I may be making the greatest mistake of my life," he said, "but I believe you and I trust you. I shall wait for results here. How long do you think it will take?"

"I have no way of knowing," Martin said. "It could be a week, or it could be several months. Meanwhile, have faith and wait patiently."

Lucien and Ninette stood up as well. Lucien shook Martin's hand solemnly.

"Good luck," he whispered.

He then shook Anne's hand politely.

"I won't be calling my mother," he told her. "But if you see her, give her my love."

Ninette stood facing Martin, a little embarrassed. Then she stepped forward and embraced first him and then Anne.

"Give my Lucien his life back," she said. "Please."

♋

Martin and Anne walked up rue Saint-Denis in silence. It was clear to both of them how they happened to meet under such bizarre circumstances. No explanations were necessary. Anne slipped her arm into Martin's.

"Let's take a taxi to my place," she said almost cheerfully. "I think I need a stiff drink."

Martin refrained from suggesting they stop at a nearby bistro. He certainly preferred going to Anne's. *Screw the rented car*, he thought. *Let them tow it away and fine me ten thousand euros for all I care.*

In Anne's apartment, the first thing she did was to take out a bottle of whisky and two glasses from the cupboard. She put them on the table and went to the fridge for ice. A sixth sense told her to turn around. There was Martin, standing right behind her, his eyes gazing directly into hers.

Time seemed to stand still. An eternity, which may have taken all of two seconds, passed before she fell into his arms and their lips met in a passionate kiss. They clung to each other, both starved for the all they had missed these past few months. They both came up for air, and Martin covered Anne's face with kisses and soft nips. She held his head in both her hands and planted kisses wherever her lips could reach.

It took a while, but they calmed down eventually. They both realized that they couldn't return to the position they were in before the breakup, without clarifying certain issues. Martin had a lot of questions he wanted to ask. Anne dismissed earlier thoughts of "explaining" her behavior as resulting from the hard time she was having, the police, the investigation, and other excuses, and decided to brazen it out with the plain truth.

"I was a bloody fool," she said. "And I possibly still am! Worthy of the utmost contempt. I saw you in a café with a beautiful young girl, and something inside me snapped. I became blind with jealousy and rage at you. A woman of my age could never compete with the girl I saw you with. With the police trailing and questioning me, I guess I went over the edge. I retreated into myself and shut out any possible means of ever seeing another point of view. It never crossed my mind that I might have been mistaken, that I may have jumped to an erroneous conclusion. But that's exactly what had happened. When I visited Mrs. Bahtyar and met Patricia Welles for the first time, the shock of being proven wrong was so intense that I couldn't face you and set matters straight. So, I went into denial and avoided you."

Martin squeezed her hand silently.

"And look at me now," she said. Tears began to roll down her cheeks. "I acted like an adolescent schoolgirl then, and I'm blubbering like one now. Can you ever forgive me?"

He pressed her to him and kissed her gently on the forehead. She laid her cheek on his shoulder, her arms around his back, clutching him fiercely. They remained motionless for several minutes.

"Annie," Martin said finally, "I highly appreciate your telling me all this. I realize what it must have cost you. You have no idea how relieved I am—as if a heavy load has been removed from my shoulders. I was driving myself mad trying to figure out what I had done to justify the way you treated me. But I was also so angry with you for rebuffing me that I had no wish to initiate communications with you."

He pushed her gently to arm's length and looked deeply into her eyes.

"Annie, Annie, my darling," he said softly. "I love you so much! I'm not interested in other women. It's you I want to spend the rest of my life with."

She tried to embrace him again, but still he held her so that their eyes were locked.

"Will you marry me?" he asked.

This time he did not prevent her from throwing herself into his arms again.

"Oh, yes, Martin, my darling, yes!" And then the tears came. Relief and joy were released, as she pressed herself to him and nuzzled her face into his chest.

She pulled away suddenly. Her face was a mess—tears and embraces had smudged her heavy disguise makeup into an aborigine's war mask. But her eyes, still wet with tears, had the tension and alertness of an operative in action.

"Martin—what about Bernard Webb?" she said.

"If what Lucien told us is true," Martin said, "and I'm inclined to think it is, we need to take action. Come to think of it, I now remember that at about the time of Tanya's murder, Bernard came to work with a bandage on his head. He said he was drunk and had walked into a door. Bernard is now on the yacht with the others, and we can expect them back in about a month. Why don't we bring Sir Cedric into the picture and consult with him?"

"Set the meeting with him for this weekend, my darling," Anne said. "I'm visiting my children." She took him by the hand and smiled at him. "Meanwhile, we have a lot of catching up to do."

"Not until you wash your face first," Martin grinned at her.

## *SEVENTY-THREE*

Anne told Sir Cedric the entire history of Tanya Gerard's murder and everything that happened in its aftermath, including the recent conversation with Lucien. Martin sat on the couch and listened without interrupting. Sir Cedric was understandably surprised, but also not a little amused by Anne's antics in addition to her job and her duties to the association.

But faces became serious again, when Bernard Webb was discussed. Lucien could not have known, of course, how close to home his revelation was. Bernard Webb, at this moment on the yacht somewhere in the Yellow Sea, was a murderer and a corpse looter. He knew most of their secrets. In about a month he would join them in London.

"What shall we do about him?" Anne asked.

"We have no choice," Sir Cedric said, "but to dispose of him quietly ourselves."

"In principle, I have to agree with you. However, that would leave poor Lucien as the only suspect for Tanya's murder, and he's sure to be imprisoned even though he is completely innocent."

"May I suggest," Martin said, startling the other two by breaking his silence, "that we conduct a search of Bernard's residence before making a decision? We might discover things we know nothing about."

"Good idea," Sir Cedric said. "I'll go along with you."

"Actually," Anne said, "I think it would be better if *I* went with Martin. I might identify things that belonged to Tanya. Besides, a man and a woman together would arouse less suspicion."

"You know," Martin said pensively, "now that I think of the time we spent in Iraq, I recall incidents that I had thought insignificant at the time."

"Such as?" Anne asked.

"I remember that Bernard would disappear from time to time for a few hours. Sometimes for a whole day. And once he was missing all night, too—I happened to wake up, and I saw his bunk was empty. He always had an explanation for being absent. He would say, kind of matter-of-fact, that he was a nature lover, and was looking for exotic plants. He once told me he could sit on a rock and watch the landscape for hours without getting tired. We paid these things no attention—everyone has his idiosyncrasies. In hindsight, after hearing Lucien's story, it is quite possible that Bernard could have been out robbing dead enemy soldiers."

Martin paused. The enormity of the accusation was almost beyond comprehension.

"I assume," he continued, "that if he had, indeed, taken souvenirs off Iraqi casualties, he would have gotten rid of them long ago. However, we should still search his place."

"And just what was Bernard doing in Paris?" Anne asked. "According to Lucien, he was quite a frequent visitor."

"Before we established the gym and the shooting range, we had all gone our separate ways. Bernard lived in Paris for a while, and learned to speak French with almost no accent. He tried his hand at business a couple of times, but he could never get off the ground."

"But Martin, that was years ago," Anne objected. "Lucien told us that Bernard was in Paris several times in the past few months."

"You're right. It is customary for us to take a couple of days leave now and then. We're not in the habit of inquiring where we've been. But thinking back, now, I believe that Bernard made more than average use of this privilege."

They decided that they would visit Bernard's apartment the next day.

## *SEVENTY-FOUR*

On D-day, the Mimosa sailed southward along the North Korean western coastline, far outside that country's territorial waters. The skies were clear and the sea was exceptionally calm. The tension within the team intensified as the launch hour approached.

"Raise the UAV on deck and assemble its wings," the admiral commanded.

George and Philip brought the wings on deck. Bernard opened the deck hatches and went below to attach the hook on the crane to the UAV. He deftly guided Spencer, operating the crane, to lower the hook onto the right place, and then gave him the signal to lift.

The aircraft rose slowly. Once it had cleared the deck, the hatches were closed again. The UAV was then lowered, and its wings assembled, without disengaging the crane. George made a final inspection of all the electric and electronic connections. The console was carried onto the yacht's bridge and switched on.

As Philip read out item after item on the manual's checklist, George flipped switches, pressed buttons, and took readings of the screen to ensure everything was functioning properly. Bernard checked the UAV's fuel tank.

Philip and Bernard had completed their jobs, and stood aside. George sat by the console on the bridge. Spencer was at the crane's controls. All eyes were directed at the admiral. A little to his left, they could see Patricia and Olaf looking on excitedly.

"Lower the plane into the water!" Admiral Stone's command was loud and clear.

Spencer smoothly maneuvered the crane so that the UAV swung slowly off the starboard bow. Then it was let down delicately until it touched the water's surface, where it rocked gently with the wavelets lapping around the floats.

"Detach the crane! Switch motor on! Taxi alongside the yacht!" The admiral barked the commands, and the team reacted immediately—each doing his part. Everything functioned like clockwork.

This was the moment they had all made the long trip for. They watched the light aircraft sailing alongside the yacht, bobbing and dipping in the ship's wake. They expected the admiral to give the command at any moment. They could see him consulting his watch.

Timing was the most important factor, and the admiral had it all figured down to the second. The UAV had to arrive and activate Excalibur above the first military base in full coordination with the commencement of the festivities in the capital—that is, about five minutes *after* commencement. There should be no information of explosions prior to the leader's speech, which was when the other prepared "surprises" were supposed to be activated. Later, yes—but not before! The UAV would then arc southward over the other two bases, with the hope of leaving a trail of exploding ammunition depots. The bases were too far for the explosions to be observed or heard on the yacht, but if the video-cams on board the UAV functioned as planned, they should be getting good imagery of what was happening.

"George," the admiral said. "You know what to do." Another glance at the watch. Then: "Do it now!"

George swiped his finger on the "throttle" on the monitor, and the UAV picked up speed. The onlookers held their breath. Water sprayed to the sides of the floats. George pulled the joystick and the aircraft took off.

જ80

Anne and Martin decided to visit Bernard Webb's apartment after lunch. It would look like an innocent visit—after all, Martin was Bernard's boss. Martin had broken into homes as part of his commando training, and though he was a bit rusty, he brought along the relevant gear—gloves, lock picks, a large ring of keys, etc. Entering would be swift and noiseless, he could always claim that Bernard had given him the key.

As it turned out, nobody noticed them entering the apartment. They put on surgical gloves, just to make sure they left no fingerprints in case they touched anything. Besides the small entrance hallway, there were two rooms—a large living room, which had a tiny kitchenette against one wall, and a smaller bedroom. All the rooms were spotless and tidy. Martin drew the curtains on the windows.

"Let's begin with the bedroom," Martin whispered.

Martin opened the clothes closet, while Anne examined the drawers of the dresser. Martin began going through the pockets of the three sports jackets he found.

"Martin!" Anne hissed suddenly. "Come and take a look at this!"

Anne had pulled out the third drawer halfway out of the dresser. She had piled the undershirts she had found to one side. On the bottom of the drawer were a little, flat wooden box and two small plastic bags. The bags contained what looked like gold coins with Arabic inscriptions.

Martin removed a coin and examined it closely.

"What do you make of it?" Anne asked.

"Looting museums," Martin said, "was commonplace when we were there. Sometimes we were given circulars with pictures of stolen items. I remember that on one occasion gold coins were stolen—a valuable set from the Umayyad Caliphate."

"Are you saying that Bernard looted a museum?" Anne asked horrified.

"Hardly," Martin said grimly. "He probably took it off the body of a looter. This coin would be recognized as plunder by any numismatist. That is why it's still here—Bernard must have found buyers for all his other stuff, but not for these few here. Or he may have a sentimental attachment to them. Who knows?"

He examined the other coins. They were all different, but all obviously of Middle Eastern origin.

"The pillaging bastard!" Martin hissed under his breath.

He heard a loud gasp. Anne had opened the wooden box. In it lay a golden amulet in the shape of a two-thumbed hand attached to a delicate chain. Anne clutched at Martin's sleeve.

"That's the one Tanya wore the last time I saw her," she whispered hoarsely. "I'm sure of it."

Martin knelt down and picked it up carefully. It was speckled with dried bloodstains.

"You despicable sonofabitch, Bernard!" he muttered. "Lucien told us the truth. I have no doubt that forensic examinations will verify that those bloodstains are Tanya's. The brute didn't even clean up after murdering her." He looked up at Anne. "I'm sorry, Anne. I know how much you loved her."

He stood up and held her as she trembled uncontrollably. He led her to a chair, and then fetched her a glass of water from the sink. She took a sip.

"I'm all right now," Anne said getting up determinedly. "Let's see what that piece of excrement has in the bottom drawer."

They found a brown envelope encircled with a rubber band. Inside were a few hundred pounds in bank notes.

"I think we have more than enough incriminating evidence," Martin said. "Let's go."

"In a minute, Martin," Anne said. "We might as well complete our search. Take a look in the toilet, while I check," she stooped by the bed, "under the … *Martin!*"

Anne had not intended to shout, but that's what came out.

"Shh, Anne," Martin said. "Take it easy. You don't want the neighbors coming down on us, do you?"

She pointed dumbly under the bed. Martin laid himself on the floor and let out a whistle. He reached in and dragged out a large blue traveling bag with two red carrying handles. He threw the bag onto the bed, and then brushed himself off.

"My bag!" Anne said softly with her hand over her mouth. She opened the zipper slightly, and then added, "Empty, of course."

She looked at Martin. His face was dark, his brow furrowed deeply, and the muscles of his jaw twitched. His hands clenched and unclenched, and his breathing was ragged. She had never seen him so furious.

"So Bernard was not only a murderer," Martin rasped, "but also a blackmailer who got half a million euro out of the association. By law, I expect he should be locked away for life. But according to the association's rules, he shall be executed." *And I hope*, he added to himself, *that I'll be the one to do it!*

Anne shut her eyes.

"What now?" she asked.

"We get out of here," Martin said, "and meet with Sir Cedric."

"Don't you think we should wait for the admiral to return, and get his opinion as well?"

"No. It will be too late then. We have to prepare ourselves to nab that murdering ghoul the minute he arrives. He should not be afforded the slightest chance of escape."

ༀ

The events that occurred during North Korea's birthday celebrations for its Great Leader made headlines the world over.

Never before in human history had such a humiliating debacle ever befallen a nation. The printed press carried the item in giant fonts on their first page, with pictures and first-hand reports of the colossal fiasco by on-the-spot journalists. Billions of people worldwide witnessed the first few disastrous minutes on television, after which communications were abruptly cut off.

A concise description of what happened could be encapsulated as follows: the Great Leader ascended the podium with half a million of his subjects cheering from the huge square and the adjacent streets. Sixty blocks of infantry, four-hundred soldiers to a block, marched in perfect formation toward the grandstand. Behind them, a column one kilometer long of giant trucks towing intercontinental ballistic missiles, followed by more conventional armor and artillery units. At the crucial moment, when the Great Leader lifted his hand for silence and began his speech, *that* was when all the loudspeakers of all the amplification systems emitted an ear-piercing, nerve-shattering screech!

As the saying goes, all hell broke loose! The multitudes covered their ears and ran—the direction didn't matter, just as long they thought they were distancing themselves from the intolerable noise.

The geometrically accurate infantry blocks suddenly disintegrated into a jumble of apathetic soldiers who wandered aimlessly about, some sitting down, others hanging on to each other, a few vomiting by the roadside.

The column of trucks halted. Their drivers exited their cabins and, almost simultaneously, all the bonnets of the vehicles were raised.

The Great Leader, his hands over his ears, his eyes bulging in astonishment and horror, was obviously attempting to make himself heard—his face, now purple with fury, was contorted into a mask of lividity, and flecks of spittle flew from his mouth—but there was no one there to listen. Two generals, their faces twisted in pain from the continuous shriek from the public address systems, took him by the arms and escorted him off the podium.

Rumors flew that explosions had been heard from outside Pyongyang.

It grew worse. The crowd panicked. People were trampled by the stampeding hordes, and shots were fired by the helpless police, mainly in self-defense. The wooden reviewing stands erected for the public were smashed to pieces, shop windows were shattered and looted, and the dead and injured lay in their hundreds, strewn where they fell.

Pandemonium reigned in Pyongyang.

಄಄

"Just wait until you hear what we found out," Anne said breathlessly when a beaming Sir Cedric admitted her and Martin into his house.

"I believe it can wait a couple of minutes." Sir Cedric pointed to his work desk, which was covered with every national newspaper in England. An ice bucket containing a bottle of champagne stood by the desk. Sir Cedric still had on the silly grin he wore when greeting them.

Martin and Anne each snatched up a newspaper, read the headlines with popping eyes, then picked up another paper. They looked at each other with wild joy, and then went into an ecstatic embrace. Anne let go of Martin, jumped into Sir Cedric's arms and kissed him on both cheeks. Martin playfully pulled her out of her clinch with Sir Cedric, and exchanged a heartfelt hug with him.

Sir Cedric, still grinning, poured out three glasses of champagne.

"To us," he said, lifting his glass. Anne and Martin repeated the toast, and took sips of their drinks.

"Are they all safe?" was Anne's first question.

"I believe they are," Sir Cedric said. "Admiral Stone called on the satellite phone a few minutes ago. They're moored in one of the tiny South Korean fishing ports, and they'll set off on the way back in a couple of days, when all the brouhaha has died down. Of course, no details of the operation were mentioned. Now, what was the important news you wanted to tell me?"

Anne looked at Martin. The mood sobered instantly. Sir Cedric looked quizzically at them both.

"Come on," he said impatiently. "Out with it. Apparently you discovered something in Bernard Webb's apartment."

"We have," Martin said. He gave Sir Cedric all the sordid details.

"That clinches it," Sir Cedric said. "We're dealing with an unscrupulous psychopath. But he's smart—if he gets the slightest inkling of what we know about him, I have no doubt he will expose us in a flash. After today's operation, we are no longer a bunch of harmless intellectuals. They'll find us guilty of several crimes, and we'll all probably end up in jail."

"We've considered executing Bernard," Anne said, "which, in principle, I support. However, that would leave poor Lucien defenseless. Sooner or later, the French police are going to get to him, and they'll never believe his story. He'll be tried, convicted and sentenced for Tanya's murder."

"Unfortunately, Anne," Sir Cedric said, "there's no way we can testify on his behalf. Only that son-of-an-unwashed-bitch could do that. Which, of course, he won't!"

"Because I'll kill him first," Martin muttered.

Sir Cedric ignored him.

"We need to think this out very carefully," he said. "This could turn out to be quite a dilemma."

Martin looked out of the window.

"To think that I called that monster my friend," he said aloud, but obviously addressing only himself. "We were together for twenty years—fighting together, living together, working together. It'll be a blow for the others as well. How could we all be so blind?"

Anne went up to him and put her arm around his waist.

"Don't blame yourself, darling," she murmured in Martin's ear. "Bernard probably has years of practice in fooling other people."

"I remember once in Iraq," Martin continued his musings, "I stopped him from taking something off a dead Iraqi soldier. I intended him to stand court martial. A few minutes later, he saved my life from an assassin, and I withdrew my intentions. I suppose that incident desensitized me to his faults. What a rude awakening!"

Anne brought Martin back to the desk.

"Let's sit down," she suggested. "I think the only choice we have is to make a deal with Bernard."

"A deal?" Sir Cedric flared up. "With that cad? Never!"

"What kind of deal did you have in mind, Anne?" Martin asked.

"I haven't a clue," Anne said. "Let's think this out. If I were to meet him face to face, I'd probably say something like, umm, 'we know you're a criminal, we've got you now, we're about to execute you, but we'll give you one last chance to stay alive if you'll clear Lucien with the French police.' I don't know, something along those lines. And Bernard would wind up in prison, but alive."

"Where he would probably reveal all our secrets," Martin said with some anger. "He'd have nothing to lose."

"Yes, that's true," Anne said. "So what do we do?"

Martin stood up, and began pacing the room.

"I'm going to suggest something you probably won't like," he said. "But it could possibly be our only way out."

Anne and Sir Cedric waited attentively. Martin stopped pacing and faced them.

"We can extend no moral behavior or decency to a monster like Bernard," he said calmly. "He deserves to die, and it is up to us to see that he does. Soon. His apartment contains enough evidence to not only connect him with the Tanya Gerard murder case, but also to positively incriminate him as the murderer."

"But how the devil will Scotland Yard know about this evidence," Sir Cedric blustered. "Worse—even if they find it, how will they connect it to a homicide that occurred outside the UK?"

"Very good, Sir Cedric," Martin smiled grimly. "I had asked myself the same questions. The answer is an anonymous letter to Scotland Yard. It will say that the body they just found is of the murderer of Tanya Gerard in Paris. That's all. The identification of the body will be definite because he'll be carrying all his identifying papers. They'll get to his apartment, find the pendant with the bloodstains, contact the Paris prefecture, match the blood type with Tanya's, match the body's fingerprints with those on the razor—and Lucien is free, without even having to tell a story!"

"The plan has some merit," Sir Cedric said. "You realize, of course, that the investigation will eventually arrive at Webb's place of employment. Meaning that you and your lads will be questioned."

"Correct," Martin said. "We'll need to brief the men beforehand, and have their stories more or less correlate. Just generalities—something like: they met Bernard in the army, and he worked with them. Yes, he was absent more frequently than the rest of them. Apart from that, there was nothing special about him. Everyone leads his own life, and there wasn't much mingling. Certainly no mention of a recent yacht voyage!"

"And then we'll inform Lucien that he's no longer—" Anne began.

"Certainly not!" Martin snapped, though not unkindly. "Lucien is not to be contacted by us again. He'll read the papers and put two and two together. He might look you up, Anne, as he knows who you are, but I think that's unlikely. If he does, congratulate him and deny any involvement whatsoever. Pure coincidence with a 'crazy Tony who loves to shoot off his mouth.'"

Anne nodded.

"Martin," she said, "I'll leave you to work out the method and the … execution of Bernard Webb. I really don't want to know."

"Leave it to me," Martin said. His voice indicated that this particular assignment would be carried out flawlessly.

Sir Cedric brought a bottle of whisky and three shot glasses to the desk.

"A bit more appropriate than champagne, I dare say," he said. "I think we could all use a slug of this stuff."

They drank in silence. All of them felt uneasy about the whole business of condemning to death someone they knew.

"Listen, my friends," Sir Cedric said finally. "We have just completed a colossal international coup successfully. True, many people lost their lives in the square and in the military bases. But we should not feel guilty about this—we *knew* this would happen, and concurred with it. Our association's laws have considered the price of human life, and have come to conclusions we have all adopted. This also includes eliminations such as Professor Allier and Bernard Webb. We cannot afford to be merciful softies— those are exactly the characteristics we accuse the democracies of having!"

"You're absolutely right, Cedric," Anne said. "Thanks. I needed that."

"Martin, you'll welcome the yacht in Nice when it arrives. Meet with the admiral discreetly, and tell him everything—the story and our resolutions. I'm sure he'll agree with everything we've decided. Then brief our lads with your plan, and prepare the execution."

"What if the admiral has questions?" Anne asked. "What if he wants a board meeting before taking any action?"

"Then everything goes on hold, and we have an emergency board meeting in Nice," Sir Cedric said. "Perhaps Martin will have to devise another plan. However, I doubt that will happen. Oh, and Martin—I think we'd prefer to leave Patricia and Olaf out of the picture altogether. Find some way to circumvent them. Agreed?"

Martin nodded.


## SEVENTY-FIVE

The Iranian president, Mr. Mahmoud Ahmadinejad, has announced that there are three thousand centrifuges currently operational in Iran. Three thousand more will shortly be added, with the final target of fifty thousand. He stated that Iran has greatly improved the guiding systems of their long-range missiles, and that if attacked by the US or Israel, the latter would be within range for counterattacks.

೦೩೪೦

The day after the North Korean catastrophe, the international media continued to report new stories that leaked out of that country. Apparently, in addition to the fiasco in Pyongyang, explosions were heard outside the city. Unconfirmed reports claimed that ammunition and explosive depots "just blew up suddenly." These explosions happened within minutes of each other, and coincided with the panic in the capital. The authorities tried to forbid the publication of such news, but the leakage was massive. Then they denied everything, but by now it was a fact—a mysterious hand had orchestrated a gigantic blow against the North Korean regime. It was as yet unclear whether the Great Leader would resign or replace most of his ministers. Mass executions were expected.

For the next few weeks, the world media continued to report on the Pyongyang debacle. Publicists analyzed and reanalyzed the events. All of them circled around the question: Was this the beginning of a revolution? Was there a powerful underground movement in North Korea? Was a foreign Western power, perhaps Japan, at work here?

The North Korean press made no official statement regarding the historic events. There were attempts to soothe the local populace by underplaying the importance of what occurred, promising a richer future, and finally by blaming the capitalists for everything that went wrong. No one saw or heard anything about the Great Leader—according to rumors, he had committed suicide or suffered a heart attack.

CRBO

Nine weeks after their departure, the Mimosa and its crew returned to the Nice marina. They were all deeply suntanned—the outdoors had done a lot to their complexions—and in high spirits. No wonder, the mission had succeeded without a hitch, and they were rightfully very proud.

Martin was waiting for them on the pier. There were shouts of welcome as he climbed on board, cheers, and backslapping, and he even got a kiss from Patricia. Martin grinned and spread his arms for silence.

"Guys," he said, "you certainly have a lot to be proud of. First, I would like to salute Admiral Stone, on a difficult job carried out brilliantly!" He turned to the admiral and gave a military salute, which was copied by the other men, including Olaf. The admiral saluted back in style, but could not conceal the slight smile on his lips. "Don't run away," he grinned at the "crew." "I'll be right back after I have a chat with the admiral."

Martin followed the admiral into his cabin.

"Quite a show you put on there," the admiral said, smiling.

"I hope it covers the severity of what I am about to tell you," Martin said gravely. They sat at the admiral's desk, and Martin related everything regarding Bernard Webb, beginning with the Tanya Gerard murder case and ending with emergency board meeting at Sir Cedric's.

The admiral kept a serious visage during most of Martin's narrative, but toward the end, his face reflected the shock he felt.

"Yes, I see," he said, when Martin had finished. "There doesn't seem to be any alternative."

"I'll have private interviews with my lads tomorrow before the general debriefing. It's the only way I can talk to them and exclude Bernard. I'll tell the boys what I told you, and we'll agree on a plan of action. Oh, I'll interview Bernard, too, of course, but that will only be the expected report on the cruise and the mission, and anything else of a more 'personal' nature. Do I have your agreement, admiral?"

"Yes, Martin. Indeed you have!" The admiral shook Martin's hand firmly. "Good luck."

"Thank you, admiral," Martin said.

Back on deck, Martin assembled the team again.

"I am announcing a debriefing meeting at the 'cowshed' in London tomorrow morning at ten," Martin said. "We'll all fly back to London tonight on our executive jet after George finishes up the business with the UAV and has it put into storage. It is imperative that you *all* attend. In addition, starting at nine a.m., I shall want a private, ten-minute tête-à-tête with each of you separately, where you can state anything personal you may want to say. Philip, please see to the sequencing of these interviews. Olaf, you need to remain with the yacht for a day or two for maintenance. Therefore, I would like to talk to you right after this meeting. Okay?"

Olaf Gunnarson, pipe stuck between his teeth, grinned and touched his cap.

"All right, the rest of you," Martin said, "off you go. Have a good time, but don't be late for the flight tonight."

They all left the yacht. Martin and Olaf went into one of the cabins, where Olaf reported on how thrilled he was to have taken part in the mission. Martin went through the motions of a thorough debriefing, and then patted Olaf on the back, and said he hoped to see him in a couple of days in London.

Martin stepped out onto the deck, and was surprised to see Patricia and John waiting for him.

"Hello, hello," he greeted them. "Why aren't you having a good time in town?"

"Martin," Patricia said, "could you excuse my absence from tomorrow's meeting? I just spoke with my mother in London and she's taken ill. She wants me and George to visit her, and I told her George was busy. But I think I should visit her very soon in fact, I shall go to the hospital directly from the airport."

*Thank goodness!* Martin thought. *I needed an excuse for* not *having her at the meeting.*

"Well," he said very seriously. "In that case I shall make an exception and interview you now."

The interview with Patricia was, of course, for show only—the same as with Olaf. It was over in twenty minutes.

⊰⊱

Three days after the team's return to London, the press announced that the body of a man in his forties, one Bernard Webb, had been fished out of the Thames. Scotland Yard reported that the man was wanted for murder in France. Investigations were continuing in cooperation with the French police.

It didn't take long for Scotland Yard to arrive at the premises of Fit and Trim. Martin was interrogated, and he told them all they needed to know of Bernard Webb's association with his company. "Yes, he was an ex-soldier under my command. Yes, he worked with the rest of the team in my company. He was well behaved, and no one had any complaints against him. No, I know nothing of his private life—he did not care to share it with me. Yes, his terms of employment enabled him to take several days off if pre-coordinated with the others."

The police officers got similar responses from the other employees. There was no need to go any deeper—after all, the main show was in Paris, not here.

⊂⊃⊃⊂

Commissaire Duval leaned back in his chair, his feet on his desk, deep in thought. The package from Scotland Yard was like a bolt from the blue, even though he had been forewarned by Commissioner Neville MacLeod. So many pieces of the puzzle were falling into place, and yet the picture was incomplete. The package contained the name and description of the corpse, his fingerprints, samples of his blood, and a bloodstained amulet found at his residence. The amulet was the one Madame Dupré had described to Marnier at their first meeting—it had definitely belonged to Tanya Gerard. The laboratory had already made all the tests: the blood on the amulet was also Tanya Gerard's, and the killer's blood sample matched the blood the police had found on the shattered mirror in Tanya's flat. Most amazing of all were the lab reports on the killer's fingerprints—not only did they match one of the sets found on the razor that killed Tanya, but they also matched the fingerprints found inside the device that electrocuted Professor Allier!

*Of course! Because the Allier case was closed, we could only compare the fingerprints to those on file with owners. But now, the computer must have made a comprehensive search, and came up with identical fingerprints in two unsolved murders!*

The press had been notified that the Gerard murder case was solved. Commissaire Duval's reputation with his superiors had been restored. He had personally called Professeur Dupré and informed her that Tanya Gerard's killer had himself been killed.

No mention of the Allier case, of course, to anyone—that one had been closed a long time ago.

*For the first time I have a substantial link between the two deaths. But how? Why? It makes no sense.*

There was a knock on his door, and Inspecteur Marnier's head popped around it.

"There's a young man out here who says he has urgent information regarding the Gerard case."

Duval resumed a dignified seated posture.

"Show him in."

A tall, well-built blond man shuffled in hesitatingly.

"Sit down," Duval said gruffly. "Who are you?"

"My name is Lucien Laval, sir," the young man said uneasily. "I was Tanya Gerard's last lover, and I witnessed her murder."

Duval was speechless. So many new revelations in such a short time.

"Indeed, young man?" Duval had finally found his tongue. "Tell me about it."

Lucien related the succession of events leading to, and culminating in, the murder. He made no mention of the lady professor or of her friend, Tony, but he confirmed every single bit of evidence that Duval already had.

"Why did you wait so long before coming forth?" Duval asked.

"Isn't it obvious? That monster would dispatch me much in the same way as he did Tanya if I came out of hiding. I was protecting my life."

*If there was any doubt before*, Duval thought, *there certainly isn't any now. Just one more shot in the dark ...*

"Tell me, Lucien—did this Webb fellow ever mention the name Albert Allier?"

"No, sir."

Duval sighed.

"Oh, well ..."

"But Tanya did. She screamed at Webb that she had connections. One of her most ardent admirers was a certain Professor Allier, who had a lot of influence, and that she told him everything, including about Webb. That was just before she called him a perverted monster for looting corpses. And those were the last words she uttered."

"Can you think of anything else I should know?" Duval asked, barely able to conceal his excitement.

"No, sir. Begging your pardon, sir—is this the same Professor Allier who had an accident some time ago?"

"Yes. Why do you ask?"

"I ... well ... I never made the connection until you asked me just now."

"Quite understandable, young man. I thank you for your testimony. Please submit a statement of everything you have told me to Inspecteur Marnier. You are free to go."

Lucien had barely shut the door behind him, when Duval jumped out of his chair, spread his hands to the ceiling, and crowed out loud. The Allier case was solved, and he had been right all along!

When Marnier poked his head in to see what all the noise was about, he found Duval at his desk, fiercely pounding his report into the computer. Duval glared at him, and Marnier backed out hastily.

The report would include the solution of the Allier murder. Murder, not accident! Allier was a patron of the arts and one of Tanya's greatest admirers. Bernard Webb learned from Tanya that Allier knew all about him. Allier also knew, naturally, of Tanya's murder, but he did not alert the police regarding Webb at once, because then he would have to expose his relations with Tanya. But Webb could not take the chance of this continuing indefinitely. So he devised the electrocution apparatus—his fingerprints were found inside the device. Why go to such lengths and such an elaborate murder? Well, who knows what a deranged mind considers the best way to do things.

Case solved!

## SEVENTY-SIX

The next board meeting was held in the admiral's office five days after the yacht's return to Nice. The admiral embraced Anne and shook hands heartily with Sir Cedric.

Martin threw a bunch of newspapers and magazines on the table.

"The resolution we made at our last meeting," he said dryly, "was carried out successfully."

"That's that, then," Sir Cedric said decisively. "We're under no threat now. Well done, Martin. Patrick, I'm dying to hear about the mission."

Admiral Stone reported on the cruise and the functioning of the UAV. He heaped praise on George Graham, who operated the aircraft as if he'd been flying them all his life.

"One thing I found curious," he said. "We observed no attempt to intercept the UAV. The chaos must have been so intense, and communication so severely disrupted, that I believe the North Korean air force was not even *aware* of our incursion. All in all, I think we did a pretty good job."

"You're not the only one to think so," Martin said. "The lads call you a 'virtuoso' playing a 'Stradivarius.'"

"Shows what good planning can do," the admiral said humbly.

"That's not enough," Sir Cedric said jovially. "It takes perfect execution as well. If we were in the habit of distributing medals, I would certainly nominate you for one!"

"Come on, guys," the admiral said, bursting with pride. "As the Americans say, it was no big deal. Any retired officer of the British Navy would have done the same." He grinned broadly.

The board then discussed reports from the world press. Nothing, of course, directly from North Korea, where they had a total blackout on news pertaining to the calamity they had experienced. It must have had catastrophic proportions. The rest of the world played guessing games: was it a failed attempt to overthrow the government? Or was it the action of a very well equipped underground movement? Here and there, the CIA was mentioned, too.

Anne tried to sum things up.

"I too wish to congratulate Admiral Stone on a remarkably well-done mission. I think we all agree that we have pulled off an astounding tour de force. As we can see, speculations as to *who* actually did the deed are still rife, and nobody is anywhere near the truth. We have proved that within us there is a secret power with which we can face almost any challenge. I admit that this has gone far beyond anything I had imagined. Now that we're all together, I suggest we begin making plans of what our next steps should be."

"What about our financial benefactors?" Sir Cedric asked.

"They are no doubt tuned in to the current news. But yes, they deserve the personal touch. I shall call Andrew Dodson and—if you don't mind, admiral—please call Neil Bennett. We'll also call our other collaborators and thank them for their contributions. And the first to thank is you, Cedric—for your fantastic laser beam! Even though we didn't use it for this mission."

Sir Cedric's face was radiant.

"That's going to change when we get to work in Iran," he said. "It's not going to be a blueprint repetition of what happened in Pyongyang. Our strike there will hurt much, much more!"

"There are a few open questions," Anne continued. "First, were our acoustic disrupters discovered? What about the other stuff we shipped? Is anything left over, that might fall into the wrong hands? If discovered, will friendly nations be alerted? Martin, I'm beginning to think you'll need to pay Charlie and Sing another visit, and wrap things up neatly over there."

"I agree," the admiral said.

"If no one has anything more to say …" Anne said and got up.

"Just a minute," Sir Cedric said. "I wonder if you've seen the latest report on Iran." He pulled a folded newspaper out of his pocket. "I bought this on my way here and read it in the taxi. It could be of significance."

"Please read it to us," Anne said, sitting down again.

"Sources in Washington," Sir Cedric read aloud, "report that the USA has withdrawn its resolution not to negotiate with Iran, as long as the latter continues with her nuclear program. After years of obstinate insistence that a precondition for negotiations was the total cessation of uranium enrichment, the USA has now agreed to deal with Iran. No explanation was given for this reversal of policy. The USA has even agreed to open a low-level diplomatic presence in Tehran, probably under the assumption that such a delegation would convince the Iranians to agree to have their nuclear program supervised ..."

Sir Cedric refolded the newspaper and looked at his colleagues. Anne jumped to her feet.

"This is a direct sequel to the 'March of Folly,'" she almost shouted. "Won't they ever learn?" Then she added softly: "I think we need no further confirmation of how proper and fitting our path is."

"And how justified our future operation in Iran is," Sir Cedric said. "We need to find out if the Iranians plan to take preventive action as a result of the Pyongyang disaster. The North Koreans just might share what they know with them."

"Very true," Martin said. "And after Iran—then what? We have no other target set up."

"We haven't finished with these two yet," Anne responded immediately. "The Pyongyang business is far from over. Frankly, I do not see the present government changing right away. In fact, it's quite likely that state oppression will increase now. We may have to act there again! So—we need to wait for Martin to report back after he talks with Charlie and Sing again. *Then* let's see what's going on in Iran."

"And what do you suggest *we* should do while waiting?" Sir Cedric asked.

"What we did when we just started the association. Investigate additional targets. We have Cedric's report on Venezuela and the papers are full about the reign of terror in Myanmar. We'll need to recruit more scientists, get new inventions. We have very good resources on hand today, but I think we should go for even better stuff." Anne emitted a long sigh. "I sincerely hope that what happened in Pyongyang will be studiously analyzed by every military and security agency in the world. Perhaps it will give the democracies an inkling of how dictators should *really* be treated!"

"Right you are!" the admiral said. "That, in itself, will help us in obtaining even more researchers and inventors of the highest quality."

"Hear, hear!" Sir Cedric said.

# EPILOGUE

Preparations for the operation in Tehran were in an advanced stage. The material and equipment had arrived safely and was distributed by the Iranian collaborators. They were all ready for the twenty-four hour alert signal, which would start the ball rolling. D-day was not far away now.

Of course, they had all heard of what had happened in Pyongyang. And they prayed that they would have at least the same success.

The association decided to employ additional inventions this time. The scientists were encouraged to discover new methods and techniques to embarrass power-crazy tyrants of the world, and to search among their colleagues and acquaintances for more brilliant minds that contribute to the cause.

Two weddings had occurred at the same church not more than a week after the North Korean operation. Anne Dupré married Martin Cooper, and Patricia Welles wed John Carmichael. They had a modest celebration attended by Anne's parents and children, Martin's parents and his team, Sir Cedric Norton and Retired Admiral Patrick Stone.

## THE END

www.ingramcontent.com/pod-product-compliance
Lightning Source LLC
Chambersburg PA
CBHW071338020726
47502CB00001B/150